Tails, You Lose

Books by Carol J. Perry

Tails, You Lose

Caught Dead Handed

Available from Kensington Publishing Corp.

Tails, You Lose

A WITCH CITY MYSTERY

CAROL J. PERRY

KENSINGTON PUBLISHING CORP.

http://www.kensingtonbooks.com

KENSINGTON BOOKS are published by

Kensington Publishing Corp.
119 West 40th Street
New York, NY 10018

All Kensington Titles, Imprints, and Distributed Lines are available at special quantity discounts for bulk purchases for sales promotions, premiums, fund-raising, and educational or institutional use.

Special book excerpts or customized printings can also be created to fit specific needs. For details, write or phone the office of the Kensington special sales manager: Kensington Publishing Corp., 119 West 40th Street, New York, NY 10018, attn: Special Sales Department, Phone: 1-800-221-2647.

Kensington and the K logo Reg. U.S. Pat & TM Off.

ISBN-13: 978-1-61773-371-0
ISBN-10: 1-61773-371-7
First Kensington Mass Market Edition: April 2015

eISBN-13: 978-1-61773-372-7
eISBN-10: 1-61773-372-5
First Kensington Electronic Edition: April 2015

10 9 8 7 6 5 4 3 2 1

Printed in the United States of America

For Dan, my husband and best friend

"Death ends a life, but it never ends a relationship,
which struggles on in the survivor's mind
toward some resolution, which it may never find."

Gene Hackman in
I Never Sang for My Father (1970)

CHAPTER 1

It was the first white Christmas I'd seen in a long time. My recent winter holidays had featured lighted boat parades, palm trees, beach volleyball, and lawn flamingos decked out in Santa hats. But New England Christmases were the ones I'd grown up with, and Florida seemed very far away from Salem, Massachusetts.

I'd pulled a big wing chair up close to the window overlooking Winter Street as snow swirled in bright halos around the streetlamps and tree lights cast colorful dots onto wind-sculpted drifts. Snow-muffled church bells rang, calling the faithful to evensong at St. Peter's, just a few blocks away. O'Ryan was stretched out full length on the carpet beside me, tummy up, eyes squeezed shut, a cat smile on his face, large yellow paws clutching a damp purple catnip mouse.

I'm Lee Barrett, née Maralee Kowolski. I'm thirty-one, red-haired, Salem born. I was orphaned early, I married once, and I was widowed young. I lived in Florida for ten years, and since I returned to Salem a few months back, my aunt Isobel Russell and I had been sharing the fine old family home on Winter

Street . . . the same house where she raised me after my parents died.

I'd been working in television, one way or another, ever since I graduated from Emerson College. So far I'd been a weather girl, a home shopping show host, and even a phone-in TV psychic. That last gig, a brief stint at Salem's cable station WICH-TV, was on a show called *Nightshades.* I dressed up like a Gypsy and, in between scary old movies, pretended to read minds, find lost objects, and otherwise know the unknowable. I'd been hired as a last-minute replacement for the previous host, Ariel Constellation, a practicing Salem witch who apparently could *really* do all that psychic stuff. Unfortunately, I was the one who'd discovered Ariel's body floating facedown in Salem Harbor.

Not an auspicious start to a new job.

It didn't end well, either. Ariel's killer set a fire that pretty much destroyed the top two floors of our house, and if it hadn't been for O'Ryan's timely intervention, Aunt Ibby and I might not have been around to celebrate Christmas.

After the unpleasant publicity, *Nightshades* was canceled, and I was once again unemployed. An inheritance from my parents had left me well enough off financially, so I didn't need to work at all. Being between jobs wasn't a problem. I just prefer being busy.

On a positive note, I was sure that when my sixty-something, ball-of-energy aunt got through redesigning the entire upstairs and driving contractors and decorators nuts, the upper stories of the house would once again be livable and we could stop tripping over paint cans, fabric samples, and wallpaper books.

I angled the wing chair a little to the right so that I could watch for headlights rounding the corner onto Winter Street. Not just any headlights. I was hoping for a Christmas night visit from a special friend. Well, maybe Detective Pete Mondello had become quite a bit more than just a friend—but I was trying to move slowly in that area of my life.

My aunt Ibby appeared in the doorway, bearing a tray with two chintz-patterned cups and a matching teapot.

"You and O'Ryan certainly look comfortable. Ready for a spot of tea?"

"Sounds good," I said, returning the chair to its original position. "I was just enjoying watching the snow. It's been a long time."

"Too long." She placed the tray on the antique drum table between us and sat in the wing chair facing mine. "And at last you're home for Christmas."

She filled our cups with fragrant jasmine tea, and we tapped them together in a toast.

"Here's to the end of a strange year," she said. "And let's hope that the next one is a lot less stressful."

"Amen," I said. "I'll drink to that."

Aunt Ibby smiled and gestured toward the sleeping cat. "Looks as though O'Ryan is enjoying his Christmas mouse."

O'Ryan opened one eye and rolled over, still hugging the mouse.

"He loves it," I said. "And he seems to have quite a catnip buzz going on."

"Pete will be pleased that his gift was such a big hit," she said. "Too bad he couldn't have joined us for dinner."

We'd had the usual holiday house full of relatives and friends for the festive meal, but the gathering snowstorm had sent them all home early.

"He said he'd try to stop by later."

"I'll bet a little snow won't keep him away," she said with a knowing smile.

I turned my chair just enough so that I could still see the headlights on any car turning onto Winter Street. It wasn't often that Pete had a holiday off, and this year he'd had to choose between Christmas Day and New Year's Eve. We'd already exchanged Christmas gifts. I hadn't wanted to give him anything too personal at this early stage of our relationship, so I'd decided on a pair of tickets for good seats at an upcoming Bruins hockey game. His gift to me, a vintage brooch with an oval miniature painting of a yellow cat, was pinned to the deep V-neck of my white silk blouse. I wore dark green velvet jeans and had tucked a sprig of holly into random red curls escaping from my attempt at a French twist.

"You know, Maralee," Aunt Ibby said, "I have a very good feeling about the New Year. The house is coming along beautifully, and the fact that you're going to start January with a good deed for the community is an excellent omen."

"An *omen?*" I laughed. "Maybe you've watched too many episodes of *Nightshades!*"

My aunt was a recent, and still pretty skeptical, believer in things paranormal. We both had reason to know, though, that some things are just beyond our understanding. O'Ryan was an outstanding example of that. The handsome cat snoozing happily at our feet had once been Ariel Constellation's pet . . . some say her "familiar." As many folks in Salem will testify, a witch's familiar is far from being an ordinary house cat!

She shrugged. "Well, omen or not, your volunteering to help out at the new school will be such a blessing for the students."

"I hope so," I said. "I'm looking forward to it."

The Tabitha Trumbull Academy of the Arts was due to open at the start of the New Year, and I'd been invited to be a volunteer guest instructor. The school was located in the sprawling old building that had once housed Trumbull's Department Store in downtown Salem. The store had been closed since the sixties and had been slated for demolition until government grants and a historical site designation saved it from the wrecker's ball. Already dubbed "the Tabby," the school would soon be bustling with the activities of aspiring dancers, poets, painters, actors, and, in my department, television performers and producers.

"Your mother and I used to go to Trumbull's with your grandmother Russell when we were little girls," Aunt Ibby said. "We loved it. There was a grand staircase to the second floor, with wide bannisters, which I always wanted to slide down."

"Did you ever do it?"

"No, I never did."

"Now that I'm officially a staff member at the Tabby, I'll give you permission to slide whenever you want."

O'Ryan's ears perked up. He stood, stretched, and trotted toward the front hall.

"Someone's coming," Aunt Ibby said. "O'Ryan always knows before we do."

She was right. The gleam of headlights glinted on the frosted windowpane as a car rounded the corner from Washington Square.

"It's probably Pete," I said. When the door chime sounded, I followed O'Ryan into the hall and opened the front door. Pete Mondello stood there, smiling, hatless, holding a huge poinsettia plant under one arm while fat snowflakes fell all around him.

"Brrr. Cold out there." He hurried inside, pulled me close for a quick hug with his free arm, and stamped his feet on the woven rope mat. "Merry Christmas, Lee," he said, tossing his coat onto a hook on the tall hall tree. "You look good."

"You look good, too," I said, brushing a snowflake from his dark hair. An understatement. He looked wonderful. "How was your Christmas?"

"Fun," he said, bending to stroke O'Ryan's head. "My sister's kids had a ball opening presents."

"So did O'Ryan," I told him. "He had the wrapping off of his purple mouse before we were up this morning. He's been playing with it all day. I think he's still a little bit drunk. Come on inside and get warm."

Aunt Ibby greeted Pete with a welcoming smile, a "Merry Christmas, Pete," and an offer of pumpkin pie.

He patted perfectly flat abs, claiming he'd already eaten too much, wished her a Merry Christmas, and handed her the poinsettia.

"Thank you, dear. It's lovely." She placed the plant on the sideboard and stood back to admire the effect. "Pete, I was just telling my niece about the old Trumbull's Department Store."

"I've seen pictures of it," he said, "but I've never been inside."

"It was a beautiful store. All those gleaming hardwood floors and racks of the latest clothes, a great big book department, hardware and notions and linens and toys and jewelry and just about anything a person might want. There was a player piano on the mezzanine-floor landing, and a man in a tuxedo played the popular tunes all day. But I guess the old stores just couldn't compete with the malls."

"I'm sure it looks quite different now," Pete said.

"I guess it must," I said. "The school director, Rupert Pennington, says a lot of the old fixtures will be moved out by the time school starts. My classes will be in the old shoe department."

"I always got my back-to-school shoes at Trumbull's," my aunt said, reminiscing. "I wonder if the old bentwood chairs are still there. Thonet, I think."

"I've heard the city plans to reuse as much of the furniture and fixtures as they can," I said, "and some of the things will go to auction."

My aunt nodded. "Maralee, remember our handyman, Mr. Sullivan?"

I did. A big man, probably in his seventies. He was the neighborhood handyman, always available if we needed a fence repaired or a drain unclogged.

Aunt Ibby went on. "He and his son were working on taking some of the smaller pieces to a storage locker today."

"On Christmas? How do you know that?"

"Mrs. Sullivan is one of my Facebook friends. They went to work right after dinner. She's not pleased. She seems concerned about them working there after dark."

"I remember being afraid to walk past the Trumbull building at night," I said. "All the kids said it was haunted."

"I've heard those stories, too," Pete said. "Something about a lady in white in the upstairs window, strange lights flickering on and off, and a piano playing in the middle of the night. Down at the station they think it's just a trick the Trumbull family used to keep vandals away. I know they could never keep security guards very long."

A slight buzzing sound interrupted us, and Pete reached into his pocket for his phone. "Oops. Sorry. I'll take this in the hall."

When he came back into the room, his expression

was serious. "Afraid I have to leave. Something's going on at your new school."

"What's wrong?" I asked.

"Don't know yet, exactly. Seems your Mr. Sullivan went down into the basement, and his son says he just disappeared. Never came back up the stairs."

CHAPTER 2

"Disappeared? How can that be?"

"I wouldn't worry too much," Pete said. "He probably just wandered off someplace when his son wasn't looking. It's a big building."

"Mr. Sullivan isn't the wandering type." Aunt Ibby sounded a tiny bit indignant. "Just because a person is over sixty doesn't mean he *wanders*."

"I didn't mean . . . I'm sure he's safe somewhere." Pete sounded apologetic. "That's what I meant. Gotta go."

"He's an old friend of the family, Pete," I said. "I hope he's okay."

"Mr. Sullivan was one of the first people to come over to help us after the fire," Aunt Ibby said.

"Does Mrs. Sullivan know that he's missing yet?" I wondered aloud.

"I'm sure her son must have told her. I'll call you just as soon as I know anything."

I walked Pete to the front door, with O'Ryan tagging along behind, carrying the catnip mouse by one damp and tattered purple ear.

Pete shrugged into his coat, then reached into an

inside pocket. "Oh, I almost forgot. I have another little gift for you."

"Another one? What is it?"

"Sorry it's not wrapped," he said, handing me a small book.

I read the title and laughed. "*The Official Nancy Drew Handbook*. Just what I needed!"

"I don't want you to fall behind in your studies just because school's out for the holidays."

When Pete and I first met, he thought I was just being nosy, because I asked so many questions about police work. That was when he'd started comparing me to that famous girl detective. Later, though, when he found out I was really interested, he convinced me to take an online course in criminology. I'd just begun, while Pete was in his third year of the same course, and I'd become more fascinated with his job than ever.

"I promise to study," I said with a smile.

"Good," Pete replied. "There'll be a quiz later."

"I look forward to it."

After a quick kiss, he went out into the snowstorm, which was gathering intensity. The big, soft snowflakes that had been falling earlier had been replaced with the hard, stinging kind.

He should have worn a warm hat. And mittens.

The cat and I returned to the living room, and I looked around for Aunt Ibby. Her voice came from the den, which housed her computer, printer, fax, and other technical toys. She looked up from her phone when I entered the room.

"Of course I will," she said into the receiver. "Don't worry, dear. I'll be right over to pick you up."

"What are you doing?" I asked, although I knew

exactly what she was up to. My busybody aunt was planning to brave the weather and drive the distraught wife to the Tabby.

"That was Mrs. Sullivan," she said with an innocent smile. "She needs a ride to the Trumbull building. I told her I'd be right over."

In this storm? I don't think so.

"Aunt Ibby," I said, "I know your Buick is a very safe car, but I doubt that the roads are all plowed yet. Driving in this storm just isn't a good idea."

"I told her I'd be there. And I will." She stood and headed for the hall, then looked back at me. "Unless you'd like to drive?"

I'm not the best driver in the world, and I hadn't had a lot of recent experience driving in snow, but my late husband, Johnny Barrett, had been a rising young star on the auto-racing circuit. I'd spent enough time around racetracks to know a little about handling cars.

Reluctantly, I agreed.

"Oh, thank you, Maralee. We'll just pick up Mrs. Sullivan and dash right over to Essex Street."

No dashing through the snow this Christmas night, thank you. Slow and steady. And prayerful.

It took only a few minutes to don coats and hats, boots and gloves, and to head out the back kitchen door toward the garage, where Aunt Ibby's car was housed. By then the snow had acquired a gleaming frozen crust on top of a foot or so of wet base.

Great for snowball fights or building snowmen. Not so much for walking.

We crunched our way past the vegetable garden, where dried, white-coated cornstalks loomed like bent rows of arthritic ghosts and the winter-killed remains of tall sunflowers crackled under their coating of ice.

Aunt Ibby stopped suddenly. "Shhh. Oops. I thought I heard the cat door. O'Ryan, that nosy boy, has followed us."

She was right. The cat raced past, skimmed along the snow, and sat in front of the garage.

"Go home, O'Ryan. Bad boy. Scat!" I pointed toward the house. "It's too cold for you out here."

Aunt Ibby pressed the garage door opener, and the cat trotted inside, looking back at us.

"Shall we take him with us?" Aunt Ibby asked. "I think he wants to come."

I shrugged. "Sure. Why not? He likes to ride."

She climbed into the passenger seat, and O'Ryan curled up on her lap. I eased the car out of the garage, and we headed slowly toward Bridge Street, where the Sullivans lived. Happily, Bridge Street had been plowed, and when we pulled up in front of the apartment house, Mrs. Sullivan was already waiting at the curb. A tiny little bird of a woman, she looked very small in the big backseat.

"Thanks so much, Ibby, and it's so kind of you to drive, Lee, on such a dreadful night. I'm terribly worried about Bill. Junior sounds worried, too. It's just not like Bill to go off and not tell anyone." The thin voice broke.

Aunt Ibby murmured comforting words. I concentrated on the road as the windshield wipers tried to keep up with the icy droplets pinging on the glass. O'Ryan purred.

Even though Essex Street is practically around the corner from our house, Salem's eccentric pattern of one-way streets and pedestrian malls made a roundabout route to Trumbull's necessary. The plows had done a good job of clearing the main streets, though, and the trip wasn't as bad as I'd expected. The parking lot next to the old store was nearly empty. There was one police cruiser, Pete's unmarked Crown Vic, an old red van marked SULLIVAN AND SON with an attached U-Haul trailer, and a couple of other cars I didn't recognize.

I parked as close to the building as I could, and we climbed out, leaving O'Ryan in the driver's seat, peering out the window. There were lights on inside the building, and a uniformed officer stood outside the glass double doors. For as long as I could remember, those doors had been covered on the inside with some kind of thick fabric, preventing anyone from seeing in. All the display windows had been covered, too, but now light shone from each one and newly polished glass gave a clear view of the grand staircase Aunt Ibby had described. Pete Mondello stood just inside the door, in apparent conversation with a man who wore a black, velvet-collared topcoat and a gray fedora hat. I recognized Rupert Pennington, the new director of the Tabitha Trumbull Academy of the Arts. Mr. Sullivan's son, Junior, sat on the bottom stair, his head in his hands.

Aunt Ibby spoke to the uniformed officer. "This is Mrs. Sullivan. She needs to talk to her son, to help you fellows figure out what's become of her husband."

CHAPTER 3

The officer tapped on the glass and motioned to Pete, who held up a finger, signaling, "Wait a minute," then, seeing us standing outside, quickly approached the double doors. He frowned as he pulled one of them open . . . not a grouchy frown, but one that meant "What the hell are you doing here?"

Pete stood in the open doorway. "Lee? Ms. Russell? What's going on?" He caught sight of the woman with us. "Is this Mrs. Sullivan? Please come in, ma'am. I've been trying to call you."

He bent to take Mrs. Sullivan's elbow and guided her toward the stairs where Junior sat. His cop face firmly in place, he turned and spoke to us over his shoulder. "You two can come in. Can't leave you standing out in the cold. Don't touch anything."

So there we stood, as Aunt Ibby says, "Like a tree full of owls," in the middle of that vast, nearly empty, hardwood-floored, retail time capsule, Trumbull's Department Store. I looked around. There was very little not to touch.

Mr. Rupert Pennington, who stood nearby and was

also carefully not touching anything, broke the awkward silence.

"Ms. Barrett? Is that you?"

"Yes, sir. Aunt Ibby, this is Mr. Pennington, the director of the school. Mr. Pennington, my aunt, Isobel Russell."

The director carefully removed one gray leather glove, and we shook hands all around.

"We drove Mrs. Sullivan here," I explained. "She's terribly worried about her husband."

"Ah, yes, indeed. The dear lady appears quite distraught." The director's voice was clearly that of a trained stage actor. I'd met Mr. Pennington before, when I was first approved by the board to be an instructor at the Tabby, so I wasn't surprised by his Shakespearean tone. I could tell by Aunt Ibby's expression, though, that she didn't know whether to be impressed or amused.

"How did you happen to be here on this dark and stormy night, Mr. Pennington?" my aunt asked.

"The young constable there"—he waved in Pete's direction—"asked me to come and perhaps be of some assistance." He reached into his overcoat pocket and produced a jangling ring of keys. "Apparently, I possess the only extant complete set of keys to this little kingdom."

"Do you know if they've figured out where Mr. Sullivan might have gone?" I asked. "Whether he might have left the building for some reason?"

"Aha!" He'd replaced his glove and pointed his index finger into the air. "We traversed the perimeter of the main floor and unlocked each and every egress onto the street level. Not stepping outside, the officer examined the newly fallen snow to see if there were any footprints indicating that any person had recently exited the building."

"And?" Aunt Ibby asked. "Were there?"

"Alas. Not a one. The only footprints were those at the front door, made by the missing gentleman and the strapping lad on the stairs"—he pointed at Junior—"as they went in and out, to and fro, so to speak, loading items into the truck."

"Junior said his dad went into the basement," I said. "Did you check the exits down there?"

Mr. Pennington shrugged. "There are none. It was explained to me that the basement was never used as a sales area for just that reason. No exits. Unsafe in case of fire, you know. So it's just a storage place. The school can't use it for classrooms yet, either. But someday, with sufficient funding, we'll make it into a state-of-the-art sound and lighting studio. But for now, it's a huge expanse of wasted space."

"It's like one of those 'locked room' mysteries," Aunt Ibby said. "As in 'Colonel Mustard did it in the library with the candlestick.' What's down there?"

"Mannequins," he said. "Rows of mannequins. Men and women; boys and girls; headless torsos; assorted arms, legs, hands, and feet; various heads and other body parts. All naked, of course, but discreetly covered with sheets, each and every one."

"That must be a strange sight," Aunt Ibby said. "But isn't the city going to sell the mannequins along with the other old fixtures? Perhaps that's why Bill Sullivan went down there."

"Originally, that was the plan," he said. "But the costume division of the Theater Arts Department asked if they could have them, and the city agreed."

"So we still don't know why he went into the basement," I said. "Maybe he was just curious."

"Sorry to keep you people standing here." It was Pete with a sobbing Mrs. Sullivan at his side. "Lee, maybe you and your aunt could talk to Mrs. Sullivan for a minute to help her calm down."

"Well, certainly." My aunt put an arm around the woman's quaking shoulders. "Could you find her a chair, Pete? And maybe a glass of water?"

Rupert Pennington, looking distinctly uncomfortable, backed away from Mrs. Sullivan, whose loud sobs were interspersed with hiccups. "I'll get a chair. There are still quite a few in the old shoe department." He hurried away toward the staircase, motioning to Junior, who still sat at the foot of the stairs. "Come along, young man. We'll get a chair for your poor mother."

"Pete," I said. "I have some bottled water in the car. I'll get it. And would you mind if I brought O'Ryan inside? I didn't think we'd be here this long, and it's very cold out there."

"You brought the cat." It was a statement, not a question. But he couldn't keep a straight face and broke into a half smile. "Sure. Why not?" He shook his head. "I'll come with you." He shrugged into his coat.

A wintry blast of air hit us as soon as we pushed the door open. He took my hand. "Watch it," he said. "This sidewalk is getting slippery."

He was right. With unsteady steps and short strides, we approached the Buick. The light from an overhead streetlamp showed O'Ryan stretched out along the top of the backseat. His pink nose was pressed against the glass, fogged from his warm, probably catnip-scented breath.

I unlocked the door, and O'Ryan, with a happy "mrrup," hopped over into the front seat.

"Pete, there's a six-pack of bottled water on the floor

in back. I hope it hasn't frozen. If you'll grab a bottle, I'll carry O'Ryan."

"Do you always carry water in the car?"

"Yep. Ever since Aunt Ibby got caught in a three-hour traffic jam on Route 128 on a hot summer day."

"Makes sense." Pete stuffed the plastic bottle into his coat pocket, while I held the big cat against my shoulder with one hand and Pete's steadying arm with the other. Still walking gingerly, we approached the old store. O'Ryan suddenly shifted his position, and I grasped him more tightly.

"Hang on, boy," I said. "We're almost there. Stop wiggling. You won't like it if I drop you into a snow-bank."

"Mrrow," he said and, poking his head over my shoulder, strained to look up at the roof.

"Do you think he's looking for the top-floor ghost?" Pete teased. "You keep telling me he's a witch's cat."

"Well, he is. He can't help it." I let go of Pete's arm and looked upward, too. "Is that where the ghost is supposed to be? On the top floor?"

"So they say. But what town in New England doesn't have a lady in white haunting a house or two? That story must be number one on the urban legend list. Crazy, isn't it?"

"Uh-huh," I agreed. "Absolutely crazy." I grasped his arm again, a little more tightly.

I still don't like walking past this place at night.

Even after we were back inside the Tabby, I held O'Ryan in my arms. If a big man like Bill Sullivan could disappear in there, how hard would it be to find a wandering cat? Aunt Ibby and Mrs. Sullivan were each seated in vintage bentwood chairs. Pete handed the water to the no longer sobbing, but still sniffling woman and after a moment, speaking in low tones, led her back toward the stairs.

With O'Ryan curled up on my lap, I sat in the vacated chair. Junior Sullivan and Mr. Pennington stood a few feet away, in conversation with the uniformed officer, who had come inside and was stamping his feet and blowing on cold-reddened hands.

"Mrs. Sullivan seems better," I said. "What made her start crying so hard? She sounded almost hysterical."

"They asked her if she and Bill were getting along. She thought they made it sound as though he was running away from her."

"Well, I guess it's a fair question. Were they? Getting along, I mean?"

"That's what made her cry so," my aunt said. "Seems they'd had a little tiff about him leaving home to come here on Christmas Day. Junior's wife was upset about it, too, so the whole family was squabbling the last time she saw him."

"I don't see a man like Bill running off over a little thing like that."

"She doesn't, either. She's just afraid the police will think so, and they won't seriously try to find him."

"Don't worry," I said. "We'll make sure Pete understands."

"Make sure I understand what?" Pete's voice came from just over my shoulder. Mrs. Sullivan stood silently beside him. Mr. Pennington, the uniformed officer, and Junior moved closer to us, and Mr. Pennington rubbed his gloved hands together.

"Well, boys," he said in his most sonorous tone, "we've a man's work ahead of us this day."

"Pardon?" said Pete.

"Huh?" said Junior.

"What'd he say?" asked the cop.

"*Fort Apache,*" said Aunt Ibby. "Victor McLaglen. 1948."

The look the new director of the Tabby bestowed on my aunt was one of pure adoration. "Dear Lady," Pennington intoned, "what an honor to meet a fellow motion picture aficionado!"

Aunt Ibby gave a polite nod. "Not really. Just an old reference librarian with a head full of trivia."

Mr. Pennington beamed. "You are too modest, Miss Russell. Or is it *Mrs.*?"

Oh my God. My boss is hitting on my aunt.

Pete cleared his throat. "Yes. Well. We're going to take a closer look at the basement. Something has turned up that no one bothered to tell us about." His cop-face stare was directed at Mrs. Sullivan. In his hand he held a purple cloth bag—the kind liquor comes in around the holiday season. It bulged with lumpy contents and clanked slightly when he shook it. "This bag is apparently the property of Mr. Sullivan. Your son says it has something to do with a hobby of your husband's. Is that right?"

The tiny woman seemed to be on the verge of tears again. "Oh, dear. I told Bill he should have asked permission, but he said nobody would care if he did it." She reached for the bag. "Did you find it down there, in the basement?"

Junior went to his mother's side. "It's okay, Ma," he said. "I told them already. I told them what Dad was doing."

Bill Sullivan doing something shady?

"Mrs. Sullivan," Pete said, handing the bag to the uniformed officer, "we'll hold on to this for the time being. You and your son may as well go home while we keep looking for your husband. We'll do one more sweep of the building tonight. If you think of anything at all that might help . . ." He handed her a card, and his voice softened. "I've put my cell phone number on the back, so you can call me anytime."

"We'll drive you home, Mrs. Sullivan," I said, "unless you'd prefer to ride with your son."

"It's hard for me to climb into the van," she said, "so, if you don't mind . . ."

Rupert Pennington volunteered to stay so that he could be sure everything would be "locked up tight" when the police left, even though Pete assured him that they'd secure the place. O'Ryan had been uncharacteristically passive during the time we'd been inside, making no cat comments, no moves to get down from my lap to explore this cavernous place. Instead, his unblinking, golden-eyed gaze had remained fixed on the narrow door that, apparently, led to the basement. Even when I stood to leave and shifted his weight to my shoulder, he twisted his head and continued to watch that solid panel with its faded NO ADMITTANCE sign.

Rather than have Aunt Ibby and Mrs. Sullivan trudge through the deepening snow, I handed the cat over to my aunt and set out to get the car, while the two waited inside the glass doors. I resisted a strong temptation to look up at the row of dormer windows protruding from the mansard roof of the weathered brick building.

I have no desire to see a ghost this Christmas night. What was it Scrooge said when he saw all those ghosts at Christmas? Something about a crumb of cheese, a blot of mustard? Aunt Ibby would know. So would Mr. Pennington.

The Buick's windshield had acquired a thin coating of ice, requiring a couple of minutes with the plastic frost scraper—one chore I hadn't missed in Florida. I turned the heat on full blast, backed the Buick out, and chugged slowly to the front of Trumbull's. Normally, I'm not a nosy person, but I hoped that on the ride home Mrs. Sullivan would tell us what it was that Bill had done and what was in the lumpy purple bag.

Pete escorted the two women onto the sidewalk, and he helped each one into the passenger side of the car, then came around to the driver's side and motioned for me to lower the window a crack. Leaning close to the glass, he whispered, "If that offer of pumpkin pie is still good, I'll drop by when we finish up here."

I smiled my reply, and with my passengers buckled in and O'Ryan again curled up on Aunt Ibby's lap, I headed back to Bridge Street. We'd barely started when Mrs. Sullivan began to talk.

"It was because of the coins, you know. That's all it was. That's how come Bill and Junior gave the low bid for the job. Bill wanted the silver."

"Silver coins?" Aunt Ibby prompted.

"Oh, yes. There should have been lots of them in an old store like that. Coins roll under the counters all the time, and those big wooden ones probably hadn't been moved in years. And since they closed the store in the sixties, Bill figured all that loose change would be the real silver kind." She sniffled. "He's been finding them all week. I told him he should've asked permission. They prob'ly would've said he could keep whatever he found. He wouldn't listen. Said the city would figure it was theirs."

"Is that what's in the purple bag?" I asked. "Money?"

"Sure. But at least now I know that Bill isn't running away from me. He'd never run off and leave all that silver behind. Anyway, Junior says he didn't even take his coat. He's in that old store somewhere. They'll find him."

"They found the bag in the basement," I said, thinking out loud. "There aren't any counters down there."

"Wouldn't matter to Bill. Not a bit." Her voice sounded stronger. "When he's hunting for coins, he'll go anywhere. He's searched the whole place. The basement must have been the only part he hadn't checked. He even took a flashlight one night and looked in the attic."

"The attic?" Aunt Ibby turned and faced the woman.

"Sure. The part with the funny-looking windows. Where they used to keep the old woman."

CHAPTER 4

Aunt Ibby and I exchanged surprised looks.

Where they used to keep the old woman?

We'd reached the Sullivans' apartment house, and the red van with the U-Haul trailer was already parked in front of the building. Before we could question his mother further, Junior Sullivan stepped over a snowbank, extending an assisting hand as she climbed from the backseat.

She thanked us again for our help and hurried away.

"What was she talking about? What old woman?" I asked as we pulled away.

"I'm not quite sure," my aunt said, "but I think I remember hearing that back when the store first opened, there was a fancy apartment on the top floor, where the family lived. Kind of an early version of a penthouse. It would have been sometime in the nineteen twenties, I should think. I'll see if there's anything about it in the old newspapers next time I'm at the library."

Although Aunt Ibby was semiretired as the head reference librarian at Salem's main library, she still put in a few hours most weeks, helping out and training staff.

"I'll bet it was nice. You could probably see the whole city from up there."

"Probably still can," she said. "When you start your new job, you'll likely have the run of the building. You can go up there and check it out."

"I might," I said, pulling up in front of our garage. "If I can get someone to go up there with me. Don't want to run into any ghosts all by myself."

"Muurree," said O'Ryan, wide awake, standing on Aunt Ibby's lap, with his paws on the dash.

"See?" she said. "O'Ryan says he'll go with you." She tapped the door opener, and I drove the big car inside the garage.

"I think what he said was, 'Is there any of that turkey left over?'"

She laughed. "You're probably right. There is, and pumpkin pie, too, for Pete, when he gets here."

"You were listening."

"Of course I was." A big smile. "There isn't much that gets by your old aunt."

"Including lines from old movies, apparently. What was that all about? I think you've made a big impression on the Tabby's new director."

"Oh. The *Fort Apache* thing? Years ago I helped a woman compile a book on famous movie quotes, and for some reason, a lot of them just stuck."

"Amazing," I said as we hurried through the icy yard. "That kind of total recall is hard to believe."

"I find your lack of faith disturbing," she said, turning the key in the lock on the back door.

"What?"

"*Star Wars,*" she said. "James Earl Jones. 1977."

With the cat leading the way, and with me still marveling at my aunt's remarkable memory, we hurried into the kitchen, with its welcome warmth and light and good holiday smells of home.

I made a fresh pot of coffee, and Aunt Ibby headed back to the den and her beloved computer. "Want a cup when it's ready?" I called. "And maybe something to nibble on?"

"Thanks, dear. Coffee will be wonderful. And maybe a teensy one of those little Christmas cookies. I'm going to see what I can find online about the history of Trumbull's."

A few minutes later, when I carried a tray with our two mugs of hot coffee and more than a few of the teensy shortbread cookies into the den, she was diligently making notes, fingers flying over the keyboard. O'Ryan sat on the desk, as close to the monitor as he could get, in the manner of cats everywhere.

"Find anything good?"

"Pretty much just the general stuff the chamber of commerce put out about them back when the store closed. But don't worry. I'll get the nitty-gritty from the old newspapers. It's all on microfilm at the library." She tapped the screen with a French-tipped forefinger and smiled. "The old newspapers printed all the dirt."

"Anything there about the lady upstairs?"

"Just about the way I remembered. It says that the Trumbull family had a lavish suite on the top floor, and they often entertained the cream of Salem society. Seems they had a huge ballroom up there that was a smaller-scale replica of the one in Hamilton Hall. They even had a balcony overlooking the dance floor. How elegant can you get?"

I nodded my agreement. Hardly any place is more elegant than Salem's two-hundred-year-old Hamilton Hall.

"I wonder what it looks like now," I said. "I guess I'll have to go up there, after all. Haunted or not."

"Why don't you ask River to go with you? I'll bet she'd love to see it."

It was a good idea. River North is one of our favorite people. She also happens to be a witch. My TV stint as a phony phone-in psychic hadn't worked out well career-wise, but it had brought me an interesting new circle of friends I might never have met otherwise.

"I will," I said. "We've got a kind of orientation thing going on for the staff this week so we'll know our way around the building. I'll ask Mr. Pennington if I can invite River one day."

"You don't have to tell him about the witch thing. She's so young and pretty. That ought to be enough of a reason for him to say yes."

O'Ryan hopped down from the desk and ran toward the front hall.

"Somebody's coming," my aunt said. "Must be Pete."

She and O'Ryan were right. The cat and I greeted the handsome detective at the door, O'Ryan with purrs and ankle rubbing, me with a hug and a "warmer than usual for the front hall" kiss.

"Wow," he said, returning my kiss with an equally warm one. "You could thaw out a snowman, woman." He hung his coat on the hall tree, then pulled me close again.

"We'd better head for the kitchen before Aunt Ibby comes out here, looking for us," I said, taking his hand. "Come on."

"If we have to."

"We do. Anyway, that's where the pumpkin pie is."

The coffee was still hot, and three slices of pie, each topped with a hefty dollop of whipped cream, had been arranged on the kitchen table.

"Come on, you two. Sit," my aunt ordered. "Pete, tell us what happened down there after we left. Any idea what happened to Bill?"

"Well, like I told Mrs. Sullivan, we did one more sweep of the place. I mean, we did as well as we could with just me and one officer. Didn't find anything new." Pete shook his head. "Looks like the guy got outside somehow, 'cause he sure isn't in that building. He didn't have his coat, you know."

"Oh, Pete. It's freezing out there," I said. "Maybe there's a dressing room or a small office or something you missed."

"Maybe." He sounded doubtful. "We'll try again tomorrow, when we have daylight. The lighting is pretty dim on the upper floors. No lights at all in the attic."

"Was Mr. Pennington helpful?" I asked. "He seems to know the old place pretty well."

"He pretty much followed us around and made sure we didn't leave anything unlocked. He takes being in charge of those keys really seriously." He smiled. "He told us there are a couple of them that don't seem to fit anything. It's driving him nuts."

"Aunt Ibby looked up some information on the building," I said. "The Trumbulls used to live up on the top floor. What does it look like up there? Can you tell it was really nice a long time ago?"

He seemed surprised. "Nice? I don't know. We prowled around with flashlights. There're just a lot of empty rooms. Except for one huge one, where they must have tossed all the old furniture and stuff. Oh, and one room that still had a bed and bureau and an old upright piano and a rocking chair. And a big framed picture of President Roosevelt on the wall."

"Must be the old woman's room," said my aunt.

"Mrs. Sullivan told us about some old woman who was kept up there."

"An old woman, huh? Well, Salem's full of weird stories, that's for sure," he said. "Look, I don't mean to eat and run, but I'm going to have to start the official search for Sullivan early in the morning. Thanks for the pie and coffee, Miss Russell. It was great."

He stood and, as Aunt Ibby nodded her approval, carried his dishes to the sink.

What a guy!

O'Ryan and I walked with Pete to the front hall. He delivered another of those sizzling kisses and held me close. Well, he held me as close as he could with a cat wrapped around his ankles, put on his coat, and walked again into that cold, cold night.

Bill Sullivan. I pray that you're somewhere warm.

It had been a long day, and I was ready for sleep. Aunt Ibby started the dishwasher while I turned off the Christmas lights, and then we both headed upstairs. Stepping carefully past a few paint cans and some tarpaulin-draped furniture, I wished her a good night, took a quick shower, pulled on one of Johnny Barrett's old DAYTONA RACE WEEK T-shirts, and climbed into bed, where O'Ryan was already asleep. I opened my new book to the chapter on "How to Choose Your Faithful Sidekicks." I doubted that Nancy would have chosen a witch for a sidekick, but I was sure she'd like River North. And I was just as sure my friend River would love searching for a ghost in the attic of Trumbull's.

I fell asleep with the chapter unread. The ring tone of my cell phone woke me, and a glance at the alarm clock showed that it was only six thirty. Caller ID revealed who my early morning caller was.

"Pete? What's going on?"

"Hi, Lee. Are you watching the morning news?"

"No," I said. "Haven't turned it on yet. Why?"

"It's not good, I'm afraid," he said. "I hoped I could talk to you before you heard about it from the media."

"What is it? Is it about Bill Sullivan?"

"Afraid so. We found him this morning."

"Is he alive?"

"He's dead, Lee. And the strangest thing is, he was nowhere near the store. He was down by the waterfront."

"How did he get there? And why? He didn't even have his coat."

"We don't have any details." His voice was solemn. "The ME hasn't even started working on him yet. But we were wrong about the coat. He was wearing one."

"That's strange. Everyone thought he'd gone off without it. But you must have some idea how he died. Do you?"

"Someone called 911 around three o'clock. Said there was a drunk under a tree in that little park by the marina."

"A drunk? That doesn't sound like Bill."

"That's what his wife said. But apparently, he smelled of alcohol when they found him."

"Oh, poor Mrs. Sullivan. How'd she take the news?"

"Pretty hard. I called Junior first, so he and his wife were with her when I got there. They'd called her parish priest and asked him to come over." He paused, and I heard his soft sigh. "That's a part of my job I hate. Telling people someone they love is dead."

"Did either of them have any idea how he happened to be so far away from the store?"

"Nope. We'll be putting out a call for witnesses later this morning. Maybe somebody saw something around there last night that will help us figure it out. Junior said the last thing he remembers Bill saying before he went down to the basement was that he thought he might have seen a silver half-dollar under that big pile of mannequin body parts. He was going to try to get it."

"Thanks for letting me know. I'll go and tell Aunt Ibby before she turns on the news."

I padded down the hall to my aunt's room and knocked gently. Too late. The TV was on, and she was watching the morning news.

"Oh, Lee. They've found Bill. Dead."

"I know." I sat on the edge of her bed. "Pete just called and told me."

"What happened to him? Did Pete say how he died?"

"They don't know yet. The medical examiner hasn't finished doing . . . you know. Whatever it is medical examiners do."

"How did Mrs. Sullivan take it? Did Pete say?"

"Pretty hard, I guess. Junior and his wife were with her, though, and her priest was coming over."

"That's good. I'm sure they'll let us know about funeral arrangements and such." She climbed out of bed and donned robe and bunny slippers. "If Bill walked all the way down to where they found him without his jacket, he probably froze to death." She paused. "The news anchor said that possibly liquor was involved. Did Pete mention that?"

"He did," I said. "And he says that Bill actually was wearing his jacket after all, but yes, the police report said Bill smelled strongly of alcohol."

"Imagine that." She sighed. "Falling off the wagon after all these years."

"He had a drinking problem?"

"Long ago, he did. But he's been sober for years. At least I thought so."

I went back to my room to shower and dress. When O'Ryan and I started down the stairs, I could already smell coffee brewing and bacon sizzling. My aunt, as usual, was way ahead of me.

After removing a pan of hot cinnamon buns from the oven, she waved a quilted potholder. "Sit right down, Maralee. Breakfast is almost ready."

I sat. O'Ryan approached his bowl, already filled with his favorite morning kitty kibble.

"I've been thinking," she said, "about Bill Sullivan and the drinking thing. I just don't believe it."

"You don't? Then why would the police report say there might be alcohol involved?"

"I don't know. But I knew the man."

"I hope you're right. At least his wife wouldn't have that to deal with along with everything else."

After breakfast we stayed busy with after-holiday chores. Aunt Ibby made preparations for the annual turkey soup, while I folded and stacked leftover Christmas wrapping paper for the recycling bin. It was around noon when Pete phoned again.

"I thought you'd want to know," he said, "that however Bill Sullivan wound up in that park, he didn't walk there."

"What do you mean?"

"The ME says he had a compound fracture of his right leg. Bone sticking right out. He wasn't walking anywhere last night."

CHAPTER 5

I'd barely had time to tell Aunt Ibby about this new development when the phone rang again. It was Rupert Pennington, his voice so agitated, it took a moment for me to figure out who was calling.

"Ms. Barrett, whatever are we going to do? It's a calamity of epic proportions, a total disaster, a major, most hideous tragedy."

"I know, Mr. Pennington." I kept my tone level. "I've heard about it. He was such a nice man."

"Oh, him. Yes, indeed. Very sad. I'm talking about our grand opening. Our introduction to the community. The beginning of Salem's foremost, most prestigious academy for artistic excellence in all fields. Ms. Barrett, whatever are we going to do?"

"I don't quite understand, sir."

"The police are here. There is yellow tape festooned across my freshly varnished staircase. There is some sort of fingerprint dust sprinkled like ashes upon my personal lectern, from which I intend to address the student body each and every morning. There are nasty, slushy boot prints on my genuine vintage oak hardwood floors. It is a disaster, I tell you. A full-blown, monstrous disaster." He sounded as though he was about to cry.

"Mr. Pennington," I said, "the Salem police are very professional. I'm sure they'll finish their work quickly. We still have a few days before the opening and enough volunteers to put everything to rights again. Please don't worry so. Is there anything I can do to help?"

"My dear lady, if you could only come over and give me a hand at reorganizing, reprioritizing, so to speak. We need to figure out how to have staff orientation week amid this chaos. There are students arriving in Salem already. The police have finished prowling about my office, so I'm quite sure they'll allow you to enter."

"I'm not sure how useful I can be, but I'll be glad to do what I can."

"It's all so confusing. The classrooms on the first and second floors are ready for furnishing, and the dance studio mirrors are scheduled to be installed today, but the third-floor dormitories still await painting, and the beds haven't even been delivered." A slight quaver crept into his voice. "They've installed countertops that are the wrong color in the diner, and the stage curtain in the student performance theater is four inches too short. We can't use the elevators, because they haven't been inspected yet. The whole thing is a disaster, I tell you."

"I'll be there," I promised and hung up.

"What on earth was that all about?" my aunt asked. "Mr. Pennington needs help, I take it."

"Apparently. I guess I'll have to go over there."

"Does he know about Bill being found?"

"Yes, though he barely acknowledged it. He's mostly

concerned about getting the school in shape for the grand opening."

"It's understandable. That's his responsibility, and he seems to take it seriously."

"True. I'll try to help."

"Well, you've got a nice day for it. It's so pretty here after a storm, isn't it?"

She was right. The snow had stopped and now lay like a woolly white blanket over the city. Ancient oaks and chestnut trees lined Winter Street, their ice-coated branches sparkling like diamonds against a cloudless blue sky.

"Just beautiful," I agreed. "I missed this. I think I'll walk downtown and enjoy it before it melts."

"You sure? You're welcome to use the Buick."

"Thanks. I'm looking forward to the walk, and I'm going to look for a car of my own pretty soon. There's room for another in the garage, I think."

"Of course there is. Whenever you're ready."

I dressed carefully, in layers. I'd been a New Englander long enough to know that even the prettiest snow day can be bitterly cold. In my warmest jeans, a black cotton turtleneck, a red cashmere pullover, and a flannel-lined jacket, along with gloves, knit hat, and boots, I set out for Essex Street.

Some of the shops had AFTER CHRISTMAS SALE signs in the windows, and bundle-carrying people along the pedestrian mall sidewalks indicated that plenty of bargain hunting, or maybe gift returning, was happening in Salem. I paused in front of an art gallery and was surprised to hear my name called from across the street.

"Lee. Hey, Lee! Wait up." I turned to see River North, long black braid flying, running toward me.

"Happy winter solstice, Lee." She enveloped me in a cheerful, patchouli-scented hug.

I laughed. "Happy winter solstice to you, River, and Happy New Year. Aunt Ibby and I were talking about you this morning."

"Really? I've been thinking about you, too. Want me to read your cards? See what the New Year might bring?"

River is an expert at reading the tarot. In fact, she took over the late-night show at the TV station after I left. She does readings over the phone, in between vampire and zombie movies.

"Maybe later. Did you hear about what happened at the new school last night?"

"No. I just woke up about an hour ago. You know I never watch the news. Too depressing."

I explained as briefly as I could. River fell into step beside me, and we walked together toward the Tabby.

"So the man went into a basement with no exits and wound up dead in a park a couple of miles away?"

"That's about it," I said. "Bizarre, huh? Ever hear of anything like that before?"

"Lee, I'm a Wiccan. I'm used to bizarre. Bizarre is my life."

"And that's a good thing. Because I think I'll be inviting you to a ghost hunt in the near future."

"Really? When? Where? I can hardly wait."

I smiled at her enthusiasm. "Ever hear of a ghost woman who's supposed to hang out on the top floor of the Trumbull building?"

"Of course. It's supposed to be old Tabitha Trumbull. The one they named the school after."

"It is? I mean, I knew Tabitha was the founder's wife, but I never heard that she was the lady in white."

"Oh yeah. That's her. The Trumbull family tried for

years to keep it quiet. But we all know what they did to her."

"We do?"

"We . . . the witches. We know."

We'd reached Trumbull's, and I stopped, waiting for River to go on, to say more about what it was the witches knew about the woman in the attic. I studied our reflections in the surface of the polished glass doors, only vaguely aware of activity inside the storefront. River, standing only as high as my shoulders, looked even younger than her twenty-five years.

"Wow," she said. "There are cops in there. Is this about your dead guy?"

"Yeah. It's a real mystery."

She shrugged. "Why don't you use your gift and help them out?"

My "gift." River is the only person in my life who calls it that. I didn't want to use it. I didn't even like to talk about it.

"I don't think I have it anymore," I said and waved my arm. "Poof! It disappeared. But what about Tabitha? You were saying . . . ?"

River laughed. "Don't be silly. A gift like that doesn't go away. Use it. Go ahead. Don't be such a chicken."

A uniformed officer appeared at the entrance. He pushed one of the doors open. "You waving at me, miss?"

River moved toward the curb. "You have to go to work." She put her hand next to her ear, with her pinkie and thumb extended. "Call me," she said. "I'll tell you all about that other thing later."

I turned to speak to the officer. "I'm Lee Barrett. Mr. Pennington is expecting me."

"Okay. He said you'd be here. You got ID?"

I showed him my Florida driver's license. He peered back and forth from the photo to my face several times.

"Not from around here?"

"Used to be. Just moved back."

"Okay. Pennington's office is on the right at the head of the stairs."

"I'll find it," I said. "Thanks."

He lifted the yellow tape, and I ducked under.

"Don't touch anything," he said.

I didn't even touch the wide railing, which, I had to agree with Aunt Ibby, would be great for sliding.

The thing River had called my "gift," the thing I didn't like to talk or even think about, dates back to my childhood. I couldn't have been much more than four and a half when I got my first Mary Janes. I wore them only on Sunday. A lot of kids had special shoes they wore to church, but mine were different. I saw pictures in them. They were, to me, like miniature TV sets. If I was bored in church, I could always watch the images in my shoes. I told Aunt Ibby and my parents about it, but they just figured it was my imagination. Aunt Ibby thought that was all it was when she agreed to take care of me for a weekend, while my parents took a little trip to Maine. She thought so right up until that Sunday morning, when I looked into my shoes and saw Daddy's yellow Piper Cub airplane slam into the side of a steep Maine cliff and burst into flames.

That terrible memory remained mercifully blocked right up until I got the job as host of the *Nightshades* program. That all changed the first time I looked into an obsidian ball I found on the set. It had belonged to my predecessor on the show, that broom-riding, cauldron-stirring witch, Ariel Constellation.

The pictures came back big-time in that damned black obsidian. Eventually, I learned that I was what people who know about such things call a scryer. River calls me a gazer. Sometimes, they say, in shiny surfaces a scryer can see things happening or things that have happened or even things that haven't happened yet. Once Ariel's murderer was captured, though, my visions stopped. I blamed the dead witch for the whole thing and prayed that they'd stopped for good. Everything the obsidian ball had ever shown me was bad, and I still tried to avoid looking at shiny black surfaces. River's idea that I should do it on purpose to help find out what had happened to Bill scared me to death.

The door marked RUPERT PENNINGTON – EXECUTIVE DIRECTOR was partially closed. I tapped gently. "Hello," I called. "It's Lee Barrett. May I come in?"

"Come in, come in, Ms. Barrett," came the clearly enunciated baritone invitation. "My door is never locked. Always an open door here at the academy. Come in and meet some of your students."

The dated style of Trumbull's had been retained for the office decor. A large walnut desk dominated the front of the room, and the director sat in an imposing high-backed leather swivel chair. A set of silver desk accessories—pen, inkwell, and letter opener, each monogrammed O.W.T., gleamed on the polished walnut surface. An ancient office safe with ornate gold-leaf lettering stood against the wall behind the desk, and brass-handled, varnished oak file cabinets completed the vintage look of the place. Two young women sat opposite Mr. Pennington in straight-backed wooden chairs, looking both bored and uncomfortable.

"Ms. Lee Barrett, please meet two of your students. Miss Kelly Greene and Miss Therese Della Monica have arrived a bit early for the opening of the academy."

There was the slightest hint of displeasure in his voice. I guessed it was because the dormitories were unfinished, the main floor was empty except for yellow tape and an obvious police presence, and two attractive female students had arrived well before Rupert Pennington was prepared to make his grand welcoming speech from behind a dust-free lectern, to a breathlessly attentive student body.

Both Kelly and Therese immediately stood. Whether out of deference to my position as instructor or just to move closer to the door, I didn't know. I extended my hand, first to dark-haired Kelly, then to blond Therese.

"Welcome to the Tabby," I said. "I know it looks a little confusing right now, but by the time school starts, it'll all be shipshape."

"How do you do, Ms. Barrett?" Therese Della Monica's voice was pure Beacon Hill; her handshake of the fingertip variety; her smile sweet and shy.

Kelly Greene's handshake was firm; her hands tanned and strong; nails short and unpolished. "Hi," she said. "Pleased to meet you." Her accent seemed like a blend of the Florida Panhandle and New Hampshire. Not exactly Southern, and with a hint of New England twang. I couldn't place it.

"Miss Greene is from West Virginia," Mr. Pennington offered.

"Guess you can tell I'm not from these parts," Kelly said. "But my pa and I live in Salem. We have a little tavern down near the ocean. I'm working there now. Our bartender, Thom, told me about this place. He's going to take your class, too. We both want to be on TV someday."

"Wonderful. Welcome," I said.

Mr. Pennington stepped from behind his desk. "Perhaps you could show these ladies a bit of our flourishing downtown."

Translation. Get these damned kids out of my office.

"I'd love to. Come on, you two. Put on your coats, and we'll do a little tour."

They practically raced me to the stairs.

"What'll it be?" I asked. "Museums and art galleries or shops?"

"Shops," they said in unison, then looked at one another and laughed.

"That's easy," I said. "We have all kinds. Take your pick."

"I like fashion," Kelly said. "If I'm going to be a TV star, I need to have great clothes." She gave me an appraising look. "Like yours. You're so put together."

"I'm mostly interested in anything that has to do with the witches." Therese spoke so softly, I had to lean close to hear her words. "I'm thinking about becoming one of them. That's actually why I chose this school. Salem is where I need to be."

CHAPTER 6

While I'd told Mr. Pennington not to worry, and I'd promised Kelly and Therese that everything at the Tabby would soon be shipshape, I thought I was being overly optimistic. But somehow, amazingly, I was right.

The painting of the dorms, thanks to the miracle of spray guns, was done, the paint dry, and the dorm rooms move-in ready before sundown that day. The beds and bureaus had arrived, and new lighting had been installed in each cubicle. The mirrors and ballet barres were in place in the dance studio, and best of all, the yellow tape was gone.

The police continued their investigation in the basement, since that was the last place anyone had seen Bill. A new, larger NO ADMITTANCE sign was posted on that door. It didn't lead to usable space, anyway, so school preparations weren't disrupted.

No more early students had shown up, much to Director Pennington's obvious relief. I learned that in addition to the two I'd met, there were four more registered for my TV courses. So far, I'd drawn one enthusiastic West Virginian, one witch wannabe, and a yet unseen bartender.

With the setting of the sun, the temperature plunged, and I, the typical Floridian, called a cab for the short ride home. River would call me chicken again if she knew about it. I had mixed feelings about calling her. I wanted to know about the attic ghost at the Tabby, but at the same time I didn't want to hear any more about using my gift in the search for answers about what had happened to Bill Sullivan.

Aunt Ibby and O'Ryan were waiting for me just inside the front door when I arrived home.

"Come in. Come in. It's getting colder, isn't it?" My aunt hugged me, and the cat purred and licked snow from the toe of my boot. "What's going on down there at the school? The evening news said that the police are concentrating the investigation on the park where Bill was found. They think someone picked him up at Trumbull's and drove him there, and they're asking for witnesses who may have seen him that night."

"Did they say anything about the broken leg? How it could have happened?" I took off my winter gear and headed for the warm comfort of the living room.

"Not exactly. They just said there was an indication of lower body trauma." She hurried toward the kitchen. "You just relax. I'll get us some tea, and you can tell me all about your day."

I propped my feet up on a plump ottoman and wiggled my toes. It felt good. "I don't even want to move," I told the cat, who had carried his purple mouse into the room and had dropped it next to my chair. "I played tour guide all afternoon to a couple of shopaholics." Between Kelly's countless trips to boutique dressing rooms as she searched for a "put-together" look and Therese's intensive quizzing of at least a dozen shopkeepers as to the magical properties of certain herbs, and her gathering of assorted magic spell books, I was beat. And my feet hurt.

I leaned back and closed my eyes, but O'Ryan was not going to allow such inattention. He batted at my stockinged feet with soft, sheathed paws. I pretended not to notice. He smacked a little harder and meowed a low-toned "mrruf." I shook my foot and pushed him away.

"Go away, O'Ryan," I said. "I'll play with you later."

He climbed into my lap, put his front paws on my shoulders, and did that staring thing cats do, knowing darn well it will make you open your eyes. It worked. The golden eyes focused on mine, the throaty cat sounds growing more insistent.

"Okay. What do you want?"

He jumped down, picked up the catnip mouse, and carried it toward the front hall. His yowl was long, loud, and insistent.

Aunt Ibby hurried from the kitchen. "What's wrong with O'Ryan?" she asked. "Is he all right?"

"I don't know. I think he wants me to follow him somewhere. Is that it, boy?"

The bedraggled mouse once more clutched in his teeth, O'Ryan headed up the stairs. I followed. When we reached the second-floor landing, he looked back at me, and determining that I was still behind him, he started up the curving staircase leading to the next floor.

"Oh, c'mon, cat! There's nothing up there except a big mess." The renovations were well under way, but the place was nowhere near habitable. O'Ryan trotted upward and then paused when he reached the third-floor landing, waiting for me to catch up.

The stairwells in our house curve in such a way that a person standing at the top of the stairs on the third floor can look all the way down and see the floor in the front hall. O'Ryan poked his head between the spindles, dangling his mouse over the edge of the top stair. He looked back, making sure I was watching.

The purple rodent plummeted downward, landing with a thud on the carpet two stories below. With both hands gripping the top of the railing, I leaned forward, focusing on the distant purple blob below. For a few seconds O'Ryan stood beside me, neck craned over the edge of the top tread. Apparently satisfied with what he saw, with a twitch of his tail, he trotted down the stairs. I followed at a slower pace and joined a puzzled Aunt Ibby in the front hall. O'Ryan had already retrieved the mouse and had put it back beside the chair I'd vacated.

"What on God's green earth was that all about?" my aunt wondered. "A new game he's thought up?"

"I'm not exactly sure," I said. "And I don't know how it's possible, but I think maybe he's trying to tell us how Bill got that broken leg."

"From being dropped?"

"Or falling," I said, "from someplace high."

"Last time anyone saw him, Bill was in a basement," she said with perfect logic. "Nowhere to fall from there."

"You're right," I said, feeling a little silly. "O'Ryan's probably just still catnip happy. Anyway, the police will figure it all out. Let's have that tea, and I'll tell you about my day. I met two of my students. Interesting girls."

We went into the kitchen, with O'Ryan tagging along, leaving the mouse leaning dejectedly against the chair leg. We sat at the table and I told Aunt Ibby that I'd run into River and what she'd told me about Tabitha being the one who supposedly haunted the store.

"Oh, there are lots of different versions of the 'lady in white' story," she said, pouring the tea. "I did a little checking today at the library. Mrs. Sullivan and River must be thinking of the same story. It's the one about Tabitha, old and crazy, wandering the attic in her nightgown. Some say the whole place was built on top of an ancient Naumkeag Indian burial ground and the ghost is an Indian princess dressed in white deerskin." She smiled. "I rather like that one. Then there are stories about one of the Trumbull girls, back in the fifties, who got pregnant and drowned herself. She's supposed to be wearing her confirmation dress. There are probably plenty of other nominees for the position of department store ghost."

"Urban legends. That's what Pete says they all are, and that just about every city has them."

"He's right. But tell me about the students. What do you think of them?"

"One of them, Kelly Greene, is from West Virginia. She's joining the class on the advice of a bartender friend."

"Kelly Greene. That's cute," my aunt said. "Is she Irish?"

"I didn't ask," I said. "Could be. Dark hair, bright blue eyes, fair skin."

"What about the other girl? What's her name?"

"Therese Della Monica. She's a cool blonde. Well spoken. But not really interested in the course, as far as I could tell. Says she came to Salem to learn to be a witch."

My aunt frowned. "What made her choose your class? She doesn't know about . . . that thing you can do, does she?"

"Of course not. Besides, it's just as I told River. That's all gone. I can't do it anymore."

Even if I can, I won't. What have the damned visions ever shown me except death and dying? Some gift!

"Hmmm. I hope for your sake, that's true."

"Therese just wants to be in Salem. I guess she thinks the Tabby sounds easy. No entrance requirements, no exams, no degrees. Probably signed up for it so she'd have a good story for her parents. After all, they're paying for it, and the Tabby isn't cheap."

"I know, dear." Aunt Ibby reached across the table and patted my hand the way she used to when I was a child. "But the students who go there can learn about things they've only dreamed of doing. Like oil painting or ballet dancing or writing poetry. Don't you worry. You'll make that course so interesting, she'll be thrilled that she signed up. And her parents will get their money's worth, too."

"Thanks," I said. "I hope so. And speaking of thrilling courses, I have a little catching up to do in Criminology 101."

"How's that coming along?"

"Slowly," I admitted. "But it's fascinating. I don't know exactly what I'm going to do with it, but, like Therese and her magic, it's something I really want to learn about."

"Well," she said, picking up a wooden spoon and facing the stove, where a black iron kettle simmered, "you can't study on an empty stomach. The turkey soup will be ready in half an hour."

O'Ryan and I went upstairs, and I changed into comfy gray sweats. I put the course textbook and a notepad on the desk, next to my laptop, then, smiling, added *The Official Nancy Drew Handbook*.

"There, cat. If you've sobered up after your funny little game of drop the mouse, we'll be all ready to study after dinner."

O'Ryan, tail straight up, in what might be interpreted as a cat's version of a rude gesture, turned and stalked from the room.

CHAPTER 7

Homemade turkey soup and hot baking powder biscuits on a cold Massachusetts winter night are pure bliss. My aunt and I sat across the table from one another in our warm, cozy kitchen, while O'Ryan, still ignoring me, enjoyed some bits of leftover turkey from a new, bright red Christmas bowl.

"I can't help thinking about the Sullivans and how sad their holiday turned out to be," my aunt said.

"I know," I said. "I was thinking about them, too. Trying to figure out how Bill got from the store to that park. Didn't you say the police think somebody picked him up at Trumbull's and drove him down there?"

"That's what they're saying."

"Just doesn't ring true. If he left with someone, why didn't he tell Junior he was leaving? Where are the tire tracks from the vehicle? An extra pair of footprints leaving the store?"

"Lots of unanswered questions," she said. "And how did he get that broken leg?"

"Maybe O'Ryan was right. Maybe he fell or jumped or was pushed from someplace pretty high up."

"Like the mouse?"

"Exactly like the mouse."

"Mrrip," said O'Ryan, sticking his pink tongue out at me.

"But where's there a high-up place between the school and the park?" I wondered aloud.

"It's a quandary," she said. "I don't know how much time the police can spend on it. After all, it's not a serious crime to be drunk in a public park on Christmas night, no matter how you got there or how badly you ended up. Maybe we'll never know what happened to his leg."

"I'm afraid that's true. I think they've about wrapped up the investigation at the school. There was still one officer looking around in the basement today, but the moving crew hadn't even finished carrying all the mannequins up to Theater Arts when I left."

"I hope they'll be able to give the Sullivans some closure, or the questions will haunt them forever," she said.

"Speaking of haunting, when you researched the ghost stories, did anything else interesting turn up in the old newspapers? River says that the ghost is Tabitha Trumbull. She says the witches know about something that happened to her in the attic."

"Not really. Seems every few years some writer digs up the old 'lady in white' stories for a Halloween feature. But when I just search Trumbull's, there's miles of information." She spread her arms wide apart. "Reams of it. After all, Trumbull's was Salem's main department store for nearly half a century. It would take quite a while to separate the anniversary sale press releases from the Trumbull obituaries and the nitty-gritty news stories."

"I imagine it would." I carried our bowls and plates to the dishwasher. "Thanks for trying."

"No problem. That's what I do. Research is my life."

I laughed. "When I talked to River today, she said that bizarre is her life. Quite a difference."

My aunt sounded thoughtful. "Not so much."

"Thanks for checking out the ghost stories, anyway."

"No problem. It was interesting. I found a few of those nitty-gritty things, too. Intriguing enough to make me want to check further."

"Really? Like what?"

"I want to cross-check a few things before I can verify what I've seen so far, but it seems a few of the Trumbulls may have been on the wrong side of the law."

"Sounds juicy. Want to give me a hint?"

She cocked her head to one side and looked thoughtful. "Well, bear in mind that it may be conjecture . . . even gossip . . . but—"

"Come on!" I had to laugh at the way she made me plead for information that I knew she was dying to tell me. "Give it up!"

"Hmmm. All right." She leaned forward and lowered her voice, as though someone might be listening. "Seems there was some bootlegging, back in the Prohibition days."

I nodded. "Not unusual, I guess, for the times. They got caught, huh?"

"Somebody went to jail for it. Not any of the Trumbulls, though, even though it was pretty obvious that they were involved."

"Interesting. Did you find anything else, Sherlock Holmes?"

"Not yet, but I'll keep looking." She sat back in her chair, a familiar self-satisfied look on her face.

"You're good," I said, meaning it. "Really good."

I wished her good night, and with O'Ryan strolling along beside me, I started for my room and the planned study session. We passed through the living room, where the cat paused, giving a backward glance toward his mouse, which still leaned at an odd angle against the chair leg.

Was that the way they found Bill Sullivan? Leaning crookedly against a tree?

Once in my room, O'Ryan hopped onto the foot of the bed, turned around a couple of times, and positioned himself so he was facing my desk. I lifted the cover of the laptop, clicked on the lamp, picked up a pencil, a pink highlighter, and the yellow legal pad, and prepared to take notes. Read Chapter Seven, the screen commanded. I flipped the thick book open to the assigned pages. Basically, criminology involves figuring out why criminals behave as they do, and this chapter put forth the idea that our relationships and beliefs affect our behaviors, criminal or otherwise.

It was after midnight when I finished reading, highlighting, and note taking.

"That's enough studying for one night," I told the cat as I shut down the computer and stacked the books and papers. "I'll join you on that nice comfortable bed in about two minutes."

But sleep wouldn't come. After much pillow punching, cover adjusting, turning from back to tummy, tummy to back, I gave up and turned on the bedside lamp. Random thoughts of Bill Sullivan tumbled through my head. Thoughts about how he'd wound up dead miles from where he'd started that cold Christmas night.

Too many unanswered questions. Is there criminal behavior here somewhere? But how? Where? And mostly, why?

Fully awake, I turned my radio to the golden oldies station, keeping the volume down low, and picked up *The Official Nancy Drew Handbook*. O'Ryan was awake, too, and had curled up on my lap, facing the open book. His big right paw shot out, and he turned a couple of pages gently, with claws sheathed.

"Okay, big boy," I said. "Is that the one you think I should read?"

He stared at the page he'd selected for a few seconds, then closed his eyes, put his head on my shoulder, and went back to sleep.

He'd landed on a passage from one of my old Carolyn Keene favorites, *The Ghost of Blackwood Hall.* "'I'm going to keep working on this case until all the pieces in the puzzle can be made to fit together . . .'"

Can a cat read? Even a witch's cat? Of course not. The idea is preposterous. All the same, when I put the book aside, carefully moved a sleeping O'Ryan to the other side of the bed, and snuggled down beneath the covers, the tumbling thoughts had gone away and I felt relaxed, as though I'd come to an important decision.

CHAPTER 8

Things at the Tabby had settled down. The NO ADMITTANCE sign remained on the basement door, but since Bill Sullivan's body had been found away from the building, official interest in the storage area had faded and Mr. Pennington had resumed his quest for extra funding to convert it to a sound and lighting studio.

Instructors, painters, workmen, and a few more early arriving students moved about the school as though they'd been choreographed. In fact, activity at the newly converted department store proved to be less confusing than the goings-on at the house on Winter Street. According to the head contractor, my aunt Ibby had a bad case of the "whileyas," as in "Whileya have that wall opened up, why not put another fireplace there?" or "Whileya tiling the powder room, let's put in a hot tub." I'd found that my best option was just to stay away from the project.

The perimeters of my classroom had been established within the vast open space once occupied by Trumbull's large shoe department. Without traditional walls, and with a full view of the elevator and the main staircase, my make-believe TV studio occupied much of the former retail space. Remnants of its previous use were evident in the typical shoe department chairs—too classic and comfortable to get rid of—and in a couple of display fixtures, which Director Pennington declared "fabulous kitsch" and "absolutely wonderful pop art" and "totally historic."

I had no objection to the tin lithographed cutout of Buster Brown and his dog, Tige. In fact, I found it cute. But the giant half model of a shiny, black, high-heeled patent leather pump affixed to the wall presented a problem. Fortunately, it was located behind my desk, so I could avoid looking at it most of the time.

There was little news about Bill Sullivan in the paper. There was a brief notification that the medical examiner would release the body to the family "soon." Pete didn't volunteer any information about the investigation, and I knew better than to question him about police business.

Orientation week went well, and it appeared that the New Year's Day grand opening of the Tabby would be all that Mr. Pennington had hoped for. The books for every class had been delivered on time. The heating and air-conditioning systems had been updated and were working perfectly. The electricians had rushed to finish their work. TV and radio spots ran as scheduled, and various local celebrities and politicians had been booked for the ribbon-cutting ceremony.

With just a couple of days to go before the grand opening, I met another of my students. With platinum hair, stiletto-heeled boots, a leather miniskirt, and a faux leopard jacket stretched across a more than ample bosom, Primrose McDonald brought all the activity on the main floor to a halt when she sauntered through the glass front doors and strolled toward the staircase.

Every male eye in the place was focused on the blonde, and Rupert Pennington darn near fell down the stairs as he rushed to greet her. I stood at the entrance to the mezzanine level, too far away to hear what they said to each other, but after a few moments Pennington pointed in my direction. The woman turned and, with a grin and swaying hips, made her way toward me through a still-mesmerized audience.

"Hi there, Ms. Barrett," she said. "I'm Primrose McDonald, and I'm here to learn what you can teach me." Her handshake was firm; her smile genuine. I invited her to join me in my classroom area, which by then was outfitted with a facsimile news desk, three TV monitors, two studio cameras, a green screen, and some rudimentary sound equipment.

Her makeup was expertly applied, and her outfit, although extreme, was of excellent quality: her knee-high boots were expensive, and her jewelry was probably real. I guessed that she was older than I was, but by how much, I couldn't tell.

"Have you had any TV experience, Miss McDonald?" I asked.

Her laugh was hearty. "Lord, no, honey, and please call me Primrose. I've done a little of what you might call stage and some movies you've never seen, but no TV."

"Is there a particular area of television that interests you, Primrose?" I asked. "My lesson plan at this point is flexible. I'm going to try to concentrate on the things you and the others most want to learn."

"Don't laugh," she said, "but I think I'd like to work behind the scenes. I'd like to write or direct."

I tried not to look surprised. "I like those areas myself," I said. "The assignment the school has just given me is for this class to produce a documentary about some aspect of Salem's history. We need some serious writing and directing skills if we're going to pull this off."

I wasn't kidding about the last-minute nature of the lesson plan. I'd been thinking along the lines of TV Production 101, but apparently, one of the major NEA grants the school had obtained required a history focus, and Mr. Pennington had pegged my class to deliver it.

"Sounds good to me," she said. "By the way, last night I ran into a couple of kids who say they're going to be my classmates."

"Really? I haven't even met all the students myself."

"I was at a little bar. Greene's Tavern. Cute bartender. Gay guy named Thom and a waitress who says she's the owner's daughter. Guess they're both going to be in your class."

"I've met Kelly Greene," I said. "Don't know Thom yet."

"Cute kids." She looked over her shoulder and lowered her voice. "Kelly said there were cops all over the place here, investigating some guy who disappeared. Are they still around here? The cops, I mean."

"No. They left," I said. "They found the man's body somewhere else."

"That's good," she said.

What's good? That they found a body? Or that there aren't any cops around?

By the time orientation week came to a close, I'd met all six of my students. The three women had enrolled early in the week, and all the men had finally shown up late on the last day. Thom Lalonde, the bartender, was, as Primrose had observed, both cute and gay. Sammy Trout and Duke Martin had walked in together—a truly odd couple. Martin, looking as though he'd stepped out of an old John Wayne movie, complete with ten-gallon hat, neckerchief, and leather vest, stood at least six-foot-six. Sammy Trout, an ex-jockey who thought he might have a future in television, was nearly two feet shorter. I made a mental note to be sure to get a class picture of the entire group.

Therese, Primrose, and Sammy had opted to live in the freshly appointed dorm rooms on the Tabby's third floor. Kelly lived at home with her father, in an apartment above Greene's Tavern, and Thom lived with his parents in North Salem. Duke Martin was "staying with friends."

After my quiet News Year's Eve celebration—chocolate-covered strawberries and a champagne toast with my aunt at midnight—I arrived early for the big event. I thought that Mr. Pennington might be feeling overwhelmed, but I needn't have worried. Everything looked fine, including the director, who was nattily dressed and downright jovial. His lectern, dust free, polished, and fitted with a microphone, had been placed on a raised platform at the head of the wide first-floor staircase. On the wall behind the speaker's platform was a life-size oil painting of the store's founder, Oliver Wendell Trumbull.

The superintendent of schools, the president of the historical society, and a recently elected representative from the city council posed with giant scissors behind a wide blue satin ribbon strung across the open glass doors. Reporters and photographers from the local and the Boston media roamed the place, and TV mobile units jockeyed for position in front of the

Tabby. On one side of the grand staircase was an entrance to a small student theater, complete with a lighted marquee and framed vintage movie posters. On the other side a curvy, chrome-trimmed door led to a vintage diner–style cafeteria. Both the theater and the cafeteria had street entrances, allowing public access.

At precisely nine o'clock Rupert Pennington took his position at the lectern amid scattered applause. The student body—a hundred and twenty men and women—was crowded onto the main floor, along with another hundred or so invited guests. I and my fellow instructors sat in folding chairs behind the director. I surveyed the audience, looking for familiar faces, and quickly spotted my aunt and River North standing together in the front row. Duke Martin was easy to recognize, as he towered above everyone else. Some of the news cameras were already focused on handsome Thom Lalonde, who stood next to the staircase railing, in what was clearly a professional model's pose. Pete had phoned earlier to wish me a Happy New Year and also to tell me he wouldn't be at the ceremony, because "something came up."

Mr. Pennington gave his sincere, sonorous, and long-winded welcome to the student body and the visiting dignitaries, his thanks to the many "little people" who'd worked "long and hard" to make this day come about, and then he introduced each instructor. The city councilor, the historical society president, and the school superintendent, who all must have been suffering from numb arms after holding the giant scissors for half an hour, finally got the signal to cut the blue satin ribbon. The Tabitha Trumbull Academy of the Arts was officially open.

A "meet and mingle" session with coffee and little cakes followed. Therese introduced me to her parents, a pleasant couple who were obviously clueless as to their daughter's motives for attending the Tabby.

"We're *awfully* pleased that Therese has chosen a career path," Mrs. Della Monica gushed. "She is *so* excited about studying with you, and about staying in this *marvelously* historic city."

I know she's excited about staying in Salem. We'll see about the studying soon enough.

Mr. and Mrs. Lalonde introduced themselves. Thom's mother, with obvious pride, handed me a composite photo card of her son. "Thom is a model, you know," she said. "He wants so much to get to New York City, get into TV, where they'll truly appreciate such a handsome, hardworking boy."

I murmured my appreciation for Thom's looks and work ethic.

"He's paying his own way through this school," she continued. "He has a part-time job as a bartender, and he even cuts lawns, washes cars. Works day and night, weekends and holidays. He'll do *anything* to achieve his goal."

Mr. Lalonde didn't speak but nodded his agreement with his wife's proud pronouncements.

I was surprised to learn that all my students had already met one another. Each of them had discovered Greene's Tavern during the past week, and they had all bonded so well that they'd spent New Year's Eve together there. I was even more surprised to learn that Mr. Pennington was also an occasional patron. Greene's Tavern was apparently thriving.

Aunt Ibby was in deep conversation with the city councilor, and she probably knew most of the rest of the people there, as well. I saw Mr. Pennington make his way through the crowd to greet my aunt with smiling enthusiasm, and I noticed that River had ducked out right after the ribbon cutting, giving a quick wave in my direction.

Darn! I'd hoped to get a minute with River so she could tell me what she knew about the top-floor ghost.

Primrose had disappeared early, but I hadn't noticed where or exactly when she'd gone. Duke and Sammy stood in line together at the refreshment table.

It was early afternoon by the time I rounded up most of my class—only Primrose was still missing—and we gathered in the classroom. I turned them loose to investigate the equipment and answered their rapid-fire questions as fast as I could. Therese was curious about how things worked, and displayed a surprising amount of technical knowledge.

With such a small class, it didn't seem necessary to assign seats, so I just waited until everyone had found a place where he or she felt comfortable. Therese and Kelly sat side by side, much the way they had when I first met them in the director's office, except that now they didn't look bored or uncomfortable. Thom and Sammy selected seats with a couple of empty chairs between them, and Duke Martin sat in the big leather chair behind the faux news desk.

"I don't know what's become of Primrose," I said, "but I expect she'll be back soon. Meanwhile, let's talk about you." I glanced around the room. "What made you choose this school? This class? Sammy, how about you?"

When I first met Sammy, I'd expected him to have a high voice, because of his short stature. Just goes to show how wrong generalities can be. The ex-jockey had a voice worthy of a news anchor.

"Thanks, Ms. Barrett," he began. "Most of you guys know I used to be a jockey. Pretty good one, too. Had a bad fall a little while ago and can't ride anymore. I'd like to be on TV. Maybe I'd like to be a sports commentator. Or even an actor. You don't have to be tall, you know. Look at Danny DeVito."

"Shoot, honey. You're taller than me," Kelly announced. "Don't worry about it."

"Want to tell us about yourself, Kelly?" I asked.

"Me? I'm just a coal miner's daughter. Like Miss Loretta Lynn," she said. "'Cept I can't sing a note—"

"Coal miner's daughter?" Duke interrupted. "Your daddy runs a bar. Ain't no coal miner."

"Used to be. Got sick in his lungs and had to quit it," Kelly explained. "But he likes running the tavern. I like it here, too. Closer to New York and Boston, where the big TV stations are."

"What's your story, Duke? How did you happen to choose the Tabby?" I asked the big man.

"I've done a few movies," he said. "Mostly Westerns. Small parts. I was shooting a commercial in Boston when I read about this place. Never did much TV. Want to."

"We'll do all we can to get you there, Duke," I promised.

But you might have to lose the cowboy getup.

I hesitated to ask Therese why she'd chosen the Tabby. I knew the answer, but I had to ask, anyway. "How about you, Therese?"

"Same as Kelly," she said. "I just really like Salem." She paused, then added, "Oh, and people always tell me I have a nice speaking voice, so my folks thought I should learn how to make money with it."

Thanks for not mentioning witches.

"Your voice is pleasant," I said. "And you seem comfortable around the equipment, too. That's a big plus in the TV business."

She colored slightly but didn't answer.

"And you, Thom?" I turned to the handsome young man. "Your mom says you already have a modeling career going pretty well."

"Oh, my God. I saw her handing out those darn pictures. So embarrassing."

"She's just proud of you," I said, "and of how hard you work."

He shrugged. "I get a few modeling gigs around here. And I tend bar most every night. Have ever since they opened."

Primrose chose that moment to make her entrance.

"Holy crap!" She sounded breathless. "Are all the big shots gone?" She plopped into a chair next to Sammy, red velvet miniskirt riding dangerously high. "Those ribbon-cutting dudes aren't going to be hanging around here all the time, are they?"

There were puzzled looks all around.

"Why?" Duke asked. "You got a problem with them?"

She shrugged, patting her hair and straightening her skirt. "Oh, I guess it's no big deal. Just ducking out on somebody I didn't expect to run in to. Here, of all places."

"I suppose they can visit whenever they want to," I said. "You going to be okay?"

"Sure. I can handle it. Don't worry about me." A nervous smile, a glance over her shoulder. Then, in a conversational tone, she added, "How come the cops are back? I just saw a couple of 'em going down the basement stairs."

Primrose was right. The police presence was back. It didn't take long to find out why.

Mr. Pennington, in his quest for funding the basement project, had arranged for a low-cost "feasibility study." A first-year media engineering student from Salem State, with a measuring tape and a ball-peen hammer, had discovered what the police had missed.

Junior Sullivan had been correct when he reported that his father had gone into the basement and had never come back upstairs.

Even the cat had been right. A fall from a height had almost undoubtedly caused Bill's broken leg.

The celebratory mood of opening day at the Tabby changed in minutes to one of confusion, consternation, and near panic. Mr. Pennington's voice over the newly installed loudspeaker system announced that students and faculty were to vacate the building in an orderly manner.

If my class was any example, the exodus was less than orderly. The old shoe department had its own entrance, so we grabbed our jackets, coats, and purses and were outside in less than a minute. We crossed the street and huddled together, watching people pouring from all available exits.

"What do you think happened?" Therese asked, clearly frightened.

"Probably just a bomb scare," Duke offered. "They'll call us back inside in a minute. Don't worry."

"I have a friend in the police department," I said, reaching for my phone. "I'll find out." So violating all my self-imposed restrictions on nosing into Pete's police business, I called him.

He answered on the first ring. "Hi, Lee. It's okay. The place isn't under attack. No danger. I'm on my way there now."

"Then what's going on? They've evacuated the whole school."

"I know. It's the damnedest thing. Seems some kind of a hole has opened up underneath the Trumbull building. Might explain what happened to your friend Sullivan. I'll call you later."

CHAPTER 9

We stood there for a while, clustered together, watching as police cars and fire engines converged on Essex Street.

"It's kind of pointless to just stand here in the cold," I said. "Let's go find someplace warm with a TV. That's probably the quickest way to find out what's going on in there. My friend says whatever it is isn't dangerous."

"Let's go to my pa's place," Kelly offered. "Big booths, huge TV, and even a fireplace."

"And cold beer," Primrose said.

Both Primrose and Duke had cars in the student parking lot. I called Aunt Ibby and told her where I was going so she wouldn't worry when she saw the news, and then Kelly, Therese, and I piled into Primrose's black Camry. The men rode in Duke's 2002 red Dodge Ram pickup. It had real ram's horns on the hood and an empty gun rack at the back of the cab.

Greene's Tavern was just as Kelly had described it. I could see why Salem folks had taken to the place so quickly. A lunchtime crowd of a dozen or so football enthusiasts was gathered around the giant TV. Kelly led us to a semicircular booth, grabbed an apron from behind the bar, and began assisting a man who was serving customers. I presumed he was her father, Joe Greene.

Opening day at the Tabby was all over the news. But the ribbon cutting, the welcoming speech, the interviews with the superintendent of schools and the downtown development team were not there. The featured footage on every channel showed a four-by-four-foot square panel of the basement wall moving up and down. The panel opened, then slowly closed, and each time a nervous engineering student hammered lightly on a round metal disk imbedded in the wooden floor.

"Look," I said. "Junior Sullivan said his dad thought he saw a silver fifty-cent piece under the mannequins. He must have hit that disk somehow and opened the panel."

The scene unfolding on the TV screen became even more dramatic. While a news anchor described the action, a cameraman, with a camera and a light attached to a hard hat, propped the panel open and crawled into the dark square. We watched as the man stood upright, then moved slowly along a dirt-floored passageway with aged brick walls on either side. The narrow passageway sloped downward for several feet and ended abruptly at a large, round hole in the ground. The cameraman leaned over the edge of the opening, illuminating what lay beneath.

It looked like a very long drop to the bottom of that hole.

A commercial break interrupted the story. "Stay tuned," said the anchor, "for our exclusive interview with the young man who made this amazing discovery beneath the basement of Salem's newest school and oldest department store."

"Oh, my God," Therese said. "You think that poor old guy fell in that hole?"

"Probably did," Sammy said.

"Yeah, but how the heck did he get out?" Primrose voiced the question that was on my mind.

Kelly rejoined us, sliding into the booth next to me, order pad in hand. "You guys want a beer or a soda or something? We have nachos and hot dogs and stuff, too."

"I didn't bring any money," Therese said.

"That's okay, kid. I'm buyin'." Duke flipped a credit card onto the table, waving away our chorus of protests.

By the time Kelly had written down our choices, the commercial had ended, and the camera was once again focused on the young man who'd found the moving panel.

"Tell us what happened when you went down into the school's basement this morning," the news anchor said, prodding, "and what you were doing there."

"Well, sir," came the hesitant reply, "the director at the school—Mr. Pennington—asked me to look the place over, see what it would take to make a sound studio out of it. So I was, like, taking measurements and stuff. You know, checking how much insulation it might need and if the ceiling was high enough for the equipment they're talking about."

"You have a degree in media engineering?"

"Not yet, sir. I'm working toward it."

"I see. And how did you happen to discover the moving panel?"

"I saw this round metal thing on the floor. I thought at first it was money. A coin, you know?" He made a circle with his thumb and forefinger. "But it was, like, stuck to the floor. Imbedded in the wood, really."

"So, what did you do then?"

"I took a hammer out of my toolbox and tapped it. Trying to get it out. Didn't tap it hard. And that panel in the wall kind of creaked and opened up." He smiled into the camera. "Scared me a little."

"Did you try to enter the passageway?"

"Heck no. After a couple of minutes it closed itself up again. So I ran right upstairs and told Mr. Pennington about it."

The young man was thanked and dismissed before the anchor introduced a member of the Salem Fire Department.

"We understand that the department has investigated. Can you tell us what's down there?"

"It's definitely a tunnel. An underground tunnel with another, narrower tunnel underneath it."

"Two tunnels? Where do they lead?"

The fireman shrugged. "We don't know yet," he said. "They both seem to branch out in different directions under the city."

"What does it look like down there?"

"Well, the top one looks old. Really old and well built. The other one is more recent, and the construction isn't as good."

Kelly had delivered our food and drinks and had joined us at the table. "Wow," she said. "What about that? An old tunnel under the city?"

"The tunnel might be old," Sammy said. "But that mechanical panel looks pretty darned new."

Sammy's doubt about the old age of the mechanical panel was just one of many topics that came up around the cozy tavern table that winter afternoon.

"If there are tunnels under Salem, wouldn't the city officials know about it?" Duke wondered aloud. "I mean, there must be pipes and telephone wires and stuff down there."

Therese thought the hole must have something to do with ancient witchcraft rituals, and Sammy said that it was probably just some kind of old-time aqueduct system, but he still wondered why there was a passageway to it from a department store basement.

Thom didn't offer an opinion as to the purpose of the tunnel. "This school tuition is expensive," he said, "and I'm working my way through. What I want to know is, how long are they going to keep us out because of a stupid hole in the ground?"

"That's right," Kelly agreed. "I'm in a hurry to break into TV. I don't want to waste time."

I didn't have any ready answers, and it was time for the first of the New Year's Day bowl games to start, so no new information was coming from the TV.

"They'll probably let us know pretty soon about opening the school again," I said. "But as long as we're all here, maybe we could brainstorm a little about the documentary we have to make."

"Good idea, Lee," said Primrose. "Can I call you Lee? After all, I'm older than you and we're talking in a barroom."

"Sure. At least while we're here," I said.

"Me too?" Kelly wanted to know.

"Okay. We'll keep things informal all around, but let's concentrate on the documentary."

"Salem history, right?" Therese pulled a pen and a small pad of paper from her purse. "I think it should be about the witch trials." She wrote, "Witch Trials" in neat, round letters.

Duke shook his head. "Been done a million times. How about Salem as a tourist destination? We could probably get it on one of the travel channels."

"That's a good one," Therese said, writing quickly. "But mine's better."

"Let's do it about the tunnel," Sammy said. "That's part of Salem history, isn't it?"

Therese made a face but wrote, "Tunnel."

"I know," said Primrose. "Let's do it about Trumbull's Department Store. Right from the beginning and up to when it got turned into a school."

"And got canceled the first day on account of a stupid tunnel." A frown shadowed Thom's handsome face.

"I like the idea, though," I said. "It includes pretty much everything that's happened in Salem since they opened the old store back in the nineteen twenties."

Therese looked up from her note taking. "They still had witches back then, too, didn't they?"

"Shoot, honey. There's always been witches," Kelly said. "We even had 'em down in West Virginia."

"Really?" Therese started a new page and wrote, "Trumbull's Department Store history, including witches."

The impromptu brainstorming session moved along quickly. We filled Therese's little notepad and started writing on paper napkins.

Ideas and questions flew around the table, and our stack of notes grew.

The session ended abruptly when Sammy said, "Hey! Wait a minute. If the school is closed, does that mean that me and Primrose and Therese can't sleep in our dorm rooms?"

"Oh, my God! I forgot all about that." Therese tossed down her pen and reached for her phone. "I'd better call my mom to come and get me."

"I'll call Mr. Pennington and find out," I said.

I called the director's private number. "How about

the people staying in the dorm?" I asked. "Can they come back inside tonight?"

"Oh, Ms. Barrett, what a mess." I could sense near panic in his voice. "The police and the fire department and the city engineers are all still here. They're trying to determine if that wretched hole has undermined the foundation or some such nonsense."

"I have three of the dorm students here with me," I told him, "and they need to make plans about tonight."

"I know. I know." He sounded near tears. "There are twenty live-in students altogether, and they're all trying to figure out where to stay. The Red Cross has offered to open a shelter, so at least they'll be in out of the cold. Should I sign your three up for that?"

"I'll ask. Can they go to their rooms and get clothes and toothbrushes?" I glanced around at my group. All of them except Duke were on their phones.

Mr. Pennington said that permission had been given for the students to gather their possessions. I covered the phone with my hand and asked my three temporarily homeless ones what they wanted to do.

"Therese is going to spend the night here with me," Kelly announced. "It'll be fun."

"Sammy can use our guest room," Thom said. "My mom says it's okay."

"We have plenty of room at my house, Primrose," I said. "You're welcome to stay with us."

I reported to the director that we would not need the Red Cross, but that we'd be there shortly to pick up overnight bags. I was about to call Aunt Ibby to tell her I'd invited a guest when my phone vibrated. I hoped it was Pete, but the caller ID showed River's name.

"Hi, River," I said. "What's up?"

"What's up with you is more like it! You know I never watch the news, but everyone is talking about

your old store and the big sinkhole, or whatever it is."
She sounded worried. "Are you okay?"

"I'm fine, River," I said. "Please don't worry. I'm at
Greene's Tavern with all six of my students, and we're
just about to go over to the school to pick up a few
things."

"Is it safe to go in there? Listen. I'm going to do a
quick card reading for you. I'll call you right back."

I started to protest, but she was gone. I called Aunt
Ibby and caught her up on what was happening.

"Tell your friend she's welcome to stay with us as
long as she needs to," she said. "I'll get a guest room
ready and start thinking about dinner."

Kelly brought her dad over to our table and introduced us. Joe Greene was a good-looking man, probably in his fifties. He wiped big hands on the white
apron tied around his trim waist, and we shook hands.
His voice was pleasant, and he had an accent much like
his daughter's, but more pronounced. There was
something familiar about him, and I felt as though
maybe we had met somewhere.

Impossible. I've never been to West Virginia.

"Don't be a stranger now, Ms. Barrett," he said and
waved in the direction of my six students. "I already
know this bunch of delinquents will show up most
every night."

"I'll be back soon," I promised. "Maybe tomorrow, if
the school is still closed."

"You're all welcome anytime."

"We're going over to school to pick up everybody's
clothes for tomorrow, Pa," Kelly said. "Be right back."

"Okay, darlin'. Drive careful, Miss Primrose. You too,
Duke."

I gathered up the notes and paper napkins, folded
them carefully, and put them in my handbag.

My class was off to a pretty good, if unorthodox, start.

There was an officer at the Tabby's front door when we got there. Therese, Kelly, Primrose, and Sammy showed their student IDs, and I produced the plastic-coated instructor's badge I'd been issued, and we were waved inside. Duke and Thom waited in the parking lot for Sammy.

I knew the girls would take some time to pack their necessities. I headed for my classroom to pick up my laptop. If our off-site meetings were to continue, we'd need it.

My phone buzzed. I hoped the caller was Pete, but once again it was River North.

"Hi, Lee. I read your cards. Want to hear about it?"

"Somehow your cards hardly ever have good news for me, but go ahead." I sat behind my desk, waiting for River's reading.

"Okay. Here goes. There's a moon above your card. Moon Mother is watching over your body, mind, and spirit."

"Moon Mother?"

"Yes. You need to listen to the voice of your subconscious, Lee. Moon Mother guides the spirit into material manifestation. You understand?"

"Not a word of it, River. But what about the Mother Moon?"

"Moon Mother. Here's what I think this means. Remember you told me the other day you can't use your gift anymore? That it's gone?"

"Right," I said. "Ariel was causing the visions, and Ariel's dead. Gone to the light, or wherever witches go."

"Remember when you used to see things in the shiny shoes when you were little? Then, when you were frightened by the terrible thing you saw, they stopped until you found Ariel's body?"

"I remember." She was right. I definitely saw visions in my Sunday school shoes up until I saw the plane crash. Then the visions stopped. "You think I made them stop because I just didn't want to see them anymore?"

"Exactly. Also, I think Ariel *was* making you see whatever she wanted you to until her killer was caught. But that's over now. I think Moon Mother is telling you it is safe for you to use your gift. She guides the spirit into material manifestation. Moves pictures of the past, present, and future into visions you can see and learn from."

"What if I don't want to?"

"That's the beauty of it! You can stop whenever you don't want to see them anymore." I could tell that she was excited. "Try it, Lee. Are you near anything shiny now? Black and shiny? Just try."

I took a deep breath. "Will you stay on the phone with me while I do it?"

"Of course I will. Just do it."

I spun the chair around until I was facing the toe of that giant black pump behind the desk.

Okay. Show me.

Within seconds, pinpoints of light and swirling colors appeared. A young woman with long dark hair and a flowing white dress moved toward me. She smiled, and in her open left hand she offered two keys.

That's enough. Now stop.

She turned her back and disappeared.

CHAPTER 10

I couldn't speak. Couldn't move. I heard River's voice.

"Lee. Lee? What happened? Are you all right?"

"I . . . I think so. I think it worked, River. I told it to start and stop, and it did."

"I knew it! I mean, I was pretty sure. Moon Mother is powerful, you know. Want to do it again?"

"No. That was plenty for now. Maybe sometime I'll try again. Not now." I turned my chair and faced away from the giant shoe. I heard laughter from my approaching female students. "I have to go. The girls from my class are coming. And, River? Thanks."

"You're welcome. Want to call me later and tell me what you saw just now?"

"Later," I said. "And listen, River, don't forget to tell me about what it is the witches know about the woman in the attic."

The laughter and chatter grew closer, and then the three students gathered around my desk.

"We're finally ready," Kelly said. "My God. It took Primrose forever to decide which boots to take. You wouldn't believe how many pairs of shoes she has!"

Primrose shrugged and smiled. "Hey. I love shopping. What can I say?"

"You all right, Ms. Barrett? Lee?" Therese looked concerned. "You're sort of . . . pale."

Kelly peered at my face closely. "Yeah. You are. Did you see a ghost?"

The three dissolved into peals of laughter again. It was contagious. I found myself laughing along with them. Not so much because Kelly's remark was funny, but because maybe I had really just seen a ghost.

"I'm fine," I said. "Guess my Florida tan is all gone. Did Sammy leave already?"

"Yep." Kelly shook her head. "How do guys pack so fast?"

Nobody came up with a good answer to that, and we headed for the parking lot, the three of them still giggling and me still trying to figure out what I had just seen in an old shoe department display piece.

Before we reached Primrose's car, my phone rang again. This time it was Pete.

"Hi, Lee. Where are you?"

"Just leaving the school. Where are you?"

"At the station. I just left there myself a few minutes ago. Sorry I missed you."

"Me too. Hold on a sec." I went to the driver's side window. "Primrose," I said, "would you mind dropping Kelly and Therese off at the Greenes' and then coming back here to pick me up?" I pointed to the phone and whispered, "Personal call."

She gave a knowing wink. "Sure thing. Be right back."

I stood in the shadow of the Trumbull building, next to the entrance to the new diner. "Pete? You still there?"

"I'm here. What are you doing there? I thought they'd cleared everyone out."

I explained about the dorm students and how we'd held a class of sorts at Greene's Tavern. "Pete, what's happening about the hole? Is that really where Bill Sullivan fell and broke his leg?"

"Looks that way. The body was released to the family this morning, before all this happened. Cause of death was a heart attack, probably brought on by the fall."

"And the alcohol?"

"None in his stomach at all. Just in his mouth."

"Then how . . . ?"

"I know. How did he wind up under a tree in the park, smelling of booze? We're working on that. We have one witness who said she was walking her dog in the area late that night and saw three drunks staggering along, singing Christmas carols." He sighed. "Now all I have to do is find three drunk singers who might have seen something."

"I hope you can find out what happened so the Sullivans will have some kind of closure."

"I hope so."

"So between what happened to Bill and the hole under the school," I said, "do you think the place will have to stay closed?"

"I don't think so. You folks don't use the basement, anyway, and that's where our investigation will start," he said. "And the city fathers are real anxious to keep the school open. There's some taxpayer investment there, you know."

"Quite a lot, I imagine," I said. "Is it true that the tunnels might be undermining the buildings?"

"The city engineer says no. Seems they know all about the tunnels—they've been there for over a century. Most of them are blocked off or filled in, but pieces of some of them are still used. He said a steak house over on Derby Square even made part of a tunnel into their wine cellar."

I remembered what Sammy had said about the mechanical door. "That movable door with the button in the floor hasn't been there for a century," I said.

"We're working on that, too."

I could almost see his cop face shutting me out. I wasn't going to get any more information about the case. That was clear. "I guess the Sullivans will let us know about funeral arrangements for Bill," I said.

"I guess so." The warmth was back in his voice. "Want to grab a quick supper before I have to go back to work? I miss you."

"I miss you, too, but I've invited one of the dorm students to spend the night at my place. She had no place else to go."

"Maybe tomorrow, then?"

"I hope so. Talk to you later."

"You bet. Bye."

Within a few minutes Primrose pulled up to the curb and beeped her horn. "Hop in, girl," she ordered. "It's getting cold again."

"Sure is," I said. "We don't have far to go." I sat in the passenger seat and gave her directions to Winter Street.

"Wow. Nice house," she said once we arrived. "Nice street."

"Thanks," I said. "It is a pretty street, isn't it? Let's drive around back, though, so you can park in the driveway. Don't want to get you a ticket."

"I heard you're dating a cute cop," she said. "Doesn't he fix tickets?" She pulled the Camry expertly into the narrow driveway next to the garage.

"I don't know. Never got one. Come on. I'll introduce

you to my aunt and our cat." I tucked the laptop under one arm and we hurried along the path to the house. I turned my key in the back door lock.

This key is flat and shiny. The keys in the vision were dark colored and more rounded, with a notch at the end, like old-fashioned skeleton keys.

"Something smells good." Primrose closed her eyes and sniffed the air. She was right. Something smelled wonderful.

"Did I mention that my aunt is a fabulous cook?" I hung my jacket on a hook in the back hall and motioned for Primrose to do the same. "Bring your bag, and come on into the kitchen and we'll see what's cooking."

Aunt Ibby, wearing a long red- and white-striped apron with KISS THE COOK in black letters, rushed to greet us. "Come in out of the cold, my dears!" She took Primrose's hand. "Welcome. So you're one of Mara-lee's students. I'm so pleased that you could join us."

"Aunt Ibby, this is Primrose McDonald. She's the one who came up with the idea of documenting the history of Trumbull's for our class project."

"An excellent idea," my aunt said. "And Primrose is such a pretty name."

I peeked into the iron pot simmering on the stove. "Smells great," I said.

"I didn't have time for anything fancy. That's just plain old coq au vin, but I did make a nice batch of double fudge brownies for dessert."

Primrose smiled and rolled her eyes. "Boy, Lee, are you ever spoiled!"

Aunt Ibby looked pleased. "Maralee, your friend will be staying in the pink guest room, across the hall from yours." She waved a wooden spoon in Primrose's direction. "We're doing some rather major renovations on the third floor, dear, so those rooms aren't ready yet."

I led the way upstairs, dropped the laptop off in my room, and then showed Primrose to the guest room. Aunt Ibby called it the pink room with good reason. Pale pink rosebud-sprinkled wallpaper and deep rose draperies complemented the antique mahogany dresser, wardrobe, and four-poster bed in the room, which was usually reserved for female guests. Primrose placed her overnight bag on the seat of a rosy chintz-covered chair and turned around in the center of the room, looking at every detail, with appreciation evident in her wide brown eyes.

Dinner was delicious, as expected, and the dessert of warm double fudge brownies with vanilla ice cream on top was pure heaven. We adjourned to the living room and caught the evening news, which was pretty much a rerun of the morning edition, only this time a film clip of the hole leading to the tunnel wasn't shown, and the opening of the school, with interviews of each of the ribbon cutters, had more coverage.

"They didn't show the hole where Bill fell," Aunt Ibby said. "Why not?"

"Probably because the cops are nosing around down there," Primrose offered. "Think so, Lee?"

"I think you're right," I said. "Pete says their investigation will center on the Tabby's basement and the park where Bill was found."

"Pete?" Primrose asked. "Is that the cute cop's name—"

"Look." Aunt Ibby pointed at the television screen. "There's the new city councilor, Mr. Wilson. We had a nice chat this morning. He came here from Washington, D.C., you know. Used to work for the government. He's quite interested in our downtown development."

I was glad Aunt Ibby had interrupted. I didn't want to discuss Pete with Primrose. Fortunately, the blonde had turned her attention to the TV screen and was watching and listening intently to the new city councilor.

"Just ducking out on somebody I didn't expect to run in to," she'd said this morning. *Is it Councilor Wilson she's avoiding?*

Jonathan Wilson's remarks were brief and had to do with his appreciation of those who'd made the Tabitha Trumbull Academy of the Arts a reality and his admiration for the beautiful facility itself.

And blah-blah-blah. Typical political speak, which Primrose seems to find oddly interesting.

The next interview was with the superintendent of Salem's schools, but Primrose was no longer paying attention to the newscast. "Do you know Mr. Wilson personally, Miss Russell?" she asked.

"Oh, no. We just met this morning. But I did vote for him, you know, and I told him so." Aunt Ibby smiled. "That's always a good way to get a conversation started with official types."

"I suppose it is," Primrose said. "I noticed you chatting with Mr. Pennington, too."

She nodded. "Yes. I complimented him about pulling everything together. Then he said, 'Money and adventure and fame. It's the thrill of a lifetime.'" She smiled. "So I said, 'Robert Armstrong to Fay Wray in *King Kong.*' It was the right answer. I thought he was going to hug me. But instead he invited me to attend a Woody Allen Film Festival."

My aunt and my boss? Dating?

I was sure my surprise showed. "He did? Are you going?"

She shrugged. "Perhaps. I told him I'd check my calendar and get back to him later."

Primrose muffled a yawn and stood. "Well, if you two don't mind, I think I'll turn in early. It's been quite a day."

"It certainly has," I said. "You go right ahead. I won't be far behind you. Sleep well."

"I know I will in such a beautiful room." Primrose headed up the stairs.

"She seems like a nice person, despite the unusual wardrobe," Aunt Ibby said. "What's her background?"

I thought about it for a moment. "I don't know much about her," I admitted. "Some sort of amateur acting experience, apparently."

"Amateur, hmm?" My aunt looked skeptical.

"I talked to River today," I said, changing the subject and wondering just how much I should tell my aunt about what I'd learned about using my gift.

"I saw her this morning. We watched the ribbon-cutting ceremony together."

"I know. I talked to her later." I took a deep breath. "River was worried about me, so she read my cards."

She frowned. "That doesn't often work out well for you."

"I know. But she told me about Moon Mother, who, she says, tells me it's safe to use my gazing ability. That I can turn it on and off at will, now that Ariel's gone."

There was a long pause. She turned the TV off, and the room was eerily silent.

"And do you believe it?" Her voice was disapproving.

"I'm afraid I have to."

"Why do you say that? You don't have to do any such thing!"

"I believe it," I said, speaking softly. "Because I tried it. And it worked."

She leaned forward, looking into my eyes. "You turned it on?"

I nodded. "Yes."

"And you were actually able to turn it off?"

"Yes."

She covered her face with her hands for a moment and then folded them in her lap. Her eyes were moist. "I had hoped after that thing—whatever it is—came back that you'd be able to make it stop again."

"Again?"

"Yes. After you saw what you saw in your shoes when you were a little girl, you made it stop somehow."

"That's true. But I've never known how. Or why."

"If you can actually control it now, that's a good thing. That means you don't ever have to do it again, doesn't it?" She took my hands in hers. "Doesn't it? You don't want to do it anymore, do you?"

"I'm not sure. I saw . . . something before I made it stop."

"Oh, dear. Do you want to tell me what you saw?"

I tried to describe what I'd seen in the toe of the giant shoe. "I saw a woman. She was young, with long dark hair. She wore a white gown of some kind. She held her hand out toward me and showed me two old-fashioned keys before I made her go away."

"And she went away when you wanted her to?"

"Turned her back and disappeared."

"Good," she said. "If you're wise, you'll forget about her and her keys. Good night, Maralee." She clicked the TV on, then switched the channel to the Rose Bowl game.

I knew we'd have to talk about my vision and River's card interpretation eventually, but for now I was free to hop into bed with my cat and wonder about the woman with two keys. I climbed the front stairs and tiptoed past the pink guest room, where O'Ryan paused, sniffing along the sill, and then together we went into my room.

I took a shower and got into pajamas. O'Ryan was comfortably curled up on the foot of the bed. I put my phone on the bedside table so I could reach it quickly in case Pete called to say good night. After moving my laptop from the desk to the bed, I plumped up my pillows, leaned back, and made a quick transcription of the notes, paper napkins and all, from our brainstorming session. I glanced at the TV, then at the books beside me. I wasn't in the mood for watching football or for reading about criminology or girl detective mystery solving, but I wasn't ready for sleep, either.

This year is off to a crazy start.

The happenings of the day tumbled through my mind, from the opening ceremony to the evacuation of the Tabby to the impromptu class at Greene's Tavern and finally to River's message about Moon Mother and my unwelcome gazing gift. And in the middle of it all was the discovery of an underground maze of tunnels, where our old friend Bill Sullivan had probably died.

The whole thing—Bill's death, the tunnels under Salem, the Moon Mother card, the vision in the shoe— seemed like pieces of a gigantic puzzle. I smiled when I remembered what that famous girl detective had said about puzzles.

Keep on working on the case until the pieces fit together.

"That's easy for you to say, Nancy," I muttered and pulled the covers up. O'Ryan turned, looked at me with obvious indifference, and proceeded to wash his face.

"Want to see what River's doing on TV tonight?" I asked the cat. "She says I need to watch her show more often." I clicked the set on and relaxed against the pile of pillows as my friend's smiling face appeared on the big screen. River's show, *Tarot Time with River North*, used the same set I'd had for my old call-in psychic show, but with an updated look. The midnight-blue *Nightshades* background, with its sparkling stars and planets, had been replaced by a floor-to-ceiling tapestry depicting the various tarot signs.

River, looking gorgeous in a silver, long-sleeved gown, sat in an ornate fan-backed rattan chair next to a round table, where she arranged the tarot cards for each caller. I had no intention of watching the movie—*Grave of the Vampire*—but it was interesting to listen to my friend as she interacted with her phone-in fans. She'd just begun explaining to a woman that the dark-haired and domineering young man who had recently come into her life might lead her to make a speculative investment, when my phone chimed.

I hit the mute button on the TV control and said, "Hi there" to Pete.

"Am I calling too late? Were you asleep?" His voice was warm, concerned, and very sexy.

"Nope. Wide awake. You still working?"

"No. I'm home in my apartment, trying to get warm. I spent the afternoon down in the underworld. Jesus. It's cold and dark down there. I'll be glad when they get some lights strung up so we can see what we're doing. Even then we won't be able to work at night. It's like a deep freeze once the sun goes down."

"Oh, Pete. I'm sorry. Have you learned any more about what happened to Bill?"

"Guess there's no harm in telling you. It'll all be in the papers soon enough," he said. "Bill fell into the tunnel, that's for sure. A little spot of his blood soaked into the ground where he landed."

"Then how did he get to the park?"

"Looks as though he was dragged through the tunnel for quite a way."

"All the way to the park?"

"Don't know yet. About a half mile in the damn thing was blocked with about a ton of rocks and dirt."

I tried to picture it. "You mean the tunnel collapsed somehow?"

"Not just somehow. Somebody went to a lot of trouble to hide the way they got Bill out of there."

It was a disturbing thought. I tried to erase the mental picture of Bill being dragged through that cold, dark place. By whom? Or what?

"But why?" I said. "He fell into the hole by accident. Why would somebody want to cover it up?"

Pete wasn't about to answer any more questions.

"Look, Lee . . ." The sexy voice was back. "Since we didn't get to go to supper, how about an early breakfast tomorrow morning? Pick you up at six?"

"I'd love to," I told him. "Primrose has her car, so she can leave on her own."

"Primrose? Nobody is named Primrose anymore."

"She is."

He laughed. "See you at six, then. And, Lee?"

"Yes?"

"I miss you. Good night."

"I miss you, too. Good night." I turned off the TV, set my alarm for five thirty, patted O'Ryan, turned out the light, and closed my eyes.

I'd barely begun to doze off when my eyes flew open.

Someone had moved Bill's body. *Who would be wandering around in a cold, dark underground tunnel on Christmas night? And why?*

CHAPTER 11

I woke up before the alarm sounded. After dressing quickly, I dashed off a note to Primrose telling her where I'd gone, then tiptoed across the hall and slipped it under her door. I picked up my laptop and followed O'Ryan downstairs, where the unmistakable smell of fresh coffee greeted us.

"Aunt Ibby? What are you doing awake so early? Is everything all right?"

My aunt looked up from her *Boston Globe,* smiled, and lifted her coffee mug in salute. "I might ask the same of you. And your friend Primrose was up and gone before either of us. What's going on? Am I missing something?"

"Primrose has left already?"

"Yes. I heard her car start. That's what woke me, not that I mind. I like mornings." She handed me an envelope. "She left a note for you."

I poured myself some coffee. "I'm having an early breakfast with Pete. That's why I'm up." I opened the pink envelope.

*Hi, Lee. Many thanks to you and Miss Russell for the
wonderful dinner and the beautiful room. Would you
please give me a call and let me know whether we have
class at school today or not? Thanks again.*

That was all. It was signed "Primrose McDonald,"
and she'd included her cell number.

I handed the note to Aunt Ibby. "What do you think
about this?"

"Interesting woman," my aunt said. "It's a perfectly
proper bread-and-butter letter, you know."

"I'm sure it is. But she doesn't say a word about why
she's leaving the house at . . . what? Four o'clock in the
morning?"

Aunt Ibby shrugged. "Approximately. But it's none
of our business where she goes or what time she goes
there, is it? What about school? Will you hold a class
today?"

"I don't know yet. Pete seems to think the Tabby will
be open in spite of the investigation." I repeated what
Pete had told me about Bill's body being dragged
through the tunnel. "He says it will be in the papers.
Did you see anything in the *Globe*?"

"Not exactly. There's a piece about the old tunnels
under Salem, and some information about some similar tunnels under Boston. They say that there's an on-
going investigation about a man disappearing from
Trumbull's basement, but that the police haven't established a definite connection to the tunnel."

"They have now," I said. "Blood evidence. Guess it'll
be in the *Salem News*."

"It's all so sad, isn't it?" she said. "I'll call Mrs. Sullivan
today and see if they've made funeral arrangements

yet. And, Maralee, I'm going over to the library to check the vertical files where they have the primary source information on the Trumbulls. Original letters, diaries, and notebooks and such."

"Awesome! That'll be a big help with our documentary project. Don't know what I'd do without you."

"Glad if I can contribute anything," she said, "but I admit I'm satisfying my own curiosity about that family."

"How so?"

"Well, there seems to be more than a little activity that one might call outside the law connected to the Trumbulls."

"Criminal activity? Besides some old-time bootlegging? I always thought the Trumbulls were the pillars of Salem society."

"Oh, no doubt some of them were. I could be all wet about this. But pillars of society have many ways of covering up for their black sheep."

"Sounds intriguing."

"Maybe I'm just a nosy old woman," she said, "but a little research couldn't hurt, and it's certainly interesting."

"It does sound fascinating. But are there any Trumbulls around who might not like our digging around in their past?"

"Don't think so. The Trumbull boys have both passed. And the daughter died years ago. Oliver too."

I glanced at the clock. "I'd better get going. Pete will be here in a few minutes. I'll check back with you when I know what's going on at school."

Still not sure whether I'd be conducting a regular class at the Tabby or we'd be meeting at Greene's Tavern again, I took along my laptop for note taking, sure it would be more efficient than the paper napkin method. I stood by the front door, watching for Pete. O'Ryan joined me, and as usual, the cat was the first to spot the Crown Vic rounding the corner of Winter Street and let me know with a satisfied "mrrup" and a soft-pawed tap on my boot.

I zipped up my jacket, pulled a woolen cap down over my ears, and grabbing my laptop, I stepped out into the early morning cold and hurried down the steps to the curb. I slid into the passenger seat, leaned across the police computer between the seats for a quick good morning kiss, fastened my seat belt, and we were off.

"Ready for work, I see." Pete noted the laptop. "Is the school officially open again?"

"I was going to ask you that. I haven't heard anything from Mr. Pennington one way or the other."

"The chief gave him the all clear late last night. Looks like we'll be digging around in the basement for a while, but upstairs is okay. Guess the city council pulled a few strings to keep the taxpayers happy."

"I'll go over there after breakfast, then, and see what's going on."

"Breakfast first. How hungry are you?"

"My aunt reminds me every morning that breakfast is the most important meal of the day. Feed me."

He smiled his great smile. "That's one of the things I love about you! Most women would say, 'I'm on a diet,' or 'I'll just have a piece of toast.' Not you!" He laughed. "'Feed me,' she says."

Did he just say the L word?

"Where are we going?" I asked.

"New place. They open at four a.m."

"No kidding. Who goes there so early?"

"You'd be surprised. Commercial fishermen on

their way out. Third-shift factory workers on the way home. Taxi drivers. Nurses. You'll see."

We drove down some of Salem's twisty one-way streets and parked in a small lot next to a nondescript, gray, two-story house with a neon OPEN sign in the front window. The place was furnished with high-backed booths and plain wooden tables, and most of them were filled. There was a low hum of conversation, a clatter of plates and silverware, and the good breakfast smells of coffee and bacon. We slid into a booth near the back of the room, and a smiling gray-haired wait-ress handed us plastic-covered menus.

"Coffee?"

We both nodded, and brimming white mugs ap-peared almost instantly. We each ordered scrambled eggs, sausage, home fries, and toast. Pete was right about the variety of customers. I glanced around the room and saw nurses in scrubs, lobstermen in oilskins and white rubber boots, kids in hockey sweaters, who must have had early morning practice. With jackets un-zipped and coffee mugs in hand, we began to catch each other up on the happenings of the days since we'd last been together.

"So do I understand that you actually held your class in a barroom?"

"That sounds terrible, doesn't it? But it really was a logical choice. We all wanted to get in out of the cold and to find a TV. Mr. Greene made us feel welcome. It's a pretty nice place. Maybe we could go there some-time. You and me."

"Okay. We will. I'm having a hard time picturing it as a classroom, though. Did you use textbooks or what?"

"No books. We just talked about what topic we'll

choose for the documentary we'll make. It has to have something to do with Salem history."

"That's a pretty big field."

"We decided on the story of Trumbull's Department Store from the time it opened until it became a school. What do you think of that?"

"I like it. That covers most of a century, right?"

"It does. Now it's your turn. Tell me what you've been doing. Besides being in a big dark hole."

Our food arrived, and our mugs were refilled. "My New Year's Eve wasn't any fun," Pete said. "Just reading drunks their rights, mostly."

"Guess you haven't found the three carol-singing drunks you were looking for."

He laughed shortly. "Nope. Still looking. How was your New Year's Eve?"

"TV. Times Square. Champagne toast with Aunt Ibby. O'Ryan and I were in bed by twelve fifteen."

"Whoopee."

"I know. Maybe we're getting old."

We finished our breakfasts, and while Pete went to the front cash register to pay the check, I zipped my jacket, gathered up my purse, and slid out of the booth. I glanced around to be sure we hadn't dropped anything. That was when I noticed the Manolo Blahnik boots on the woman in the booth behind us.

I knew immediately that the feet in those gorgeous boots belonged to Primrose McDonald. Her back was to me. The great legs were covered by dark blue sweatpants. A gray hoodie covered most of the platinum hair. The man seated across from her leaned forward, his eyes on her face, speaking in tones too low for me to hear. I was pretty sure they hadn't noticed me, and I hurried to catch up to Pete.

Why is Primrose having an early breakfast with city councilor Jonathan Wilson?

I didn't say anything to Pete about what I'd just seen. True, it was a bit strange, but as Aunt Ibby had reminded me, it was none of my business where the woman went or who she met when she got there.

It wasn't quite eight o'clock when Pete dropped me off in front of the Tabby.

"Want me to wait until I'm sure you're safely inside?"

I tucked my laptop under one arm and waved with the other. "Nope. I'm fine. If they don't let me in, I'll hang out in the diner until they open the doors. Thanks for breakfast."

"I'll call you later," he said. "I have the night off. Maybe we can do something."

"Great. See you then."

I had no trouble getting into the school. I tapped on one of the glass doors, showed my instructor's ID to a burly man wearing a security badge, and walked right in.

"Is Mr. Pennington around?" I asked.

"The guy who runs the place? Yeah. He's downstairs with a couple of gents who look like big shots. One of 'em's a cop." He pointed to the basement door, where the discreet EMPLOYEES ONLY plaque had once again been replaced with a small hand-lettered NO ADMITTANCE sign.

"I need to talk to Mr. Pennington for a just a minute," I said. "Is it okay if I go down?"

He shrugged. "Okay by me. That badge says you work here."

I opened the door and started down the steep staircase. The space below was well lit, and the hum of conversation echoed in the huge empty room below. I paused after taking just a few steps. The conversation below sounded confrontational, and I didn't want to walk in on a dispute.

"Listen, Pennington, you and the rest of your people are going to have to do exactly as we say, or I swear, I'll shut this place down." The man's tone was angry; the voice familiar. "I came in early this morning and found a couple of your so-called students wandering around down here. Apparently, your security guard thinks anyone with a school ID has the run of the place."

"I apologize for that," I heard the director say. "I'll reprimand both young men. I'm sure they were just curious. Meant no harm." He cleared his voice. "Let's not make a federal case out of it."

Another man spoke. "Look here, Pennington," he growled. "What you don't seem to understand is that it *is* a federal case. Now, you keep everybody out of here. That means everybody. Including you. Do I make myself clear?"

I began to back up. My question about school opening time could wait. I'd almost reached the door when my phone chimed. I grabbed it and turned it off. Too late. The conversation ceased abruptly, and all three men moved to the foot of the stairs.

"Ms. Barrett? Is that you?" Mr. Pennington shielded his eyes with one hand and peered up to where I stood in the shadows.

"Who is it this time? Another curious student? Come down here, ma'am, and identify yourself." The man's voice was firm.

Making my way down the stairs seemed to take forever, like one of those slow-motion shots on TV. The room below was silent, and the three men stood looking up at me. I recognized the tallest one as Salem police chief Tom Whaley.

Uh-oh. Chief Whaley and I have crossed paths before, and he's definitely not one of my fans.

"So. Ms. Barrett." His look was stern and disapproving. "Why am I not surprised to see you?"

Mr. Pennington looked from the chief to me and back. "You know one another? How nice." He quickly introduced me to the other man, a serious-looking fellow wearing a black suit. "Mr. Friedrich is here to help with the local investigation of that poor man who fell into the hole."

Mr. Friedrich is here from where to help with the investigation? What do they mean, it's a federal case?

Mr. Friedrich acknowledged the introduction with a curt nod, while Chief Whaley folded his arms and frowned.

"Yes, well, I'll be going," I said. "I just wanted to know if we're using the building for classes today, Mr. Pennington. I need to inform my students."

Chief Whaley answered my question. "The classrooms and dormitory are open as of noon today. The announcement will be on local radio and TV. Under no circumstances are you or any of the students to enter this basement. Do I make myself clear?"

"Yes, sir."

"Pennington, we'll replace your security guard with a police officer. Maybe that will keep out the curious students, and also Ms. Barrett, who has a habit of interfering with my investigations."

If Mr. Pennington wondered what the chief was talking about, he didn't say so. I knew exactly what he meant. I'd been unintentionally in the way of his investigation of Ariel's murder, and he clearly hadn't forgotten it.

I scurried from the basement to the relative shelter of my classroom. I put the laptop away in my desk and checked the phone to see who'd called and given away my presence on the basement stairs. River North's name popped up.

I called her back, wondering what she was doing awake so early. I knew how late she'd been up, since I'd worked the same hours at WICH-TV when I was pretending to be a psychic.

"Hi, River. Why the early morning call? You okay?"

"I'm fine. Just couldn't sleep, wondering what you saw in your vision. Come on. Tell me."

"All right. It doesn't make much sense, though."

"Come on. I'm dying to know."

I described what I'd seen in the toe of the shoe. The woman, the white dress, the two keys. "Make any sense to you?" I asked. "Any ideas?"

She sounded thoughtful. "You know, it reminds me of something I heard a while ago from the oldest member of the coven. Megan is over a hundred years old, nearly blind, and walks with a cane. She's a very powerful witch."

"No kidding? A hundred years old?"

"She sure is. And, Lee, Megan and Tabitha Trumbull were childhood friends. Now, this may be a coincidence—and you know I don't believe in coincidences—but the story she told us about Tabitha involved two keys."

CHAPTER 12

"Since you're already up, want to come over to the school?" I was anxious to hear about Megan and Tabitha. "I don't have a class until noon. You can tell me your story, and maybe I can show you around the place."

"Love to," she said. "Want me to bring the cards? Read you again?"

"Uh, no thanks. Let's just talk this time."

"Okay. Be right over."

I texted my six students, telling them school would officially be in session at noon.

They'll probably be disappointed. Having class in a barroom is kind of cool.

I pulled six textbooks and the teacher's edition from the bookcase, pushed seven chairs up to the round table, put markers beside the whiteboard, then headed down to the first floor so I'd be there to get River past security. Giving a nod to the portrait of Oliver Wendell Trumbull, I approached the double glass doors. The security guard had already been replaced by an officer, who checked my ID badge. I told him I was expecting a prospective guest speaker, which was sort of true.

Therese would love it. A real witch to talk about spells and magic. Wonder if River will do it?

The officer stood beside me until she arrived. He unlocked the door, recognized River right away from her show, warned us both to stay away from the basement, and resumed his post next to the NO ADMITTANCE sign.

"Come on upstairs first," I said. "Let's check with Mr. Pennington to be sure it's okay for us to look around."

"Good idea. I wouldn't want to get into trouble in this place," River said, glancing back over her shoulder. "Enough trouble here already."

"You've got that right." We reached the director's office, and I tapped lightly on the partially open door. "Mr. Pennington? Hello?"

"Yes. Hello," came a muffled answer.

I pushed the door open, glanced around the room, but didn't see him. "Hello?" I said again. "Mr. Pennington?"

I fought an urge to laugh when the man suddenly popped up from behind his chair, reminding me of a Whac-A-Mole game.

"Oh, Ms. Barrett, excuse me. Just doing a little housekeeping." He stood erect, patted his hair, adjusted his jacket, and smiled in River's direction all in one smooth move. "And who is this lovely lady? Another student?"

I introduced River and, while they shook hands, peeked at the space behind the chair where he'd obviously been sitting or kneeling. The only thing there was the antique safe.

Permission to tour the building, all of it except the basement, was given quickly and graciously. "I'm sure you'll be impressed with our facility, Miss North." Again the big smile. "Or is it Mrs.?"

He'd used the same line on Aunt Ibby.

We retraced our steps to the mezzanine landing, where River paused. "Megan says there used to be a piano here, and there was a man in a tuxedo playing popular tunes for the shoppers."

I nodded. "Aunt Ibby mentioned that, too."

River pointed toward the portrait of Oliver Wendell Trumbull. "This must be the founding father of Trumbull's. Right?"

"That's him. He was Tabitha's husband."

She lowered her voice. "The money to build the store all came from her family, you know. The Smiths."

"No. Really?" I was surprised. "I didn't know that."

"Yep. Seems Mr. Trumbull was just a guy who worked for Tabitha's dad. Megan says the wedding was the high point of Salem's social season. Eight bridesmaids, reception at Hamilton Hall, gown imported from London. A real big deal."

"Must have been quite a party. Was Megan one of the bridesmaids?"

"Nope. Megan's mother was a cook at the Smith family's mansion. The two girls were raised together and were best friends, but in those days you didn't include servants in the wedding party." There was a trace of annoyance in her voice at the long-ago injustice. "Megan was thrilled to even be invited to the wedding."

"I'd like to meet her. She must have some wonderful stories to tell," I said.

"I'll introduce you," she promised. "Want to show me where you work?"

"Sure. Come on. You can see the giant black shoe, and you can tell me all about Megan and Tabitha and the two keys. And I'm still waiting to hear why the Trumbulls kept the poor woman locked up in the attic."

River followed me and stood in the middle of the shoe department turned classroom. "Hey, it looks almost like a real TV studio." She turned slowly in a circle. "News desk, monitors, green screen, rolling cameras, the whole works. And you even have a little study table all set up. This is wicked cool!"

I could tell from her expression that she meant it. "I'm happy you like it. I want this class to work, to give everybody at least some of what they're looking for."

She gave me a quick hug. "You'll be great. Now, tell me about that shoe." She moved closer to the giant pump, reached out and touched it. "Feels like a real shoe. They made things better back in the day, didn't they? Now it would be cardboard or plastic."

It hadn't occurred to me to touch the thing. Right from the start I hadn't even wanted to look at it. "Guess you're right," I said, taking a seat with my back to the shoe. "The thing . . . the vision . . . whatever . . . lasted only a few seconds."

"Do you think it might have kept going if you hadn't told it to stop?" River sat in a chair opposite mine, and looked at me intently.

That possibility had crossed my mind, but I'd been trying not to think about it. "I don't know. Maybe."

"Tell me again about what you saw."

I closed my eyes, trying to see the very clear picture of the dark-haired woman. "She was young. Around your age. She had on a long dress, satin maybe, with a really high collar. Puffy sleeves at the top but tight from the elbows down."

"Sounds pretty."

I nodded. "It was pretty. Anyway, she walked toward me. Kind of floated, really. She held her left hand toward me. There were two old-fashioned keys in her palm. She seemed to want me to take them." I bowed my head. "That was when I told it to stop. She turned her back and disappeared. That was the end of it. Do you know what it might mean?" I said, hoping she'd have an answer.

"I'm sorry." She looked genuinely sad. "I'm good with the cards, but not so much with dreams or visions."

"That's okay," I said. "Now it's your turn."

"Okay. Here goes. Both stories are from Megan, but I don't think they have anything to do with each other."

"I'm listening."

"You already know about the big, fancy penthouse they had upstairs in the old days. Megan says it was beautiful. Tabitha was really proud of it and liked showing it off. I mean, they owned this great big department store, and she could have anything she wanted to decorate with. Loved shopping."

"That would be fun," I said, thinking how much Aunt Ibby enjoyed redecorating the house on Winter Street.

"Sure would," she said. "But before long, people starting saying Tabitha was confused in her mind, and the Trumbulls stopped having parties and dinners and dances." River shook her head. "It got so they couldn't let her out of the building at all. Afraid she'd wander off and get lost. So they hired a nurse to stay with her, and at night, after the store was closed, she was allowed to get dressed up and go downstairs by herself and pick up anything she wanted."

"So she could still go shopping."

"Kind of. Of course, they just put everything back in the morning. She wouldn't remember."

"Oh, that's so sad."

"I know. Mr. Trumbull moved out sometime in the

nineteen forties. He told people she didn't know who he was most of the time, anyway. She still liked to have Megan visit, though, and sometimes they'd have conversations that still made sense."

"I'm glad she still had a friend."

"Pretty soon Mr. Trumbull stopped Tabitha's nighttime shopping trips. He figured she was getting outside somehow, because a few times she came back upstairs with dirt on her shoes and clothes. After that she had to stay locked inside the apartment." River pointed toward the mezzanine landing. "The player piano that used to be out there? They moved it up to her room. She loved it. Played the old tunes all day and half the night."

"That would explain why people who think they see her ghost sometimes say they hear a piano playing."

"I guess so. Anyway, she lived up there until she died. Even after the store was closed, just her and a nurse."

"You're kidding! They kept her up there, over an empty store? All that time? And she died there?"

"She didn't die there. They were smart enough to take her to a hospital at the end." She looked around and spoke softly. "So nobody would know they'd kept her locked up all those years. We know only because of Megan. I guess the nurse never told anybody. They must have paid her to keep quiet about it."

"It's hard to imagine people treating their own mother that way."

"I know," River said. "But Megan thinks Tabitha may have been happy, in her own way."

"I hope so. Now tell me about the keys, please."

"Okay. Here goes." She leaned forward in her chair and dropped her voice. "I may not have it exactly right.

It's been a while since I heard it, and I didn't know I might want to remember it later."

"Go on."

"I already told you that Megan and Tabitha were childhood friends, practically raised together in Tabitha's family mansion down near where Pickering Wharf is now."

"It's not there anymore."

"Nope. Got burned down a long time ago. It was almost right next door to a great big yard where the coal barges from down South used to unload. Megan says most everybody burned coal for heat back then." She wrinkled her nose in apparent disapproval of coal fires in general and continued. "After the fire, the coal company bought the land and put up an office building or something. While they were having a new mansion built, Tabitha's family moved in with her grandparents in a house down the street a little ways. Anyhow, when Megan and Tabitha were little, maybe five or six, Tabitha's grandpa showed them a tunnel hidden behind his house."

"A tunnel? No kidding? Like the one they just found under this building? Pete says there are a bunch of them under the city."

"I know. I need to start paying attention to the news." She shook her head. "I didn't even hear until this morning that the hole under here was an old hunk of tunnel."

"So Megan remembers the tunnel?"

"Heck. Megan remembers everything. Tabitha's grandpa showed them a little path that led into the tunnel. She says there were electric lights along the walls and even a round cover with a small glass window in the ceiling that let in sunlight. It was part of the sidewalk up on Derby Street."

"You mean people could see into the tunnel from above it?"

"Nope. They couldn't. Megan says the two friends tried it, and the glass was so thick and opaque, they couldn't see a thing. Anyway, they liked going to the tunnel so much that Tabitha's grandpa built them a little playhouse down there."

"He let those children play underground?"

"Only when he was nearby. She says he used the tunnel a lot. Moving things from the house to somewhere in the tunnel."

"Moving what?"

River waved a hand in the air. "Who knows? They were little kids. They didn't ask. Anyway, here's where the two keys come in. That playhouse had real kid-size furniture in it. Tables, chairs, lamps, and a big toy box. They called it their treasure chest."

"Treasure? What was in it?"

"Just toys and kid stuff. But they loved it mostly because it had a real lock and key."

I realized I'd been holding my breath as she spoke. "That's one key," I said, excited. "Where was the other one?"

River smiled. "Don't rush me. I'm getting there. The other key was the key to the playhouse itself. It had a bright red painted door with a brass door knocker and a fancy brass keyhole."

"So. Two keys," I said. "You said you don't believe in coincidences, and I don't think I do, either. Does Megan know what happened to them?"

"No. There were two sets. Tabitha's grandpa kept one set, and Tabitha had the other. Megan had a chance to visit Tabitha up there in the attic just before she died." River pointed toward the ceiling. "She told Megan the keys were safe with Mary Alice."

"Who's Mary Alice?"

"Mary Alice was Tabitha's youngest daughter. She committed suicide when she was fifteen, back in the nineteen fifties."

CHAPTER 13

"The ghost in the confirmation dress," I said, hardly realizing I'd spoken out loud. "But I wonder why Tabitha thought she had the keys."

"Which ghost is that?" River asked.

"Aunt Ibby told me about three possible ghosts in white. One of them was a pregnant teenage girl who drowned herself. She's wearing her white confirmation dress."

"That would be Mary Alice, I guess. She was pregnant, huh? Guess that explains the suicide. Back in the fifties teen pregnancy was a big no-no. I didn't know she was one of the ghost suspects, though. Who's the third?"

"An Indian princess in white deerskin. Aunt Ibby's favorite."

"Oh yeah. I like that one, too. She's supposed to be buried under the building." She snapped her fingers. "Hey, I wonder if they'll find her bones down in the tunnel."

"Stop it!" I laughed. "You are so creepy."

"I know. It's fun. Listen, do you think we could go up to the top floor? I'd love to see Tabitha's room."

"I've never seen it myself," I admitted. "I've been kind of scared to go up there alone."

"Now's your chance, girlfriend. I'll protect you. Let's go."

I looked at my watch. "We still have time before the noon class. Let's take the elevator up. It still has the old department store directory in it. Ladies' wear, children's, hosiery, millinery."

"Cool."

Trumbull's elevator ran from the first floor to the third, but not down to the basement. On the third, there was another elevator, which went to the top floor. That one had been for the exclusive use of the Trumbull family, according to Mr. Pennington, and was out of service because it hadn't been inspected yet. But from a jangling ring of keys, he'd given us one for the door leading to the attic suite stairway, along with a flashlight.

"It's dark and dusty up there now," he'd warned. "But I envision it someday returning to its original splendor, providing appropriate accommodations for visiting dignitaries—important personages from the world of music, stars of the stage and screen."

Mr. Pennington would absolutely adore hobnobbing with those personages.

I smiled at the thought as River and I stood in the elevator. I glanced at the directory's third-floor entry. THIRD FLOOR: FURNITURE, DOMESTICS, NOTIONS, FABRICS, BEAUTY PARLOR. We left the elevator and climbed the stairs to the once splendid home of Tabitha and Oliver Wendell Trumbull, arriving in a high-ceilinged foyer. River aimed the flashlight upward.

"Wow. Look at that. The crown molding in here must be a foot wide, and it's full of fancy curlicues. That would cost a fortune now."

"Probably did then, too," I said. An open arched doorway led to what might have been a formal parlor. It was stripped of furniture, and the blue moiré taffeta-covered walls were water stained and dirty. The floorboards creaked as we made our way toward a row of dormer windows, where pale winter sunlight filtered through panes of purple-tinted glass.

The view of Salem from the top floor of the Tabby was, as Aunt Ibby had guessed, amazing. "Look," River said, pointing. "You can see all the way to the ocean."

She was right. Salem doesn't have a lot of really tall buildings, and most of the trees were leafless, so it seemed as though no matter in which direction we faced, there was a panoramic view of the city.

"I think these dormer windows go all around the whole top floor," I said. "I'll bet every outside room has views like this."

"Want to try 'em all?" River pushed open a paneled door, and we entered what must have been a fabulous dining room. Three chandeliers, their crystal prisms still reflecting snippets of rainbow light in spite of cobwebs and layers of grime, were spaced along the center of the vaulted ceiling and tinkled slightly as we passed.

"Let's try to find Tabitha's room," River said. "I hope at least she had a nice view to look at, even if she couldn't go outside."

"Hope so," I said, and we pushed open another door at the end of the long room. "Better use the flashlight. It's dark in here."

We hurried through several empty rooms, our footsteps and voices providing eerie echoes. At the end of a broad, carpeted hall we reached a set of ornately carved double doors.

"This must be the ballroom," I said. "Pete was up

here and says it's full of old furniture and stuff now." I pulled both latches and threw the doors open.

It was the highest ceilinged of all the rooms we'd seen so far, and even the hodgepodge of furniture couldn't obscure its "once upon a time" elegance. There was a balcony overlooking the dance floor. Huge mirrors in gilded frames, which must have once reflected ladies in ball gowns and gentlemen in tuxedos, now displayed random piles of discarded furnishings— velvet-seated chairs juxtaposed with homely kitchen cabinets, a child's rocking horse atop a satiny chaise longue. Bureaus, desks, lamps, bookcases, and hat racks loomed in precarious piles, chair and table legs sticking out at crazy angles. The general effect was unsettling. We slowly backed out of the place and closed the doors.

"Let's find Tabitha's room and then go back downstairs," I said.

Several closed doors along the hallway opened into empty rooms—except for one. We'd found Tabitha Trumbull's prison. We stood together in the doorway, neither of us crossing the threshold. Unlike the ballroom, with its unruly piles of furniture, Tabitha's room was a picture of neatness, despite a fine layer of dust shrouding everything. River stepped onto the Oriental rug first, and I followed. There was a twin-size bed next to one of the windows, with a large framed photograph of President Franklin Roosevelt above the headboard. A marble-topped dresser displayed a wooden-handled hand mirror and a brush and comb.

"Look," River said. "It's a corner room. She had windows on two sides."

Sheer once-white curtains hung in limp folds, partially covering the square-paned casements, and we hurried to see what view of Salem Tabitha had had.

Two of her windows overlooked the stores and shops and restaurants that line Essex Street. The other two offered a similar vista to the one we'd seen from the parlor, and so she'd been able to see all the way to the ocean.

River pointed. "There's her piano, the one the tuxedo guy used to play." She knelt and touched the wide pedals beneath the instrument. "I've never seen one of these before. Have you?"

"Only in antiques shops," I admitted.

"Do you know how it works?" She pulled a long bench close to the keyboard and sat, hands poised, as though she was about to perform at a recital. "Do you push on these pedals?" As she spoke, she moved her feet up and down, and a slightly out-of-tune version of "I've Got My Love to Keep Me Warm" issued from the old Pianola.

"You've got it," I told her. "Try pedaling a little faster."

River pretended to play, moving her fingers across the keys, smiling, and rocking her body from side to side in time to the music. "This is great! I want one. How does it know what song to play?"

"I think there's some kind of a roll behind that panel." A wooden section with a raised design was just about where sheet music would be displayed. I slid it aside and revealed a perforated rolling cylinder. "See? There it is. When you pedal, the roll moves and those little holes pick out the notes."

"I love it," she said.

"I'm glad Tabitha had this to help her pass the time up here," I said. "Especially after they didn't let her go shopping anymore."

"She must have had some songs besides this one. Let's find some more of these rolls."

"I know people keep sheet music in the piano bench. Maybe there are some piano rolls in this one." I investigated the contents of the bench. Pushing aside some colorful song sheets, I exposed a row of the perforated rolls, each secured with a rubber band. "There's a bunch of them here," I said, "but they're kind of tattered. I wonder what happened to the boxes."

"Let's try this tall cabinet," River suggested, tugging at the doors of an ornate armoire. "Oh, boy," she said after opening it. "Jackpot!"

Jackpot for sure. The armoire was packed full of neatly boxed piano rolls, top to bottom, side to side, each with its labeled end exposed. I put the song sheets back and closed the bench lid. Moving close to the armoire, I played the beam of the flashlight across the varicolored labels.

"I know some of these songs, like 'Heart and Soul,'" I said. "And look, there's 'Moonlight Serenade.' But I never even heard of a lot of them. How about you?"

"Uh-uh. Ever hear of 'Cornfield Capers'? These names are a riot," River said. "There must be hundreds of them. Maybe a thousand. Want me to play some more?"

I glanced at my watch. "Sorry. We haven't got time right now. Got to get back downstairs. My students will be showing up."

"I wish we didn't have to leave." She closed the piano lid while I secured the armoire doors. "Can we come back sometime? I want to see the rest of Tabitha's stuff."

I wanted to see Tabitha's stuff, too, very much. "Sure we can. And soon."

As we rode the elevator down to the first floor—the directory read BOOKS, HARDWARE, SMALL APPLIANCES, CHINA, River looked thoughtful. Just before the elevator door slid open, she said, "Lee, I hope you don't think I'm too weird or anything, but when I started to play that song, did you notice anything, um, anything kind of strange in the room?"

"Like the rocking chair rocking by itself?"

"You saw it, too?"

"I did. But it was probably just the vibration from the piano, don't you think?"

"Sure. Maybe."

I walked with River to the door, then hurried back to the elevator for the short ride to my classroom. I discovered that none of the students had arrived yet. I was about to sit behind my desk when I realized that the key to the upstairs suite was still in my pocket. I hurried to Mr. Pennington's office and knocked on his door.

"Come in, come in, Ms. Barrett. My door is always open. Did you find your excursion into the building's past enlightening?"

"Really interesting," I said. "I'd like to go back up there when I have more time." I handed him the key.

"Certainly, my dear. Absolutely." He opened his top drawer and removed the round ring full of keys. He reattached the one I'd handed him, then placed the ring on his desk. "Did your attractive young friend enjoy it, too? What was her name? River?"

"River North," I told him. "She'd like to come back, too. She was particularly interested in the Pianola."

"A fascinating instrument," he began and launched into a history of the player piano, but I barely heard his words. My attention was completely focused on the key ring. Particularly on two keys that were quite unlike the rest.

Two long, dark-colored skeleton keys.

My mind was buzzing as I hurried down the stairs.

*The same two keys I saw in the woman's hand are on
Mr. Pennington's key ring.*

Keys. An underground tunnel. A rocking chair. A
dead handyman. Primrose McDonald's breakfast ren-
dezvous. And an old woman locked in an attic room. I
realized I was beginning to frame my thoughts in a
new way. I was actually thinking, *WWND? What would
Nancy do?*

I'd have to sort it out later. It was a couple of minutes
before noon, and the sounds of arriving students
echoed through the building. Footsteps on stairs,
laughter, voices, buzzing phones, announcements over
the loudspeaker—it must have sounded something like
this when the doors of Trumbull's Department Store
opened every morning. All that was missing was a
piano accompaniment.

Sammy and Duke were the first to arrive, with Kelly,
Thom and Therese close behind. Primrose hadn't arrived yet.

"Find yourselves a seat, everybody," I said. "I hope
you've all been thinking of more ideas for our documentary."

"Duke and I took a walk around the basement early
this morning," Sammy said, "and we've got some new
ideas about the tunnel."

"Before we got tossed out by the cops," Duke said
with a smirk. "Guess we weren't supposed to be down
there."

"Yeah," said Kelly. "What part of *no admittance* don't
you guys understand?"

Duke and Sammy exchanged amused glances.

"We showed the guard our student IDs, and Duke
showed him a ten-dollar bill, and we were in," Sammy
said.

"Don't try that again, you two," I warned. "The security

man lost his job, and you've managed to tick off the chief of police."

They'd managed to tick me off, too, and it showed in my voice. Both men looked down at their feet, but whether that meant repentance or just a way to hide their smiles, I couldn't tell.

Primrose dashed into the room in a whirl of faux leopard, black velvet, fishnet hose, and the Manolo Blahnik boots. "Sorry I'm late, kids. Did I miss anything important?"

"Not really," I said, the trace of annoyance still in my voice. "Take a seat."

"You missed the part where Sammy and Duke almost got arrested," Kelly said.

"No shit? Tell me about it." Primrose faced Sammy. "What happened?"

"No big deal," Sammy said. "We didn't obey the sign. Went down in the basement, and the cops chased us out."

"Oh, is that all?" Primrose looked disappointed.

Therese raised her hand. "Do you want me to take notes again?"

"That would be a big help. I've transcribed all the notes from yesterday." I placed the laptop in front of her. "Let's get started."

"Okay," she said. "Ideas, anybody?"

Silence.

Kelly frowned. "Come on, you guys. Therese and I thought up dozens last night, while we were helping in the bar."

Primrose spoke up. "What happened, Thom? You took the night off and let the girls pick up all those tips?"

Thom shrugged. "Duke said it was about time I

relaxed a little. He took Sammy and me out to dinner. Took us to breakfast today, too."

"Really? How nice." Unsmiling, I stood in front of the whiteboard, picked up a marker, then printed a number one. "Let's get down to business. Who's first?"

"How about this?" Kelly asked. "I heard that the Trumbulls used to live on the top floor. Let's make a set that looks like Tabitha's room. One of us dresses up like Tabitha, and she tells about living up there back then."

"I like it, Kelly," I said. "As a matter of fact, I got to see Tabitha's room this morning. I'll try to arrange for all of you to see it soon." I wrote, "Reenactment" on the board, while Therese tapped on the laptop.

"Here's another one," Therese offered. "Let's see if we can get a witch, or even a coven, to come and talk to us about today's witches in Salem."

"I'll work on that one." I wrote, "Witch visit" for number two. I looked from Thom to Sammy to Duke. "Any ideas from the men?"

"I've got an idea, ma'am," Duke said, sounding so John Wayne-ish, I almost expected him to call me "pilgrim." "How about this? We do a real investigation into what the Trumbulls used that tunnel for." He lowered his voice and looked around the table. "They must have used it, 'cause the trapdoor ain't no hundred years old, like they're sayin' the tunnel is."

"Nope," Sammy said. "That sucker was put in long after that. And they must have used it for something kind of small, because the entrance panel is only about four feet high."

"Right," said Duke. "But at some time they used tunnels for big stuff."

Therese looked up and stopped typing. "How do you know?"

Sammy answered, "The tunnel entrance, the old one, is so tall that Duke here could stand up in it."

It was my turn to ask. "How do you know that?"

Duke sounded proud of himself. "Tried it."

"Are you nuts?" I felt my redhead's temper beginning to flare, and for a moment I forgot my teacher status. "Don't you two dopes realize it might be a crime scene? You actually pushed the button and opened the door?"

It was Thom's turn to confuse things even more. "They didn't actually go in," he said. "Just sort of measured the entrance."

"You too? You were in on this?"

"I didn't go downstairs. It was my job to keep the guard busy. I kinda used to date him." He flashed his gorgeous model smile in my direction. "I took off through the diner when I saw the cops pull up out front. We thought you'd be happy about it. Investigative reporting, just like on TV."

I put down the marker and sat, looking around the table at each of them. "Damn it. I'm probably going to have to tell somebody what you've done. One of the men who caught you walking around down there is a federal agent."

"No kidding?" Primrose leaned forward, exposing cleavage. "A Fed? Did you get his name?"

"Friedrich," I said. "Why? What difference does it make?"

"No difference," she said. "Just nosy, I guess."

"Are you really going to tell on them?" Kelly wanted to know.

"I'll have to tell Mr. Pennington," I said, hoping this wouldn't get half my class expelled.

"Shall I put it in the notes, though?" Therese asked. "About what the Trumbulls could have used the tunnel for? It's a good idea, even if they shouldn't have gone down there."

"Put it down," I said, "but any more investigative reporting has to be okayed by me from now on. Everybody got that?"

Heads nodded. I wrote "Trumbulls' tunnel use" at number three on the whiteboard. "How about you, Primrose? Ideas?"

"No, but Sammy and Therese have the best voices, so they could do the narration."

"Voice-over," I said. "Good idea."

I wrote "Therese/Sammy—voice-over." "Duke?" I asked the big man. "Any preference for what you'd like to do for the project?"

"I've done a little TV—commercials and bit parts. I think I'd like to learn about 'behind the camera' work. Maybe like writing or directing, you know?" He had dropped the phony Western tough guy act for the moment and sounded sincere.

"I think we're off to a good start," I said. "Therese, as soon as you've finished adding today's ideas to the ones we came up with yesterday, why don't you all get to work on putting them into logical order for our documentary."

"We'll start a storyboard," Duke said.

"Exactly. And, Primrose, you've expressed an interest in writing, so maybe you can begin a loose outline of the Trumbulls' story, using the ideas we have so far."

"You're going to help us, aren't you?" Kelly sounded concerned.

"I'll be right here at my desk if you need me," I

said. "I have a little paperwork to do. Don't worry. You'll be fine."

I left them at the round table and sat down at my desk. Still in WWND mode, I planned to write down all the puzzle pieces I had so far on index cards. Then, like my students, I'd try to put the information into a logical sequence. I pulled a stack of index cards from my purse and began to write.

1. *Bill Sullivan falls into the hole in the tunnel floor.*
2. *There's a second tunnel under the original one. Why?*
3. *How did he get to the park?*
4. *Does Primrose McDonald's connection to Jonathan Wilson mean anything?*
5. *Why is the federal government interested in Trumbull's basement?*
6. *Can Megan the witch shed any light on this?*
7. *Why is the vision showing me two keys?*
8. *Why do they look like the keys on Pennington's key ring?*
9. *Why did Tabitha tell Megan that Mary Alice has the keys if Mary Alice is dead?*

I stopped writing and shuffled the cards.

They don't make any sense, no matter how I arrange them. Not yet.

If I looked into the shoe again, would the woman still be there? Would she tell me what the keys mean if I didn't stop the picture?

I spun the chair around. I was at eye level with the toe of the shoe. Almost immediately the swirling colors and the points of light appeared. The woman was there, her back to me, exactly as she'd looked when she turned and walked away when I first saw her.

"Don't go away," I whispered. She turned, smiled, and held the keys aloft. She walked, or floated, through a wide brick archway. I felt as though I was following her. I knew that we'd entered the tunnel, not through the moving panel in the basement, but through the entrance as it must have been long ago.

She turned, raising the keys over her head. With her other hand, she beckoned me to follow her deeper into the tunnel. As I watched, the figure grew smaller and smaller, until it finally turned a corner, still beckoning, and disappeared. It was only then that I noticed the shadowy figure of a cat following close behind her.

"Lee? Ms. Barrett? You okay?" Kelly's gentle tap on my shoulder startled me. Eyes still focused on the shoe, I watched as the vision disappeared as cleanly as if it had been clicked off by a remote control.

"What? Oh, Kelly. I'm sorry. Guess I was . . . um . . . daydreaming. Woolgathering, my aunt Ibby calls it. How's the storyboard coming?"

Primrose answered the question. "Lots of holes in it, but it's beginning to make sense."

"Primrose is good at this," Therese said. "It sounds like she's telling a story."

"That's exactly what we're doing," I said. "Telling a story."

"I mean the way she's doing it. It's, like, from Mr. and Mrs. Trumbull's point of view. As though they were still alive now and have seen everything that's happened since they opened the store on the first day."

I was impressed. "Nice going, Primrose," I said. "An excellent way to frame it."

I meant it, and I was pretty sure the overseers of the grant would like it, too. Now, if I could only get my own puzzling storyboard to make as much sense as the one my students were creating. We worked until five o'clock, when the six students grabbed coats and hats and said hasty good-byes, leaving me alone with Therese's neat stack of printouts and my own meager, not so neat pile of index cards.

My phone buzzed. I smiled when I read the caller ID.

"Hi, Pete," I said. "What's up?"

"It's five o'clock," came the warm, familiar voice. "You get rid of all those little darlin's yet?"

"All gone," I said. "I'm alone and was just thinking of heading out into the cold for the walk home. You know, I've got to get serious about buying a car."

"How about I come over there now and drive you home, and then maybe later we can catch a movie or something? I've got the night off."

"You have no idea how good that sounds, Pete. It's been a strange day."

"I'll be there in ten minutes. Meet me out front?"

I wanted to say, "Make it five," but didn't. I dialed Mr. Pennington's number, dreading what I had to tell him about my students' unauthorized basement investigation, and was relieved when the voice message said he'd be out of the office until tomorrow. After scribbling "Tell Pennington" on a fresh index card and "Cat in the tunnel?" on another, I stuffed the printouts and cards into a manila envelope, made a quick trip to the restroom to freshen my makeup, then pulled on my jacket. I was standing outside the glass doors when Pete's car pulled up to the curb.

He leaned across the seat and opened the passenger door for me. "Hop in. It's cold out there."

"Dark too," I said. "Not even five thirty and it looks like midnight."

"Welcome to New England winter."

"I know. I thought I missed it a little when I lived in Florida—the pretty snowfall, the skaters on the pond, chestnuts roasting on an open fire . . . you know, all the Norman Rockwell stuff."

"And now?"

"Hmm. Not so much. I'm ready for an early spring."

"Aw, come on. It's not so bad here." He frowned. "You're not thinking about leaving? Going back to Florida?"

"Not for a minute. I'm home to stay."

"Good." He smiled as we rounded the corner to Winter Street and parked in front of the house. "Shall I come back and pick you up around seven? We can catch an early movie and maybe stop in at your friend's tavern later."

"Sounds like fun," I said. "See you at seven." I waved, dashed up the stairs, and stepped into the welcoming warmth of home, complete with purring cat weaving in and out between my feet.

"Hello, Maralee," my aunt called from the den. "You're early. I thought you might phone me for a ride home."

"Pete picked me up. I was all prepared for a nice brisk walk, though. I don't like to keep depending on you for transportation."

"It's no bother."

"I was just telling Pete, it's time for me to start looking for a car of my own."

"Whatever pleases you, dear. Are you ready for a bite of supper?"

"Just a tiny bite," I said. "Pete will be back at seven. We're going to the movies."

"I have a nice pea soup in the freezer. I was thinking of having that with some fresh hot johnnycake."

"Perfect. Need any help?"

"Not a bit. You run upstairs and get yourself prettied up for your date." She was already heading for the kitchen. "While we eat, I'll tell you what I've learned so far about the Trumbulls."

"Really? Anything juicy?"

"I think you'll be surprised. Hurry along now."

A quick shower, a change into black jeans and a white turtleneck, and I hurried back downstairs. Steaming pea soup in a white ironstone tureen and hot-from-the-oven johnnycake were already on the kitchen table. The meal, as usual, was delicious, but I could hardly wait for Aunt Ibby's report on what she'd learned about the Trumbulls.

"I think I told you," she began, "that I could access the vertical files where paper items, like notebooks and correspondence and records and such, are kept."

"You did," I said. "There'd be things there in their own handwriting, wouldn't there?"

"Absolutely. And there was plenty to look at, I'll tell you. I haven't had time yet to really study anywhere near all of it, but I did glean a few interesting tidbits."

"Tell me."

"Back in the late nineteen eighties there was a big to-do around here about a Salem commercial fishing boat running guns to Ireland for the IRA."

I shook my head. "I don't remember that."

"Well, you were very young. Anyway, the boat's captain and a couple of crew members went to jail after they got caught." She dropped her voice. "The papers said that they were exchanging the guns for cocaine. The boat belonged to one of the Trumbull boys. Oliver Jr."

"Did he go to jail, too?"

"He was never charged with anything. A Captain Gable took the whole blame. He was sentenced to twenty years in a prison in Connecticut."

"Twenty years. He must be out by now," I said.

She shook her head. "Died in jail, poor soul. But what I found today was a small packet of letters he wrote. To Tabitha Trumbull."

CHAPTER 14

For a moment I didn't say anything, doing some fast calculations in my head.

"Wait a minute. If that was in the late eighties and Tabitha died in the early nineties, she must have been pretty old by then and, well, pretty crazy. How could she carry on a correspondence?"

"That's what I thought, too," Aunt Ibby said. "But apparently, Tabitha was in the habit of sending small sums of money to the captain's wife."

"Maybe she wasn't so crazy, after all," I said. "River says that her witch friend, Megan, used to visit Tabitha regularly, and that the old woman could carry on intelligent conversations. And, Aunt Ibby, you won't believe this, but Tabitha lived in her room up over the store until just before she died."

"No! How could that be?"

"Megan says it's true. A nurse stayed with her, and I suppose her family visited her, but she lived up in that room all that time. She must have been sending the money from there."

"The notes from the captain were all brief thank-yous. Things like 'Thank you for your letter and for the twenty dollars you sent to my wife. We appreciate your help.'"

"So she wrote letters to the captain and sent money to his wife. That was kind of her," I said.

"It was," my aunt agreed, "but one of the notes was a bit confusing."

"How so?"

"The captain wrote the usual thanks for the twenty dollars. It was always the same amount, by the way." She paused and leaned forward. "He said that the money made it possible for her to buy brand-new bicycles for all four of the kids."

"With twenty dollars?"

"I know." She frowned. "Even at nineteen eighty prices, you couldn't buy much for five bucks, let alone a brand-new bike."

"Strange," I said, mentally adding five-dollar bicycles to my puzzle pile. "I'll clean up these dishes and feed O'Ryan. Pete should be along in a few minutes. Thanks for the yummy supper."

O'Ryan heard his name in connection with food and strolled into the kitchen, looking up at me expectantly. I opened a can of baby shrimp, added a sprinkle of bacon bits, and placed the red bowl on his personalized place mat.

"There you go, spoiled cat," I said as I loaded the dishwasher. "You and I have lucked into a good deal here, haven't we?"

"I'm the lucky one," said Aunt Ibby. "It's my great pleasure to have you both with me. I've been thinking of Tabitha and how lonely she must have been up there in that sad place." She sighed. "But I haven't even asked about your day." She looked at the kitchen clock. "Maybe later?"

I'd been thinking about how and what and how much to tell her about my day.

"Definitely," I said. "I'll tell you all about it. River and I went up to the top floor this morning and spent some time in Tabitha's room."

"Really? I'll wait up for you. I want to hear every detail."

"You don't have to do that," I said, knowing that she would, anyway.

O'Ryan looked up suddenly from his bowl and streaked for the front door. The cat, as usual, was right. I caught up with him and peeked from the tall windows next to the door. Pete's headlights shone as he rounded the corner of Winter Street, and seconds later the Crown Vic pulled to a stop at the curb.

"Smarty-pants cat," I muttered, taking my jacket from a hook on the hall tree. "Aunt Ibby," I called. "Pete's here."

"Have a nice evening, dear," came the reply. "Talk to you later."

By the time I opened the door, Pete had already started up the steps. "Wait a sec. I'm coming." He slipped an arm around my waist. "Might be icy. Can't have you breaking anything."

I had to laugh. "I'm fine, Pete. I've been running up and down these stairs since I was a baby."

"I know." His eyes sparkled in the glow from the overhead lamp as he pulled me closer. "I just like holding you."

"I like it, too," I said, realizing how very much I liked it.

We headed toward East India Square and lucked out with a metered parking space just a few doors down from CinemaSalem.

"What'll it be?" Pete asked, looking at the titles on

the marquee. "There's a new Bruce Willis flick. How about that?"

"Look," I said. "They have one of my old favorites. *Raiders of the Lost Ark*."

"We'll toss a coin," he said. "Want to call it?"

"Okay," I said. "Heads, it's new Bruce Willis. Tails, it's vintage Harrison Ford."

"Fair enough," he said and reached into his pocket for a quarter and tossed it.

"Tails," I said. "You lose."

He handed me the coin. "Keep it for luck."

"I will," I said, slipping it into my pocket. "I'll try to remember not to spend it."

"At today's prices, there's not much you can buy for twenty-five cents."

We bought a tub of popcorn and settled down in our seats as the title rolled and Indiana Jones began his race through a Peruvian jungle in search of a gold idol.

There, in the darkened theater, a couple of my puzzle pieces slid neatly together.

On-screen, Indy searched for a lost medallion. A gold, coin-shaped medallion. Pete's words came back to me, and I reached into my pocket and rubbed my new lucky coin. What if the twenty-dollar gifts were in the form of gold coins?

"Pete." I shook his arm. "Pete," I whispered, "what's a twenty-dollar gold piece worth?"

"Huh? I don't know. Probably around a thousand dollars, I guess. Why?"

"Thanks," I said. "I'll tell you later."

I settled back in my seat, reached for a handful of buttery popcorn, and relaxed. I could almost hear Nancy telling her father, "I'm going to keep working on this case until all the pieces in the puzzle can be made to fit together . . ."

Me too, Nancy. Me too.

The movie was every bit as good as I remembered it. Pete and I watched, holding hands like teenagers, as Indy wandered the snake pits of the Well of Souls and survived the pyrotechnic unearthing of the sacred ark.

"Okay," he said as we walked back to the car when the movie was over. "What was all that about a twenty-dollar gold piece?"

"I don't know if it makes a lot of sense yet," I said, "but maybe gold coins have something to do with the documentary we're making about the Trumbulls."

"You don't sound too sure."

"I know." I sighed. "It's still in the preproduction stage."

"Anything I can help with?" He held the door open for me, taking my elbow as I slid into the passenger seat.

"I need to mull it over in my head for a while," I admitted. "As soon as I can come up with a logical question, I'll tell you."

"Sounds mysterious," he said.

"It does? Great. I love a good mystery."

He laughed. "And I love your girl detective side."

Did I just hear the L word again?

"About the girl detective thing . . . ," I began. "Something came up today that I think I need to tell you about."

"You sound concerned. What happened?"

"I guess Chief Whaley must have told you about the two students they discovered wandering around in the basement."

He nodded. "Sure. Trout and Martin. I heard."

"They weren't just walking around, Pete. Sammy and Duke actually opened the panel that leads to the tunnel, and Duke went in a little way."

"We know about that. We're on it. Got 'em on video."

I was surprised. "There's a camera down there? Then that means . . . ?"

"Yep. Got you, too, when you came down the stairs. Chief had the camera installed right after Sullivan disappeared. He wasn't too happy to see you."

"I'm sure he wasn't. I wasn't thrilled to see him, either. Does Mr. Pennington know, then? About those two opening the panel? I didn't want to be the one who had to tell him what they'd done."

"He knows. Don't worry. We've got it handled."

"They were just playing investigative reporters," I said. "I hope it doesn't get them expelled."

"Don't worry about that. Pennington thinks they were just being curious."

"One more thing," I said.

"What's that?"

"Thom was the lookout. He kept the security guard occupied."

"Didn't know that. We'll check it out. Thanks for the tip. Guess you're picking up a lot in that criminology course."

"I'm just getting into the chapter on criminogenic traits, and it got me wondering."

"You're thinking the Trumbulls might have a criminal streak in the bloodline?" He glanced over at me, his expression serious.

"Aunt Ibby thinks so. She found a few things. One was that there were bootleggers using the old tunnel back during Prohibition. They were connected to the Trumbulls," I said. "Apparently, a lot of people know about that."

Pete nodded. "Right. You can even see the tracks in the old tunnel where they moved the booze on carts right up to the store's basement. It must have been quite a sophisticated operation for those days."

We had left downtown Salem and were headed toward Derby Street. Pete waved a hand in the direction of the harbor. "Of course, there are lots of cave-ins down there. And just to make it more confusing, whoever built the new tunnel just dug underneath the old one whenever they came to it, so the damn thing goes up and down like a roller coaster, part of it old and part of it new."

"So Bill must have fallen into part of the new tunnel," I said.

"Right. And they dug so deep in that spot that they needed a ladder to get up to the store's basement. That would have been around the nineteen eighties, and it looks like whatever they were moving then had to be smaller and lighter than carts full of whiskey bottles."

"Do you know what it was?" I asked.

"We have a few ideas. Nothing for sure."

"The old tunnel sounds more interesting," I said, thinking of the brick archway and the underground path the dark-haired woman had shown to me.

"Yeah. But both tunnels branch out all over town, and we keep coming to dead ends. We haven't explored all of them yet. There is probably a bunch of them that lead to where the boats used to tie up. That's where most of the smuggled stuff came from. Somewhere around here, I'd guess."

As we drove along the darkened street, I tried to imagine what that long-ago waterfront must have looked like. By looking between buildings as we passed, I could catch brief glimpses of the ocean and even see distant flashes from the lighthouse on Baker's Island.

"River told me that a woman named Megan was friends with Tabitha when they were little kids," I said.

"Tabitha's family lived somewhere around here. Megan remembers an entrance to the tunnel right near a house where they played together."

"That might be a good lead," Pete said. "Any idea where that house was?"

"Somewhere near a coal yard, I think she said. Maybe you could check the old maps and deeds at city hall and figure it out."

"Nice going, Lee," he said. "Maybe I should talk to your friend River. She might remember even more details."

"Sure. And you can probably talk to Megan. She's a witch." I paused to see what his reaction might be. He didn't say anything or change his expression, so I continued. "She's over a hundred years old."

"Really? Mind still pretty good?"

"River says Megan never forgets anything."

"Great. Know how I can get in touch with her?" he asked.

"Who? River or Megan?"

"Both. Either." He smiled. "Nice going, Lee," he said again.

I felt proud of myself. "Thanks," I said. "I haven't met Megan yet, but I'll ask River to call you."

"I'll be interested to hear what else you and your aunt have dug up about the Trumbulls, too," he said as we pulled up in front of Greene's Tavern.

The good smell of a wood fire greeted us even before we climbed the few steps onto a narrow porch and opened the door. The retro jukebox, complete with bubble lights, played a Carrie Underwood tune. The clinking of glasses and the hum of conversation punctuated with bursts of laughter completed the picture of a friendly neighborhood bar. My puzzle could wait until later.

The first person to notice us was Primrose. She raised a beer mug in our direction. "Over here, Lee. Come on and join us."

"That's Primrose," I whispered. "And it looks like the rest of the gang is here, too."

Thom was behind the bar, along with Joe Greene. Kelly, balancing a tray full of glasses, waved with her free hand. Sammy and Duke were huddled around the flashing numbers of a keno game, and Therese, looking darling in designer jeans and a pink velvet hoodie, sat beside Primrose.

A smiling Thom placed two Budweiser coasters in front of us. "What'll it be, folks? Hi, Ms. Barrett."

"Hi, Thom. Meet my friend Pete Mondello. Pete, Thom is one of my students."

The men shook hands, and Pete and I each ordered a light beer. I introduced Pete to Primrose and Therese, and Joe Greene came over to welcome us to his tavern. Within a few minutes Sammy and Duke joined us, and Kelly paused in her serving duties to say hi.

I watched and listened as Pete interacted with each person. Everyone received a smile and a handshake, and each one was also asked a question. Sometimes two. The questions were framed so politely, so casually, that they seemed exactly like normal tavern small talk.

"Where are you from originally?" "What kind of work did you do before you came to Salem?" "Do you like it here? Have family in the area?"

I wonder if he does this automatically because he's used to interrogating people. Or is he really digging for something? And doesn't he sometimes question me in the same way?

CHAPTER 15

I didn't pay attention just to Pete's words that night at Greene's Tavern. The answers to his questions were pretty darned interesting, too. I discovered a lot about some of my students in just those few snippets of conversation.

Kelly stopped to speak with us occasionally as she moved between the bar and the tables. In those brief moments, through Pete's gentle questioning, I found out that her mother had left her when she was a baby to be raised by her dad and his grandmother. "I've never even met my ma," Kelly said without a trace of bitterness. "Have no idea where she went."

Joe Greene was charitable when he spoke of the woman. "She wasn't ready to take care of a baby. I wasn't surprised when she took off. Life around the coal mines isn't easy for a girl. My own mother died too young." He looked fondly in his daughter's direction. "But me and Mamaw did a good job with the kid, don't you think?"

They certainly had. Joe also had kind words for his handsome bartender. "That Thom is a good kid, too," he said. "Learns fast. Works hard." He laughed.

"Money hungry, though. The boy's gonna make it to New York in record time."

Pete turned his attention to Thom. "That what you want to do? Go to New York? What for?"

"Modeling. TV. Movies. Who knows?" Thom gazed past us, watching his own reflection in the mirrored wall. "But you have to move fast in the face business. Looks don't last. The best place to get discovered, to get the big agents, is New York. So as soon as I get enough money, I'm gone." He made a taking-off motion with his hands. "See ya later."

"Burn green candles, Thom." Therese spoke softly.

"Huh?" several people said in unison.

"Green candles," she repeated more firmly. "To attract money. I read it in one of the spell books. It's a witch thing."

There were smiles and head shakes all around, but Thom said seriously, "Thanks, Therese. I'll try it. The sooner I can get to New York, the better."

Primrose had been uncharacteristically quiet, slowly sipping the same beer she'd been holding since we came in. "What about you, Pete?" she asked. "We know you're with the Salem police. Are you working on whatever's happening underneath the Tabby?"

Pete didn't change his expression or his tone of voice. "Oh yeah. I've been down there a couple of times. Cold, dark, and damp. What about you, Miss McDonald? Are you planning to head for the big city, too?"

"New York? Nope. Not me. Been there, done that, got the T-shirt, and gave it to Goodwill." She tossed back the beer remaining in her mug. "You can drop the Miss McDonald. Call me Primrose. I'm sort of liking it here, Pete. I may stick around Salem for a while."

"Primrose," Pete said. "That's an unusual name."

"My mother likes flowers."

"So does mine." He turned to Sammy. "Sammy Trout. Name's familiar. Sports pages, I think. Right?"

I raised an eyebrow.

You already know he's been snooping around the basement. And I'll bet Chief Whaley ordered a complete background check this morning. You know all about Sammy Trout. Duke Martin too.

Sammy put his elbows on the bar, supporting his chin on both fists, looking at Pete. "Used to be a jockey. Pretty good one. Took a bad fall a while back and had to quit racing."

"Tough luck," Pete said. "That must have been hard to take. When was that, exactly?"

"Oh, a few years ago." Sammy looked down, breaking eye contact. "It was a pretty bad time. But now I'm thinking about sports broadcasting. Lee here is helping with that." He looked up, aiming a weak smile in my direction.

I nodded my acknowledgment of the compliment and returned the smile. But I hadn't realized that Sammy's accident was "a few years ago." He'd given the impression that it had been recent. I wondered how long ago "a few years" might be and what he'd been doing since then.

My puzzle was getting more complicated. I'd started out visualizing one of those picture puzzles kids have, with a few big, easy to handle shapes. Now it was beginning to look more like the gazillion-piece kind that take up the whole top of a card table.

Pete motioned to Thom and ordered a round for the group. "Looks like your cowboy friend took a powder," Pete whispered. "Ducked out the door when I was talking to Sammy."

I'd been so interested in the answers to Pete's questions, I hadn't even noticed that Duke was missing. "Maybe he just went out for a cigarette," I said.

"Hmm. Maybe." Pete looked doubtful.

Joe Greene came out from behind the bar, removed his apron, and took the seat next to Pete.

"Did you say you used to work in the coal mines?" Pete asked.

"Just like my daddy before me," Joe said. "And his daddy before that." He looked at Kelly with pride in his eyes. "Makes me glad I didn't have no boys."

"I've never been to that part of the country," Pete admitted. "Seems like damned hard work."

"You get used to it, like anything else, I guess." Joe shrugged. "It's good money, but the stuff gets in your lungs after a while, you know? Makes you cough all the time. Didn't get sick enough to get the big pension, though, so I have to keep on workin'."

"You feel better living here?"

"Oh, sure. Good salt air. I feel great. Me and Kelly stayed there until my grandmother passed, and then we sold everything and moved up here."

"You've certainly made this into an attractive place, Joe," I said. "It has an old New England look."

"Always wanted to live near the ocean," he said.

Kelly came up behind her father and threw an arm around his neck in an impulsive hug. "This is the perfect place for us, huh, Pa?"

"Right, honey," Joe said. "We're just where we belong."

Primrose stood and pulled on a black leather jacket. "Well, it's time for Therese and Sammy and me to head for the dorm. Looks like Duke has ditched us. Thanks for the drinks, Pete. See you at school, Lee."

"We'll be right behind you, Primrose," Pete said. "Nice to meet you all. Ready to go, Lee?"

We said good night to Joe and Kelly. Pete left a generous tip for Thom, and we headed outside. I watched Primrose's Camry leave the parking lot. Within a few seconds another car pulled out from behind the building and followed hers onto the darkened street.

"Well, I'll be damned," Pete said. "Did you see that?"

"Yes, I did," I said. "But I'm not sure exactly what I saw."

"Looks like somebody's put a tail on Primrose. Or else on one of the other two."

The taillights of the car behind Primrose's black Camry twinkled in the distance as we drove along the curving shore road.

"Are we following them?"

There was a smile in Pete's voice. "Why? Do you want to?"

"Yes, please!"

"I think we will," Pete said, "just to be sure they get home okay."

"Is anything wrong?" I asked.

"No. Not really. But we'll catch up with the tail and run the plate through the DMV."

We sped up, and in minutes our headlights illuminated the Massachusetts plate on the late-model black Lincoln ahead of us. We dropped back a bit as Pete tapped the numbers into the notebook-size computer mounted between our seats.

"Hmm. That's strange," he said.

I waited for him to continue. When he didn't, I leaned closer and peered at the screen. He swiveled it away from me, but not before I'd glimpsed a Boston address.

"Come on," I said. "You have to tell me who's following them. After all, they're kind of my responsibility."

"Can't do it, babe," he said. "But I promise you, they aren't bad guys. Your students are all safe." The car ahead drove straight on Derby Street, while we turned right onto Hawthorne Boulevard and toward home.

"Don't you want to make sure they make it back to the dorm okay?" I asked. "What if they decide to stop someplace else?"

"I'll call the guard on duty at the school and tell him to call me as soon as they come in."

"Okay. That makes me feel better."

Pete was still on the phone when the guard reported that the three had already entered the school.

"Thanks, Pete. Technically, they're all adults. I don't know why I worry about them."

"That's the second time tonight I've been reminded that your students are all over twenty-one," he said.

"It is?"

"Joe Greene made a point of telling me he'd checked all their IDs."

"Maybe he thought that was why you were there. To see if he was selling alcohol to underage kids," I said.

"He thinks I was there for something other than an evening out with my girlfriend, that's for sure." He frowned. "Makes me wonder what that something is."

"Were we there for something else?"

"Hell, no. You said you'd like to go there sometime, so we did."

"But you think that he thinks . . . what?"

We made the turn onto Winter Street. "I don't know," he said. "But now I'm curious."

"You asked everybody so many questions tonight," I said, "I thought you were looking for something, too."

He seemed surprised. "Hey, I didn't even know they were all going to be there. I admit I wanted to hear what Sammy had to say, on account of what happened this morning," he said. "And I probably would have had a few questions for Duke, too, if he hadn't sneaked out, but I didn't mean to grill anybody. Was I that obvious?"

"Maybe Primrose noticed. She always seems to know how to dodge questions."

"She does, doesn't she?"

We'd stopped in front of the house, and I was sorry our evening together had ended. Lights shone from both the upstairs and downstairs windows, so I was sure Aunt Ibby had kept her promise to wait up for me.

We leaned toward one another across the computer and bumped heads, then laughed through an awkward good-night kiss. Pete walked with me to the front door, where O'Ryan peeked from a side window.

"That cat must like looking out that window. He's there every time I come over," Pete said.

"Actually, he goes to the front hall only when he knows someone is coming," I admitted. "He figures it out somehow before they even turn the corner of the street."

"Come on. You're trying to tell me O'Ryan has some kind of ESP?"

"I guess you might call it that. It's something he's done ever since we got him. We're used to it." I unlocked the door and patted the waiting cat. "Want to come in for a while?"

"Can't. On duty early tomorrow. Want to do something Saturday?"

"Love to. Maybe we can go car shopping."

"So you're serious about buying a car. Any idea what you want? I know most of the car dealers in town."

The image of a sharp-looking blue roadster formed

in my mind. "Um . . . maybe a convertible," I said. "A blue one."

"I'm sure we can find something you'll like," Pete said, making it sound as though I was a kid who'd just asked for a pony. "See you Saturday. Don't forget to give River my number."

"I'll remember."

Aunt Ibby called to me from the den as soon as I closed the door. "Maralee?" O'Ryan scampered ahead, to where she sat on the couch. She hit the mute button on the TV remote and patted the cushion beside her while the cat climbed onto her lap. "Come, sit down. I can hardly wait to hear about Tabitha's room."

"And I can hardly wait to hear more about the Trumbulls' shady history," I told her. "Also, I've come up with a theory on how someone might have been able to buy four bikes with twenty dollars back in the eighties."

"How's that? Don't tell me the Trumbulls were dealing in hot bicycles!"

I laughed. "No. Nothing like that. But what if the gifts to the captain's wife were twenty-dollar gold pieces?"

"Why, Maralee, I think that would explain it. But where would that old woman, locked in an attic, get gold coins?"

"I don't know. But the Trumbulls were wealthy. Maybe she'd just saved them."

"Yes, they had plenty of money, no doubt. Was her room nice?"

I thought about that. "The furniture was good quality, but nothing ostentatious, if you know what I mean."

"Tell me."

I described the single bed, the rocking chair, the

sturdy armoire, the sheer curtains. "There's a dresser with a mirror, too," I said. "And the player piano is there. The one you told me about from the store, and the armoire is chock-full of piano rolls. And there's a big picture of President Roosevelt."

"Teddy? Or Franklin?"

"Franklin. It's a big framed photo, hanging right over the headboard of her bed."

She nodded, with that wise look she gets sometimes. "Roosevelt. Gold coins. Uh-huh."

"Uh-huh what? There's some kind of connection?"

"Maybe. Let me think about it. What else did you see on the top floor? Were the other rooms furnished?"

"No, not really. A piece here and there. Except for one room with furniture piled to the ceiling. That was a little creepy," I said.

"Do you expect to go back?" my aunt asked as O'Ryan stretched, stood, and moved from her lap to mine. "Sounds a bit scary."

Not as scary as what I saw in the shoe.

"Sure. We'll go back. But now it's your turn," I said, scratching behind the cat's ears. "O'Ryan wants to hear about the Trumbulls, both naughty and nice." I decided now wasn't the time to tell her about the vision and the keys.

O'Ryan looked up and locked eyes with me. I tried not to blink. He won.

Okay. I'll tell her tonight.

"The vertical files contain all kinds of bits and pieces," Aunt Ibby began. "Newspaper clippings, photos, diaries, ledgers, old greeting cards, deeds, mostly paper memorabilia. The Trumbull family's collection takes up several files."

"Primary source material," I said. "The real documents. Not just copies."

"Right. Of course, the most important stuff has been preserved on microfilm, paper being so fragile, but I wanted to be sure we have access to everything. I even found Tabitha's old recipe cards." She looked pensive. "You know, someone should put those into a book."

"You could do it," I said. "In your spare time."

She cocked her head to one side. "Maybe I will. After I finish remodeling the upstairs."

"Go on," I said, encouraging her. "Tell me about the Trumbull bad seeds."

"It goes back to the Smiths, actually. Tabitha's folks. They had the money, you know."

"Yes. River told me that."

"Tabitha's grandfather had a little brush with the law back near the turn of the century. I found one old yellow newspaper clipping that said he'd been accused and found innocent of opium trafficking."

"*Opium?*"

"Oh, sure. It was apparently the drug of choice back in the late eighteen hundreds. You could even order small quantities of it from the Sears catalog. Anyway, the old man was accused of smuggling opium from China on his merchant ships and running an opium den. They never proved it, though. No evidence."

"Maybe that's what they were doing. Bringing opium to an underground opium den inside the tunnel," I said, recalling Megan's story.

"The tunnel?" She leaned forward. O'Ryan sat up straight. "What about the tunnel?"

I repeated, as well as I could, River's story of the two

little girls and the men who went back and forth into the tunnel and allowed them to play underground. I told her, too, about the locked playhouse and the locked toy chest that Tabitha's grandfather had given them.

"Well, for heaven's sake, I've never heard about any such thing," she said, sounding a bit miffed by the omission. "That's a great story. I wonder if it's true. You say Megan is still alive?"

"Yes. She's over a hundred, and River says she's still sharp. Pete's interested in the story, too. He wants to see if Megan can remember exactly where that tunnel entrance was. It might save them some time in exploring down there. It's not a nice place."

"I should think not, especially after what happened to Bill."

I told her what Pete had said about the new tunnel being dug underneath some of the places where the old one had collapsed. "They think each of the tunnels must have several exits close to the waterfront, so that they could move things to and from their boats." O'Ryan moved back to Aunt Ibby's lap, turned around a couple of times, and lay down, facing me.

Tunnels. Old and new. Now would be a good time to tell her about the vision in the shoe.

I opened my mouth to tell her then, but she changed the subject. "Oh, Maralee. I don't know if you've heard. Visiting hours for Bill will be tomorrow evening at the Murphy Funeral Home," she said. "And the funeral mass will be Saturday at St. Thomas's. Shall we go together?"

"We'll go to the wake together for sure," I said, "but I think I'll ask Pete to come with me to the funeral."

"That'll be nice, dear," she said. "Pete is such a fine man. How was your date tonight? Did you go anywhere interesting?"

"It was definitely interesting. We went to the movies first, and afterward, we went to Greene's Tavern."

"Tell me about it."

"Very New England. They've done a good job with the decor, and they seem to be doing a brisk business," I said. "All my students were there. Apparently, it's become their favorite hangout."

"I think you said one of them works there with her dad."

"Yes, Kelly. Thom works there, too. Bartender."

"Was Primrose there?" she asked.

"She was," I said. "And the strangest thing happened. When we left the tavern, we saw a car following Primrose's."

"Are you sure? That's frightening."

"Pete said it was tailing her or one of the others in her car. She was driving Therese and Sammy back to the dorm."

"Did he find out who was following her?"

"Sure. He checked the plate with the DMV, but he wouldn't tell me who it was. He just said they were perfectly safe and not to worry."

"But you worried, anyway."

"I did. I feel responsible for them in a way. But I got a peek at a Boston address on Pete's computer. Want to check it out? Maybe then I can understand why I'm not supposed to worry."

She headed for the computer desk, dislodging O'Ryan, who uttered a disgruntled "hrumph," and plopped himself lengthwise across my lap.

"Okay. Shoot. What's the address?"

I repeated the address I'd seen on the computer screen. Within seconds she said exactly what Pete had said when he saw it.

"Hmm. That's strange."

"What's strange? Who was it?" The cat was unceremoniously dumped a second time as I hurried across the room to look over her shoulder.

"Apparently," she said, "the car that was following Primrose belongs to the United States Department of the Treasury."

CHAPTER 16

What followed was what I guess they call a pregnant silence. My aunt and I looked at one another without saying a word.

The Treasury Department? Was that what the men in the basement of Trumbull's meant by a "federal case"?

She spoke first. "I'm thinking," she said, "that this has something to do with gold. Maybe the twenty-dollar gold pieces you mentioned earlier. The ones Tabitha might have given to the boat captain's wife."

"Really? You think a few gold coins given away back in the eighties would interest the government enough to follow people around now?"

"Could be." She shut the computer down, and I followed her back to the couch. "And I think it might have to do with President Roosevelt, too. Franklin, not Teddy, just like Tabitha's picture."

"Roosevelt? But he died back in the forties."

"Back in the Depression years, though, he recalled gold coins. People all over the country turned them in. It was the law."

"It's not against the law anymore," I protested. "You

can buy all the gold coins you want. The ads are on TV all the time."

"I know. But for a long time it was illegal to own gold coins, and of course, not everybody turned theirs in. Some people hoarded them or shipped them out of the country."

"People like the Trumbulls?" I asked.

"Not unlikely, from what I've learned about them so far," she said. "Trouble seemed to follow that family."

"Speaking of trouble, a couple of my students took an early morning stroll in the Tabby's basement, and I'm afraid they may be in trouble because of it."

"I should think they might be," she said. "Isn't there a guard there?"

"They got past him. So did I, a little later." I repeated the story I'd told to Pete earlier.

Her look was disapproving. "So you've had another run-in with Chief Whaley?" she said. "And the federal fellow, too? Friedrich?"

"Afraid so. I'm hoping nothing comes of it."

"I hope not, Maralee. That tunnel seems to be bad luck for everyone."

O'Ryan had stretched his long body across the back of the couch, momentarily avoiding the possibility of being dumped from a lap. His head was positioned behind my left shoulder, and just as Aunt Ibby said, "Tunnel," he leaned toward my left ear and said, quite plainly, "Nowww." Maybe it sounded a lot like a regular meow, but I knew it meant "Now." As in "Tell her about the vision and the keys. Now."

So I did.

"Today I looked into the toe of the display shoe." I blurted it out, barely pausing for breath. "The woman was there, with her back to me, the same way she'd been when I told her to stop last time. She faced me and held two keys out so I could see them clearly. There was an arched entrance, too, and brick walls. I'm sure it was the old tunnel. She beckoned to me to follow her, and she walked deeper into it, then turned a corner and was gone."

I watched my aunt, trying to judge her reaction. For a moment she didn't speak, and then she reached over and took my hands in hers. "I'm not surprised, Maralee, that you tried it again. I knew eventually you'd have to. I've been reading up on gazing, and apparently, according to experts in that sort of thing, if you can actually control it, some good may come of it, after all."

"You think so? You approve of my using this . . . whatever it is?"

She shook her head. "I didn't say I *approve* of it. I believe, though, that perhaps you need to explore it further. You were, for reasons I can't begin to comprehend, granted this gift. It may possibly be something of value."

I felt a warm rush of tears. I squeezed her hands. "Thank you for understanding."

"I didn't say I *understand* it, either." She gave a wry smile. "But I do accept it as part of you, an extraordinary, mysterious part of the you I love so very much."

"Thank you," I said again.

O'Ryan returned to my lap, an expectant look on his furry face. "Oh, one thing I forgot to tell you about the vision . . . ," I said. "There was a cat following the woman."

"A cat," she repeated softly. "And keys. Two of them, you say? And a woman in the tunnel, wearing a white dress and asking you to follow her."

"That's right. And later today, after River and I

returned from the attic, I saw the same two keys on Mr. Pennington's key ring."

"Remarkable," she said. "Do you think those are the ones the little girls had? The ones you told me about that opened the playhouse door and the toy box?"

"Maybe. Although River says that Tabitha told Megan that there were two sets of those keys and that Mary Alice has the other ones."

"Mary Alice?"

"Tabitha's daughter who drowned herself about sixty years ago."

"So we're all the way back to the attic ghosts," she said. "Mary Alice would be the one in the confirmation dress."

"Guess so," I said. "Everything seems to lead back to those rooms at the top of Trumbull's. Even the twenty-dollar gold coins we think Tabitha gave away."

"Right," she said. "But, of course, Pete's interested in learning about the Trumbull building in connection with what happened to Bill."

"It would have to be something about the new tunnel, I suppose, since that's the one Bill fell into."

"Maybe it has to do with the gunrunning incident. They could have used the new tunnel for that. And that all happened years after the store had closed." She had her wise expression firmly in place. "No wonder most of Salem thought the place was haunted. If there was activity going on inside the building at all hours, that certainly might explain some of the ghost stories circulating about lights and noises and spirit sightings, wouldn't it?"

"You bet it would. And all they had to do in case anyone else ever went into the basement was pile all the mannequin parts back on top of the button."

"Do you think Tabitha was aware of what was going

on down there?" she asked. "I can hardly believe she'd have any part of such a thing."

"She could have," I said. "After all, she was still able to write cogent letters and carry on intelligent conversations with Megan." I paused. "I feel as though we've been going around in circles. Don't you?"

"Exactly," my aunt agreed. "From attic to basement, from underground tunnel to rooftop apartment, from Bill's silver coins to Tabitha's gold ones. Where does it all lead?"

"I've been writing things down on index cards and shuffling them around," I told her. "So far I haven't been able to make sense of it all."

"Everything leads to the Trumbulls, one way or another, I guess," my aunt said. "Although none of them ever seem to leave any fingerprints. I like your index card idea. Maybe I'll start a card file of my own and we can compare notes. Two heads are better than one and all that."

"Fine idea," I said. "Right now, though, my head just wants a nice soft pillow. I'll see you in the morning."

"Good night, dear. I think I'll watch the late news," she said, turning the TV sound back on. I'd just stepped into the front hall when she called me back to the den. "Maralee, look at this. Councilor Wilson is in the news again, cutting another ribbon."

I returned to the couch, and together we watched as Jonathan Wilson smiled into the camera. "He doesn't look or even sound like a newcomer," I said. "He looks like genuine old Salem aristocracy."

"Yes. Quite a handsome fellow, isn't he?" she said. "He had relatives here. Inherited some property down near the Willows, I believe. He'd lived here for only about a year when he ran for the city council." The news segment ended, and a dog food commercial prompted my aunt to hit the mute button once again.

"You said you voted for him," I said. "He must have made a good impression."

"Oh, yes. He won handily. He speaks well and seems to genuinely love Salem. He retired from some sort of big government job in Washington, so he knows all about government grants and such. He was instrumental in getting the grants for your school."

"Since we're going to be sharing index cards," I said, "I have something on one of mine that concerns Jonathan Wilson."

I told her about seeing Primrose and Mr. Wilson together at the restaurant.

"Odd," she said. "They seem an unlikely couple, don't they? What did Pete think?"

"I didn't mention it to him. You said it was none of our business what she did or where she went," I reminded her. "I'm quite sure neither of them noticed me, and I doubt that Pete saw them."

"He's very observant," she said. "I don't think that man misses much. He doesn't tell you everything."

I thought about that. He hadn't even told me he'd seen me on video, coming down the stairs to Trumbull's basement and confronting Chief Whaley, until I brought the subject up myself.

"You know, you're absolutely right," I told her. "I'm going to ask him if he saw them together. Maybe he'll help me fill out that particular card."

"Go along to bed, then, dear," she said. "You've had a busy day. I'm going to stay up for a while and watch River's show."

I was surprised. "Really? I've never pictured you as a fan of vampire movies."

She gave an apologetic shrug. "I guess I've acquired

another guilty pleasure in my old age. Anyway, it's not always vampires. Tonight she's showing *The Curse of the Werewolf*. Oliver Reed is in it. Besides, that tarot thing she does is quite interesting."

I gave her a quick kiss on the forehead, picked up the cat, and headed once again for the front stairs. "You're an amazing woman, Aunt Ibby. Good night. Enjoy the movie."

I slept well and set out for school in the morning, rested and looking forward to a productive day with my class. The weather was still cold, but the sun shone brightly. Aunt Ibby and O'Ryan waved to me from the living room window—the cat waving a paw with an assist from my aunt. The short walk to the Tabby was a pleasant one. Primrose, Sammy, and Therese were already in the classroom when I arrived. Primrose spoke up before I had a chance to take off my jacket.

"Hey, Lee. Was that you checking up on us last night, after we left the bar? The security guy was on the phone when we came in, telling somebody we were home safely." She looked amused. "Were you playing mother hen?"

I wasn't about to tell her that she was being tailed by the U.S. government, and that it was Pete who was on the other end of the call, so I admitted to being the nosy hen. "The roads were slippery, and you'd had a couple of beers. I didn't mean to embarrass you," I said.

"Oh, we weren't embarrassed," Therese said. "We thought it was cute." She smiled. "And your boyfriend is totally cute, too."

It was my turn to be embarrassed. I cleared my throat. "Well, then," I said in my most professional teacher voice, "let's get organized, shall we? The others should be here any minute."

Kelly and Thom arrived together, with Duke close behind them.

"We aren't late, are we?" Kelly sounded worried. "Did we miss anything?"

"Not at all," I said. "These guys were early. After all, they live right upstairs."

"My dad dropped us off," Kelly said. "Thom spent the night at our place."

Sammy looked up from a book that lay open on the table in front of him. "Spent the night, huh? Something going on with you two that we should know about?"

Thom rolled expressive eyes. "Don't be stupid. It was late, and my ride home left without me." He aimed an aggrieved look in Duke's direction. "It wasn't the first time I've slept on the Greenes' couch. Probably won't be the last."

Duke slouched in his seat. "Sorry about leaving like that. Felt like I was going to puke, so I took off."

"You could have called." Thom sounded whiny.

Duke shrugged. "Sorry."

"We're all here now," I said, "so let's get started. Therese? Where did we leave off?"

She leafed through a neat stack of printed sheets. "Primrose had just started to tell the story of Trumbull's Department Store from Mr. and Mrs. Trumbull's point of view."

"Right," Kelly said. "And we all agreed it's a super way to tell about Salem's history for the documentary."

"It certainly is," I agreed. "Primrose, how's that coming along?"

"Got a little sidetracked, Lee, with this tunnel thing going on," she said. "I got to wondering who was using the mechanical door and the new tunnel after the store was officially closed. So I did a little research." She dropped her voice to a near whisper. "Some of those Trumbulls weren't exactly Boy Scouts."

"Did you dig up some dirt, Primrose?" Kelly wanted to know. "I love gossip—even if it's about old dead guys."

"Me too," Thom said. "The documentary will be better if it's not all goody-goody."

"Well, I found out some pretty interesting stuff." Primrose paused, looking around the room, making eye contact with each person. Sure of everyone's undivided attention, she continued. "The sneaky bastards were running guns to the IRA back in the eighties."

"Well, gunrunning is kind of glamorous, isn't it?" Kelly said. "Can't we make it sound like they were Irish patriots or something like that?"

Primrose made an unladylike snorting noise. "It's not glamorous, little girl. It's illegal and stupid, and people get killed. The Trumbull family was right in the middle of it. And if that's not enough, they were bootleggers in the thirties, and besides that, they even used to smuggle drugs."

"What's your source for all this?" I asked. "We can't make claims that might be libelous. New England bootlegging seems to be common knowledge, but were any of the Trumbulls found guilty?"

According to Aunt Ibby, they hadn't been, and it had taken her a day's digging at the library to find Trumbull connections to any of the crimes. I knew Primrose had been in class all of the previous day and at Greene's Tavern for much of the evening. When had she found time to dig up the information? And where?

"I told you I'm nosy," she said with a toss of her

platinum mane. "I ask questions. People in bars tell you all kinds of things."

"If you heard all this in barrooms, Primrose," Thom said, "I can tell you for sure that drunks make stuff up all the time. I ought to know. I listen to them every night."

"Should I write all that down?" Therese wanted to know.

"Go ahead," I told her. "But with a note to check further."

"You'll find out I'm right," Primose said with a smile. "Sometimes being nosy is really useful."

Sammy snapped the cover of his book shut. "Yeah," he said. "And sometimes it can get you into big trouble."

"You're awfully quiet this morning, Duke." I addressed the big man, who again occupied the chair behind the news desk. "Any thoughts on research methods?"

"No thoughts on anything," he mumbled. "Hung over."

A burst of laughter provided an opportunity for me to change the subject from the possible sins of the Trumbulls to the actual production of a usable script.

"I've brought in a few books on Salem's history," I said, spreading out half a dozen volumes on the round table. "I'd like each of you to take one and just browse through it. Make notes of anything that you see that might relate to what we're doing."

After a brief pileup at the table as each of them selected a book, and after a momentary tug-of-war between Sammy and Primrose over *Death of an Empire*, because it had the coolest title, the classroom was quiet. Each of them appeared to be engrossed in his or her selection, including Sammy, the smiling victor of the battle over the Robert Booth book. I sat at my desk and pulled a couple of blank index cards from my purse. Pen poised over the cards, I looked up, surprised, as Rupert Pennington approached from the mezzanine landing.

"Ah, Ms. Barrett." He beamed, rubbing his hands together. "What a very orderly classroom. I'm delighted to see all these young people engaged in such an earnest pursuit of their studies."

"Yes, Mr. Pennington," I said. "We're working hard on our Salem history project. We're tying the history of Trumbull's Department Store to parallel happenings in the city."

Each of the six students remained focused on the texts, but it was obvious that they were listening.

"A most worthy objective," he said. Then, after what might be considered a dramatic pause, he added, "We are simply passing through history." This pronouncement was followed by an expectant look in my direction.

Boom. I got it. I smiled and said, "Paul Freeman. *Raiders of the Lost Ark.* Nineteen eighty-one."

"Bravo, Ms. Barrett," he said. "You've clearly inherited some of your charming aunt's remarkable perspicacity."

Should I tell him I saw the movie last night? Nah.

"Thank you, sir," I said. "Was there something particular you wanted to see us about?"

"Hmm? Oh, yes, indeed. You've met Councilman Jonathan Wilson, have you not?"

"Briefly. At the opening ceremony. Why?"

"He's asked permission to address your class one day next week. He has an idea, a plan, actually, with which he feels your students might be able to help. And with their obvious interest in history, I agree." He glanced around the room.

Kelly, Therese, and Thom remained glued to the texts in front of them. Duke appeared to be nodding off. Only Sammy and Primrose had eyes focused on the director, with undisguised interest.

"I'll certainly try to fit it into our schedule, Mr. Pennington," I said. "I'm sure we'll be happy to help the councilor in any way we can."

"Thank you, Ms. Barrett." He gave an all-inclusive wave in the direction of the classroom. "Carry on," he said, then turned on his heel military-style and left.

"Are we supposed to make notes only about the things that happened after the store opened?" Kelly asked. "A lot of things happened here before that."

"Right," said Therese. "Like about the witches."

"We'll concentrate on the years between nineteen twenty-five and the opening of the Tabby," I said, "but the present is always influenced by the past."

Duke, hangover and all, managed a comment. "Everyone's is."

"I bet you've got a past, man," Sammy said.

"So do you, shorty," Duke shot back.

"Not me," Thom said. "I've got a future. And the sooner I get away from here, the better."

I began to feel I'd lost control of the situation. I tapped my pen on the desk for emphasis. "Take another ten minutes for reading and note taking. Then we'll brainstorm with what we've got." I waved Pennington-style. "Carry on," I said.

Before long the room was so quiet, we could hear the distant *bump-bump* of feet from the dance studio.

CHAPTER 17

The brainstorming session went surprisingly well, with everybody contributing ideas. Some were silly, some were unworkable within our slim budget, but many of them made it onto Therese's stack of papers. It was, in fact, exactly what a brainstorming session should be. I was proud of them, and I told them so.

"Good effort, you guys," I said. "I worked with professionals back in Florida who weren't as spot-on as you all have been today."

I could tell they were pleased by the compliment, and the mood was relaxed when we headed to the diner together for a lunch break. In traditional New England diner style, high-backed booths with red vinyl upholstery were situated down one side of a wide aisle. A long counter with chrome bar stools lined the other side. Therese, Kelly, and Thom sat opposite Duke and Sammy in a booth, each vying for the first song selection from the tabletop jukebox.

Primrose and I sat together at the counter. "It's quieter here," I said.

"Faster service, too." She studied the menu for a moment, then put it down. "Listen, Lee," she said, "I'm not buying that line about you checking on us last night because I'd had a couple of beers. What's the real story?"

The waitress appeared and took our orders, giving me a little time to form an answer.

"After you left Greene's, Pete saw another car pull out from behind the building. It looked like it was following you."

"Jesus. Do you know who it was?"

"Not exactly," I said, more or less truthfully. "Pete wanted to be sure it wasn't some creep, so he checked the plate on his computer."

"And?"

"We followed you for a mile or so, and he said you'd be okay," I said. "But I made him call the security guard just to be sure you got home all right."

"Thanks," she said. "But didn't Pete tell you who it was?"

"Uh-uh. He sure didn't." Our meals were delivered quickly, and I busied myself by putting tiny oyster crackers into my cup of clam chowder, hoping her questions were over.

They weren't.

"Did he say it was me they were following? Could it have been one of the others? Therese or Sammy?"

"He didn't know."

Primrose took a bite of her chicken salad sandwich, then gave me a hard, searching look. "You know something you aren't telling me. Don't you?"

If it were me, I'd want to know.

"I saw the address on Pete's computer. Aunt Ibby looked it up. The car following you belongs to the Treasury Department. Boston office."

She put down her fork, looked me straight in the

eye, and smiled. "Treasury? No shit. For a minute there I thought it was something bad."

Was she being sarcastic? I couldn't tell. "Something bad?"

"Don't worry, Lee." Again, the big smile. "It's okay. And thanks for telling me."

"You're sure you're okay? Is there anything going on I should know about?"

"Really. There's no problem." Her smile was almost convincing.

Nothing about this made sense. My puzzle pieces were getting more jumbled, instead of coming neatly together. I was actually relieved when it was time to go back to class. At least there, among the books and props, cameras and mikes, monitors and screens, there was some sort of order. We paid our checks and went back into the Tabby, hurrying past the scowling officer in his chair next to the basement door, and up the stairs to the mezzanine.

The brainstorming continued. Lunch fueled, it was even better than the morning session. Ideas flew around the table. Therese's fingers flew over the keyboard. By four o'clock we were ready for the rough draft script preparation to begin.

"Primrose and Duke," I said, "you two are designated writers. I've printed out a copy of the notes for each of you. Why don't you read through them separately? Then you can get together and try to come up with a workable outline for us."

"How long do we have?" Duke asked.

"Things move fast in TV land," I said. "Shoot for Monday. That'll give you the whole weekend to work on it."

"Not fair," Primrose grumbled. "Nobody else gets homework but us?"

"That's showbiz," I said. "Their time will come, I promise."

The room cleared quickly. I retrieved a few wadded bits of notebook paper, gathered a couple of left-behind pens, and generally tidied up the place.

"Oops. Somebody dropped a history book." After grabbing a large hardcover volume from under a chair, I read the title, tried to remember who had which history book, and realized this wasn't one I'd handed out.

Sammy had been engrossed in reading when I arrived in class that morning. This was probably his. But what was so fascinating about *Massachusetts Atlas and Gazetteer?* I flipped through the colorful pages of maps. The corner of one page was folded down, an absolute sin in the eyes of my librarian aunt. The detailed map of Salem's streets was not only folded but was otherwise marred with scribbled notes in ink and fluorescent marker.

I hope this isn't a library book, Sammy, or you're going to do time in hell!

I put the book in my top desk drawer, planning to give it to the culprit on Monday. With a last look around the room, to make sure we hadn't left a mess for the custodian, I put on my jacket, hat, and gloves, preparing for the walk home in the fading winter daylight. My cell phone had been turned off all day, and I turned it on and checked for calls I'd missed. There were only two. One was from River, and the other from Jonathan Wilson.

I figured that when I called him, the councilman would echo Mr. Pennington's request that I make time for him to speak to the class. I called River first.

"River? You called?"

"Hi, Lee. I've been thinking about Tabitha's room," she said, "and I talked to Megan about it."

"Really? What did she have to say? Did she remember how it looked?"

"Of course she remembered it," River said. "I told you, Megan never forgets anything. Anyway, I told her about the rocking chair and the piano and all, and you know what she told me?"

"No. What?"

"She said she wouldn't be a bit surprised if Tabitha was still up there. Waiting."

"Waiting? For what?" The idea of the old woman's spirit still inhabiting that lonely place was impossible to accept. "Come on, River. You mean you actually think Tabitha's ghost is still wandering around on Trumbull's top floor? That all those urban legend 'ghost in white' stories are true?"

"Gee, I didn't say I thought so. I said Megan thought so." She sounded apologetic. "I just want to know what you think. After all, you're the one who can see things."

"You want me to look at the damned shoe again, don't you?"

"Sort of. I mean Ariel used to show you things after she was dead. Maybe Tabitha can, too." Another pause. "You don't have to, if you're afraid."

"I'll think about it, okay? Meanwhile, would you call Pete? I told him about how Megan and Tabitha played in the tunnel when they were little. He's interested in finding out if Megan can show him where the entrance used to be."

"He wants to talk to me? Wow. Makes me feel important."

I gave her Pete's number. "I'll talk to you later, River. Oh, by the way, my aunt has become one of your fans. I caught her watching the werewolf movie last night."

"That makes me feel even more important."

"River," I said quietly, "I'll think about the shoe thing, but I'm not making any promises."

"I understand." Her tone was sympathetic. "If you do it, though, maybe you can figure out what Tabitha's waiting around for."

The daylight was fast disappearing, and the street-lights along the pedestrian mall, artfully disguised as old-fashioned gas lamps, dispelled the gathering darkness. I decided to wait to return Jonathan Wilson's call until I reached home, and hurried in that direction. There'd be plenty of time to shower and change clothes before Aunt Ibby and I would have to leave for Bill's wake.

O'Ryan was at the front door to greet me with much purring and ankle rubbing. I could hear my aunt rattling pans and humming happily in the kitchen and knew immediately what was happening there. In Salem, when there's word of a funeral, casseroles, stews, and meat pies, cakes, cookies, and sweet rolls issue from ovens all over the city. If her freezer was large enough, Mrs. Sullivan wouldn't have to cook for a month.

I helped my aunt fill a sturdy carton with a foil-covered casserole, a plate of cookies, and a couple of pies, to be carried to the Sullivans' apartment after the wake.

"I'll just take all this out to the car now," I said as Aunt Ibby loaded mixing bowls into the dishwasher. "The temperature's still in the thirties. The trunk of the Buick will make a perfect refrigerator."

"Thanks, dear. Hurry back. I want to hear about your day."

I didn't need to be told to hurry. With the setting of the sun, a bone-chilling wind had whipped up. I grabbed the car keys from one of the hooks on the apple-shaped plywood keyboard I'd made one summer at Girl Scout camp and, balancing the carton, dashed through the backyard to the garage.

Although the front door of our house faces Winter Street, the back door and the garage face the next street to the west, Oliver Street. After depositing the box of goodies and securing the trunk, I stepped back out into the yard, where the sturdy trunk of a maple tree offered a moment's shelter from the bitter wind. Oliver is a narrow one-way street, and a winter parking ban is usually in effect there while snow is still on the ground, so I was surprised to see a small green Ford parked just across from where I stood.

That guy's begging for a ticket, I thought as I hurried back toward the house and into the welcome warmth of the kitchen.

Aunt Ibby motioned toward the vintage oak table. "Here, sit down and relax for a minute. Visiting hours for Bill are from six to eight, so we have a little time to get dressed and get to the Murphy Funeral Home. I've made fresh coffee, and I saved a batch of peanut butter cookies just for us."

Hot coffee and warm cookies. Who could resist? I kicked off fleece-lined boots, wiggled my toes, and relaxed, just as she'd ordered.

"How was your day?" she asked. "Did the class go well?" She looked at the kitchen clock. "You're home a little early."

"It went awfully well. Better than I'd expected," I said. "We had kind of a marathon brainstorming session. I let them leave a little early. By the way, I told Primrose about the car following hers last night, and her reaction was sort of odd."

"How so?"

"She smiled, thanked me for telling her, and said not to worry."

"That *is* odd. She didn't seem upset about it at all?"

"Not a bit. My next index card will say, 'Primrose doesn't mind if there's a T-man following her around.'"

"Very curious," my aunt said. "Did anything else interesting happen today?"

"I actually recognized one of Mr. Pennington's old movie quotations. I think he was impressed."

"Good for you. What line was it?" she asked.

"It may not have been exactly fair," I admitted. "I saw the movie last night, so the line was fresh in my mind. It's 'We are simply passing through history.'"

"*Raiders of the Lost Ark*," she said with satisfaction. "Paul Freeman. 1981."

"You're good," I told her.

"I know," she said, brushing a few cookie crumbs away. "Shall we get ready to leave?"

"Sure." I stood and pulled out my phone. "First, I have to call Jonathan Wilson. Apparently, he wants to address my class." I dialed the number, and he answered promptly.

"Hello, Ms. Barrett." His tone was hearty and friendly. He sounded as though he might be smiling. "Thanks ever so much for returning my call."

"You're welcome, sir," I said. "I understand that you'd like to address my class."

"I would indeed," he said. "Will next Monday be convenient for you? I know this is short notice, but I'd like to speak to them about a matter of importance. To me, to them, and to the great city of Salem."

"How much time will you need? Will half an hour do?"

I had listened to politicians before and needed to make it clear that we didn't have time for a long-winded dissertation, no matter how important the matter might be to the great city of Salem.

"Thirty minutes will be fine, Ms. Barrett," he said. "I have an interesting old map to share, and I'm in hopes that your students might be able to aid me in a bit of research. It concerns Salem history, and Mr. Pennington tells me that's your area of expertise."

"I'm hardly an expert, Mr. Wilson. But we'll help you if it's at all possible without interfering with our regular class work. Will nine to nine thirty Monday morning work for you?"

"Yes, indeed. Thank you. I look forward to seeing you and the students on Monday morning."

"Well?" Aunt Ibby was at my elbow when I hung up.

"Well what?"

"What's he going to talk about?"

"Something about an old map he has."

"Sounds interesting. And kind of mysterious." She smiled. "Hurry along now. We don't want to be late."

Once in my room, I filled out one index card with the information about Primrose and the Treasury Department and another with Sammy's name and the title of the map book and added them to the stack. Fanning my cards out, I noticed that there were several with Primrose's name on them, so I grouped those together. There were a few bearing Therese's name, and I put those together, too. Maybe organizing the cards by the names of the people involved would help me with my puzzle.

I knew I should be getting ready for the Sullivans' visiting hours, but the array of oblong cards began to assume a pattern of sorts. Jonathan Wilson's name appeared more than once, and Rupert Pennington's did, too. Tabitha Trumbull and Megan the witch each had almost as many cards as Primrose did. Thom and Kelly had three apiece, and Joe Greene had one: Duke had two cards, one about the early morning walk in the basement and another noting that he'd left the bar early the previous night. There were three cards for Sammy. The first one questioned when he'd had his accident; the second was about the basement excursion. The newest one was about the map book.

I made a note on another blank card.

Jonathan Wilson has an interesting old map to share.

Pete was planning to check some maps at the city hall. Maybe I needed a separate category just for maps.

Scratching at the bedroom door broke my concentration. As I let the cat into the room, I checked my watch. I was supposed to be ready to leave in just a few minutes, but I was still in my stocking feet and the clothes I'd been wearing all day. Seconds later Aunt Ibby knocked.

"Maralee? Are you ready? It's five forty-five."

"Just give me a few more minutes," I called, pulling my sweater over my head and peeling off my jeans.

"I'll bring the car around to the front." She didn't sound pleased. My aunt liked to be punctual.

"Sorry," I said. I took the world's fastest shower, tore a navy blue skirt and a white blouse from a dry cleaner's bag and put them on, donned tights and leather boots, did a speedy makeup job, and put on a gray midi coat. I dashed down the front stairs and checked my watch again. *Six and a half minutes. Not bad.*

I climbed into the waiting Buick. "We can get there in ten minutes," I said. "It's only over on Federal Street."

"I know," she said. "It's just a matter of finding a

parking space when we get there. Bill had a lot of friends."

She was right. The funeral home's lot appeared to be full, and cars lined the right side of the one-way street.

"We'll drive around the block again," she said. "Maybe somebody will move. Watch out on your side for a space."

I lowered my window as we moved slowly along Federal Street. "Look," I said. "There's a car right across from the funeral home with the motor running and two people in it. Maybe they're getting ready to leave."

"Good," she said. "I'll go around once more, and they may be gone when we get back."

The car was still there when we made the second pass. It was still running, and the two people were still inside. The man in the backseat had lowered his window, too, and as we rolled slowly past, I found myself eye to eye with Mr. Friedrich, the same man in black I'd met in the basement of the Tabby.

Slinking down into my seat was reflexive, involuntary, and pointless. The man had seen and recognized me just as surely as I had him.

"What's wrong, Maralee?" Aunt Ibby asked.

I told her what I'd seen. "That man, Friedrich, must be watching to see who attends Bill's wake. But why would Bill's friends interest the government?"

"I'm sure I don't know. Look, there's a space." She expertly parallel parked the Buick, and we walked a short block back to the building. I peeked across the street. The car was still there, but the rear window was closed.

The place was crowded, as we'd expected. Bill had made many friends over the years, and it seemed as though most of them had turned out this night. Aunt Ibby and I joined the group offering condolences to the Sullivans. We moved along in baby-step fashion toward the place where Bill lay in peaceful repose, clean shaven and dressed in his best suit. Mrs. Sullivan, pale and tired looking, brightened when she saw Aunt Ibby.

"Oh, Ibby. Thank you for coming. And you, too, Lee. It's a wonderful turnout of Bill's friends, isn't it?"

It was certainly a wonderful turnout. But I wondered what they'd all say if they knew they were being watched by the occupants of the car parked across the street. My aunt and I spoke the usual consoling words one uses on such occasions.

Mrs. Sullivan whispered an invitation to come over to the apartment later. "I can't invite everyone," she explained. "Not enough room."

"We'll be there," my aunt promised. "And I've made you one of those apple pies Bill always liked."

That brought a smile to the wan face. We made our way to the guest book and left after signing. I was almost afraid to look across the street, but the black car was gone. *No surprise there,* I thought. *They're probably on the way to Bridge Street, looking to score a good parking space in front of the Sullivans' place.*

CHAPTER 18

As Aunt Ibby and I walked past the orderly row of beautiful homes lining Federal Street, she spoke thoughtfully. "About that man you saw . . . Friedrich, you say his name is?"

"Right."

"Do you think that could be the same car that was following Primrose?"

"Quite likely," I admitted. "Same model, same color, same year."

"Are you going to tell Pete about those men being here?"

"I will, but I'm betting he already knows about it. He knew all about that episode in the basement and never mentioned it until I told him what had happened."

"Don't be timid about asking him questions, Maralee. You have an interest in figuring all this out, and situated as you are at the school, you're literally right on top of the situation." We pulled into a space marked GUEST behind the Sullivans' building. "You may find that you learn things the police miss," she said. "Pete'll probably be glad for your help."

She popped open the trunk of the Buick. I picked

up the still-cold carton of goodies and closed the trunk, and then we started up the stairs to the Sullivans' second-floor apartment.

We were among the first to arrive. Aunt Ibby quickly busied herself with Mrs. Sullivan and some of the guests, arranging the various food offerings on the dining room table. I joined a small knot of women I recognized from Aunt Ibby's church, and listened politely as they debated the merits of the many floral tributes we'd seen at the funeral home. Their discussion, involving the comparative beauty and worth of carnations versus calla lilies, was less than stimulating, and I found my attention wandering. I stood next to a lace-curtained window overlooking Bridge Street. Trying not to be too obvious, I pulled the curtains apart. Streetlamps illuminated the area, and reflective patches of snow made the scene even brighter.

The big government car wasn't there.

But that little green Ford was.

What in blazes is going on here? Is someone tailing me, too?

I wanted to tell Aunt Ibby about the car I'd seen on Oliver Street, and I very much wanted to talk to Pete, too. I needed to hear some of his coolheaded logic. There was probably a valid reason for the presence of the green car, and for Mr. Friedrich and his companion loitering outside the funeral home. But I couldn't think of one.

I separated myself from the flower discussion group and headed to the dining room, where guests had begun to fill paper plates with goodies from the feast displayed on the Sullivans' dining room table. I had barely eaten all day, and I was hungry. I chose a big square of beyond wonderful homemade lasagna and looked around for my aunt.

I found her in the kitchen, in an animated debate with one of the Sullivans' teenage grandsons on the relative merits of social networking. I caught her eye and tapped my watch. She took the hint, excused herself, and joined me next to a Formica counter where assorted canned soft drinks shared space with a good-size bottle of Irish whiskey.

"Ready to leave?" she asked.

I swallowed the last bite of lasagna and dropped the paper plate into a nearby wastebasket. "I'd like to, if you don't mind," I said. "Something strange just happened."

She raised one eyebrow. "Happened here?"

"Not in here. Out on the street. I need to get out there and check on something."

She asked no questions but nodded her agreement. We excused ourselves, saying good-bye to our hosts and promising to join them for Bill's funeral mass at St. Thomas's in the morning. We hurried down the stairs and climbed into the Buick.

"I think there's a car parked across the street that might be following us. Me, I mean," I said as she backed the Buick out of the guest parking area.

She turned to look at me. "Is it that Friedrich person again?"

"I don't know. Don't think so. Go slowly so I can see. It's a small green Ford."

She took me literally. Doing barely five miles an hour, we rolled onto Bridge Street.

"If I can get a look at the license plate," I said, "I'll get Pete to run it through the DMV."

"Do you see it?" she asked. "Is it there?" The driver behind us leaned on his horn. "I think I need to go a little faster."

"Never mind. It's gone," I said, and we headed for home.

"What made you think it was following you, anyway?" she wanted to know.

"When I put the food in the trunk, I saw the same car parked on Oliver Street, across from our garage. I noticed it because of the parking ban."

"Of course, you know more about automobiles than I do." My aunt sounded thoughtful.

"I can't tell one car from another . . . but . . ." She paused.

"But what?"

"Remember when O'Ryan and I waved good-bye to you from the window this morning?"

"Sure. That was cute."

"When you were walking toward the common, a green car was driving along right beside you."

"It was? Are you sure?"

"I'm sure. And, Maralee, O'Ryan growled until it was out of sight."

"At this rate I'm going to need another package of index cards," I told my aunt as we pulled into the garage.

We hurried, almost running, through the backyard, past the vegetable garden, where dead cornstalks loomed like ghostly sentinels, to the back stairs, where a welcome pool of brightness glowed from the lantern-shaped light over the doorway.

"You get your feet warm," Aunt Ibby said as we entered the back hall, where O'Ryan sat with an expectant look on his fuzzy face. "I'll make a pot of tea and meet you in the dining room. You gather up your index cards, and I'll get mine." She smiled. "We'll put all our cards on the table and see if we can make some sense of all this."

"Good idea," I said, bending to pat the purring cat. "O'Ryan, how do you always know which door to run to when somebody's coming?"

I headed for my room, O'Ryan close behind me. Ten minutes later, warmly pajama and slipper clad, with index cards in hand, I took my place at the dining room table.

Aunt Ibby was already there, her stack of cards, smaller than mine, neatly fanned out in front of her. "Have you made your new notes yet?" she asked, filling my cup with fragrant chamomile tea. "I put down a few words about the car at the funeral home, and I noted what you said about that other green one. I made a card for the car I saw from the window this morning, too. That's all I had for new entries."

I hadn't made mine out yet. I picked up a pen and pulled a few cards from a new package. The first three duplicated my aunt's notes. "I'm separating mine by the names of people mentioned," I said, "but I don't think I need a special stack for you."

"Probably not. Who has the biggest stack so far?"

"Primrose does," I said. "And Duke has the smallest."

"Duke is the man in the cowboy outfit?"

"Right. He seems to think he's channeling John Wayne," I said. "His cards say only that he was in on the early morning basement exploration, and that he left the bar that night before Pete could talk to him."

"Duke's not one of the people who lives in the dorm, I take it?"

"No. He says he's staying with friends."

"I see." She cocked her head to one side. "With friends, hmm? And what attracted him to your course? Did he say?"

I thought for a moment, trying to recall what Duke had said when I asked him that question. "He said he'd been shooting a commercial in Boston when he read about the school and decided to sign up."

"Just like that? What does he hope to learn? You say he's already doing commercials."

"Movies, too, apparently. Mostly Westerns," I said. "But he's interested in directing. He and Primrose are working together on the script for our documentary."

"I see. Now, what about Sammy? What does he hope to learn?"

"Sammy is looking for a career in sports broadcasting," I said. "He was injured in a fall and can't work as a jockey anymore."

"Makes sense," she said. "He was along on the basement excursion?"

"Yes. He was."

"Who do you think was the ringleader there? Duke or Sammy?" she asked.

"I haven't thought about that," I admitted, "but I'm sure the police and Mr. Friedrich have."

"We're back to him again," she said. "Everything seems to point in that man's direction."

"Whatever direction that might be." I gathered my cards into a neat stack and just stared at them.

"Oh, one thing Mrs. Sullivan told me tonight may be worth a card."

"What's that?"

"She said that the police had returned Bill's things to her. You know, his ring and watch and such."

"I'm sure they always do that. It's a normal procedure."

"I know. But she said that the coat they say Bill was wearing when they found him wasn't his."

"Wasn't his?"

She shook her head. "Nope. She said she'd never seen it before in her life."

"Funny, Pete didn't mention that. I wonder where it came from."

We drank our tea and nibbled on a few more peanut butter cookies. Then, satisfied that we'd done everything possible with what little information we had, we put away our cards and rinsed our teacups.

"I'm going to call Pete and ask him to come to the funeral mass with me tomorrow," I said. "Then I guess we'll go car shopping afterward."

"Sounds like a good plan, dear," she said. "And maybe Pete will give us a few tidbits of information for our card collections."

"Maybe." I was determined to ask him for help with my puzzle, but I was doubtful that he'd share much of anything with me. "He's pretty tight-lipped about police work."

"As well he should be," she agreed. "But try, anyway. He may surprise you."

I was snuggling comfortably in my bed, with O'Ryan stretched out across my feet, when I called Pete. He answered after the first ring.

"Hi. I was just thinking about you," he said, his voice low and sexy.

"You were? That's nice. I like it when you think about me," I said.

"You must be thinking about me, too. That's why you called."

"I was. And it is. Want to go to a funeral with me tomorrow morning?"

He laughed. "Wow. That's romantic. How can I resist?"

I laughed too. "Oh, Pete. I'm sorry. That was awful!"

"No, it wasn't. It was honest. You want me to go with you to Bill Sullivan's funeral?"

"Uh-huh. I do. Will you?"

"Sure. I was planning to go, anyway," he said. "I really like that family. Sorry I never got to know Bill. Shall I pick you up, say, around eight? The service isn't till ten. We can have breakfast, and then, after the funeral, we can look at some cars."

"I'd like that a lot," I said. "And maybe you already know about this, but remember that man who was in the basement with the chief when you saw me on the video? Friedrich?"

"Yeah. What about him?"

"He was in a parked car across from the funeral home tonight. And it could have been the same car we saw following Primrose—the one from the Treasury Department."

There was a long silence on his end of the phone. Too long.

"Are you surprised I know who that car is registered to? You wouldn't tell me, so I memorized the address and Aunt Ibby looked it up."

More silence.

"Are you still there, Pete?"

"I'm here. Just thinking." Sexy voice gone. Cop voice activated.

"Look," I said. "Please don't keep shutting me out. I seem to be right in the middle of something, and I need to know what's going on. You know you can trust me."

Another silence. O'Ryan's ears perked up, and his eyes opened slightly.

"You do know that," I said. "Don't you?"

"I do, Lee. It's just, well, I don't want you involved in something dangerous."

"Dangerous? Damn it, Pete. I *am* involved." My redhead's temper began to flare. "And so are my students. Every day we're all sitting right on top of a place that needs an armed guard to keep people away! Primrose is being stalked." I heard my voice rising. "And maybe somebody's stalking me, too."

"What do you mean by that? You think you're being followed?"

Is there such a thing as a sexy cop voice?

O'Ryan sat up straight, eyes locked on mine.

"Yes. I mean, maybe. I don't know for sure." I felt myself veer from temper to near tears.

"I'll tell you about it in the morning. Okay?"

"Want me to come over now? I'll be off duty in a few minutes."

"No thanks, Pete. It's late. Don't worry. O'Ryan and I are safe in bed. I'm going to read a chapter in my criminology book and go to sleep. I'll see you in the morning. Okay?"

His "Okay" was hesitant. "I'll pick you up at eight. We'll spend the day together. And, Lee?"

"Yes?"

"I do trust you. I care about you. A lot. Good night."

"Good night, Pete."

O'Ryan resumed his prone position at the foot of the bed and closed his eyes. I plumped up my pillows and picked up the Criminology 101 textbook. I propped the book against my knees, then opened it to the chapter entitled "Genetic Influence on Criminal Behavior." I stared at the pages, trying to force myself to concentrate on the printed words. But my thoughts were too scattered for study.

I was achingly aware that Pete had just said he cared for me a lot. I didn't know whether to be pleased or scared by that. It was awfully soon for any real emotion to have developed between us. We'd met only a few months ago, and Johnny had been gone for less than two years. But when Pete held me close and kissed me the way he did, I had to admit that I felt something pretty powerful—real or not.

I grasped the textbook tightly with both hands, willing myself to stop thinking about Pete and his kisses. I focused on the page.

> *There is significant scientific evidence that criminal behavior has genetic as well as environmental sources.*

Would this explain why several generations of the Trumbull family had been connected to a variety of crimes?

I read the required chapter, jotted down a few notes for the online quiz I'd have to take soon, snapped the book shut, and turned off the bedside lamp. O'Ryan changed his position and curled himself into a furry yellow ball beside me.

"Good night, fur ball," I said.

His answering purr sounded like a tiny engine idling. Within seconds I was in a half-dream state, watching little metal cars race around on a circular track. Friedrich's car was there in miniature, followed by the green Ford, with a blue roadster convertible bringing up the rear. Around and around they went. Were Friedrich's car and the Ford chasing the roadster? Or was it the other way around?

CHAPTER 19

The next day, I opened the front door before Pete had a chance to ring the doorbell, and stepped out into the cold but sunny morning. Pete took my hand.

"Careful. The steps are a little slippery."

I was pretty sure-footed, but the hand-holding was nice, anyway. "Are we going to have breakfast at the restaurant we went to before?" I asked.

"Nope. Too crowded. I want you to tell me what had you so spooked last night." He held my arm and helped me into the car, as though I were made of glass. "We'll go someplace quiet." He wasn't smiling. "I worried about you all night. What's all this about somebody stalking you?"

I'd been sleepless for a while, too, until I found out that watching imaginary little cars on a circular track works better than counting sheep. I felt surprisingly rested.

"It's probably no big deal," I said as we pulled away from the curb. "And I'm sorry if I snapped at you last night. Maybe it's all just a big coincidence. But . . ."

"But you don't really believe that."

I sighed. "Not really."

"Let's grab some takeout. Then we can park someplace quiet, and you can tell me what's going on."

"Sounds good to me," I said.

He drove to the nearest fast-food place, ordered our coffee and bacon, egg, and cheese biscuits, then headed for the park at the Salem Willows. In the summertime the Willows is a hive of activity—arcades, music, bumper cars, cotton candy, seafood restaurants, all within sight of the ocean. But in the dead of winter you could hardly find a quieter place.

We parked beside a curving section of beach next to a sheltered cove, where the only sound was the cry of gulls. "Start at the beginning," he said, "and tell me everything."

I began with my walk out to the garage to put the food in the Buick's trunk and how I'd noticed the green car parked across the street. "I noticed it because of the parking ban," I said, "but I didn't think much about it."

Pete put his coffee cup in a cup holder and took out a pen and notebook. "Go on," he said. "Don't leave anything out."

I thought for a moment as I took a few bites of my breakfast. "Aunt Ibby brought her car around to the front and picked me up, and we drove over to Federal Street, to the funeral home. It was crowded, so we went around the block a couple of times, looking for a parking space. That's when I saw Friedrich. His window was rolled down. I'm sure he recognized me."

Pete nodded, still taking notes. "He probably did. Then what?"

I told him about going to the Sullivans' apartment. "I was kind of bored, so I looked out the front window, wondering if Friedrich would be out there," I said. "He wasn't, but that same green car was. The one I saw parked on Oliver Street."

"You're sure it was the same one?"

"Pete," I said, "I know a little about cars. It was the same one. It's a two thousand six Ford Focus. Dark green. Dented right front fender."

He smiled. "Sorry. Sometimes I forget what a gearhead you are."

"That's okay. Anyway, Aunt Ibby and I left in a hurry. I wanted to try to get the plate number."

"Good girl. Did you get it?"

"No. The darn car was gone when we got outside."

"And you have no idea who it was?" He put the pen down and unwrapped his breakfast biscuit. "And it wasn't on Oliver Street when you got home?"

"Never saw it again," I said, "and I haven't a clue who it was."

"If you do see it again, snap a quick picture with your phone, but don't be obvious." He frowned. "I don't like the idea of somebody following you."

"Or maybe they're watching Aunt Ibby," I said. "That idea bothers me even more."

"Don't worry, babe," he said. "We'll figure it out."

"There's one more thing. But I don't know if it's important."

"Tell me about it, anyway."

I told him about the green car Aunt Ibby had seen from her living room window. "She's not sure what kind of car it was," I said. "Just that it was green, so probably it's nothing."

"Probably," he agreed, still taking notes. "Anything else?"

"Not about that." I sipped my coffee. "Just some school stuff."

"Like what?"

"I got a call from Jonathan Wilson," I said, watching his eyes, still wondering whether he'd recognized Primrose and the city councilman the last time we shared breakfast.

"Wilson? What did he want?"

"He wanted to talk to me about addressing my class. He says it's something important to 'the great city of Salem.'"

"Sounds like a politician. What did you tell him?"

"He's going to come on Monday morning for half an hour," I said. "He wants to talk about an old map."

"No kidding? Would you mind if I audit your class on Monday? I've developed an interest in maps lately myself," he said.

"You're welcome anytime," I said. "Sammy Trout likes maps, too. He was studying an atlas yesterday, with a map of Salem all marked up."

He nodded and wrote in the notebook. "What about the big guy? Duke."

"He was pretty quiet. Said he was hungover. This weekend he and Primrose are supposed to be working on a preliminary script for our documentary."

"Duke and Primrose, huh? Odd couple."

"I know. It'll be interesting to see what they come up with."

We sat for a while in companionable silence, broken only by the strident calls of the gulls. It seemed like a good time to try out my interrogating skills.

"Pete," I said, "do you mind if I ask you something?"

"Go ahead."

"That last time we had breakfast," I began, "when we went to that new place, were you . . . I mean . . . did you see . . . um . . . notice—"

"Wilson and Primrose getting cozy behind us? Sure I did."

"You didn't say anything. Weren't you going to tell me?"

He smiled. "I didn't even know who Primrose was then. Weren't *you* going to tell me?"

"Aunt Ibby says it's none of my business where Primrose goes or who she meets."

"Aunt Ibby is right."

"Another thing about Aunt Ibby . . . ," I said. "She's been digging around in the Trumbull files at the library."

"Come up with anything new?"

"Have you been thinking about the gunrunning in the eighties? That they might have been using the new tunnel, the one Bill fell into, and the trapdoor in the store basement?"

"She found the same information we did."

"Seems so," I said. "And one more thing . . . although I'm sure you already know about that, too."

"What is it?"

"The jacket that the police returned to Mrs. Sullivan with Bill's things."

He frowned. "What about it? We always return personal belongings."

"She says it wasn't his. Said she'd never seen it before in her life."

I could tell from his expression that he was truly surprised, and I felt a speck of satisfaction that I knew something he didn't.

"You're sure about that? Good work, Lee."

"Thanks," I said.

He looked at his watch. "Hey, we have some time before the funeral. Want to check out a car dealership on the way to St. Thomas's?" Pete gathered up our wrappers, cups, and napkins, tossed the food bag into a trash barrel, and we headed back to the city.

"Have you been thinking about what kind of car we should be looking for?" he asked on the way.

"Well, I'm not thinking about a Ferrari or a Bugatti," I said. "I like American cars. I think a Corvette would be fun."

He laughed. "Everybody thinks a Corvette would be fun. Seriously, are you thinking about a new car? Or used?"

"New," I said, picturing Nancy's roadster. "And blue."

Pete drove to a dealership I'd seen advertised on television. "I know the manager," he said. "Nice guy. He'll take good care of you." We climbed out of the Crown Vic and Pete motioned toward shiny rows of cars displayed on the huge lot. "Why don't you take a look around? I'll see if he's in his office."

I didn't need to look far. There it was in the showroom window. A long, swoopy Corvette Stingray convertible. Laguna Blue. No need to wait for the manager. I pushed the glass doors open and walked straight over to my dream car.

"A beauty, isn't she?" The salesman spoke from behind me. I didn't even turn to look at him.

"Mind if I sit in her?"

"Go right ahead," he said, reaching past me and opening the car door. I slid onto the smooth leather seat, put one hand on the race car–style steering wheel and the other on the seven-speed manual gearshift, and fell in love. I read the price sticker, blinked a couple of times, and stayed in love, anyway.

"How about taking her out for a test-drive?"

"I want to, but I don't have time right now," I said.

"No problem." He handed me a business card. "How about this afternoon?"

"I'll be back," I said, reluctantly getting out of the

car and looking around the showroom for Pete. "My name is Lee Barrett, and I'll definitely be back." I stuck out my hand, and we shook on it. "And if she drives as good as she looks, you've got a sale."

Pete and his manager friend arrived just in time to overhear the "you've got a sale" part. The manager beamed. "I'm Chuck," he said. "Pete here said you have great taste, Ms. Barrett. You sure do. Under that hood is 450 horsepower. She goes from zero to sixty in four seconds. You got your V-8 engine. You got your seven-speed manual. You got your—"

Pete interrupted. "Thanks, Chuck. Unfortunately, Lee and I have to head out right now. Funeral. Old friend." He took my arm and steered me toward the glass doors. "She'll be back another time to talk about it."

Once outside he put his arm across my shoulders. "Sorry to rush you out like that, but I wanted to give you a little time to think before you sign anything."

"I appreciate that, Pete. I really do. But I do want to test-drive it. Who wouldn't?" Just thinking about it made me smile. "Ride with me this afternoon, while I try it out. I double-dog dare you!"

I was surprised when he agreed right away. "Can't let a double-dog dare scare me," he said. "You're on." He looked at his watch. "Now let's go say good-bye to old Bill, shall we?"

Neither of us mentioned the Corvette on the way to the church. I knew Pete had some doubts about my buying such a high-powered car, and I was sure he had some concern about my ability to pay for it. I'd never talked about money with him, and I was sure he had no idea just how well set financially I was. Between my parents' estate, Johnny's insurance, and the counsel of some shrewd financial advisers, I'm what most people would consider a wealthy woman. I'm also quite a thrifty one. Other than using some of the money for college, I'd barely touched it. I could easily afford to buy the Laguna Blue beauty, and I fully intended to have it.

Saint Thomas the Apostle Church is in Peabody, just over the Salem line. It's a little jewel of a place, Old English, with lots of curved arches and carved wood inside. Soft organ music played as we made our way down the center aisle, and the sun shining through stained glass made pastel patterns on the wooden pews. It was a few minutes before ten o'clock, and the chapel was crowded with Bill's friends. We were lucky to find two seats together. I searched for familiar faces and spotted my aunt a few rows behind the Sullivans.

"There's Aunt Ibby," I whispered to Pete. "And a lot of our neighbors are here, too."

"Nice turnout," he whispered back. "And at least one person I'm surprised to see here."

I looked from side to side. "Who? Where?"

"Shhh," he said. "Tell you later."

The ancient ritual of the funeral mass had begun. The rhythmic words, the tinkling bells, the scent of incense filled my senses. When the service ended, and we stood to leave, Pete spoke softly.

"Look at the guy at the far end of the last row on the right." I looked in the direction he'd indicated. No one in the last row looked familiar. "The man with the dark glasses," he said. "Wearing a watch cap pulled down low."

I peered more closely at the man, who held a handkerchief to his face, wiping first one eye and then the other. As I watched, he quickly removed his glasses, wiped them, then put them back on.

I realized in those few seconds that I was looking at the tearstained face of Thom Lalonde.

"It's Thom," I said. "But why? I'm quite sure he didn't know Bill."

"Why is a good question," Pete said. "After all, if he didn't know Bill, why is he here, crying?"

CHAPTER 20

Bill's burial in nearby St. Mary's Cemetery was to be a private affair for family only, so after we left the church, we went straight back to Pete's car. I looked around for Thom but didn't see him anywhere.

"Thom was really upset," I said. "I don't understand it."

"Are you going to ask him about it when you see him on Monday?" Pete asked. "Tell him you saw him here?"

"Does that mean I'm on the case?"

"What case?" He grinned.

"I'm not sure," I said, laughing. "It's kind of a 'secret tunnel, broken leg, city councilor, map book, barroom, green Ford' federal case!"

"Something like that." He laughed, too. "Seriously, though, Thom might just be one of those people who like to go to funerals. Like a professional mourner."

I considered that. "Could be, I guess. After all, a funeral mass is a fairly public event. He must have known he'd be seen by people who'd recognize him, in spite of the cap and shades."

"That's true," Pete said. "But don't forget, he was in on the basement caper, along with Sammy and Duke.

Thom may not be as innocent as he looks. Life is full of surprises." He gave me a long look. "Speaking of surprises, do you mind if we stop by the station? I want to talk to the chief about the coat they found on Bill. I think the chief might want to take another look at it."

"Do I have to come in with you? I'm not one of Chief Whaley's favorite people, you know."

"Oh, don't take anything the chief says personally. He's all business all the time. Come in with me. He might want to hear about this from you."

I agreed reluctantly, and that was how I happened to spend part of my Saturday off in the Salem police station, face-to-face with what the comic books would call my arch nemesis. I got a curt nod acknowledging my presence, but he addressed Pete.

"So, Detective," he said, "to what do I owe the pleasure of seeing Ms. Barrett once again? So soon." There was no mistaking the unfriendly glare he sent in my direction.

"She told me something about the Bill Sullivan case today. Something I guess we missed."

"Sullivan?" Whaley said, looking at the clock on his wall. "By this time I presume he's six feet under."

"Well, sir," Pete said, "Mrs. Sullivan claims the coat he was wearing when we found him wasn't his."

The chief's icy blue eyes narrowed. "You know that to be a fact, Ms. Barrett?"

I could feel my temper rising. "Mrs. Sullivan says the coat isn't Bill's. She ought to know."

"She told you this?"

"She told my aunt."

"Thirdhand information, Detective Mondello," he said, turning his stare in Pete's direction. "But it may be worth checking. Get on it. Interview Mrs. Sullivan again and pick up that coat."

It was my turn to be surprised when Chief Tom Whaley stuck out his hand. "Thank you, Ms. Barrett," he said.

"You're welcome, Chief Whaley," I said, shaking his big paw.

We left the station and headed for Pete's car. "Chief wants me to get right on it," he said. "I hate to barge in on the Sullivans right after they just buried Bill. Maybe I should wait until tomorrow."

"Maybe, but, Pete, when I was at the Sullivans' place last night, I saw a Goodwill box in the downstairs lobby. Since the coat wasn't Bill's, she might have already tossed it."

"Good observation, Lee," he said as we returned to his car. "Did anybody ever tell you you'd make a good cop?"

I had to laugh at that idea. "Never. But at least Chief Whaley shook my hand."

"What do you say we grab some lunch, then head over to the Sullivans'?" he said, smiling, as we turned onto Margin Street. Then his expression changed. "But what about your test-drive? Can we skip it for now?"

"Not a chance," I said. "You're not going to chicken out on me. We'll do both."

"Whatever you say. Where to for lunch?" Pete asked. "Not a drive-through this time."

"Have you tried the diner at the Tabby yet? I had lunch there yesterday. Good food."

"Sounds okay to me," he said, and we headed toward Essex Street.

The diner was busier than I'd expected it to be on a Saturday. It was obvious that more than the student body of the Tabby had discovered the place. All the booths and most of the seats at the counter were occupied. I glanced around, looking for familiar faces, and spotted Mr. Pennington sitting alone in one of the wide booths.

"Let's see if my boss wants to share his table with us," I said.

The school director didn't look up as we approached. His attention seemed to be focused on multiple sheets of lined yellow paper strewn all over the table, barely leaving room for the full cup of coffee, which appeared to be untouched.

"Sir?" I said, gesturing toward the crowded counter. "Busy place. May we join you?"

"Huh? What? Oh, Ms. Barrett. Detective Mondello." He swept the papers together into a ragged pile and attempted to stand, knocking a few pages to the floor. "Please do. Glad for the company."

Pete gathered up the fallen sheets while I slid into the booth, facing Mr. Pennington. Pete sat beside me, adding the yellow papers he'd picked up to the pile. "You look busy, sir," he said. "Preparing a math test?" I realized then that the pages were completely covered with numbers. Row upon neat row of numerals marked each sheet.

"No. But it is a test of sorts," Mr. Pennington said, running a hand through thinning hair. "Perhaps I need a detective like yourself to help me figure it out."

"I'm not much on math," Pete admitted. "What's the problem?"

"Know anything about safecracking?"

I blinked, surprised.

"A little," Pete said. "Why?"

I knew what the answer was going to be. Mr. Pennington was trying to figure out how to open the safe in his office.

"It's that huge safe in my office," the director said. "I've tried listening for clicks. I've tried random combinations. Now I'm trying to figure out possible configurations of numbers to try. But there must be a million of them."

"Probably more than a million," Pete said. "Have you called a locksmith?"

"Of course. He offered to drill it. Can't do that. It's city property."

"Do you know what's in it, Mr. Pennington?" I asked. "Something valuable?"

"Maybe. I don't know." He shrugged. "That's not the point. It bothers me when I don't know things like that. What's in the locked safe? What do my spare keys open? How did that man get out of the tunnel? I don't like mysteries. Never did. Except in the movies, of course."

"Still haven't found out what those old keys go to?" Pete asked. "You were trying to figure that out when we first met."

"Still trying," he said. "They've got to fit something in the old store."

Or somewhere under the old store. Maybe in a tunnel. Or even something belonging to a pregnant, dead teenager.

"Are you talking about the two old skeleton keys I saw on your key ring, sir?" I asked.

"Ah, you are perceptive, my dear. Indeed. The very ones."

"They came with all the others? The ones that open the doors and cabinets all over the building?"

"Absolutely. With patience and diligence I've learned what each and every one of them unlocks—with the notable and unfortunate exception of the two you noted." He looked proud of himself. "No easy task. There are almost twenty keys on that ring."

"I remember it," Pete said, "and I was impressed

with how you knew exactly what each key opened when we searched the building on Christmas night."

"Keys, like people, have distinct personalities of their own," he declared.

"Is that from a movie?" I wondered aloud.

Mr. Pennington beamed. "It sounds like it, doesn't it? No, I made that one up myself."

"I don't know if I can be helpful with your safe-cracking problem or with your mystery keys," Pete said, "but we may be close to finding out exactly how Bill Sullivan got out of the tunnel."

"Oh, I do hope so. All that activity beneath the school is quite disconcerting. The daily parade of workers up and down the basement stairs, the presence of the armed guard, the general atmosphere of unrest cannot be beneficial to the student body." He looked at me. "Do you not agree, Miss Barrett? Do your students seem uneasy because of it?"

I hadn't really thought about it. My students, like Mr. Pennington's keys, each had a distinct personality. How much they'd been affected by the commotion at the Tabby, I didn't know.

"I can't honestly say that, sir. I don't know what any of them was like before they enrolled here."

Pete gave the waitress our orders and offered to buy Mr. Pennington lunch, as well.

"Oh, no thank you, Detective," he said, gathering up his papers. "I've already eaten and have occupied this space far too long already. You young people enjoy your day, and thank you for listening to an old man's ramblings."

He stood, about to leave, then turned. "Ms. Barrett," he said, "do you happen to know whether your delightful aunt has decided to accompany me to the Woody Allen Film Festival?"

"Um . . . she did mention it. I'll have her call you."

"Excellent," he said. "Thank you. Miss Russell is a charming woman. Charming." He left the diner, using the Tabby's first-floor entrance.

"Your aunt and old Pennington?" Pete raised an eyebrow.

I shrugged. "Who knows? Pete, is that true about Bill?"

The waitress appeared with our food. I was hungry and it all looked delicious. "Is what true?" he asked, pouring ketchup onto hot onion rings.

"Is it true that you're close to figuring out how they got Bill out of the tunnel and into the park?" I put ranch dressing onto my salad.

"We've broken through that pile of rubble I told you about."

"The rocks and dirt you said were deliberately put there?"

"That's right. We had to be careful taking it all apart. Didn't want to cause another cave-in. Somebody really doesn't want us to see where they dragged Bill's body to."

"But you'll find it," I said.

"Of course we will. But the mess of rubble gave whoever it was time to clean up any tracks they might have left, and the damned thing branches out in about forty different directions. Up and down. Old tunnel blocked. New tunnel dug underneath. They all probably exit in different places along the waterfront." He held up the menu. "You want dessert? Boston cream pie looks good."

Pete had pie, and I had Grape-Nut pudding. We both had coffee, and then, with his assurance that he didn't have a worry in the world about riding in a Corvette with me, we left for the Sullivans' place.

"God, I hate doing this," Pete said, lifting the door knocker on the second-floor apartment.

Junior Sullivan answered and, with only the slightest expression of surprise, invited us inside. "Come in, Lee, Detective," he said. "What can we do for you? Do you need to see Mother?"

"I don't want to disturb her," Pete said. "Maybe you can help me. I'm really sorry to bother you about this, but the chief would like to take another look at that coat your dad was wearing when we found him."

"That ratty old thing? It wasn't his, you know."

"We know that, but do you still have it?"

"I doubt it. It was dirty and smelled of booze. But we can ask Mother what she did with it," he said. "Everybody's in the kitchen. Come on."

I didn't know what to expect when we followed him through the dining room, where the table, with a fresh white linen tablecloth and a centerpiece of red carnations, displayed an assortment of covered dishes and baked goodies.

Mrs. Sullivan hurried across the kitchen to greet us. I'd been afraid we'd intrude on a group of heart-broken people, sad and tearful, having just buried a dear one. But what we found was a true celebration of Bill's life. There was laughter and storytelling, and maybe a nip or two of Irish whiskey.

Junior explained to his mother why we'd come. "You want that nasty old jacket? Bill wouldn't have been caught dead in that thing." With a rueful smile, she sighed. "Though I guess he was." She motioned us toward an adjoining laundry room. "I planned to give it to the Goodwill, so I washed it first. Here it is."

Neatly folded on top of the dryer, the brown quilted jacket looked quite presentable. "It cleaned up right nicely, didn't it?" she said and handed it to Pete.

We thanked her, declined the invitation to stay for a "bite of food," expressed our condolences once again, and left.

"Too bad she washed it," Pete said as we headed back to the police station. "Probably destroyed any evidence we might have found."

"At least you have it, though," I said. "It's not in a landfill somewhere."

"You're right. And it may be of some use, even clean. I'm going to show it to that woman who told us about the three drunks she saw near the park that night."

"The carol-singing drunks?"

"Yeah. It's a pretty slim chance, but if she recognizes it, maybe she saw Bill."

"Bill? But Bill couldn't have been walking down the street, singing or otherwise," I reasoned. "You said his leg was broken when he fell. Besides, the medical examiner said he wasn't even drunk."

"True," Pete said. "But suppose you've got somebody who needs to be moved from one place to another. And suppose that somebody has passed out. Unresponsive. Even dead." His voice dropped. "And suppose you've got a friend handy who's willing to help you move him."

I saw the picture in my mind. One person on each side of Bill, with an arm around him, pulling him along across the snow. An irreverent flash of a scene from *Weekend at Bernie's* popped into my head.

"And you think those were the three drunks the woman saw on Christmas night?" I asked.

"Could be. Worth checking, anyway."

We reached the police station, and this time Pete agreed that I didn't have to come inside while he delivered the coat. I turned on the radio, and smiled when I realized that Pete had it tuned to a country and western station. There wasn't much to look at from the car window besides a flagpole and some bare-branched trees, so I pulled a few index cards and a pen from my purse.

I made notes about the jacket that wasn't Bill's, Thom Lalonde's tears, the three drunks singing Christmas carols, Mr. Pennington's search for the old safe combination, and the pile of rubble obstructing the tunnel.

I was scribbling on a sixth card when Pete returned.

"How did it go?" I asked, switching off the radio. "Was the chief glad to get the coat or mad because it was clean?"

"A little of both, I think," he said. "Let's go test-drive your dream car."

"Yes!" I said. "I can hardly wait. You ready for a quick trip to Gloucester?"

"You picked that ride because you know there's a nice little stretch there where you can open her up."

"Exactly," I said. "And I promise I won't go over eighty."

"Seventy," he said. "I don't want to have to write you a ticket."

CHAPTER 21

Pete aimed the car in the direction of the dealership, while I searched the bottom of my purse for a rubber band to keep my newly written index cards together. I caught myself happily humming an off-tune version of "My Heroes Have Always Been Cowboys" when Pete suddenly executed a fast U-turn, reversing our direction, activated the hidden red, white, and blue flashing lights in the windshield and grill, hit the siren, and floored the Crown Vic.

OMG! I'm in a high-speed chase with a cop!

"Hang on, babe," he said. "That's your green Ford."

No high-speed chase, after all. The green car ahead of us was already slowing down.

"That's it," I said. "But what are you going to tell him you stopped him for?"

"Mud splashed all over his front license plate," Pete said. "Unreadable. That's against the law."

The Ford pulled over to the curb. Pete parked behind it and climbed out of the Vic. There was mud smeared on the back plate, as well. Pete kicked it, making the numbers visible. He stood there for a moment, tapping on his phone, then approached the driver.

From where I sat, I couldn't get a clear view of the man in the driver's seat, except to see that he had long hair and a beard. He handed something to Pete, his license and insurance, I supposed. Pete leaned closer to the window. He appeared to be listening, not talking.

It seemed as though a long time had passed when Pete came back and opened the car door, but a glance at the clock told me it had been only about five minutes. I saw the Ford start up and drive away.

"That is the damnedest thing I've ever seen," he said, sitting behind the wheel but not moving the car. "You're not going to believe it."

"Who is it?" I said. "I know I've never seen him before. Why is he following me?"

Pete shook his head. "First," he said, "you *have* seen him before. And second, he isn't following you."

"I don't get it."

"I didn't, either, until I got a look at his driver's license."

"Come on, tell me," I said. "Whose car is it?"

Pete turned off the flashers and moved us smoothly into traffic. "Nope. I think I'll make you play detective for a while. I'll tell you this much. The car is registered to a person who you probably don't know and who has no record of any kind of legal trouble."

"Darn it, Pete. Don't play games with me. I've been worried about that stupid car for days."

He smiled. "Uh-uh. You want to study criminology. Consider this a midterm exam."

"You're terrible. Okay, but at least give me a clue."

"Fair enough. Let me see." Again the smile. "Try this. The driver of the green car is wearing a disguise. Fake beard and hair."

I thought about that. "How's this? It's probably

someone from the Tabby who has access to the costume and makeup divisions Right?"

"Right. Go on."

"And if the car is registered to someone I don't know, it's borrowed. Right?"

He nodded. "Yep. Right again."

"You said he *isn't* following me."

"He isn't."

"If he isn't following me, yet he's hanging around my house, and he followed us to the Sullivans', then he's following someone else."

"Correct," he said. "I told you you'd make a good cop. Keep going."

"He's stalking my *aunt*. My God. Who is he?"

"You're almost there. Stay with it."

"Who at the Tabby has any interest in Aunt Ibby?" I answered my own question immediately. "Rupert Pennington. That old dog!"

"Nice going," he said, taking one hand off the wheel and offering a high five. "The disguise was so good, I never would have recognized him if he hadn't shown me his license."

"But why? Why is he watching her?"

"He thinks he's in love. Isn't watching her so much as checking for boyfriends. He wants to be sure he has a clear field before he . . . um . . . begins courting her."

"Amazing," I said. "And what about the car?"

"Belongs to his nephew. He's on the way to return it and pick up his own," Pete said. "He's really embarrassed. I didn't have the heart to ticket him for the muddy plates."

"Did you tell him he has to stop? That he can't keep watching us?"

"He promised. But what is your aunt going to think about all this?"

"I don't know," I said honestly. "I truly don't. She might think he's just a silly old fool. Or she might be flattered."

"Women," he said, with a mock sigh. "You never know what they're thinking."

"This woman is thinking it's about time to take a ride in my new car," I said. "With you as copilot."

I could tell that they were happy to see us back at the dealership. The salesman hurried to the door to meet us, inviting us to sit down and have coffee while he explained all the new features on the Corvette. Chuck spotted us from his glass-walled office and rushed out to greet us.

I was sold already, but I sat politely and listened to the tag-team recitation of heart-thumping statistics on horsepower, torque, and navigation.

"Sounds wonderful," I said. "I can hardly wait to test it out. Can we do it now?"

"Sure," the salesman said. "But since she's a two-seater, we'll have to leave you behind, Pete. Sorry."

"Oh, no. I promised Pete he could come with me."

"That's okay," Pete said quickly. "No problem. I understand. The salesman always goes along on the test-drive. That right, Chuck?"

"Not in this case." Chuck held up both hands. "No worries about a customer riding with one of Salem's finest. I'll get the keys and meet you out front."

"Great," Pete said. "Thanks a lot."

"You don't sound as excited as Lee does." The manager smiled. "Relax. You'll love it." He turned to me. "Top up or down, Lee?"

"Down, of course. We'll just blast the heat."

Within a few minutes, with my jacket zipped, hat and gloves on, and with Pete in the seat beside me, I slipped on my sunglasses and turned the key, loving the sound of 6.2 liters of American V-8 muscle roaring beautifully in my ears. I headed for one of the nice clear stretches of Massachusetts freeway that tolerated a heavy foot, booted her up to a little over seventy, and knew for sure this was my car. We traveled as far as the rotary in Gloucester, where I turned and slowed down for the ride back to Salem.

"Well, what do you think?" I asked Pete, hoping he thought as I do, that riding in a good convertible with the top down on a clear, crisp day is one of life's great pleasures.

"Not bad," he said as I pulled up in front of the dealership. "Not bad at all. And you're one hell of a good driver."

Reluctantly, I slid out of the driver's seat, took off my hat and gloves, and pushed my sunglasses up onto the top of my head. "Wow! That was fun!"

Inside, I wrote a check for the deposit, arranged to come back on Monday to finish up the paperwork, and shook hands with the manager and the beaming salesman. Then Pete and I climbed back into the Crown Vic.

The sun was low in the west by then, and darkness was closing in fast. Lights began to appear in windows, and the temperature dropped. I looked at my watch. "It's only four forty-five," I said. "It gets dark here way too early."

"I know," he said. "Not much like Florida. What shall we do with the rest of our day? Dinner and another movie? Hot dogs and beer at Greene's Tavern?"

Another visit to the cozy, old-fashioned bar sounded good to me, and the blazing fire in that big stone fireplace would be welcome, too.

"Hot dogs and beer, please," I said. "And maybe

later we can go back to the diner and have a big slice of apple pie. Hot dogs, apple pie, and Chevrolet. The perfect all-American day."

"I like it," he said.

When we pulled into the Greene's Tavern parking lot, Pete didn't make a move to leave the car. "Do you think your whole class may be here tonight?" he asked.

"I wouldn't be surprised," I said. "Why?"

"There're a couple of things you might need to know about some of your students."

"All right, if you think so. Who?" I didn't want to hear anything bad about any of them.

"I guess you know we ran a check on Sammy and Duke after they were caught nosing around in the basement," he said.

"Sure. You had to do that."

"Sammy has a record," he said. "He's served time in jail more than once. Oh, he's paid his debt to society, as they say, but I think you need to know that he might not be exactly trustworthy."

"He's not dangerous, is he?" Sammy had kind of a smart mouth, but I couldn't imagine him hurting anyone.

"No violent crimes. Don't worry about that. But he was convicted once of doping horses, fixing races. He served a short sentence, and he was suspended from racing for a year on account of it."

"What else? You said more than once."

"While he was suspended, he went to jail again. That conviction was for selling cocaine. Then he got back into racing. Small tracks, some overseas. Like he said, he got hurt a few years ago. No other trouble since."

"Well, that's something," I said. "What about Duke?"

"First of all, Duke's not his real first name."

"That doesn't surprise me. Going to tell me what it is?"

"Nope. But he has no police record that we could find. Small-time actor."

"That's what I thought. Anyone else I need to know about?"

"Just Primrose."

"Primrose? What's she done?"

"Absolutely nothing. That's the problem. There's nothing about her anywhere that we've been able to find. It's as though she dropped here from Planet X. She has a legit New York driver's license, but no work record, no Social Security information. We're still looking into it."

"What about the others? Kelly and Therese and Thom?"

"They've checked out okay so far. Seem to be just who and what they say they are."

"Why all the interest in my class, anyway?" I wanted to know. "Does it have anything to do with the tunnel?"

Pete opened his door. "I've already told you more than I should."

When we walked into Greene's Tavern, Kelly was busy waiting tables and Primrose was seated at the bar, on the same stool she'd camped out on the last time we were there. Therese and Sammy sat side by side at the keno machine. I didn't see Thom anywhere, but behind the bar, serving customers, were Joe Greene and Duke Martin.

Pete and I took our back-to-the-wall seats at the end of the bar, and Duke put a couple of coasters in front of us. "What'll it be?" he asked. "It's still happy hour."

Pete ordered light beer for both of us, then pointed to the rotisserie hot dog cooker behind the bar. "We'll have a couple of those hot dogs, too."

"I'm surprised to see you tending bar, Duke," I said. "You're a man of many talents."

"Struggling actors hold down lots of different jobs, ma'am," he said. "I learned to bartend in a little joint in L.A. years ago. When Thom called in sick, Joe was kind of stuck, so I said, 'Aw, shucks, I'll do it.'" He wasn't wearing his ten-gallon hat, but the John Wayne accent was firmly in place.

"What do you think of my new bartender?" Joe Greene asked. "Other than being so tall he keeps hitting his head on the wineglass rack, he does a pretty good job."

Duke looked pleased. "Glad to help out. Mustard and relish on the dogs?"

Primrose picked up her drink and moved to the vacant stool next to me. "You guys must like this place."

"Lee had a craving for hot dogs," Pete said. "Want one?"

"Don't mind if I do," she said. "Duke and I have been working on our storyboard all day. I forgot to eat."

Pete signaled to Duke and ordered another hot dog as Primrose turned and faced me. "What's up with the sunglasses, Lee?" she said. "It's dark outside."

Embarrassed, I reached for the glasses on my head and yanked them off. "I forgot all about them," I said. "I was wearing them while I was test-driving a new convertible this afternoon."

"No kidding? I love convertibles. What kind?"

I launched into a happy description of the Corvette, probably telling her far more than she wanted to know. My automotive babbling was interrupted by Sammy.

"Hi, guys," he said, then motioned to the bartender. "Hey, Duke, I need some more change. That Therese is the luckiest woman I've ever seen. I may take her to Vegas!"

I turned to look at Therese, who was tapping numbers onto the flashing video screen, her fingers flying as fast as they did on a keyboard. She lifted one hand for a nanosecond wave in our direction, then focused again on the game.

"I never thought of Therese as a gambler," I said. "But she looks as though she's seriously into it."

Sammy picked up his change. "This is her first time." He shook his head. "Never saw anything like it before." He hurried back to join the luckiest woman he'd ever seen, and I turned my attention to my hot dog and beer.

"So, Primrose," Pete said, "you say you and Duke have been spending your weekend doing homework?"

"Right. We worked all day over at the dorm. We'll be working on it tomorrow, too."

"Good for you," I said. "How's it coming?"

"Pretty good, I think," she said. "I really enjoy the research part."

"I like it, too," I said. "Of course, it helps that I have a research librarian for an aunt."

"Is that what Miss Russell does? You never told me that." Primrose looked pleased. "Maybe she'll give me a hand with a little extracurricular project I'm helping a friend with."

"I'm sure she'll be glad to," I said. "What's the project?"

"My friend is a writer. Lives in California. She's calling her new book *Hot Prez*. It's about our hottest presidents. I'm helping with the East Coast hotties. By the way, I'm going to have to skip school for a day pretty soon to check out the JFK library in Boston."

"I'm sure we can arrange it," I said. "Kennedy sure belongs on that list. Who else is on it?"

She paused and took a bite of her hot dog. "I haven't seen the whole list yet. I know Reagan's on it. And Obama. Bill Clinton, of course. Oh, yeah. Roosevelt."

"Teddy or Franklin?" Pete asked.

"Franklin," she said. "I did the research on him at the FDR Library when I was working in New York."

"What kind of job did you have in New York?" Pete asked. I knew where that line of questioning was going. After all, Primrose hadn't dropped here from Planet X.

Primrose waved a dismissive hand in the air. "Oh, I was just freelancing. A little stage work. A little film work. You know. Amateur stuff."

"Hard to make a living that way," Pete said.

Primrose shrugged. "I did all right. I always do."

"You'll be interested when we go upstairs to Tabitha's room," I told her. "She was a big fan of President Roosevelt."

"How do you know that?" she asked, frowning.

"She had a big framed picture of him. It's hanging right over her bed."

"Really? She must have thought he was a hot prez, too. When can we go up there and take a look around?"

"Maybe sometime next week," I said. "After we've heard Councilor Wilson's . . . um . . . presentation."

"Have you met the councilor yet, Primrose?" Pete asked. "He seems like a nice guy. Real interested in Salem history, apparently."

Another hand wave. "Yeah. We've met. He seems okay. I'm not much into local politics."

But are you into local politicians?

"Hi, Lee. Hi, Pete." Therese slid onto the stool

next to Primrose. "Sammy taught me how to play keno. It's fun."

"Come on back and play some more." Sammy stood behind her. "Don't quit now. You're on a roll."

"Don't want to play anymore." Therese pointed at Primrose's hot dog. "I'm starving. Can I have one of those, Duke?"

"Sure thing, kid," Duke said. "Don't let Sammy teach you any bad habits. Gambling's really harmful for some folks."

"Man, you should see her play! She's a phenom, I'm telling you," Sammy said. "She says she can see the numbers before they come up."

"Duke's right, Therese," Pete said. "Gambling can get to be a real bad habit. You don't want to throw your money away like that."

"Oh, I wouldn't," Therese said. "It's not my money. Sammy was just teaching me how to play. It's all his."

"Jeez, Sammy. The least you can do is buy the kid a hot dog with your winnings," Primrose said.

"Yeah, sure." Sammy put a few bills on the bar. "Have a glass of wine, too."

"Thanks, Sammy," Therese said, all smiles.

Duke, ducking his head and avoiding the wineglass rack, delivered Therese's drink and dog, then jerked a thumb toward the tavern's front door. "Hey, look who's here."

Nodding and smiling to the left and the right, wearing a velvet-collared topcoat and a gray fedora, and carrying an ebony walking stick, Rupert Pennington made his grand entrance into Greene's Tavern.

CHAPTER 22

"Good evening. Good evening." The director strolled the length of the bar, greeting patrons along the way.

Joe Greene called out, "The usual, Mr. P?"

"Indeed, my friend. All things remain as usual on this fine night." He carefully placed his hat on the bar, leaned the walking stick against the wall, nodded to me, and sat next to Therese.

"A pleasure to see you, Ms. Barrett. Detective Mondello, Miss Della Monica," he said. "How nice that several of our favorite students are also here in this most convivial atmosphere."

I could only stammer, "Hello," astonished that the man was apparently going to pretend that nothing had changed. That "all things remained as usual," even though only hours ago he had been wearing a wig and a fake beard and had admitted to Pete that he'd been stalking my aunt for days.

Joe delivered Mr. Pennington's drink—bourbon and water—and leaned across the bar. "Good to see you, Mr. P. I've been wanting to tell you how much my girl is liking that school. Hell, she's been glued to a history book all day. Never liked to study that much back home."

"Mostly due to her excellent teacher." Pennington raised his glass toward me.

"Did Kelly work as a waitress when you lived in West Virginia, Joe?" Pete asked.

"No, but she learned waitressing right quick."

"And what was it you did down there?" Pete wanted to know. "Some sort of coal mining, was it?"

Kelly appeared with a drink order, putting her tray on the bar. "Pa wasn't just a regular miner," she said. "He was a specialist. Probably still be doing it if he didn't get the cough."

"We're well out of it, honey," Joe said. "Things are much better here."

"A specialist . . ." I began to ask a question, but Duke had loaded the tray with drinks and Kelly headed back to her tables, while Joe waited on a customer at the other end of the bar.

"Duke," Pete said. "What's wrong with Thom? You say he called in sick?"

"Don't know exactly," Duke said. "I didn't talk to him. Joe says he sounded bad, though. Probably some kind of flu. Lots of that going around."

"You say young Thom is ill?" Mr. Pennington said. "That's odd. I saw him just a little while ago over by the new train station. I stopped and offered him a lift, but he declined."

"By the train station?" Primrose asked. "Did he look like he was going somewhere or just waiting for someone?"

"Good evening, Miss McDonald," Mr. Pennington said. "I really can't say what his intentions might have been, but I do recall that he was carrying a satchel."

"He wouldn't just take off without telling us." Therese shook her head. "Would he, Sammy?"

Sammy shrugged. "Dunno. He was in a real hurry to get to New York."

"That's right," Duke said. "Maybe he finally got enough money together and headed on out."

Joe Greene joined the conversation. "When I talked to him, he sure sounded sick. All snifflin' and breathin' hard."

"He wouldn't run off somewhere without telling me," Kelly insisted. "He's my best friend. He's the nicest person I've met since we moved here."

Mr. Pennington downed his drink and signaled to Duke for another. "I found out what the secret to life is," he said. "Friends. Best friends." He looked around expectantly, and his gaze settled on me. "Ms. Barrett?"

"Yes, sir?"

He leaned forward, looked into my eyes for what seemed like a long time, then sighed.

"Oh, Ms. Barrett. I am disappointed. Your sweet aunt would have had that one in two seconds. Jessica Tandy. *Fried Green Tomatoes.* 1991."

Therese looked mystified. "What do tomatoes have to do with Thom running off and leaving us?"

"It's a movie, honey," Sammy told her. "Don't worry about it. Come on back and play keno."

"I don't want to. Can we go home now, Primrose? I'm tired. And I'm worried about Thom." She closed her eyes and put her fingers on her temples. "I think something's wrong with him."

I'd seen that gesture before. Ariel had often used that same pose when she pretended to do her TV psychic hocus-pocus. The warm feeling I'd felt when Pete and I entered the bar was disappearing fast.

"You about ready for that apple pie, Lee?" Pete asked. "I know I am."

Bless you, Pete. I really want to get out of here.

"Absolutely," I said, forcing a smile. "Good night, everybody. See you all at school on Monday. And, Duke, when Thom calls you back, would you text me?" Mentally crossing my fingers, I added, "I'm sure he's okay."

Pete and I hurried out into the cold and climbed into the Vic. He turned on the heater, and we waited there for the car to warm up. "That Pennington is a strange one," he said. "I guess he's just going to pretend the whole green Ford thing never happened."

"Well, he is an old actor," I said. "Pretending is his business. But I'm going to have to tell Aunt Ibby everything. She can decide whether to confront him about it or not."

We pulled out of the parking lot and headed downtown. "Are you really up for that pie?" he asked.

"Of course I am," I said. "But I'm worried about Thom."

"Me too," he admitted. "Between the way Thom behaved at Bill's funeral, then pulling this disappearing act, it makes me wonder exactly what his connection to Bill's death might be."

"I'm afraid I'm thinking along the same lines, and I don't like it." I ran a hand through my hair. "Oh, damn," I said.

"What's wrong?"

"My sunglasses. I left them on the bar."

"Want to go back and get them?"

"No. It's not important. I have more at home," I said. "I'm sure Joe will put them away for me."

The diner at the Tabby appeared to be as busy at

night as it was during the daytime. We were happy to find two seats together at the counter.

"You're in luck," the waitress said, taking our order. "The apple pie is still hot. Just came out of the oven."

"In that case, we'd better have some vanilla ice cream on top," Pete said. "You agree?"

I did, of course. As I sipped my coffee and savored the pastry treat, I tried to put thoughts of Bill's death and Thom's disappearance and Mr. Pennington's strange pursuit of my aunt out of my mind.

But anxieties don't melt away as easily as ice cream on hot apple pie.

It was still fairly early when Pete brought me home, but he turned down my invitation to come in, as he'd drawn morning duty. He walked me to the door, where we shared a discreet good-night kiss—the 100-watt porch light discouraged anything more.

"I'll see you Monday morning at the school," he reminded me. "Is nine o'clock early enough for me to catch Wilson's talk?"

"Nine is perfect," I said. "See you then."

O'Ryan greeted me in the front hall with purrs and mrrows, Aunt Ibby close behind him with questions. "Did you find a car you like? Where did you go after the funeral? I looked for you, but you disappeared so quickly. Did you tell Pete about that green Ford? Do you want coffee?"

"Whoa!" I laughed. "Slow down. No thanks to the coffee. I just had some at the diner. Let's go sit somewhere, and I'll tell you everything." I took off my boots and jacket and followed her into the living room. "It's been quite a day. This may take a while."

I'd picked up a few brochures at the dealership, so while Aunt Ibby leafed through the colorful pages of pictures of the Corvette, I told her all about it. "I can hardly wait to take you for a ride, Aunt Ibby. You're going to love it."

"From the looks of these pictures, I think your Johnny would have loved it."

"He would have," I agreed. "He left me with a passion for fast cars, that's for sure."

"Your daddy would have loved it, too," she said. "He had a Corvette, you know."

"Daddy had one?" I was surprised. "I didn't know that."

"Oh, yes, indeed. It was bright yellow, just like his plane. A 1986 Stingray Corvette. You were probably too little to remember it." She nodded. "How he loved that car. And you, in your little car seat, squealing with delight whenever he took you for a ride."

"I like it that he had one. Maybe it's a genetic thing."

I told her about picking up the coat that wasn't Bill's, but there didn't seem to be a gentle way to tell the truth about the green car—to let her know that it was she who was being followed. So I just blurted out the whole story. "It seems Mr. Pennington thinks he's in love with you." I described how Pete had chased the Ford and unmasked the bearded driver. "And when we saw him later at the tavern, he behaved as though nothing had happened."

I watched her face. At first her eyes narrowed, and her mouth formed a straight line. She swallowed a couple of times, then lowered her head and began to chuckle softly. "He actually wore a fake beard and a wig?" She rocked back and forth and laughed out loud. "He was creeping around, watching to be sure I didn't have any boyfriends lurking in the bushes? The damned old fool!"

Her hilarity was contagious, and I found myself giggling along with her at the silliness of the whole thing, my anxiety melting away. Between gasps of laughter, she said, "Maralee, I haven't had a man behaving so foolishly over me since third grade, when Billy Stewart wrote, 'I love Isobel' in colored chalk all over the sidewalk in front of our house."

"What are you going to do?" I asked. "Are you going to tell him I told you about it?"

She wiped her eyes. "I'm going to do just what he's doing. I'm going to behave as though nothing has happened. And I'm going to that Woody Allen Film Festival with him." Smiling, she shook her head. "The damned old fool."

I told her then about Thom and how we'd seen him crying at the funeral and how he'd called Joe and said he couldn't work, because he was sick. "But Mr. Pennington saw him near the train station, and he was carrying a suitcase," I said. "Some of the others think he's gone to New York."

"What do you think?" she asked. "Would he do that without telling anyone?"

"It seems out of character to me," I said. "Kelly says he'd never leave without telling her. She felt terrible about it. Says he's her best friend."

"Poor Kelly."

"I know. Then Mr. Pennington quoted some line about best friends from *Fried Green Tomatoes*. Said you would have recognized it in a minute."

"I found out what the secret to life is. Friends. Best friends," she said. "Jessica Tandy."

"You're a wonder."

"Yes, I am," she said, smiling. "I suppose with all this going on, you'll have some notes for your index cards."

"I've already written a few," I said, pulling the rubber-banded pile from my purse and showing her the half dozen cards I'd filled out. "I'll do one more about Thom being missing. Can you think of anything else?"

"Not offhand," she said. "I'll go back to the library on Monday and dig around in the vertical files some more. It's been fascinating to research so far."

"It seems that Primrose has an interest in research, too," I told her. "She's helping a friend who's working on a book about America's most attractive presidents. She's planning a trip to the JFK library, and she's already done the FDR library in New York. She may ask you for some help with the project."

"The Roosevelt library, hmm? He keeps turning up lately, doesn't he? Tell her I'll be glad to help."

We climbed the stairs together, with O'Ryan scampering ahead. Just as we reached the top, Aunt Ibby snapped her fingers.

"Maralee, there was one thing I found in the vertical files that has me puzzled."

"What's that?"

"It was a birthday card sent to Tabitha, signed 'Love, Ma.'"

"A card from her mother? What puzzled you about it?"

"It was one of those Disney cards, with a picture of the Little Mermaid on it."

"Ariel. Cute."

"Maralee, that movie came out in nineteen-eighty-nine. Tabitha died a few years after that. So how old would that make her mother?"

Was it possible that Tabitha's mother had lived to be that old? If Tabitha was in her eighties when she received the birthday card, and her mother had married young, say, at sixteen or seventeen, it was surely a possibility. After all, Megan was over a hundred.

"I guess she could have been in her late nineties," I

CHAPTER 23

I lay in my comfortable bed with a warm cat curled up on my feet, trying to make sense of that topsy-turvy day. Jumbled thoughts of a teary-eyed bartender, a joyous freeway ride, a folded brown jacket, an unmasked aunt stalker, maps of Salem, old and new, and a dead woman's dead mother's birthday greeting tumbled around in my brain like fractured images in a kaleidoscope.

Put first things first, I told my inner Nancy. *What's the most important thing?*

Clearly, the answer was to find out what had happened to Thom.

Where has he gone? Why was he crying? Is he all right wherever he is?

With a vow to start finding answers to those questions in the morning, I fell into an uneasy sleep.

I awoke the next day to the sound of robins squabbling as they stripped red berries from a winterberry bush below my window. A glance at the clock told me it was too early to call Thom's mother, but not too early to call Primrose—the only other person in the class who'd talked about New York. If that was where Thom said as we paused outside my bedroom door. "But where was she? Was there a postmark on the envelope?"

"No. I'm afraid some stamp collector had cut it out," my aunt said. "They do that. Take the whole top of the envelope. No stamp. No postmark. No return address."

"It all just gets more confusing, doesn't it. Goodnight, Aunt Ibby."

O'Ryan ran ahead of me into the bedroom, staking out his spot at the foot of the bed. I turned on the TV—he seemed to enjoy it—then sat at my desk and spread out my growing collection of index cards in a random configuration.

I sat there staring at the cards, registering nothing at all. A delicate tap at my door roused me from the so far fruitless effort.

"Maralee? Are you still awake?"

"Sure. Not even undressed yet. Come on in."

My aunt hadn't changed into nightclothes, either. She waved a sheet of copier paper. "Look at this. I couldn't wait to find out about Tabitha's mother. I went online and looked her up. It was easy. I know exactly where she was when that card was sent."

"You do? Where?"

"Greenlawn Cemetery. Been there since nineteen forty-seven."

had gone, maybe she'd have some idea of where he might be.

It was a good guess. Primrose and Thom had had several conversations about the Big Apple, one quite recently.

"He asked me if I knew any agents," she said. "I don't, but I knew a couple of models who have agents, and I gave him their numbers. But hell, I thought he was just getting info for the future."

"Do you have any idea where he might be staying? Does he know anybody there?"

"I don't think so," she said. "God, Lee. That city's no place for a beautiful boy like Thom to be wandering around by himself. Does he have any money?"

"I think he must. He seems to be saving all his pay from the tavern. I'm going to call Joe and see what he thinks," I said. "I'm really worried about him."

"Me too," she said. "Let me know if you find out anything. I'll see you tomorrow at school. Is Councilor Whatshisname still on?"

Councilor Whatshisname? Come on, Primrose!

"Councilor Wilson. Yes, as far as I know, he'll be there at nine tomorrow."

I said good-bye to Primrose and rang Joe Greene.

"Greene's Tavern, where the elite meet. Joe Greene speakin'," Joe said.

"It's Lee Barrett, Joe," I said. "I'm worried about Thom. Have you heard anything?"

"Not a word. Guess I'll have to see about getting Duke to work Thom's schedule. I mean, until he turns up."

"Have you talked to Thom's mother?" I asked.

"Sure. Freaked the poor lady out. She thought he'd come to work as usual and spent the night here. He does that sometimes."

"She had no idea where he was?"

"Nope."

"Do you think he had enough money to leave town, Joe?"

"Well, he stopped by here yesterday morning and asked for his paycheck." He paused. "Besides that, he's been savin' for a long time. If he cashed in everything, he's got quite a lot."

"Thanks, Joe. You'll be sure to let me know if you hear anything, won't you?"

"Sure thing."

At least if Thom was in a strange place, he had enough money for a hotel room. That made me feel a little better. If we didn't hear from Thom soon, I'd get those models' numbers from Primrose and see if they'd heard from him.

Next puzzle piece. Who would sign a card "Ma" when the recipient's real mother was dead? A mother-in-law? No. Oliver Wendell Trumbull's mother would have been even older than Tabitha's. The captain's wife? Tabitha was in correspondence with her, at least to the extent of sending her money, most likely in the form of twenty-dollar gold pieces. They could very well have been on a greeting card–sending basis. Could the woman have been nicknamed "Ma"? Sometimes people with a lot of kids answer to the name, and we knew she had at least four. *Worth checking.*

What about that brown jacket? If it wasn't Bill's, whose was it? Somebody had dressed him in it, dragged him through the tunnel, and left him in the park. Maybe the police could find some evidence on the jacket, even though Mrs. Sullivan had laundered it so carefully.

At least I wouldn't have to worry about the green

car anymore. No doubt Mr. Pennington would be able
to walk right up to our front door from now on.

O'Ryan and I went downstairs together. Still in
pajamas, I picked up the Sunday *Globe* from the front
steps and started the coffeemaker, hoping for a normal
Sunday with aunt and cat—and without any more
random puzzle pieces. I prepared O'Ryan's breakfast,
poured myself a cup of coffee, and opened the paper.

"You two are up early." My aunt helped herself to a
cup and joined me at the kitchen table. "Didn't you
sleep well?"

"I'm okay," I said. "Just had a lot on my mind last
night. Mostly I was worried about Thom." I told her
about my conversations with Joe Greene and Primrose.

"He's a grown-up young man," she said. "Undoubtedly, he's just gone off to seek his fortune, as they used
to say. He'll get in touch with you soon, I'm sure. May
I please have the crossword puzzle section?"

I searched through the paper and pulled out the
Lifestyle section. As I handed it to her, a headline
caught my eye. BOSTON COIN COLLECTORS' CONVENTION
DRAWS CROWDS. A black-and-white photo at the head of
the column showed a group of people looking at a
display of coins.

"Wait a minute," I said. "Do we have a magnifying
glass?"

"Look in the junk drawer," she said.

I looked among the safety pins, paper clips, bottle
openers, pens, and pencils and found a big, long-
handled one worthy of Sherlock Holmes. "Perfect," I
said and held it over the photo. "Yes. I'm pretty sure
that's him."

"Who?" she asked, looking over my shoulder.

"I could be wrong," I admitted, "but that looks a lot
like Mr. Friedrich. The Treasury man we saw across

from the funeral home. What do you suppose he's doing there?"

"I suppose the Treasury Department has a particular interest in coins," she said, perfectly logically. "Or maybe he's just a collector. It's a very popular hobby, you know."

"Hmm. Maybe. But I'm going to fill out a card about it, anyway."

"Good idea," she said. "Will you get me a pen while you've got the junk drawer open?" Not too many people work the *Globe* crosswords in ink, but my aunt does. She looked up from the paper. "Funny how certain topics keep coming up in our conversations lately, isn't it?"

I nodded. "Uh-huh. Like coins."

"And President Roosevelt," she added.

"And the tunnels."

O'Ryan pushed his empty bowl to one side with his nose, meowed something that sounded very much like "Ma," and formed his long tail into a question mark.

"Right, O'Ryan," my aunt said, not looking up from her paper and without a trace of surprise in her voice. "Ma too."

"You sound as though you think he's really speaking English," I said, reluctant to admit that I had often thought the same thing.

"Of course he is," she said. "What other language would he know?"

I shook my head. "Want to drive over to the Chevy dealership and see my new car after breakfast?" I asked. "I can't pick it up until tomorrow, but I'd like to show it off."

"Love to," she said. "And you know what? I'd like to get a peek at Greene's Tavern, too. A lot of the build-

ings in that part of town date back to the seventeen
hundreds."

"Looks pretty old to me," I said. "And you can meet
Joe Greene. Interesting guy. Used to be a coal miner,
you know."

"Really? From coal miner to tavern host. Quite a
career switch."

"The coal mining was starting to affect his lungs," I
told her. "He and Kelly both feel better here."

"I imagine they would," she said. "Good New England salt air can do wonders."

"After we eat and get dressed," I said, "we'll go for a
ride and breathe some of it."

I was feeling pretty good about myself. I had the
sports car I'd always wanted, a volunteer position doing
something useful, a fine old home to live in, an aunt I
adored, a handsome man in my life, and even a most
remarkable cat. The weather felt almost springlike, the
robins had started to arrive from the south, and—
index cards be damned—my life in Salem at that
moment was sweet.

Aunt Ibby finished the crossword to her satisfaction—which meant correctly, in ink. I'd dressed in
jeans, a red sweater, and my NASCAR jacket, and
within the hour we were in the Buick, on the way to
visit the Corvette.

My salesman greeted us with a big smile, told Aunt
Ibby about the great trade-in possibilities of her Buick,
and escorted us to the detailing department, where my
car was getting what amounted to an automotive spa
treatment.

"Oh my, what a lovely color," she said. "You always
did look pretty in blue."

"Anybody would look good in this car," I said,

stepping back to admire it again. "I'll take you for a ride as soon as it's officially mine."

"I'll look forward to it," she said. "Shall we go to visit the Greenes now?"

With a promise to return on Monday to seal the deal, Aunt Ibby and I left the dealership and headed for Greene's Tavern.

We arrived just before noon. There were only a few cars in the parking lot, so I was quite sure Joe Greene would have time to talk with us before he got too busy with customers.

"What a charming building," Aunt Ibby said as we approached the door. "Mid-eighteen hundreds, I'd guess."

Joe was alone behind the bar, polishing glasses. He looked up when we entered. "Good morning, Ms. Barrett," he said. "Surprised to see you here so early."

"My aunt is interested in this handsome old building, Joe. Aunt Ibby, meet Joe Greene. Joe, this is my aunt, Isobel Russell."

Joe wiped his hands on his apron and reached across the bar to shake hands. "Welcome to Greene's Tavern, Miss Russell. Yep, me and Kelly, we really like the old place. I'll have Kelly show you around if you like."

"Thank you, Mr. Greene. How old is it? Do you know?" Aunt Ibby said.

"It says eighteen forty-something on the deed. Hey, Kelly!"

I hadn't seen her at first, but Kelly's head popped up from one of the booths. "What? Oh, hi, Ms. Barrett. Come back for your sunglasses?"

"Actually, I brought my aunt for a visit, but I'll take them. Thanks. Come meet her. She's interested in learning about your tavern."

Introductions made, Kelly began what sounded very much like a prepared speech. "The house was built in eighteen forty-three," she began. "It was the home of a Salem merchant and ship owner named Zephaniah Smith." She gestured for us to follow her toward the fireplace.

"You sound as though you've done this before," I said.

"Oh, sure. People ask about it all the time. I found an old script about the place all typed out when we first got here. I've read it so many times, I've got it memorized."

"Remarkable," Aunt Ibby said. "Was it always a tavern? I don't remember seeing it before."

"No. Just a house. This used to be the living room and the old kitchen." Her gesture included the length of the room. "Pa took out some walls and built the bar and the booths, and he cleared a whole bunch of trees in the backyard for a parking lot. It was a lot of work, huh, Pa?"

"Lots of work is right, honey," Joe said. "But the place had been pretty well maintained all those years. Taxes paid, lawn mowed, curtains in the windows."

"How fortunate you were to find such a place for sale," Aunt Ibby said.

"Oh, we didn't buy it," Kelly said. "Pa inherited it from Mamaw Greene."

Aunt Ibby and I looked at one another.

"Your grandmother owned it, Mr. Greene?" my aunt asked. "Was she a Salem girl?"

He shrugged and went back to polishing glasses. "Don't know where she got it. We didn't even know about it until Mamaw was dyin'. Anyway, it's ours now."

"Come on," Kelly said. "I'll tell you about the fireplace. It's made mostly from native fieldstone." Kelly tapped the massive mantelpiece. "And there's a stone wall all around the property that's made out of the same kind of rocks."

"It's a wonderful old fireplace," I said.

"Want to see upstairs?" Kelly asked. "That's where we live."

"Oh, we don't want to intrude on your private space," Aunt Ibby told her.

"It's okay. Isn't it, Pa?" Kelly had already headed for the narrow wooden staircase at the far end of the long room.

"Sure, honey. Take 'em up if you want to."

We followed Kelly up well-worn stair treads to the second story. Wide floorboards were accented by a colorful braided rug. Kelly pointed to a sofa upholstered in dark red.

"That's where Thom used to sleep when he stayed over. I'm so worried about him, Lee." Tears appeared in her bright blue eyes. "I tried to call his cell all night. It's just going to voicemail."

"We're all concerned, Kelly," I told her. "Primrose has a couple of New York phone numbers that might give us a lead, and I'm sure Pete will help us any way he can. Thom's going to be okay," I said, with more confidence than I felt.

"That's what Pa says." She wiped her eyes, then straightened her shoulders. "But you want to know about the house." She resumed her memorized lecture, explaining sills and lintels and soffits in detail as we moved from room to room. We finished up in the kitchen, where modern appliances shared space with a soapstone sink and a long maple harvest table.

"Thanks so much for the tour, Kelly," I said as we returned to the downstairs bar, where customers had begun to congregate. "I'm really impressed with your knowledge. You'll be able to contribute a lot to our Salem history project, I'm sure."

"I'll do my best," she said. "Wait a sec. I'll get your sunglasses out of the lost and found closet." She pulled open a tall closet door behind the bar and reached for a box on the top shelf. "Lots of glasses here, but yours are right on top." She pulled them out and handed them to me.

"Hey, Kel," called one of the customers. "I'm missing one of my jackets. I'm thinking I could have left it here."

"What jacket was that, Ronnie?" Kelly asked. "There's about a dozen of 'em in here." She slid wire hangers along the closet pole. "What color is yours?"

"Kind of brown," said Ronnie. "An old quilted brown jacket."

"Nope. Nothing like that here," she said. "You haven't seen it, have you, Pa?"

"Not that I can recall, honey," said Joe Greene. "You must have left it someplace else, Ronnie."

We said our good-byes to the Greenes and hurried across the parking lot, neither of us saying a word until we were inside the Buick.

"The brown jacket," I said. "What do you think? Is it the one they found on Bill?"

"A bit too much of a coincidence, isn't it?" she said. "I think Pete and your newfound friend Chief Whaley would appreciate hearing about this. Even if it *is* just a coincidence, they might want to talk to this Ronnie person."

"I think I'll call Pete now," I said. "Maybe he can get here before Ronnie leaves."

"I hope this won't cause Mr. Greene any trouble,"

Aunt Ibby said. "Such a nice man. It's the strangest thing, Maralee. I have a feeling that I've met him somewhere."

"I had the very same feeling the first time I saw him, too. But since I've never been to West Virginia, I'm sure we've never met."

Pete answered after a couple of rings. "Hi, Lee. What's up?"

I told him we'd picked up my sunglasses at Greene's Tavern and what we'd just heard about a missing quilted brown jacket. "I thought you and the chief would want to know about it," I said.

"Good going," he said. "Is the man still there?"

"We're still in the parking lot, and he hasn't come out."

"Okay. I'm coming over there right now. You two go along home," he said. "I'll call you later."

"Are you going to bring the jacket?" I asked. "To see if he can identify it?"

"Maybe," he said. "Now you two get going. No need for anyone to connect you to the cops showing up."

Aunt Ibby had already backed the Buick up. "We're on our way," I said. "Be sure to call and let us know what happens."

We did as Pete had suggested and went home. It wasn't as though we didn't have plenty to keep us occupied there. After a quick lunch of sandwiches, Aunt Ibby grabbed a tape measure and began measuring for draperies for one of the new third-floor rooms, while I headed for our bookshelf-lined study, in search of some more books about Salem. Each volume there was cataloged according to the Dewey decimal system, courtesy of my librarian aunt. I pulled open the drawer marked 900 – GEOGRAPHY AND HISTORY in the old wooden card catalog cabinet and found a handful of Salem history titles.

I selected half a dozen books, sat down behind Grandpa Forbes's old desk, and began to read. O'Ryan had followed me and found a patch of afternoon sunshine on the Oriental rug. He proceeded to give himself a good wash, then settled down for a nap.

The only sound was the ticking of the brass ship's clock on the wall and the whisper of pages being turned as I refreshed my knowledge about the Witch House, the Ropes Mansion, and the House of the Seven Gables. A slim volume of black-and-white photos offered reminders of long-ago Salem buildings—the beautiful Paramount Theater, the old Gothic-style train depot, the original Parker Brothers game factory—all gone in the name of progress.

"If it hadn't been for the government grants, the Trumbull building would be gone, too," I told the sleeping cat, who twitched his ears but kept his eyes closed. "I'll be sure to thank Councilor Wilson for his part in getting the funding to save the place."

It was when O'Ryan jumped up onto the desk and performed his favorite cat flop on top of the book I was reading that I realized that he'd run out of sunny spots and that darkness was approaching.

"Are you trying to tell me something?" I asked and was rewarded with a pink-tongued lick on my chin. "Okay. Enough reading."

Together the cat and I headed downstairs and rejoined Aunt Ibby.

"It's been an eventful day, hasn't it?" she asked. "I had pizza delivered. Want to just relax and watch a movie on TV?"

"Good idea," I said. "But I'll keep the phone handy. I can hardly wait to hear about what happened at the tavern when Pete went to find out about the brown jacket"

It wasn't long before the call came. Aunt Ibby hit the mute button in the middle of the first commercial as I picked up the phone.

"Hello, Pete," I said. "What happened? Did you go to the tavern?"

"Sure did," he said. "I told Joe I just happened to be in the neighborhood, and I thought I'd stop by to get your sunglasses."

"Good excuse."

"Kelly said you'd already come in and picked them up, so I said something like, 'I guess people are always leaving things here,' and right away this guy Ronnie spoke up, complaining about his lost brown jacket."

"So did you tell him you knew where it was?" I asked. "Did you bring it with you?"

"Nope. I told him we have a ton of lost and found down at the station, which is true. I told him if he'd like to take a look, I'd give him a ride over and back."

"So did you?"

"Yep. He came right along with me. I put the coat on a hanger, wrinkled it up a little, and showed it to him. He ID'd it right away. Wanted to know where it was found."

"What did you tell him?"

"I told him somebody found it down by the marina."

"Well," I said, "that was kind of true, too."

"Of course it was. So I asked him if he could remember leaving it around there."

"Did he?"

"Not exactly. But he did admit that he sometimes drank in several other bars in the neighborhood besides Greene's Tavern," Pete said. "Could have left it in any one of them."

"Oh, wow. That doesn't help much, does it? Did you give it back to him?"

"No. Couldn't do that. I told him he'd have to talk to the chief because his jacket might be involved in a case we're working on. He wasn't too happy about that."

"You don't think Ronnie had anything to do with what happened to Bill, do you?" I asked.

Pete sighed. "At this point, I don't know what to think, Lee. We'll just keep the investigation going, no matter how long it takes. Bill got from the basement of the store to the park near the waterfront somehow, and now it's our job to put all the pieces together."

Put all the pieces together. That's what I'm trying to do, too. If I could find just a few pieces that fit into one another, I'd have a clue about what the picture on the front of the puzzle box was supposed to look like. So far, nothing.

CHAPTER 24

I dressed extra carefully for Monday's class, not so much because an important representative of city hall was going to be there, but because Pete was. I decided to borrow the Buick, too.

"I'll bring your car back at noon," I told Aunt Ibby. "Then, if you'll give me a lift to the dealership, I'll pick up the Corvette."

I skipped breakfast at home, deciding instead to grab a quick bite at the diner. I was nearly an hour early for the nine o'clock class when I parked the Buick in my assigned space. The anticipated arrival of Jonathan Wilson for the morning session had apparently inspired some special housecleaning efforts at the Tabby. The grand staircase, wide bannisters and all, shone from a recent buffing. The tables and chairs, the monitors, and the whiteboard in my classroom fairly sparkled. A new potted philodendron had appeared on my desk, and the giant patent leather pump glowed with reflected light from the ceiling fixtures.

Assured that all was shipshape for the great man, I headed for the diner. The before-school crowd was there, mostly students and instructors. I looked around for my group.

"Hey, Lee! Over here." I recognized Primrose's voice and spotted most of my class crowded into one booth. Therese, Sammy, and Kelly sat on one side, with Primrose and Duke on the other. Duke drew his lanky frame closer to the window, while Primrose moved to the center, patting the space next to her. "Come on. Sit with us."

"Big day, huh?" Duke said. "We get to listen to a big shot from city hall."

"Be nice," I told him. "I've heard that he's pretty much responsible for getting our funding."

"Maybe we can get a few extra bucks for our project." Duke pretended to punch Primrose's arm. "The lady has come up with some expensive ideas."

Primrose smiled and gave a thumbs-up. Gone were the miniskirt and the cleavage-revealing top. Primrose wore a gray pin-striped pantsuit, and her platinum hair was neatly pulled back with a silver barrette.

"I bet he'll be impressed," Kelly said, "but I wish Thom was here with us."

I changed the subject. "What's everybody having for breakfast? What's good?"

A chorus of good-natured replies broke the tension as the waitress appeared to take our orders, and before long the normal chatter between classmates resumed.

By 8:45 a.m., breakfast was finished and we were gathered in the classroom, where a few more changes had been made. Mr. Pennington's podium now stood in front of my desk, and two rows of vintage chairs were lined up, facing it.

"I guess we're supposed to sit here, huh?" Sammy sat in the first row, directly in front of the podium.

"I hate these little seats," Duke said, slouching into

a chair in the back row, with a glance at his favorite, much larger chair behind the news desk.

Primrose took the seat closest to the rear, and Therese and Kelly sat side by side next to Sammy. I looked toward the mezzanine entrance, expecting to see Pete at any minute. The new furniture arrangement was confusing. If I sat at my desk, I'd be behind the speaker's back. Apparently, I was expected to sit in the audience with the others.

I walked to the back of the room, where I'd have a clear view of the staircase and could watch for the arrival of our guest. It was a couple of minutes before nine when I spotted Pete bounding up the stairs, two at a time, looking more like a student than a detective. In jeans and a sport coat, with an open-collared white shirt, he fit right in with the students milling around on the first floor below. I was so busy looking at Pete, I completely missed the councilman's entrance. Accompanied by Mr. Pennington, he had arrived via the elevator from the second floor.

Jonathan Wilson was a good-looking man, and he undoubtedly knew it. His golden tan, in midwinter Massachusetts, had to be either sprayed on or of the tanning bed variety. He had good hair, brown and wavy, with the perfect amount of gray at the temples.

Mr. Pennington went straight to the podium and gave an open-palmed gesture indicating that everyone should stand. Pete got there just in time to stand in the second row, next to Primrose, while I moved forward, right hand extended, to greet the councilman.

His handshake was firm; his smile, genuine. It was easy to see why Salem, including my aunt Ibby, had voted for him.

"Ms. Barrett," he said. "Thank you so much for allowing me this opportunity to address your students.

The creation of the Tabitha Trumbull Academy has been my dream for a long time. Inviting all of you to accompany me on what I think may be an exciting journey into Salem's past is a rare privilege, indeed."

"You're most welcome," I said. "And we thank you for all you've done to save this beautiful building."

"My pleasure," he said and then joined Mr. Pennington at the podium, passing Primrose on the way without so much as a sideways glance, while I slipped into the back row and stood beside Pete.

"You may be seated," the director said. "Let us proceed. With us this morning is a man who needs no introduction, city councilor Jonathan Wilson, whose considerable influence in Washington, D.C., was largely responsible for the creation of this school. His words will surely provide a noteworthy addition to our Salem history documentary—which, as you know, is required as a condition of the NEA grant he was instrumental in obtaining for us."

"Thank you, Mr. Pennington." A smiling Wilson lifted a slim briefcase, placed it on the podium, and lowered his voice. "What I have in this briefcase is the only copy of an artifact that, I believe, has not been photographed or duplicated in any way for many years. I intend to share it with you. I believe it to be a rough, hand-drawn map of some area of Salem." He tapped the top of the briefcase. "It is my hope that by identifying the unmarked streets and roads on the map, we can figure out exactly the area it depicts, and then we may be able to recover valuable government property that has been lost for several decades." His pause was dramatic. "If we can do it, your contribution to the great city of Salem, and, indeed, to the United States of America, may be significant."

Sammy raised his hand and voiced the obvious

question. "Why don't you just get a current map and match up the streets and roads on your map?"

"Of course I've done that," the councilman said. "And bearing in mind Salem's extensive urban renewal projects, I know that the topography of the city has changed over the years."

"I don't get it. Why are you going to show it to us?" Therese wanted to know. "Most of us can't even find our way around Salem yet. How can we help?"

"Because I have reason to believe that the map is in some way connected to the Trumbull family. When I heard about your history project, I realized that the six of you could supply the extra eyes and ears this investigation needs." His broad gesture took in all of us, and I realized that not knowing Thom was absent, he probably thought Pete was the sixth student.

"If it's that big a deal, why doesn't the city just go for it?" Duke said.

"Because," said the councilman, "they don't know anything about it yet."

Jonathan Wilson's pronouncement was met with silence. Even the voluble Mr. Pennington didn't speak. The *thump-thump* of dancing feet from the floor above was the only sound in the room, until Primrose stood and, hands on hips, demanded, "But you can't do that! You can't just turn over some kind of government document to this bunch of amateurs."

That shocked Mr. Pennington out of his momentary loss of words. "Miss McDonald! A little decorum, please. I'm sure Councilor Wilson will elucidate his position."

"Primrose," I heard Pete whisper. "Cool it."

The blonde sat, her expression sullen, and I stood, prepared to apologize for the disruption.

"Mr. Wilson," I began, "I'm sure Primrose—Miss

McDonald—meant no offense, but perhaps you could give us a little more detail before we sign on to anything. We need your assurance that this project is completely . . . well, legal."

"It is indeed, Ms. Barrett." He pushed a small gold key into the briefcase's lock, turned it, and opened the case a crack. "I came by the document honestly, I assure you. I found it, quite unexpectedly, while doing some routine research at city hall on maps of various Trumbull properties in the geographic information department. I made a copy of it, along with some other less important papers, not realizing what it might be until much later." He opened the briefcase wider and removed a single sheet of paper.

Sammy, who was closest to the podium, leaned so far forward, he nearly fell from his chair. The councilman lifted the paper above Sammy's line of vision.

"I'll let all of you see it in just a moment. But please know that I'm telling you all this in confidence. If this is as important a find as I think it may be, and if the city benefits as much as I believe it will, you'll all be heroes."

"Sure. But what's in it for you?" Duke asked.

Jonathan Wilson smiled. "They'll probably elect me mayor," he said, "but that's not why I think this project is important."

"Wouldn't it be easier to turn the information over to the other members of the council?" Pete asked. "It seems like something they'd like to be involved in."

"True enough. But there's a real possibility that I'm completely wrong about this. It may be nothing. A council investigation that turns up nothing would be hard to live down. But a school project flies under the radar, so to speak. What do you say? Are you people in?

It could make your documentary something of real value."

Kelly was the first to respond. "I think it'd be cool. I think we should do it."

"Ms. Barrett?" The councilman looked at me. "What do you think? It couldn't do any harm, and it surely adds a new dimension to something you're already working on."

I knew he was right about that. "May we see the map?" I asked. "Then we'll talk about it among ourselves and let you know what we decide."

"Fair enough," he said. "You may pass by, one person at a time, and look at it." He placed the paper on my desk. "But there will be no surreptitious cell phone photos." The councilman continued, "As I said, I believe this is the only copy. I'd like to keep it that way for the time being. Meanwhile, if anything on this map rings a bell with any of you, please let me know. I'll give you each my card, including my private number."

We lined up like kids at a water fountain during recess and approached the desk one at a time. Since I was last in line, I could watch each person's reaction.

Sammy was the first to view the paper. He leaned close to the desk, his eyes darting back and forth as he studied the map. "Are you sure it's right side up?" he asked. "There's no north point here."

"It may not be," Mr. Wilson admitted. "I don't know. You may turn it around if you want to."

"No, that's okay," Sammy said. "C'mon, Therese. Your turn."

Therese stood at the desk, leaned forward, and looked down at the paper. Then she closed her eyes, touched a spot on her forehead with her right hand, and backed away quickly. It was Kelly's turn next. She moved the paper in a circular motion, viewing it from all angles, then pointed at something on it and looked at Jonathan Wilson. She seemed about to speak but shook her head and returned to her seat.

Primrose took her turn, followed by Pete. Primrose barely glanced at the paper, then glared at the councilman and walked to the back of the room, where she leaned against a row of file cabinets, still scowling. Pete, like Kelly, turned the paper around, then put it back in its original position. Then it was my turn.

It was, as Jonathan Wilson had described it, a rough drawing, probably done with pencil. There were lines, some curved and some straight, that seemed to represent streets or roads, and there were some squares here and there along the lines, which I decided must mean buildings. As Sammy had pointed out, there was no indication of direction. In fact, there were no words on the thing at all. But when I looked closely, I could see a faded number on a small square. It was a six or a nine, depending on which way one viewed the map. To the left of the numbered square, there were some crude stick figure things that looked like Christmas trees and a circle with a dollar sign in it. Like most everything else I'd looked at that was related to the Trumbulls, it made no sense.

We each received a business card with the promised personal number scrawled on the back. Mr. Pennington accepted one, too, although he hadn't looked at the map. Jonathan Wilson, still smiling, returned the map to his briefcase, placed the gold key in his breast pocket, and followed the director to the elevator. He shook hands with each of us as he passed. Primrose managed to return his smile and received an extra-long handclasp.

At the elevator door, he turned to face us. "Thank you all for your kind attention," he said. "Please consider this challenge carefully. It may lead to an exciting adventure for all of us." He shrugged well-tailored shoulders. "On the other hand, it may lead nowhere at all. But it would still be an adventure." He waved and the elevator door slid shut.

"What a nice guy." Kelly was enthusiastic. "I think we should help him out if we can."

"He seems nice, sure," Therese agreed, "but do we have time to fool around with that old map and still get our own work done?"

"Oh, I don't know," Duke said. "I kinda like the looks of that little dollar sign."

"I'm with you on that, brother," Sammy said. "Looks like an old-fashioned treasure map to me. Except it's got no skull and crossbones."

"Speaking of maps, Sammy," I said. "You left your book here on Friday." I pulled the top desk drawer open, took out the *Massachusetts Atlas and Gazetteer,* and handed it to him. "And what do you think about it, Pete?" I asked. "Is there anything wrong with our looking into this map thing?"

"Nothing illegal, if that's what you mean. The map itself is apparently a matter of public record. Looks like it's been lying around for years over at city hall and nobody's bothered to try to figure it out until now." He looked closely at the card Jonathan Wilson had handed him, turned it over, then put it in his wallet. "And, like the man said, it may not lead anywhere at all."

"So you think it will be all right for us to get involved with it?" Primrose asked. "It's not going to get him—or us—into any trouble with anybody?"

"That depends," Pete said. "If there's private property involved, naturally, you can't trespass."

Kelly glanced at the business card, which she still

held in her hand. "Now that I've got his number, I'm going to call him up."

"Remember, he's a busy man," I warned. "I'll ask him to come back and speak to us again, and we can prepare questions ahead of time." I saw Pete look at his watch. "Pete, you're busy, too. I know you have to leave. Thanks for coming."

"It was interesting. Thanks for inviting me." He headed toward the stairs. "See you guys. I'll call you later, Lee."

I waved, said, "Later," and turned back to face the class.

"Can we put the room back the way it was now?" Duke asked. "This little chair is killing my back."

"Sure. Everybody sit where you're comfortable. Duke? Primrose? Do you want to use Mr. Pennington's podium for your presentation, or should we put it on the mezzanine landing?"

"I guess we'll keep it," Primrose said. "I'm going to do the talking, but we worked together on the script."

There was a little flurry of activity as the podium was moved to one side. Duke took his regular seat behind the news desk, and Primrose stepped to the podium, facing the rest of us, and shuffled a thick sheaf of papers.

"Here goes," she said. "We've found quite a few old pictures to illustrate our script. Duke's going to put them up on a monitor while I read what we've got so far."

A vintage black-and-white photo showing the exterior of Trumbull's Department Store flashed on the big monitor screen.

"Oh, wow. Look at the cool old cars parked out front," Kelly said. "When was that taken, Primrose?"

Primrose read from her script. "People came from

miles around when we opened the store. It was a cool fall day in nineteen twenty-seven."

The room was silent as Primrose continued to read. She and Duke had prepared their script as though the store's founders, Oliver Wendell Trumbull and his wife, Tabitha, were telling the story. More photos flashed on the screen from time to time as she read. Women with boyish figures in the slim flapper fashions of the twenties. Interior photos of the store, showing prices so low, they brought a collective gasp from the group.

"Look at that," I heard Therese whisper. "Those cute T-strap shoes were only two dollars!"

The presentation took nearly an hour, and Primrose closed with an explanation of the time line involved. "We've taken it only from the store's opening up to just before the Second World War," she said. "There's a bunch more we need to research, and we have a lot more pictures, too. Mr. Pennington found these for us. Duke, want to run through a few more of them, just to show what else we have?" Primrose returned to her seat beside Therese amid well-deserved applause as pictures continued to appear on the monitor screen.

"Primrose and Duke, you two have done a great job," I said. "This documentary is going to be outstand—" I stopped midsentence when a photo of a woman in a long white dress flashed by.

"Duke," I said. "Can you back that up, please? To the picture of the woman?"

"Sure," he said. "This one?"

For a moment I couldn't answer. I stared at the screen and, hardly recognizing my own voice, breathed, "Who is she?"

Primrose looked at the screen. "Her? That's Tabitha Trumbull. It's her wedding picture. Great dress, isn't it?"

It was more than a great dress. It was satin, with a high collar. The sleeves were puffy at the top, tight from the elbows down. The woman had long dark hair and a shy smile. I'd found my mystery woman. She of the long white dress, the keys, and the tunnel was a young Tabitha Trumbull. I looked around the classroom. There was no one there for me to share the amazing revelation with. In fact, besides River North and Aunt Ibby, there was no one I *could* share it with. At least no one who wouldn't think I was crazy.

The clock over the news desk told me that we had about fifteen minutes before the noon lunch break. "I'm going to dismiss you a little early," I said. I was faster than my students in heading for the exit. "Gotta run. Picking up my new car."

That was true, but foremost on my mind was the photo of Tabitha in her wedding dress and my need to share this new information with someone who'd understand.

I called River as soon as I was inside the Buick. "River," I said when she answered. "The woman in my vision is Tabitha. I saw a photo of her in her wedding dress. It's the dress she was wearing when I saw her in the tunnel with those keys. But she's young, not a crazy old lady."

"Wow! I was hoping it would be her." She was clearly as excited as I was. "You've got to get us all up to that top floor. To contact her. It'll take the whole coven to do it."

To actually contact the spirit of a dead woman only I could see?

"How, exactly, would you do that? Would you be able to talk to her? Would you all see her the way I do?"

"I think so. I've never done it myself, but I know there's a way to do it," she said. "I guess Megan would lead, because she knew Tabitha on the physical plane."

"That makes sense," I said, knowing perfectly well that it didn't make any sense at all. None of this did.

"Sure it does. You get Mr. Pennington to say we can do it, and I'll get in touch with the coven." She paused. "And listen, Lee, I'm going to ask my boss at WICH-TV to send a film crew. I think he'll go for it. Big ratings."

"Wait a minute. You can't tell anybody about . . . you know . . . the things I've seen."

"Of course not." She sounded indignant. "I would never do that. Half the people in Salem already think the place is haunted, anyway. Heck, some of 'em think the whole city is. This'll just be an investigation into who the woman in white is."

"I'll talk to Mr. Pennington," I said, starting the Buick's engine. "I have to go now. I want to tell Aunt Ibby about it, and I'm going to pick up my new car."

"Okay. And, Lee, don't worry," she said. "It's the right thing to do. Remember, you helped Ariel to cross over by catching her killer. Maybe you can help Tabitha to move on, too."

Aunt Ibby didn't see things quite the same way River did. "The dress in the photo matching the dress on the woman you've seen in those visions of yours does seem to indicate that you've been seeing a young Tabitha," she said. "But don't you think involving a coven of witches is a bit . . . exploitative?"

"I guess it is," I admitted. "But Mr. Pennington will probably like the publicity for the school, and maybe the witches can figure out how to get poor Tabitha out of the Trumbull building and on to wherever she's supposed to go next."

She looked dubious about that but nodded her head and changed the subject. "So how was your speaker this morning?"

"Interesting," I said. "He brought us what he claims is the only copy of an old Salem map. He wants us to help him figure out what part of the city it represents. There aren't any street names, just some square building shapes. One of them has a number on it."

"Another mystery. And is there any further word on young Thom?"

"I'm afraid not. Joe Greene spoke to his mom, and she didn't even realize that Thom hadn't gone to work."

"It must be a dreadful feeling, not knowing where your child is," she said. "I feel so blessed to have you here, safe with me."

I gave her a quick hug, then handed her the keys to the Buick. "I parked out front so we can leave right away to get my car. I have only an hour before I have to be back at the school."

"Let's go," she said. "I'll have you there in a jiffy."

Sometimes my aunt has a bit of a heavy foot, and we reached the dealership with time to spare.

"I'll just drop you off, dear," she said. "I'm going to put in a little time at the library."

"Thanks for the ride," I said. "I'll see you at home later."

"Oh, by the way," she said as I was about to close the car door. "There was a little piece in the *Globe* this morning about that coin show."

"Really? What about it? Was that Mr. Friedrich's picture in the paper?"

"The article didn't mention him, but it said that the dealers had been given special instructions to get photo identification from everyone selling gold coins. Seems there have been some turning up around here that the Treasury Department is interested in."

Coins again. Bill was looking for silver ones. Friedrich was looking for gold ones. Tabitha gave away twenty-dollar ones. What did it all mean?

The sight of my new Corvette parked in front of the showroom, top down, sunlight glinting on sweet sweeping curves, chased all the puzzling thoughts away. I filled out the usual paperwork, arranged for the transfer of funds from my bank to the dealership for payment in full, and the Laguna Blue beauty was all mine.

If I skipped lunch, I'd have time to drive around for a while before heading back to the Tabby. A Corvette ride beat an egg salad sandwich any day. I headed down Derby Street toward the Willows, where Pete and I had shared breakfast. There wouldn't be much traffic, and a short ride beside the beach, with the radio blaring rock and roll, the sun on my face, and the wind in my hair, would be fun.

It was fun. Of course, the wind in my hair completely destroyed the chignon I'd fashioned so carefully, but that didn't matter. I was happily driving toward the park exit when I noticed a black Camry partially hidden by the low-hanging branches of a willow tree.

The branches didn't hide the occupants of the car. Primrose and Jonathan Wilson, together again.

I was sure they'd noticed me. Who wouldn't notice a wild-haired redhead in a convertible with Michael Jackson's "Billie Jean" blasting from a ten-speaker audio system with a bass box and subwoofers?

I turned down the radio, pretended to look the other way, and left the park at a decorous pace, heading back toward the school. When I reached the Tabby, I brushed my hair into some sort of order, put the Corvette top up, and got out.

Should I pretend I hadn't seen Primrose and Jonathan Wilson? Or should I confront her and ask what was going on? As it turned out, I didn't have to make that decision. Primrose was the first of the students to arrive for the afternoon session. The conservative pin-striped number she'd worn in the morning had been replaced with one of the miniskirt outfits. She pulled a chair up opposite mine, put her elbows on the desk, looked me in the eye, and said, "Lee, I guess we have to talk. Coffee in the diner after school?"

"Good idea," I said. "I'll meet you there."

My afternoon lesson plan involved some of the technical aspects of the documentary preparation. We used the school-supplied textbooks to study the proper script format, then did some classroom experiments with a fixed camera versus the handheld variety. We decided that the Trumbull story would be most effective if we used the handheld camera and a direct cinema technique, something like they did in *The Blair Witch Project*.

"I loved that movie," Therese declared. "Just loved it."

Of course you did, I thought.

Sammy clipped a lapel mic to his shirt and read Oliver Trumbull's first few speeches from Primrose and Duke's rough script. Therese did the same, reading Tabitha's parts. I was happily impressed with both of their performances. Even at this early stage of production, the proposed documentary showed promise.

"They sound perfect," Kelly said. "But they don't *look* like the real Trumbulls."

"I know," I said. "I'd thought that you and Thom

would play Oliver and Tabitha in tableau mode, while Sammy and Therese told the story. But now that Thom's not here, I don't know. Duke's much too tall. Maybe we'll have to recruit someone from the acting class."

"You mean you don't think he's ever coming back?" Kelly started to tear up again.

"No. Of course I don't think that." I tried to reassure her. "But what if Thom's managed to find work in New York? We have to have a plan B."

"Don't cry, Kelly," Primrose said. "I'm going to call some model friends of mine in the city and see if they've heard from him. I'm sure he's all right."

Kelly accepted a tissue and returned to the study of how to formulate a TV script, while I struggled to formulate some questions I could ask Primrose at our planned after-school meeting.

"Ms. Barrett! Fabulous news!" I looked up, surprised to see Mr. Pennington hurrying into the classroom.

"That's always good to hear," I said, hoping it was about Thom. "What news is that?"

"I just got a telephone call from Bruce Doan," he said. "He's the manager of WICH-TV, you know."

"Yes. I know."

"He's interested in producing a TV show right here at the Tabitha Trumbull Academy."

That pronouncement grabbed everyone's attention. Books snapped shut. Cameras stopped mid-frame. Voices and sniffles ceased. Rupert Pennington had center stage.

"We are going to—if you all agree to participate, that is—host an entire coven of our brothers and sisters of the Wiccan persuasion, witches, that is, as they attempt to contact a spirit, ghost, that is, on the top floor of this very building." A dramatic pause followed. "And the entire episode will be filmed for the viewing pleasure of millions."

Everyone spoke at once.

"When?"

"Will we be in it?"

"*Real* witches?"

Mr. Pennington held up his hands. "I'll present all the details later," he said, glancing at the clock. "You are all dismissed. Ms. Barrett, will you come with me?"

I picked up my purse and followed him to the elevator. "This could put the Tabitha Trumbull Academy on the theatrical map," he said. "Such a production might even draw a national audience, according to Mr. Doan. Think of it, Ms. Barrett!"

I was thinking of it. What if they did actually contact the long-dead Tabitha? Would I find out at last what it was she wanted from me? What the two keys meant?

"Sit down, Ms. Barrett," he said. "Be at ease, and tell me what you think of Mr. Doan's idea."

River North's idea.

"A TV show about a coven of witches gathering here at the Tabby would certainly bring attention to the school," I said truthfully. "And it *is* the type of TV people seem to enjoy."

"I'm glad you agree," he said. "So we'll proceed with it?"

"Won't you have to check with the city? They may not want that type of attention."

"You're correct, of course. I'll call Councilman Wilson first thing tomorrow and get his input. But I'm sure we're doing the right thing."

"I hope so."

"Be always sure you're right—then go ahead." He followed the words with the expectant look I'd seen before.

"Movie quote?" I asked.

"I admit, it's a bit obscure. *Davy Crockett, King of the Wild Frontier.* Fess Parker. 1955. Even your dear aunt might have missed that one."

CHAPTER 25

Skipping the elevator, I hurried down the stairs to the diner and my appointment with Primrose. She was already there, sitting alone in a booth, with enough books and papers spread over the surface of the table to discourage anyone from sharing the space. She looked up as I approached, and swept the papers aside.

"Hi, Lee. Sit. I'll try to explain."

"I don't want to pry into your business, Primrose," I said. "You don't owe me any explanations."

But I sure am curious.

"Well, here it is in a nutshell, Lee. Jonathan and I have met before."

"I figured that might be the case the first time I saw you together."

She frowned. "The first time? You mean you've seen us together before today? When?"

"The morning after you spent the night at our place. Pete and I had breakfast at the same restaurant you two did," I said. "We sat in the booth right in front of yours."

She smiled. "Damned high-backed booths. Could you hear what we were talking about?"

"Nope. Too noisy for that."

"Okay. Here goes. We met years ago in Washington, D.C. We both had State Department jobs. Mine was a much lower level than his. Minimum security clearance. A glorified file clerk, that's what I was. Anyway, we had kind of a thing going on." She shrugged. "Kind of a big thing, actually."

"I understand. That happens."

"I didn't look like this then," she said, looking down at her skimpy outfit. "Anyway, he was married. Still is."

"Uh-oh."

"Yeah, uh-oh is right. We decided we should break it off. And we did. Honest to God, Lee, I about fainted when I saw him at the Tabby on opening day. That's why I beat it out of there so fast."

"I wondered about that," I said.

"I had to duck out before he had a chance to recognize me. Blow my cover."

"Your *cover?* What kind of cover?"

"I can't explain it entirely. I work for the government. I'm here on an assignment." She raised both hands in a gesture of helplessness. "I can't tell you much more than that."

"Is Primrose McDonald your real name?"

That brought a smile to her face. "No, it isn't. And blond isn't my real hair color."

"So you contacted Wilson and told him . . . what?"

"The truth about why I'm here. It's a big coincidence that we both wound up in the same place again."

River doesn't believe in coincidences.

"You seemed annoyed when he suggested that the class get involved with that old map he showed us."

"I was," she said. "I don't know anything about that map, but I thought it was dumb to involve us in city business. He explained it to me, but I still don't like it."

"I guess you're not going to tell me about that, either, are you?"

"Can't. But don't worry about it too much. It'll probably work out fine."

"Primrose," I said, "is it all right with you if I tell Pete what you've told me? He's already been checking on your background. Seems you have none."

"I know. We didn't have a lot of time to set this up. I was happily looking at flower seeds in an Ace Hardware store in New York's beautiful Hudson Valley when the call came. Next thing I knew, I was on a plane, heading for Massachusetts, with four suitcases full of miniskirts, hair dye, great shoes, and push-up bras."

I had to smile. "Flower seeds. Is that where Primrose came from?"

She nodded. "Right across the street from a McDonald's. They were in a hurry to get going on my fake ID. I guess it might be okay for Pete to know about this so he'll stop digging into it. I'll ask Friedrich to fill Pete in."

"Friedrich?" That surprised me. "He's part of this, too?"

"Oh yeah. I'm kind of on loan to the Treasury." She gathered her scattered papers and books and tucked them into a backpack. "Please don't ask any more questions. I may have talked too much already. Let's get that coffee now, okay?"

And that was that. She signaled to the waitress. We ordered our coffees, and the conversation became a normal chat between student and teacher.

I had a lot on my mind when I drove home from the Tabby. I pulled into the garage and hurried through the backyard to the house.

"Aunt Ibby, I'm home," I called. I bent to pat O'Ryan and was treated to a welcoming "mrrow."

My aunt answered from the kitchen. "Hello, Maralee. Come right on in, dear. I've made your dinner, and it's in the warming oven."

"Thanks," I said, shedding boots and coat and entering the warm, fragrant room. "You look lovely. You going out?"

She patted "fresh from the beauty shop" hair and did a graceful turn, flaring the skirt of her soft green, long-sleeved dress. "You like it? It's new. I have a date."

"It's perfect." I knew without asking who her date was, but I asked, anyway. "Who's the lucky guy?"

"It's Rupert," she said, blushing just a tiny bit. "We're going to a special screening of *My Dinner with Andre*. It's one of my favorites, and Rupert was an extra in that film—a patron in the restaurant scene."

"Sounds like fun," I said, attempting enthusiasm. "When is he picking you up?"

She consulted the tiny gold wristwatch with real diamonds marking the twelve and the six. I remembered it from my earliest childhood. She wore it only on very special occasions. "Any minute now," she said. "You don't mind being alone, do you?"

"Of course not. O'Ryan is here. You run along and have a good time." I laughed. "Oh, Aunt Ibby, I sound like you, talking to me!"

"Yes, you do. I've taught you well. Look, there goes O'Ryan, heading for the front door." She picked up her purse and followed the cat. "Rupert must be here already."

I brought up the rear of the parade, then joined O'Ryan at one of the long windows beside the door. My aunt was right. Rupert Pennington stood on the brightly lit landing, smiling, impeccably dressed, pressing the doorbell.

I reached for the doorknob, but Aunt Ibby held up a finger. "Wait a second." She shrugged into her beige cashmere coat. "Let it ring once more. I don't want to appear anxious."

O'Ryan, apparently not interested in Aunt Ibby's gentleman caller, gave a little sniff and strolled back toward the kitchen.

I gave her a hug, let the bell chime one more time, opened the door, and wished them both a pleasant evening. Resisting the strong temptation to add, "I'll wait up for you, Isobel," I watched as he took her arm and helped her down the stairs, pretty much the same way Pete liked to help me.

I had picked up my purse and was headed up to my room when my cell phone buzzed. Duke Martin's name popped up. Surprised, and with the missing Thom still on my mind, I said, "Duke? Is everything okay?"

"Oh, sure," he said. "I'm fine. Listen, Lee, I'm here at the bar, still filling in for Thom, and I got to thinking about that map. The one Mr. Wilson showed us."

"Yes, Duke. What about it?"

"Well, when I was looking at it, I knew it reminded me of something I'd seen before," he said. "Something recent."

"What was that, Duke?"

"The maps of the Boston subway system," he said. "I'm not sayin' that's what it is. But I think it's a map of something like that. Something underground."

"The tunnels," I said, knowing that he was right. "It's a map of tunnels under Salem."

"Yep," he said. "I reckon."

"I think you're right, Duke. Have you called Mr. Wilson yet?"

"Nope. Wanted to run it by you first."

"I think he'd want to hear your idea. It's not too late to call him now," I said. "Go for it."

"I will. Thanks, Ms. Barrett," he said. "I'm going to call him as soon as I get a break. We're busy tonight."

"Duke, is Primrose there?" I asked.

"Sure is. Want to talk to her?"

I sat on the bottom step and fished a pen and an index card from my purse. "Yes, please," I said. "She has a couple of phone numbers she offered to share with me."

"Okay. Hang on." I could hear music and muted conversation while Duke managed the phone handoff, and then Primrose answered.

"Hi, Lee," she said. "What's going on?"

"I forgot to ask for the phone numbers of those models you know in the city," I said. "I think I'll give them a call and see if either one has heard from Thom."

"Sure." She repeated the 212 area code numbers and I jotted them down on the card. "I've called them both and left messages on their voice mails so they'll know we're trying to track Thom down," she said, "and I left word that you might call. Maybe you'll have better luck."

"I hope so," I said. "Are the others there tonight?"

"Kelly and Duke are working, and Sammy and Therese are glued to the keno game. Why don't you drive those fancy wheels over here and keep me company?"

I laughed. "That's tempting," I said. "But I haven't even changed my clothes yet. I just want to put on sweats and sneakers and play couch potato with my cat."

"Sounds boring," she said. "See you at school."

I did exactly what I'd told her I wanted to do. Before

long, comfortably dressed and shod, I leaned against plumped-up couch cushions and put my feet on an ottoman, while O'Ryan paced back and forth along the back of the couch.

"Come on, cat. Settle down," I said. "We have things to do."

I called the first number on the index card and got the same response Primrose had. Voice mail. The perky voice announced that Tasha was on a shoot and that I should leave my name and number and a brief message and she would get back to me soon. I did as she asked, and hoped that she would.

I called the second number, and the phone rang for such a long time, I assumed that the voice mail was full. I was about to hang up when a tiny click told me that someone in New York City had picked up the phone.

"Hello?" I said. "Hello? Is anybody there?"

Long pause. Then a hesitant voice. "Ms. Barrett? Is that you?"

"Thom?"

"Yes. It's me. I recognized your number."

"Thom, what in the world is going on? Everyone here is worried sick about you." Relief, all mixed up with anger, flooded over me. "Are you all right? What are you doing there?"

"Tasha and Mira are on a shoot in Barbados. Mira said I could stay here and watch her cat," he said.

"That's fine, Thom," I said, trying to speak calmly. "But what I meant was, why did you run off like that without telling anyone? Your poor mother must be going crazy, and Kelly is close to tears all the time."

"I had to get away from there." His voice broke. "I'm sorry if everyone is worried. I couldn't stay there, knowing . . . knowing what I know."

"I don't understand," I said. "What is it you think you know?"

"That poor man. He didn't walk to the park by himself that night."

"That's what the police think," I said.

"Huh." He made a short, unfunny laughing sound. "The police think they know everything. But they don't."

I tried for a normal tone. "Would you like to tell me about it, Thom? Maybe I can help somehow."

"No. I'll never tell anyone. I promised, so I can't tell. But I went to his funeral, Lee. I heard his wife crying." Thom's voice dropped to a whisper. "It was terrible."

"I know, Thom," I said. "I was there. I knew you were sad, and I tried to find you afterward, but you were gone."

"I ran away," he said, his voice becoming stronger. "And I'm not coming back. Will you give my mother a message? And Kelly, too? Just tell them I'm fine. Not to worry."

"Of course I will. But please listen to me. This isn't a good way to handle things. Would you like to talk to Pete about what it is you think you know about Bill getting to the park that night?"

"No. No police." He was almost shouting. "I shouldn't have talked to you, Lee. I thought you might understand, but you don't. No one does."

I tried to speak soothing words, to tell him that everything could be worked out. But I was talking to dead air. He'd hung up.

"I have to call Pete," I said aloud. "And Thom's mother. And Kelly."

O'Ryan had stopped his pacing and now sat on the ottoman, where I'd put the phone and the index card with the telephone numbers on it. He put a big paw on the card and flipped it onto the floor. There was writing on the back. The card I'd pulled at random from the stack in my purse read, *Who are the three drunks singing Christmas carols?*

"Is that what you think Thom knows about?" I asked the cat. "Does he know who they are?"

He cocked his head to one side, blinked a couple of times, then curled up on the cushion beside me and closed his eyes.

"Never mind," I said. "I'll call Pete and tell him what Thom said. He'll know what to do."

I retrieved the phone and punched in Pete's number, shaking my head when I realized that I'd been speaking aloud to a cat and, worse than that, halfway expecting an answer. Pete answered after a couple of rings.

"Hi, Lee. What's up?"

"I've located Thom," I told him. "He's in New York, staying in an apartment that belongs to one of Primrose's friends."

"That's great," he said. "Good work. How did you find him?"

I told him about Primrose's model friends and how Thom was cat sitting for one of them. "He answered the phone because he recognized my number," I said. "And he wants me to tell his mom and Kelly that he's okay, and I told him I would, but, Pete, there's more. He ran away because he knows something about what happened to Bill Sullivan on Christmas night."

"He saw something?" I heard Pete's voice change into cop mode. "Exactly what did he say?"

I repeated what Thom had said about Bill not walking to the park by himself. "I told him that the police already knew that, and he laughed and said the police don't know everything. I asked if he'd like to talk to you, and he said he'd never tell anybody what he knew, because he'd promised."

"Promised who?"

"I don't know. I tried to tell him it would all work out, but he hung up on me. I probably didn't handle it right."

"You did fine, Lee. Do you know where Thom is now?"

"Just that he's in an apartment in the city that belongs to a model named Mira, who's on a shoot in Barbados." O'Ryan opened his eyes. "And she has a cat." He closed them again.

"Good. Do you have Mira's last name?"

"Primrose probably does. She gave me the number."

"Do you know if Primrose is at the dorm?"

"No," I said. "She's at Greene's with the rest of the gang."

"Okay. I'm still on duty, so I can't pick you up. Want to meet me over there? You can tell Kelly and the others that Thom's safe, and I can see what else Primrose knows."

"See you at Greene's," I told him. I changed my clothes, promised the cat I'd be back soon, and left a note for Aunt Ibby in case she beat me home.

The parking lot at the tavern was almost full. I looked around for Pete's unmarked Crown Vic but didn't see it. After pulling the Corvette into a space partially illuminated by a streetlight, I locked her up and, after one backward admiring glance, climbed the few steps to the bar's front door.

Primrose was the first to greet me. "Lee! I'm so glad you came. Come sit by me." She tapped the shoulder of the man next to her and, with a smile and a jerk of her thumb, indicated that he should move. He did, and I slid onto the vacated stool. "Look at that," she said, pointing toward the keno game, where Therese and Sammy had drawn a small crowd. "It turns out that Therese is some kind of a whiz at the game. She's making Sammy rich."

"Nice for Sammy," I said. "But I need to tell you about Thom. I talked to him. He's at your friend Mira's apartment."

"Oh, my God. For real? Is he okay?"

"Depends on what you call okay, I guess," I told her. "He's warm and safe and dry. Mira's away on a job, and Thom's taking care of her cat."

"Jesus. Have you called his mother yet? She calls me ten times a day, wanting to know if I've heard anything."

"Oh, good. Then you have her number. Why don't you call her now, while I give Kelly the good news?"

"I will," she said, then stood up. "Hey, Kelly! Come over here. Lee has something to tell you. It's about Thom," Primrose yelled.

Primrose's loud pronouncement brought not only Kelly to the bar, but Therese and Sammy, as well. Duke and Joe Greene hurried over to where I sat, too, all of them talking at once.

"Have you heard from him?"

"Do you know where he is?"

"Is the kid okay?"

I held up my hands, signaling them to be quiet. "Listen, everybody," I said. "I talked to Thom less than half an hour ago. He's in New York, and he's safe. Primrose is calling his mom, and I've already told Pete."

Tears streamed down Kelly's face, and Joe Greene

hugged his daughter. "See, honey? I told you he'd be all right."

"When's he coming back?" Duke wanted to know, perhaps thinking that his new position as bartender might end. "Or did he get a modeling job?"

"He didn't mention anything about a job," I said, "and we talked for only a few minutes. I think he just wanted to let you all know he's safe and well."

I hadn't seen Pete come in, so I was surprised and pleased when he sat beside me on the stool Primrose had vacated. "They all look happy," he said. "Everybody relieved about Thom?"

"Absolutely," I said. "And, Pete, after you talk to Primrose, you might want to speak to Duke. I think he's figured out what Jonathan Wilson's old map is all about."

Duke put coasters in front of us. "What'll it be, folks?"

"Just a Pepsi for me, Duke. Lee?"

"Sounds good."

"Lee tells me you've got the old map figured out," Pete said.

"Think so." Duke drew our sodas and placed them dead center on the round coasters. "It looked like a subway map to me," he said. "And a subway is just a whole mess of little tunnels, kinda like the ones under Salem."

Pete nodded. "I think you might be right about that, Duke," he said. "Good work. Did you tell Jonathan Wilson about your theory?"

"Sure did. I called him tonight and told him about it. He thinks I'm right, too."

"A tunnel map, huh?" Sammy said. "Why didn't I think of that? I should have seen it. I thought it was regular streets." He slapped his forehead. "But do you know where the tunnels are?"

"Not a clue," the bartender said. "Could be any-where under the whole dang city."

"Gee, Duke," Therese said. "Did you figure out what the square box with the number on it means?"

"Nope. Not yet."

"I did. I called Mr. Wilson tonight, too," Kelly said.

"Really?" Primrose had persuaded another bar patron to give up the seat on Pete's other side, and she leaned forward, her elbows on the bar. "What does it mean?"

"It's a six, not a nine," Kelly said firmly, "and it means this house."

CHAPTER 26

"How the hell do you figure that?" Sammy asked. "You think the square with a six on it belongs to you somehow?" He grabbed Therese's hand. "She's nuts. Come on, kid. Back to the game."

"No, really. This house is number six," Kelly insisted. "Tell them, Pa."

Joe Greene poured drinks as he spoke. "It's a little complicated, but this place is kind of on the lot backward. When you came in here from the parking lot, you came in the front door, right?"

Most everyone nodded.

"Well," Joe went on, "the parking lot used to be the backyard, and you came in here by what used to be the back steps." He pointed to the wall behind him. "See, the front of the house was over there, facing that street around the corner. You can't even see the old front door from the street anymore. It's all covered up with bushes and trees and stuff. But Kelly's right. There's a rusty old number six on that side of the place, and this side got a whole new street number."

"Uh-huh," Kelly said. "I told Mr. Wilson about it, and

he believed me. Sounded excited, too. He's coming over here first thing in the morning to see for himself."

"Is that right?" Sammy said. "Well, maybe you ain't so nuts, after all."

Sammy and Therese returned to their game, Kelly went back to waiting on tables, and Pete spoke in low tones to Primrose. He pulled out his notebook and pencil, and made notes, nodding his head as she answered.

As soon as Pete returned the notebook and pencil to his inside coat pocket, Primrose left us to join the group congregated around Sammy and Therese.

"Looks like young Therese is some kind of keno genius," Pete said.

"I know," I said. "She says she can see the numbers before they come up on the screen. But tell me about Thom. Are you going to bring him back to Salem? Find out what he knows about Bill?"

"We'll handle it." Pete's cop face was firmly in place.

Clearly, he wasn't going to talk about that topic, so I tried another. "Did you ever learn any more about Primrose's background? Besides the fact that she has a valid driver's license?"

"Yeah, Friedrich and Chief Whaley checked her out. No problem. Nothing there for you to be concerned about."

He knows, but he's not going to tell me about it.

I tried once more. "Duke's idea about the map is interesting, isn't it?" I said. "If it's a map of part of the tunnel, what do you think it means?"

"I think he's right," Pete said. "Don't know why I didn't see it myself, since I've been working down there on and off since this whole mess started."

"And what about Kelly's claim that the number on the map means this place? You think she's right, too?"

"I doubt it. But I'll go back to city hall and dig up the old deeds to this property. Then I'll look up whatever tunnel maps the city engineer has. If they match up with Wilson's map, and if Kelly's right about the six being this place, the circle with the dollar sign in it is pretty close by." He smiled. "If word gets out about that, Joe's parking lot is going to be full of treasure hunters with metal detectors."

"Nothing surprises me anymore. My little TV production class in the Trumbull building is turning out to be a lot more interesting than I thought it was going to be," I said. "And not always in a good way."

"I know." Pete looked at his watch. "I'm still on duty for a couple more hours, and I've done what I came here to do. Gotta run," he said. "What about you? Can't make Aunt Ibby stay up late, worrying."

"Aunt Ibby isn't home. She had a date with Mr. Pennington. I'm going to be the one staying up late, worrying."

He laughed. "So the beard and wig thing didn't scare her off, huh?"

"Guess not. I think she's flattered by the attention."

He took my hand. "Wish I could stay, but I can't."

"Walk me out to my car?" I asked.

"You bet." He paid for our sodas and left a tip for Duke. We said good-bye to the others, who were all focused on Therese, the keno wizard, and headed for the parking lot.

"So the back stairs are the front stairs, and the front door is the back door," I said.

"And if the new tunnel is partly underneath the old tunnel," he said, "does that mean up is down, and down is up?"

"Why not?" I laughed. "It makes as much sense as anything else around here."

He gave me a quick peck on the cheek, and we climbed into our respective cars. I reached home before Aunt Ibby did, and made sure the porch light was blazing—to discourage any untoward senior citizen hanky-panky. I fed O'Ryan his before-bedtime saucer of warm milk, donned flannel pajamas, turned the TV to *Tarot Time with River North,* and prepared to wait up for my aunt.

I had no intention of watching one of River's creepy vampire movies, but I liked the tarot segments. Her first card reading involved the Two of Pentacles. River advised the caller that he had the ability to juggle two situations at once, and complimented him on his industrious nature.

Must be nice. I can't even juggle one.

"Stay tuned during the first break in our feature film, *Love at First Bite,* starring George Hamilton." River smiled. "I have some exciting news to share with all of you."

I decided that watching George Hamilton would never be really creepy, and it occurred to me that River's exciting news might be about the promised coven gathering on the top floor of the Tabby.

I heard our front door close softly just before Dracula's coffin got lost. I hit the mute button. "Aunt Ibby? Is that you?"

"Oh, are you still awake, dear? You didn't have to wait up for me."

"Wouldn't miss this for the world," I told her. "Come right in here and tell me all about your date. Shall I make us some hot chocolate?"

"You sound just like me," she said, appearing in the doorway in stocking feet, holding her high-heeled shoes in one hand.

"Of course I do," I said, looking pointedly at the

shoes and trying hard to keep a straight face. "Were you going to tippy toe up the stairs so I wouldn't know how late you stayed out?"

"You're teasing me."

I laughed. "Still, tell me, was it fun?"

She sat in one of the wing chairs with her feet curled up under her. "It really was, Maralee," she said. "Rupert is such an interesting man. He's been so many places and done so many things." Her eyes sparkled. "Why, did you know he's made arrangements for a big TV company to come and stage one of those ghost-hunting programs right there in the Trumbull building? He's even negotiating for a coven of witches to take part in it."

"Great," I said, even though I was confident that covens don't negotiate, WICH-TV was not a big TV company, and Mr. Pennington hadn't arranged much of anything. But I wasn't about to spoil the lovely glow Aunt Ibby had going on.

She glanced toward the mute TV. "Oh, you're watching River's show. Don't let me interrupt you."

The image of the tanned but distraught Dracula loomed on the silent screen. "I wasn't really watching the movie," I said. "But River is going to make a special announcement after the first break. And, Aunt Ibby, I have good news about Thom. He's safe, staying with a new friend in New York."

"That's wonderful!" she exclaimed. "His mother must be so relieved. You know, Rupert is quite fond of that class of yours. At least he's fond of most of them." She frowned. "Maralee, did you know that one of your students has a police record?"

"Sammy? Yes. Pete told me."

"I'm glad you're aware of it. Rupert is aiding the police in a top secret crime investigation. Naturally, he's sworn to secrecy on the details, but he's quite concerned about having an ex-convict on the premises."

"Sammy has paid his debt to society, as they say," I told her. "But I appreciate Mr. Pennington's concern." I managed to cover a smile. So the Tabby director had portrayed himself to my aunt as not only a television show producer, but as some kind of undercover cop, as well.

"Oh, look," she said, pointing at the TV. "There's River. Doesn't she look pretty? Let's hear her special announcement."

I turned on the sound. River, exotic in bright red satin with a sprinkling of silver stars in her long braid, smiled into the camera. "Dear friends of the night," she said. "Most of you know me as a reader of the tarot, a seer of past and future happenings as revealed to me by the cards. But some of you also know me as a witch, a proud practitioner of the Wiccan tradition."

She paused, leaning closer to the camera. "Rarely are members of the Salem community invited to observe the inner workings of a coven. But later this week, a commercial-free episode of this show, *Tarot Time with River North,* will give you a live look at an actual attempt to contact a departed spirit, to free a ghost from her earthly bonds."

River's excitement was evident. "Yes, dear ones, thirteen of us will gather on the top floor of the Trumbull building in downtown Salem. There we will reach out to the ghost of Tabitha Trumbull. Some of you may have seen her in the upper windows or heard her playing her piano late at night." River gave a dramatic hand gesture. "You all know her as 'the lady in white,' a gentle spirit who has for many years wandered that dusty attic in her white wedding dress. Watch for further announcements about this special event on

WICH-TV. But now back to gorgeous George Hamilton in *Love at First Bite.*"

Aunt Ibby clapped her hands together. "How exciting! Rupert must have arranged for River to host the show."

"Could be," I said, knowing that now both Bruce Doan and Mr. Pennington were claiming competing credit for River's idea. "Anyway, if it works out well, it'll be a big plus for River's television career."

"You're right. But it's entirely possible that Tabitha won't show up on cue, isn't it? Probable, actually." Her smile faded. "Rupert will be disappointed."

"Even so, it's good programming," I said. "River's ratings that night will be huge."

"True. I wonder how they know Tabitha's wearing her wedding dress. I'd never heard that before."

"I guess River got that from me," I said. "I haven't had a chance to tell you. I saw a photo today of Tabitha in her wedding dress. She's definitely the woman in my vision, and she's wearing that dress."

"If that offer of hot chocolate is still good," Aunt Ibby said, "and you don't really want to watch the movie, let's adjourn to the kitchen."

I whipped up a couple of cups of hot chocolate—instant, not the made-from-scratch kind my aunt served—and we took our usual places at the table.

"Poor lonely Tabitha," my aunt said. "I'm beginning to feel as though I know her. But tell me about Thom."

"Thom's new friend is a model. He's taking care of her cat while she's on a shoot in Barbados."

"It's good that he has a friend who took him in."

"Actually, she's Primrose's friend," I said. "I called a number Primrose gave me to see if the woman might have heard from Thom, and he answered the phone himself."

"Has he found work, or will he be coming home soon?"

"He told me he's not coming back. It has something to do with how Bill Sullivan got from the bottom of that tunnel to the park."

"What did Pete say about that?" she asked.

"Primrose gave Pete the model's address," I said. "I suppose the police will want to question Thom about whatever it is he knows about Bill."

"The tunnels seem to be a part of everything we talk about lately," she said. "Bill Sullivan, the woman in your vision, the gunrunners, and now young Thom."

"You're right," I said. "And Duke thinks he knows what Jonathan Wilson's map means."

"Really? What?"

"Oddly enough, it could be a map of some underground tunnels."

"Didn't Mr. Wilson know what the map represents?"

"He thought it looked like city streets somewhere in Salem, but he couldn't figure out where. It has some squares on it, which are probably buildings. One is marked with either the number nine or the number six, and Kelly Greene is convinced that it's a six, and that it refers to their house. Mr. Wilson is going over there first thing in the morning to check it out."

She frowned. "There must be plenty of houses in Salem numbered six. Seems like a shot in the dark to me."

"To Pete too. But he's going to look for some old deeds and maps of the tunnels, anyway."

"Pete will get to the bottom of it," she said.

"The bottom of the tunnel?" I asked. "I hope not. It's cold and dark down there."

I meant it as a joke, but as I said the words, I shivered.

CHAPTER 27

The weather felt almost springlike as I drove to the Tabby in the morning. Most of the snow had melted, and the sky was cloudless. There'd be more snow coming our way, for sure, but for the moment at least, it was a "blue sky, convertible top down" kind of day. There wasn't a hint of rain anywhere in the sky, so I parked, left the top down, and went inside. The dorm dwellers Primrose and Therese were already in the classroom, and Sammy arrived a short time later.

"I'm not late, am I?" Kelly called from the mezzanine landing as she hurried forward and took a seat at the table.

"No," I said. "We're all early. I've put your textbooks on the table. We're going to review some of the technical aspects of producing our documentary."

Kelly opened her book, then snapped it shut again. "It's too nice a day to stay inside, reading. We should go on a field trip."

"Too muddy outside." Primrose closed her book, too. "I've got good shoes on."

"You don't have any bad shoes." Kelly shrugged one shoulder. "Hey, I guess Mr. Wilson doesn't, either."

"Mr. Wilson?" She had Primrose's attention. Mine too.

"Oh yeah. You should have seen him prowling around our place first thing this morning. He looked so goofy. All dressed up in his nice suit and shoes, carrying his skinny briefcase in one hand and a big set of hedge clippers in the other, slopping through the mud out behind the house."

"Hedge clippers?" Sammy's smirk had disappeared. "What for?"

Kelly threw her hands up. "Beats me. Guess he wanted to cut some of those tree roots and tangled-up weeds and bushes to try to find that number six. After that, he was walking along on top of the stone wall. But Pa ran outside and yelled at him to get out of there."

"He did?" Therese's eyes widened. "Why?"

"Something about insurance."

"So did Jonathan . . . Mr. Wilson . . . leave when your dad told him to?" Primrose asked.

"I don't think so. He came down off of the wall and went around to the back of the house again. I mean the front." She giggled. "You know what I mean."

"He's wasting his time," Sammy announced, standing up. "There have to be hundreds of number six houses in Salem. Right, Lee?"

"I'd have to say yes to that, Sammy. Maybe if some of the other squares had numbers, we could figure out the location of the streets or tunnels, or whatever they are." I took the teacher's copy of the textbook from the shelf. "Shall we get to work now?"

"Where's Duke?" Sammy looked toward the landing. "We're two men short now. Am I going to be the only rooster in this henhouse?"

"Huh. You should only be so lucky," Primrose muttered.

"No kidding, Ms. Barrett. He should be here."

Sammy frowned. "Mind if I step outside and try to see what's up with him?"

"Go ahead," I said. "But don't take all day."

"Thanks." He pulled on his jacket, holding his phone to his ear. I watched through the old shoe department's empty display window as he hurried out of sight.

"Looks like it's just us hens," Kelly said, opening her book. "What page are we on?"

We read a few chapters, practiced filming with the handheld camera, and checked the sound levels. I was surprised when I looked at the clock over the news desk and saw that it was nearly noon.

Duke wandered in a few minutes before twelve, looking disheveled and unshaven. "Sorry," he mumbled, slumping into his favorite chair. "Overslept."

"You look terrible," Kelly said. "Where did you sleep? In your truck?"

"Yep. I did." He leaned forward, cradling his head on folded arms. "I feel like shit."

"You want to come to lunch with us, Duke?" Therese asked.

The big man just groaned.

"Maybe we'll bring you something," Kelly said, and she and Therese and Primrose headed for the diner. "Coming, Ms. Barrett?"

I was about to join them when my phone buzzed. Pete was calling.

"You on your lunch break?" he asked, his tone serious. "Can you talk?"

"Sure. What's wrong?"

"Looks like your boy Thom has skipped town again."

"What do you mean?" I dropped my voice and walked toward the stairs. "Where'd he go?"

"We tried to contact him by phone last night, and

when we couldn't, I asked for a New York uniform to go over there this morning to roust him. Chief's through screwing around with this kid."

"Did that scare him away?" I asked.

"Nope. Already gone. The doorman says Thom took off last night. Probably right after he talked to you." Pete sounded disgusted. "Damn."

"Oh, Pete. I'm sorry. Maybe I shouldn't have called him."

"Not your fault, babe. The doorman says the kid came down carrying a suitcase, gave him twenty bucks to check on the cat, got into a cab, and left."

"Maybe he decided to come home," I said. "Did you see if his mother's heard from him?"

"She hasn't. Now we've got her all upset and crying and calling the station every two minutes again. What a mess." He exhaled audibly. "Want to eat lunch with me? I'm at the drive-through right now. I'll bring you a cheeseburger."

"Good deal."

"I'll be there in a minute," he said. "You want fries with that?"

"Sure. And you might bring an extra coffee for Duke. He's not feeling well today."

Pete arrived with the promised burgers, fries, and coffee. "Let's go outside and sit in your car," Pete said, glancing at Duke. "Nice out there. Depressing in here."

"You've got that right," I said. "Let's go."

We walked out to the parking lot and climbed into the Corvette with our food and drinks, as if we were going to a picnic. I leaned back in the driver's seat, eyes closed, enjoying the feeling of the warm sun on my face.

"Pete," I said, "what are you going to do about

Thom? You're going to have to find out what he saw Christmas night."

"We'll find him. We have more than one reason now to bring him in."

I opened my eyes and sat up straight. "What does that mean?"

"I reinterviewed the dog walker. Remember the one who saw the three drunks?"

"Did you show her the brown jacket to see if she could identify Bill?"

"She didn't recognize it. But she did notice something about one of the drunks. The one that passed by closest to where she was walking."

"What about him?"

"She says he was extremely good-looking. Like a movie star," he said.

"Thom." I didn't have to ask. "It was Thom."

"She ID'd his photo."

"So Thom was one of the men carrying Bill that night." I paused in the middle of biting into my cheeseburger. "Do you know who the other one was?"

"Not yet. But we'll get Thom to tell us."

"If you can find him."

"Oh, we'll find him. Here. I brought you a hot apple pie." He handed me the tissue-wrapped treat.

"I'll split it with you," I said, cutting it in half with a plastic knife. "Kelly says Jonathan Wilson was over looking around Greene's Tavern early this morning."

"I have an appointment with him this afternoon," he said. "Wilson's found some old surveyor's maps of all the properties along the waterfront. If Duke is right about Wilson's map showing underground tunnels, they might match up somehow."

"You never told me what you're looking for there."

"It's kind of a cold case thing your friend Friedrich is working on."

"So did you talk to Megan yet?"

"Only on the phone. I'd like to show her the surveyor's map first to see if that will help her locate the tunnel entrance," he said. "She sounds old. Really old."

"She's quite blind, too," I said. "I don't know how useful a map is going to be."

"She says she can see close up with her glasses pretty well. It's worth a try, anyway. I have to head back to the station." He looked up. "Might want to put the top up. Clouds moving in from the nor'east."

"I'll take your advice on that. Let me know if you hear anything about Thom, will you?"

"Sure. I'll call you tonight." He dashed across the parking lot to his own car while I put the top up on mine.

Caffeine had improved Duke's attitude and appearance, and Kelly, Primrose, and Therese had returned from lunch smiling, with shopping bags from a nearby boutique. So when Tabby director Pennington dropped in for a surprise visit, the mood in the room was upbeat.

"I have a wonderful surprise for you and your students, Ms. Barrett," he said, beaming, "though I see that one has not yet returned from the noon repast." The smile lessened slightly. "No matter. You can relay my message to the tardy one."

"I'm sure he'll be back soon, Mr. Pennington," I said, hoping I was right and trying not to worry too much about Sammy. Hopefully, he was just skipping class, but with everything going on lately . . .

"There's exciting news for all of us here at the Tabitha Trumbull Academy." A dramatic pause, while he made eye contact with each person. "Tomorrow night a professional television crew will be on the premises to record a milestone in paranormal reality TV programming—"

Therese's happy squeal interrupted his speech. "Is it the one River North talked about last night on the show? Oh, my God! That's fabulous!"

"Yes, my dear. Miss North is somewhat involved." He cleared his throat. "At the stroke of midnight tomorrow night there will be a gathering of some of our Wiccan friends on the upper floor of this very building. Thousands of viewers will see an actual attempt to contact the departed spirit of our own Tabitha Trumbull."

"Will we be there?" Kelly wanted to know. "It's kind of part of our project."

"There will be a few invited guests on the actual set," he said, "and yes, of course, this class will be among them."

"I don't believe in ghosts," Duke stated flatly. "And I don't believe in witches, either. Do I have to go to it? Anyway, I have a night job."

Mr. Pennington looked surprised. "No one is required to attend. You may be excused if you wish." He made a small bow in my direction. "Ms. Barrett, I'll have complete information for you later in the day. Good afternoon to you all." He hurried to the elevator, turned, and waved. "Carry on," he said, stepped inside and the door slid closed behind him.

"Well, I'll be damned," Primrose said. "Are they really going to film up there in her room? We haven't even seen it yet."

"I know," I said. "I'm sorry. I wanted you all to see it together."

"Hey, where's Sammy, anyway?" Duke looked around the room.

"He's supposed to be out looking for you," Kelly said. "I think he's just skipping class. Too nice a day."

"Gee, first Thom disappeared, and now Sammy's gone," Therese said. "There's something totally weird about this place." She dropped her voice to a whisper. "I just love it."

By then we'd all slipped out of study mode, so books were re-shelved and the conversation was all about the upcoming ghost hunt. I debated whether or not to announce that Thom had gone missing again, and decided to delay the bad news. After all, it had become a real police matter and was no longer just a case of a mixed-up runaway kid. And maybe, with luck, they'd have Thom back in Salem by the end of the day.

"How do the witches do it?" Kelly wanted to know. "Is it like a séance, or do they chant magic words or what? Therese, you bought all those witch books. What are they going to do?"

"I watch those ghost shows on TV all the time," Primrose said. "I think they set up special cameras and microphones and look for orbs and try to record voices from dead people."

"Witches don't need cameras and recorders." Therese dismissed such technology with a wave of one well-manicured hand. "They each have their own gifts, and when they work together as a coven, the power can be enormous. I can hardly wait to see what will happen."

"Will we be on camera at all when the witches are doing . . . whatever witches do?" Kelly wanted to know. "I mean, what are we supposed to wear?"

The talk among the women turned to casual versus dressy dark colors and then to light versus regular stage makeup. Duke sat behind the news desk, looking bored, and took his phone out of his pocket.

"Hey, you guys," he said. "I just got a text from Sammy. He's coming back." He laughed. "Says he's been looking for me all this time. Checked every bar on Derby Street. Good excuse, huh?"

My own phone vibrated. I peeked at the caller ID. It was a text from Pete.

Call me when you get a chance.

I tapped in OK and slipped the phone back into my pocket.

"Maybe there'll be some information about proper attire in Mr. Pennington's instructions," I said. "If not, I'd say wear whatever you like. But I warn you, it's dusty up there. Dirty, actually, so white is out of the question."

"Except for the ghost," Therese said.

"Of course," I said. "Except for Tabitha."

It was nearly an hour later when Sammy sauntered into the room, wearing a Boston University sweatshirt, and took his regular seat at the table.

"Hi, guys," he said. "What's new?"

"It's about time, man," Duke said. "You left me alone all day with these women, talkin' about clothes and witches and ghosts and shit. And me with a king-size hangover."

"I like your shirt," Kelly said.

"Thanks. Had to change. Somebody spilled a beer on my jacket," Sammy said. "What's all this about ghosts and witches? What did I miss?"

"We're almost famous," Therese said. "We're going to be on TV. River North's show. The witches are going to contact the ghost of that lady in white who haunts this place. Awesome, huh?"

"Who's River North? And when is all this supposed to happen?"

"Tomorrow night." I gave him a brief rundown on what Mr. Pennington had told us, and Therese added details about River's show and Wiccan practices.

"I'm not goin'," Duke told him. "You don't have to, either. It's all a load of hocus-pocus crap."

The clock above the news desk showed 4:45 p.m. "It's nearly five," I said. "I think I'll dismiss you a little early. I want to check with Mr. Pennington about the information he promised."

All of that was true, but I was also anxious to find out what Pete wanted. As soon as the classroom had cleared, I called him. He picked up on the first ring.

"I got your message," I said. "Is anything wrong?"

"I hope not. Have you heard anything from Jonathan Wilson?"

"No. Why?" I asked. "I thought you had a meeting scheduled with him."

"That's just it. He never showed. I called his wife, and she says he left early this morning, before she was awake, and they haven't seen him at city hall all day."

People keep disappearing around here. Thom's gone missing twice. Now Wilson. Bill was missing for a while, and that certainly didn't turn out well.

"Kelly says he was at the Greenes' early this morning. It was about that map and the number six on the house, I think."

"Already checked with Joe Greene. Last time he saw Wilson was when he left to drive Kelly to school. Says he stopped to pick up some groceries, and Wilson was gone when he got back. Hasn't seen him since."

"I wonder if the councilor contacted Mr. Pennington. Do you want me to check with him?"

"I'd rather you checked with Primrose. Seems there

was an affair some years ago, and Mrs. Wilson knows all about it. She thinks maybe it's on again."

"Oh, boy. That could be awkward."

"I'll do it if you don't want to. Just seems it would be easier on Primrose if you ask her if she knows where he is, instead of it being like a police interrogation."

"You're right," I said. "I've already dismissed everybody, but she's probably still in the building."

"Thanks, Lee. Did I ever tell you you'd make a good cop?"

"Once or twice. I'll let you know what she says. Anything on Thom yet?"

"It won't be long before we find him. He landed in Boston early this morning. We're not the only ones looking for him. Agent Friedrich from the Treasury ID'd him from a photo taken at a coin show. Seems he sold a marked twenty-dollar gold piece to a dealer. The Treasury'd like to know where he got it."

"Thom did? A twenty-dollar gold piece?"

Another coincidence? I don't think so.

"That's right," he said. "Didn't you tell me that twenty-dollar gold pieces had something to do with the documentary your class is making?"

"I did say that. I still think they do. I just haven't figured out exactly how. I never connected Thom with gold, though. What a mess. I'm glad I didn't tell anybody here that he left Mira's apartment," I said. "They were all so excited about the ghost-hunting thing, I didn't want to destroy the mood. Did you know they're doing it here tomorrow night?"

"I heard all about it at city hall. Seems Wilson personally walked Pennington through the permitting process yesterday."

"They need permits for ghost hunting?"

"Sure," he said. "It's a public building. You need permits for everything. Insurance too."

"Kelly said that her dad chased Wilson away from that wall next to the tavern because of insurance," I told him.

"Could be," he said. "It's muddy out there. If Wilson slipped and fell, it would be Joe's liability. I'll ask him about it."

"You might want to come to the witch thing," I told him. "Megan will probably be here, and maybe you can show her that surveyor's map you have."

"Good idea. Thanks, Lee."

"You're welcome. I'll talk to Primrose and call you back."

I set out to hunt for Primrose, hoping she wouldn't turn up missing, too. Happily, all it took was a phone call to locate her. She answered on the first ring.

"Hello?"

"Hi, Primrose. It's me. Lee Barrett."

"Oh. I was expecting someone else. What can I do for you, Lee?"

"I'd rather not discuss it over the phone," I said. "Are you still in the building?"

"In my room, but I may have to leave in a hurry. Expecting a call."

"May I come up for a minute? It's important," I said. "And I think you should know, Thom's gone missing again."

"I've heard about Thom," she said. "Mira called. She's really pissed. He went off and left her cat all alone. Didn't even leave a note. Last time I give that ungrateful little twerp a friend's phone number."

She gave me the number of her dorm room, and I

took the elevator to the third floor. I hadn't seen the inside of the dorm since the students had moved in. Primrose's room was neat and attractive, with a colorful bedspread and matching draperies. A framed photo of the U.S. Capitol building during cherry blossom season hung on the wall. Primrose sat on the edge of the single bed and motioned for me to sit in the only chair. She was dressed once again in the pin-striped pantsuit, and her purse was next to her on the pillow.

"What's going on, Lee?"

"I need to ask you a question, but I think I already know the answer," I said. "You haven't seen Jonathan Wilson today, have you?"

"Why do you want to know? Has something happened to him?" Her voice rose, and she twisted the strap of her purse.

"Pete had an appointment with him this afternoon to look over some papers at city hall," I said. "Jonathan didn't show up, and his staff says he hasn't been there at all today. You know he was at the Greenes' early this morning, but Joe chased him off. That seems to be the last anyone's seen of him. Pete is concerned."

"Oh, dear God. I never should have involved him in this." She rocked back and forth, as though she was in pain.

"Involved him in what, Primrose? What's going on?"

"I can't talk about it. I can't."

"If it's about his wife . . . ," I said. "Apparently, she knows about the affair you two had. She thinks it's on again. Do you want to talk about that?"

"No." She stood, then opened the door and motioned for me to leave. "It's none of your business, Lee. Stay out of it, for your own sake. You'll have to go."

So I left. I went back to my classroom, called Pete,

and repeated the conversation. "She hasn't heard from him, and she's worried."

"She may have good reason to worry, Lee," he said. "We found Wilson's car out behind the tavern, hidden by all those trees and overgrown bushes. No sign of him."

He promised to call me later, and I made a fast check of my area, tossing a couple of empty Styrofoam coffee cups and picking up a long manila envelope, which had been left on my desk while I was visiting Primrose. I looked inside it, confirmed that these were the papers Mr. Pennington had promised, and stuffed the envelope into my purse. With no reason to stay at the Tabby any longer, I hurried to the parking lot, climbed into the Corvette, and headed home.

I parked in the garage, noting that the Buick was missing. O'Ryan met me at the back door.

"Hello, big boy," I said, patting his soft fur and accepting a pink-tongued lick on my fingers. "It's always nice to be welcomed home with purrs and kisses." I followed him into the kitchen. A note from Aunt Ibby on the kitchen table informed me that a shepherd's pie was in the warming oven and that she'd gone to meet Rupert at the library to help with some "last-minute research."

I changed into fresh jeans and a Tampa Bay Rays T-shirt, then returned to the kitchen and helped myself to some dinner, putting a big spoonful of the gravy-drenched meat and vegetables into O'Ryan's red bowl. I opened the manila envelope while I ate. It was an itinerary of the projected night's event in standard outline form, indicating the times for seating guests, greeting the arriving TV personnel, delivering props for witches, arranging lighting, and the like. There was a section about Wiccan protocol, which still had a few blank spaces in it, and I guessed that might be the reason for Mr. Pennington's research trip to the library. He'd be a stickler for using the proper forms of address. Ariel had been a coven queen. Had she been addressed as "Your Highness?" Was a boy witch a warlock or just a witch? I didn't know.

The TV show was scheduled for midnight, but River and the witches would arrive hours earlier to become familiar with the place.

"Therese is going to be thrilled to meet some real witches," I told the cat.

I heard the click of the back door opening as my aunt arrived. "Hi, Aunt Ibby," I called. "We're in the kitchen."

"Did you get your dinner all right? Oh, I see you did. Let me get out of these heels, and I'll join you." She draped her coat over the back of a chair, kicked off her shoes, and took a plate from the dish cabinet.

"You look especially pretty tonight," I told her. "How'd your library date with Mr. P. go?"

She wrinkled her nose. "An hour or two in the stacks does not constitute a date. It went quite nicely, thank you. Rupert wants to be sure everything goes well tomorrow, whether the spirit world cooperates or not. This event came about sooner than he'd anticipated. The timing has to do with the waning moon or some such Wiccan tradition."

"I know there's a lot of preparation for an off-site production like this for the TV station," I said. "Watching it unfold is going to be a real treat for my TV production students. It's something they could never get from textbooks."

"From what Rupert says, this TV show is much more involved than I'd realized," she said, putting a couple of spoonfuls of food on her plate. "With everything going on around us, it's hard to focus on any one thing."

"That's truer than you know," I said. "A lot has happened in the past twenty-four hours. I've been dying to talk to you about it."

"I can tell from your face, it isn't good. Tell me."

I started with the news that Thom was missing again, and that a witness had identified him as one of the men Pete suspected of moving Bill Sullivan from the tunnel to the park.

"I'm so sorry to hear that," she said. "He seems like such a nice lad."

"I know. Not only that, but Mr. Friedrich is looking for him in connection with a gold coin Thom sold recently."

"I guess that explains the picture of Mr. Friedrich at the coin show."

"I guess so," I said. "And now Councilman Wilson has disappeared."

"No! Jonathan Wilson? Why, he's one of the most popular people on the city council." She looked genuinely sad. "I do hope nothing has happened to him."

"Hope not. But it seems he and Primrose were romantically involved at one time. Mrs. Wilson knows about it, and she thinks it's still going on."

"What does Primrose say?"

"She says she doesn't know where he is, and she won't comment on the affair at all."

"That's probably wise," my aunt said. "You're just full of bad news today, aren't you?"

"I know. I guess we'd better fill in a few new index cards."

We sat together at the kitchen table, scribbling notes on the familiar oblongs, and managed to go through a pot of coffee and half a loaf of banana bread before I noticed the time.

"Holy smoke. It's after eleven," I said. "Want to watch the late news and maybe see what River has to say about tomorrow's ghost hunt?"

"Yes, let's. Maybe there's news about Thom or Mr. Wilson." She raised a hand with crossed fingers. "If there is, I hope it's good."

"Hope so," I agreed, gathering up my cards. "You know, the more notes I make, the more confused I get."

"Same. But my notes about Thom are beginning to make a little bit of sense."

"What do you mean?"

"It's the gold coin thing. Somebody must have paid Thom for something with a gold coin. But it was marked somehow, and Mr. Friedrich traced it to him."

"I see that."

She continued. "Pete thinks Thom may have helped someone move Bill's body." She tapped one of the cards she'd written that evening. "And this one says that Thom cried at Bill's funeral," she said. "I may be completely wrong, and I hope I am, but at least it connects one card to another."

We carried our coffee cups into the living room, and Aunt Ibby turned on the television set. We each gasped when a full-screen picture of handsome Thom Lalonde filled the screen. I recognized the pose right away. It was from the composite photo card Thom's mother had displayed so proudly.

"Have you seen this man?" I recognized the voice of Scott Palmer, the WICH-TV field reporter. "Thom Lalonde, twenty-five, is a person of interest in the matter of the Christmas night death of William Sullivan. A police spokesman emphasized that Lalonde is not a suspect at this time, but he may possess relevant information. He was last seen in New York City but now is believed to be in Boston or Salem. If you see him, call 911 or notify the Salem Police Department."

Thom's picture faded away, and Palmer moved on to another story. Aunt Ibby turned down the sound.

"This looks very serious, Maralee," she said. "The best thing that boy can do is turn himself in."

"I hope he will," I said. "Kelly will be heartbroken over this."

When River North's theme music, *Danse Macabre*, issued faintly from the TV, Aunt Ibby turned the volume up.

I watched and listened as River smoothly introduced her show and then leaned toward the camera, eyes sparkling. "Before I take your calls, dear friends of the dark, I want to tell you about tomorrow night's very special show. You will be privileged to witness something few ever see. A coven of Salem witches will gather at the scene of one of our city's most haunted places." She paused, and the camera pulled closer. "You all know about the lady in white. She has appeared to many over the past decades. This gentle spirit haunts the building once known as Trumbull's Department Store in downtown Salem."

River's voice dropped dramatically. "The coven, of which I am a fortunate member, will attempt to free the spirit from whatever earthly bonds hold her here. We believe that the lady in white is Tabitha Trumbull. Watch my program tomorrow night, dear friends, and see for yourself a possible miracle. Blessed be."

She returned to the regular programming format, and my aunt once again lowered the volume. "River's viewership tomorrow night will be enormous," she said.

"That'll be good for River and the station," I said.

"And if they can pull this off, I guess it'll be good for Tabitha Trumbull."

"I'm hoping they can send Tabitha away forever," my aunt said. "That'll be good for you."

"I wonder if she'll have time before she leaves to show me what she wants me to do about the keys." I made my tone light, but I was deadly serious.

CHAPTER 28

The atmosphere around the Tabby felt electric the next day. Word of the event had spread far beyond WICH-TV's coverage area, and mobile units from Boston and Worcester were already in the parking lot when I arrived in the morning. The usual contingent of protesters had positioned themselves across the street from the school, waving signs bearing slogans like "Thou shalt not suffer a witch to live."

Inside the building roving reporters with cameras and microphones interviewed people at random, and in a school where much of the student body had stage or screen aspirations, the attention couldn't have been more welcome.

Mr. Pennington had stationed himself on the mezzanine landing, in front of the founder's portrait, and was shaking hands with everyone he could reach. It was not an environment conducive to study, but I had a plan B in mind for my group. I pulled five spiral-bound notebooks from the supply cabinet and handed them out, along with ballpoint pens. "We can't lick 'em today, so we might as well join 'em," I told my group. "You're going to be reporters. Go on out there and ask questions. Find out what people think about what's going to happen here at midnight."

"Do I have to do it?" Duke asked. "I'm not going to the thing. There are no such things as witches and warlocks, and I think you're all nuts."

"If you're afraid, Duke, I can make you an amulet to keep the witches and ghosts away from you," Therese offered, all dimples and smiles. "And we don't say warlocks. They're all called witches. Come with us. It's going to be fun."

Duke didn't answer, just pulled his Stetson lower and accepted a notebook.

Overnight Primrose had changed from pinstripe-suited government agent back to her miniskirted self. She took off, her platform boots with four-inch-high heels clattering down the stairs. Kelly, still subdued, tucked her notebook under one arm and followed Therese into the elevator.

Alone at my desk, except for the intermittent parade of Tabby students, guests, and members of the press passing by, I propped up a textbook, pretending to read. I wasn't aware how long I'd been hiding behind the book, thoughts wandering, when I felt, rather than heard or saw, a sudden shift in the atmosphere. I walked over to the stairwell leading to the lobby, trying to figure out what was different, why the vibes in the place had changed suddenly.

Mr. Pennington came over to where I stood. "Do you know what's going on, Ms. Barrett? All the media people are leaving. Look at that!" He pointed toward the glass doors, where cameramen and reporters were pushing one another out of the way in their efforts to get outside. From the parking lot came the rumble of trucks and cars starting. "Something very peculiar is happening here."

"No, sir," I told him. "Something is happening *away* from here." I'd worked at enough TV stations to know that a mass media exit like this one almost always meant that a better story was going on somewhere else. "Come on. Let's turn on the TV and see what it is."

I clicked on the TV and the giant flat-screen behind the news desk glowed. A BREAKING NEWS banner flashed green across the top of a picture of Jonathan Wilson. An announcer's voice boomed from the Tabby's taxpayer-funded state-of-the-art speaker system.

"Popular Salem city councilor Jonathan Wilson is dead at the age of fifty-three. His body was found this morning near a popular waterfront tavern. Foul play is suspected, and a possible suspect is being detained for questioning. Stay tuned for details as they become available."

Primrose McDonald's scream could be heard throughout the building.

A small group had joined us in front of the TV. Primrose, her boots clicking loudly on the polished floor, pushed Mr. Pennington aside and, sobbing, reached across the desk, as though trying to touch Wilson's image on the screen. "No!" she screamed. "No!" She slumped forward, and I put both arms around her, pulling her away from the desk and guiding her to a chair.

"Primrose," I said. "Shhh. Here, sit down." Racking sobs shook her body. A crowd had begun to gather, some glued to the television, most staring at the crying woman. I looked at Mr. Pennington. "Help me get her out of here. Can we take her to your office?"

"Of course. Certainly." With one of us on each side, we guided her toward the elevator. With an officious wave of his hand, Mr. Pennington cleared everyone out of our way, and within seconds we were riding up to the second floor.

By the time we reached the director's office, Primrose had grown quiet, except for a tiny whimpering sound. We seated her in the swivel chair behind the desk. She stared straight ahead as I held her hand.

"You'd better get back there and keep things in order," I told Mr. Pennington. "I'll stay with Primrose."

"Should I send for a doctor?" he asked. "Will she be all right?"

"I'll take care of her," I assured him. "We'll be fine."

As soon as the door had closed, Primrose began to talk.

"He's dead, isn't he? Jonathan is dead, and it's my fault. I never should have involved him. I should have left the damned letters there, and none of this would have happened."

I squeezed her hand, struggling to find words to comfort her. "We don't know what's happened, Primrose. Surely, you can't blame yourself."

"My fault," she said again. "My fault for going to him when I found them. I thought he'd be impressed. Thought he'd think I was smart."

"You *are* smart, Primrose," I said. "I'm sure nothing you found could have caused this."

"Hundreds of them," she whispered. "She must have sent them to him for years."

"Hundreds of letters? To Jonathan?"

That brought a disdainful look. "No. Not to Jonathan. To the president!"

"The president? I don't understand."

She sighed. "The letters were from Tabitha Trumbull. To President Roosevelt. There was a whole file drawer full of them right there in the FDR library research room. If anyone had ever bothered to read them, they would have known about it."

"About what?"

"The gold. The goddamned gold." She began to cry again.

Tabitha. Roosevelt. Gold. Puzzle pieces began to click together.

"Shhh. Please don't cry so, Primrose. Tell me about the letters."

"I was up there on an assignment for the National Archives and Records Administration, to help with sorting out some files." She wiped her eyes with the back of her hand and sat up straight. "Lee, did you know they save all that stuff people write to presidents? They just stick it all in file folders, and it winds up in gigantic file drawers in their libraries after they're dead."

"Go on."

"I knew about my friend's book project, so I started to read some of the president's personal mail. There was a big stack of letters from somebody named Tabitha Trumbull."

"A big stack of them?"

"Right, and they all started out like regular fan letters. That's probably why nobody bothered to read them to the end." She gave a short laugh. "Tabitha put all the good stuff at the end of hers. And I had to be the one to find them."

"What did they say?"

"Oliver Wendell Trumbull was hoarding gold. Big-time. And Tabitha knew where it was. So she ratted him out to the president. Nobody was supposed to have gold back then, you know." Then she laughed out loud. "And the president never got the message. Hundreds of times she tried to tell him, and he never got the message."

I was beginning to get it. "What happened to the gold?"

"Don't you see? Tabitha stole it. So she could save it for President Roosevelt."

"But he never got it. The president never got the gold."

"Nope. Neither did anybody else. It's still wherever she hid it." A terrified look came into her brown eyes. "Jonathan must have gotten too close. And now he's dead."

A gentle knock sounded at the office door.

Damn. What a bad time to be interrupted.

"Who is it?" I snapped. "We're busy."

"It's Kelly," came the soft reply. "Let me in. Thom's been arrested. They think he killed Mr. Wilson."

I leaped to my feet and pulled the door open. Kelly Greene stood there, her fair skin drained of color, her blue eyes clouded. "They think Thom killed Mr. Wilson," she said again.

I pulled her inside and led her to one of the wooden chairs facing the desk. "Here. Sit down. Who told you that?"

She sat calmly, hands folded in her lap. She seemed to be looking past us. "Pa called me. He says I need to come home. There's cops all over the place. They took Thom away in handcuffs."

"Thom was at your house?" I sat beside her. "He was hiding at your house?"

"No. He was out back. In the shelter."

"The shelter? What do you mean?" I asked, thoroughly confused.

Kelly seemed to notice Primrose for the first time. "Are you crying, Primrose?" she said. "Don't worry. Thom wouldn't hurt anybody."

Primrose's voice was sharp. "How did the little sneak

kill Jonathan?" Kelly's face contorted, and she began to weep silently, while Primrose continued to demand an answer. "Tell me how he did it, Kelly. And why?"

"Stop it, both of you," I said and stood between them. "I'm going to call Pete. He'll know what's going on." My phone buzzed before I could pull it from my pocket.

Great minds.

"Pete," I said. "What's happened?"

"I'll explain later. I'm on my way there," he said. "I'm bringing Joe Greene over so he can take Kelly home."

"She's here with me, in Mr. Pennington's office," I said. "Primrose is, too."

"Good. I'll want to talk to both of them. Stay where you are."

He hung up before I could say anything more.

"Pete's on his way," I told the two. "Your dad's coming with him to take you home, Kelly. It'll be all right." I knew it was a stupid thing to say. Nothing about this was going to be all right. I went to the window and looked outside. The TV mobile trucks were gone from the parking lot. People moved along on the sidewalk, pushing strollers, carrying shopping bags. It looked like a perfectly normal day out there. As I watched, Pete's Crown Vic rolled onto the lot. He and Joe Greene got out and hurried toward the front of the building.

"They're coming," I said. "Wait here. I'm going to meet them downstairs and bring them right up."

I took the elevator to the first floor, bypassing the mezzanine. Joe Greene and Pete were coming through the glass doors. Joe still wore his apron, drawing curious looks from people in the lobby. I met them at the foot of the main staircase, and we started up the stairs together.

"I'm so glad you're here," I said. "I left Primrose and Kelly in Mr. Pennington's office. They've calmed down some, but they're both terribly upset. Is it true? Thom's been arrested and Mr. Wilson is dead?"

We reached the mezzanine landing, with its life-size portrait of the old store's founder. Pete began to answer my question, but I wasn't able to focus on his words. Instead, I stopped short, staring at Joe. I knew without a doubt why I'd felt as though we'd met before.

Joe Greene was the spitting image of Oliver Wendell Trumbull.

Had Pete noticed it, too? Had anybody? Joe looked younger than the man in the portrait, but to me, the resemblance was unmistakable.

Pete's words began to filter into my consciousness. "A pretty grim scene. Thom was just sitting there in the backyard, holding the weapon."

"The weapon?" Even to my own ears, my voice sounded thin, wavering.

Pete gave me a searching look. "You okay? Yeah, the weapon. Hedge clippers."

We'd reached the director's office. I pushed the door open, trying to process what Pete had just said. The mental image was terrifying.

Kelly and Primrose were still there but had changed their positions. Primrose had moved from the swivel chair to the one next to Kelly. She had put one arm around the smaller girl and was speaking softly. "Don't cry, Kelly," she murmured. "Look. Your dad's here."

Joe Greene went to his daughter and stood there with her in his arms, her head nestled on his broad shoulder, tears in his eyes. "Let's go home, darlin'," he said. "Pa will make everything all better. Don't cry."

Pete knelt down beside Primrose. "You going to be okay, Primrose?" he asked. "You feel up to answering a few questions?"

She nodded. "I'm okay, Pete. Sorry, Lee. I lost it for a minute down there, didn't I?"

"I understand," I said. "What now, Pete?"

"Can you take a couple of hours off?" he asked. "I'd like you to follow me back to the Greenes' in your car. The tavern's closed up for now, and I need you to stay there with Kelly for a little while. The chief wants to talk to Joe and Primrose."

"I'm sure I can," I said. "I'll tell Mr. Pennington what's happening."

"You don't have to go into any detail," Pete said. "Just tell him you need the afternoon off."

"Okay," I said. "I'll meet you at the Greenes' as soon as I can. Do you want me to drive the girls?"

"I think Kelly would rather stay with Joe. You can drive Primrose if you want."

"Primrose?" I looked at the blonde, who nodded her agreement. "We'll be right behind you."

I walked down the stairs to my classroom, while Pete and Joe, one on each side, escorted Kelly to the elevator. Primrose went to the third floor to get her coat and purse and said she'd meet me at my car. I found Mr. Pennington and Therese among the dwindling crowd watching TV and saw that regular programming had resumed.

I told the director that I'd need most of the afternoon off. "I'll be back as soon as I can," I promised, "and I'll be here for the program tonight, of course."

He didn't ask for an explanation, and I didn't offer one. "Kelly's dad has already picked her up, and Primrose is coming along with me," I told him. "My class has their reporting assignments. Therese, I'm leaving you in charge. Just call me if you have any problems."

Therese was clearly pleased with the new responsibility, but still concerned about her friend. "Is Kelly going to be all right? She's awfully worried about Thom."

"We all are," I said, and then, suppressing an urge to say, "Carry on," I left.

Primrose was waiting beside the Corvette when I got there. "Nice wheels," she said as I unlocked the doors. She'd shed the platform heels and the miniskirt in favor of jeans and ankle boots. "I'm guessing Pete wants to talk to me about Jonathan, right?"

"He didn't tell me, but I guess so."

"I haven't done anything wrong." She gazed out the window for a moment. "But I called Friedrich, just in case."

"Probably not a bad idea," I said. "Want to tell me the rest of the story behind Tabitha's letters?"

"Okay. That old woman had a wicked crush on the president, for sure." She smiled briefly at the thought. "She must have been pretty mad at her husband for breaking the law, too. About the gold, I mean."

"You said she was stealing it. That doesn't sound like something Tabitha would do."

"She wasn't stealing it for herself. She was trying to save it for the president. She even scratched a tiny *T* on every coin." Primrose gave a helpless palms-up gesture. "Nobody paid any attention. Must have been frustrating."

"I should think so. But what became of the gold?"

"That's the big question. That's what Jonathan and I tried to figure out back then. Friedrich too. They figure the gold still belongs to the Treasury. Friedrich's been racing all over town, trying to figure out what happened to it. Hell, he even tailed me that night. Went to the old guy's wake, too, watching who came and went." She gave a short laugh. "Anyway, we knew it had to be in Salem someplace, and we were pretty sure it was in the Trumbull building. But it was still private property as long as it was kept up and the taxes were being paid."

"But who would be paying taxes on it after Tabitha died?"

"Part of Tabitha's estate. Payments were made through a Boston law firm. Right up until a couple of years ago."

A puzzle piece slid into place. "That's why Mr. Wilson was so determined to save it from the wrecking ball," I said. "That's why he moved here and ran for city council."

"When I got this assignment, I didn't even know he was here, honest to God. I thought he'd gone on to other things." She looked down. "And now he's dead. All because of President Roosevelt's gold."

"You don't know that," I said. "Nobody's mentioned gold at all."

"Thom had a marked gold coin, remember? Friedrich pegged him for that. He's . . ." Her words broke off as we pulled into the parking lot at Greene's Tavern.

A uniformed officer signaled for me to stop. Bright yellow tape was stretched across the entrance to the lot. More of it was draped along the low stone wall beside the tavern. I stopped the car and rolled down the window.

"Where can I park, Officer? I'm Lee Barrett." I handed him my license. "Pete Mondello asked me to meet him here."

"Yes, ma'am. He just got here. You can park it right

here and walk on back. I'll take your keys, just in case we have to move it." He moved one hand along the fender. "Sweet ride."

I handed over the keys, and Primrose and I started across the muddy parking lot toward the bar. The neon beer signs had been turned off, and the place looked deserted.

"Do you know what Kelly meant by the 'shelter out back'?" I asked, looking around the property. "And I wonder if 'out back' means this side of the house or the other."

"I asked her about it when you left us. It's some kind of old World War II bomb shelter they found on the property when they moved in." She stopped walking and looked at me. "Why? Is that where they found Jonathan? That where he . . . died?" The brown eyes filled with tears again, and I put an arm around her waist.

"I don't know," I said. "Come on, Primrose. Hang on. You can get through this."

Pete opened the tavern door. No music or wood smoke, no friendly clinking of bottles or smell of hot dogs greeted us as we stepped inside the darkened long room. Joe Greene and Kelly sat close together in one of the booths. For a long moment nobody spoke.

Pete tapped Kelly's shoulder gently. "Kelly, why don't you and Lee go upstairs for a while? You'll be warmer and more comfortable there while I talk over some business with your dad and Primrose."

Kelly rose, almost trancelike, and moved toward me. I reached for her hand and led her toward the stairway. Pete was right. It was warmer and more comfortable in the Greenes' upstairs kitchen. Kelly and I sat together at the harvest table on a long bench. We were next to a window, made cheerful with red- and white-checked café curtains.

Kelly pushed the bottom tier of curtains apart. "That's the bomb shelter . . . right there," she said. She pointed toward the base of the hillside just inside the low wall of fieldstones. "See? The door is open."

I moved closer to the pane and peered out. "Where?"

She pointed again. "Right there. See where that yellow tape is tied to a tree? That's where Thom was hiding."

I could see it then—a neat oblong outlined by weathered boards amid a tangle of low bushes, dead grass, and stunted trees. As I watched, a uniformed officer emerged, followed by two men with CSI lettered on white jumpsuits.

That must be where it happened.

I pulled the curtain shut. "Tell me about the shelter, Kelly," I said. "Have you ever been inside?"

"No." She shook her head. "Pa said I couldn't go in there. It isn't safe."

"How did Thom know about it? Did you tell him?"

"No. Pa told him. It was because of the Christmas presents, I guess."

"Christmas presents?"

She nodded. "Uh-huh." She dropped her voice. "I wasn't supposed to know that the shelter was where Pa hid my Christmas presents. I figured it out when I heard some noise out there Christmas night and saw Thom and Pa closing it up."

"Did they know you saw them?"

"Sure. I asked Pa about it the next day. He told me he'd hidden my presents in there because I'm so nosy." A quick shy smile. "It's true. I am. Anyway, Pa told me that he got them all out okay Christmas morning but couldn't get the door back on straight by himself. It's pretty heavy. So he asked Thom to help him with it that night—so nobody would see where the shelter was and go in there and maybe get hurt, you know?"

"I see," I said, trying to put it all together in my mind.

"They must have been really drunk, though," she said. Again the little smile.

"Why do you say that?"

"Well," she said, "what woke me up was the two of them singing 'O Come, All Ye Faithful.'"

CHAPTER 29

Things were coming together. The witness had seen three men that night. She'd identified Thom as one of them. If Kelly was right, Joe Greene had been the man on the other side of Bill Sullivan.

Did that mean Bill had been inside the bomb shelter? Why? And how did he get there?

I didn't believe for a minute the story about hidden Christmas presents. I needed to tell Pete what I'd learned. I went to the head of the stairs. Another male voice came from below, and I guessed that Mr. Friedrich had arrived. He wouldn't appreciate being interrupted right now. Especially by me.

Kelly had grown silent again. At least I could jot down what she'd told me so that I could relay the information to Pete as accurately as possible. I returned to the table, pulled an index card from my purse, and began to write, trying to quote her exact words. I covered both sides of the card, finishing with "O Come, All Ye Faithful." I'd just finished texting an abbreviated version to my aunt when Pete appeared in the kitchen. He motioned for me to join him beside the soapstone sink, out of Kelly's earshot.

"Lee, I have to go over to the station. Chief Whaley wants to get statements from Joe and Primrose. Friedrich is here, too, and he's coming along with us. Will you be all right here with her?" He motioned toward Kelly. She sat quietly, looking down at the tabletop, absently twisting her hair. "There's an officer right outside, if you need any help," he said.

"We'll be fine," I said. "Here." I handed him the index card. "Read this when you get a minute, okay?"

He tucked it into his pocket. "Sure. Thanks, Lee. I'll be back as soon as I can. I appreciate your doing this."

"No problem," I said as he left, knowing that there were plenty of problems, but none that I knew how to solve.

"Where's Pete going?" Kelly asked.

"He'll be back soon. They had to go over to Pete's work for . . . something." I returned to the long bench, sitting close to her.

"Probably something about Thom, I guess."

"Maybe. Kelly, if Thom didn't do anything wrong, Pete will find out. I promise."

"Good. I'm sure he didn't do what they're saying he did to Mr. Wilson."

"What have you heard about that?" I asked, hoping she didn't know yet about the murder weapon.

"Before you got here, I heard the policemen talking." Her tone was matter-of-fact. "They said Thom shoved those big old hedge clippers right up into Mr. Wilson's throat. Got blood all over himself, then just sat out there on the stone wall until somebody saw him and called 911."

"You don't believe it," I said, knowing as I spoke that she truly didn't. I took her hand. "Mr. Pennington says the secret to life is best friends," I told her, hoping

Jessica Tandy wouldn't mind my giving the director credit. "You're the kind of person who stands by her friends, no matter what."

She lifted her chin, her expression brightening. "That's what I am. Thom is my best friend, and he didn't do it. I'm sure."

"I pray that you're right," I said. "I really do."

"Pete'll figure it out," she said. "I'm sure he will. I'm going to try not to worry anymore."

"Worrying doesn't do much good, anyway, Kelly."

"I know. Lee, do you think the witches will still come to the school tonight? Even if Mr. Wilson is dead?"

"Why, yes. I expect that they will. Sad as it all is, it really has nothing to do with them, does it? Besides, the TV station has already done a lot of preparation for the show. River's show."

"Is River your best friend?" she asked.

I thought about that for a moment. "Yes, she is," I said. "The show tonight is very important to her, and I'll do everything I can to make sure it's a success."

"I hope all of our class will be there. I know Therese will," she said. "I think Sammy will come, but I'm not sure about Duke. And probably Pete won't be able to get Thom out of jail in time for it. What do you think?"

"These things take time," I told her, sidestepping the question. "I'm sure everybody is working hard, trying to figure it all out."

"That's good." She pushed the curtain aside again and looked out the window. "Can I go back to school when Pa gets back? It's going to be boring around here until they say we can open the bar."

"All right with me," I said. "We'll see what Pete and your dad say."

"Will we be able to watch them set up the television

stuff? And can we meet the witches before the show?"
The sparkle was beginning to come back to her blue
eyes. I was glad about that, but fearful of the disap-
pointment she was going to have to face when Pete
couldn't pull off the miracle it would take to set Thom
free.

"I'm not sure about all that," I told her. "Maybe. But
I promise I'll introduce you to River."

"If anybody told you River had done something
really, really bad . . . something terrible, you wouldn't
believe it." It was a statement, not a question.

I pictured River in her red satin dress, silver stars in
her braid. Then I pictured her holding blood-soaked
hedge clippers and quickly shook the thought away.

"You're absolutely right," I said. "I wouldn't believe
it for even one second. Because I know her."

"See?" she said. "I know Thom."

I heard the tavern door open and the sound of footsteps climbing the stairs. It was Pete, and he was alone.
"Where are the others?" I asked. "Where's Primrose?"

"Mr. Friedrich is going to give her a ride back to the
school." Pete looked across the table. "He said you can
come along, too, Kelly. They're waiting out front. I
need to talk to Lee for a minute."

"You sure it's okay?" she asked. "Where's Pa? Did
he say I could go?"

"Yes, he said it would be all right. He's still down at
the station, helping the chief out with a few details."

"Oh, good," she said. "He'll tell the chief Thom
couldn't have done it."

He caught my eye, and his expression was serious.

Kelly picked up her coat and started downstairs.
"You're coming back to school, too, aren't you, Lee?"

"I'll be right behind you," I told her, then waited
until I heard the tavern door close. "What's going on?"

I asked Pete. "Are they talking to Joe because of what Kelly told me?"

He nodded. "That was really important, Lee. Looks like Joe and Thom are the ones who dragged Bill down the street to the park."

"I thought so. But that would mean Bill was in the bomb shelter that night. How can that be?"

"Sit down," he said. "This might take a while. Remember when I told you the city engineer said parts of the tunnel are still being used? Like the guy who used part of it as a wine cellar for his steak house?" I nodded. "Well, more than one family thought about using a piece of it as a bomb shelter."

"So the bomb shelter is an entrance to the tunnel, and that's how Bill got there," I said. "And Thom was in on it, too?" Puzzle pieces were slamming together.

"Maybe. But we know for sure that Joe was. He's admitted to causing the pile of rubble blocking the thing."

"Of course." I slapped my forehead with the heel of my hand. "He was a miner. He'd know exactly how to do it."

"He was more than just a miner," he said. "Joe was what they call a blaster, and that means just what it sounds like."

"Kelly said he had a specialty," I said, recalling her words. "That must be what she meant. But wouldn't people around here have heard an explosion like that? Reported it?"

Pete shrugged. "He seems quite proud of that part. Says it didn't make any more noise on the surface than a door slamming."

"Did he tell you what he was doing down there on Christmas night? How he found Bill in the first place?"

"That's the strange part. Said he was looking for

the gold that his grandmother left him when he heard Bill fall."

"The grandmother who left him this house?"

"Right. I found the deed at city hall this morning. Place belonged to an M. A. Greene."

"M. A.," I repeated, an imaginary lightbulb flashing over my head. "Not Ma, as in Mother, but M. A., as in Mary Alice."

Naturally, Pete didn't know what I was talking about. I told him about the birthday cards Aunt Ibby had found, the ones signed *Ma,* in the Trumbull files. "It means that Mary Alice didn't commit suicide," I said excitedly. "And Tabitha knew it. Kept it a secret all those years."

"Mary Alice? The kid who got pregnant and jumped overboard back in the fifties?"

"But they never found a body, did they?"

"I don't know," he said. "I could look it up."

"Don't bother," I said. "She didn't drown. She got to West Virginia somehow and had her baby. That would have been Joe's father. And Tabitha knew all about it." The thought made me happy. "Good for her."

"In that case," Pete said, reaching for his notebook, "I'm thinking that the baby's daddy could have been part of the crew on one of the coal barges that used to dock down the street. The ones from West Virginia."

"And he smuggled her aboard somehow!" I exclaimed, adding to Pete's story. "And before she left, she told her mother where she was going."

He put the notebook down on the table. "But what does that have to do with gold?"

"It's the gold Primrose and Friedrich and Jonathan Wilson have been looking for. Tabitha hid it so she could give it back to President Roosevelt."

"She hid it somewhere in the tunnel," he said.

"Right. And she gave the keys to Mary Alice. Joe probably has them now."

"The keys? To what?"

"You'd better talk to Megan," I said. "Come on. She may be at the school now, getting ready for the show." I picked up my jacket and purse. "She'll tell you about the treasure chest in the tunnel."

I reclaimed my Corvette, and Pete took off in the Crown Vic. By the time I got back to the Tabby, the TV mobile unit from WICH-TV was there, along with a utility van full of equipment. TV trucks always attract attention, but the real spectacle was going on inside the Tabby, where a procession of black-robed witches moved slowly, single file, up the main staircase. Each of them wore a hood, and a few had their faces heavily veiled. I spotted River right away as she assisted one of the witches toward the elevator. Wispy snow-white hair escaped from beneath the black hood, and the woman, bent and wizened, leaned on her cane. As tiny and frail as the witch was, she seemed to give off an unmistakable aura of strength and power.

Megan.

I looked around the main floor for Pete, but so many people had gathered there to watch the arrival of the witches, I knew it would be impossible to spot him. I hurried through the crowd, hoping to catch up with River and Megan.

"River," I called. "Wait for me."

River and Megan both turned toward me at once. River waved and motioned for me to join them, while Megan smiled, illuminating her wrinkled face.

"I'm so glad to see you both," I said. "You must be Megan."

Megan's voice was soft and almost musical. I leaned forward to hear her.

"You're River's friend Maralee," she said. Her use of my full first name was a surprise.

"I am," I said, "and I'm so pleased to meet you at last."

"Ride up with us, Lee," River said as the elevator doors slid open. "Mr. Pennington said we could use the Trumbulls' private elevator to go to the top. Look, he gave me the key," she said, waving a key attached to a brass tag.

Megan wore an old-fashioned gold lorgnette on a chain around her neck. She held the handle with bony fingers, brought the lenses close to her opaque pale blue eyes, and then brought her face close to the directory on the elevator wall. "Ladies' wear, children's, hosiery . . . Many times I shopped here with Tabitha," she said. "That was a long time ago. It's nice to be back."

"You must miss her," I said.

"Every day," she said. "Every day." Then her expression brightened. "Tonight I can finally see her again."

We'd reached the third floor. I held Megan's arm and helped her out into the corridor, while River opened the ornate door to the Trumbull family's private elevator. It was about the same size as the ones that served the store, but the similarity ended there. A plush red cushioned bench ran along the back wall, a gilt-framed mirror above it. The other walls held framed oil paintings. There was no dust and no sign of neglect anywhere. It was like riding in an elegant time capsule.

The top floor of Trumbull's looked much different than it had when River and I last saw it. The open arched doorway revealed a fully furnished formal living room. TV techs moved about efficiently, most of them acknowledging River with a smile, a nod, or a word or two of greeting.

"Wow. Look at that," River said. "They must have found all the furniture in that ballroom and put it back where it belonged." She held Megan's hand. "I wish you could really see this, Megan. I'll bet it looks just like it did when Tabitha lived here."

"If Tabitha's ghost comes back tonight," I said, "she's going to feel right at home."

With the electricity turned on, the cobwebs removed, and the furniture in place, the change was startling. The ballroom, with the furniture gone and the floor buffed, looked ready to receive dancers.

"Mr. Pennington must have worked crews around the clock to get this done," River remarked, marveling at the transformation. "This is going to look fabulous on TV. I can hardly wait to see what they've done to Tabitha's room."

"I hope they haven't changed anything," I said. "It was perfect just the way it was. Without the dust, of course."

As we moved from room to room, Megan was silent, running a gnarled hand along the edge of a mahogany sideboard, touching the carving on a rosewood chair, gently tapping a cut-glass wine decanter.

The door to Tabitha's room was partially closed. I hesitated, then—holding my breath—pushed it open. The curtains and the bedding had been laundered, and President Roosevelt smiled benignly through sparkling glass. The piano and bench had been polished, and the rocking chair had a yellow velvet cushion on the seat. A small bouquet of fresh flowers on the dresser was the only change besides the electricity and the cleanliness.

"Oh, Megan, it's perfect," River said. "I'll bet it looked just this way when you used to visit Tabitha back when she was, uh, sick."

The old woman smiled. "You mean back when she started acting crazy?"

Megan and River entered the room, while I still stood in the doorway. River sat on the piano bench, and Megan sat on the edge of the bed. Was I supposed to sit in the rocking chair?

No thanks.

"Scoot over," I said to River and sat on the piano bench beside her. "Megan," I said, "I hope you won't be offended, but I have to ask you a question. It's about Tabitha."

"Go ahead, dear," said the witch. "I'm far too old to be offended by anything anymore."

I took a deep breath. "You said she was *acting* crazy. I want to know . . . I *need* to know . . . Was Tabitha ever really crazy?"

"Who's to say what's crazy and what isn't?" she said. "That's not for you or me to judge." She held a finger up to her lips. "But I think I know what you mean. Was she crazy in the way that most people thought she was? No. She never was."

"Then why did she pretend all those years? She let them keep her prisoner here." Megan had given me the answer I'd anticipated, but I still couldn't imagine why anyone would voluntarily do such a thing.

"Perhaps you see what I mean about what's crazy and what isn't," she said. "Dear Tabitha was never crazy the way people believed. She always recognized her own husband and talked gibberish only if she thought someone was listening."

"So she was acting all that time," River said. "That's amazing."

"Amazing indeed." The old witch nodded. "She fooled them all."

"What about the nurse?" I asked. "There was a nurse here all the time."

Megan shrugged thin shoulders. "Bribed her. With gold coins and good Scotch. She's dead and gone now. Don't know what killed her, the alcohol or the money." She shook her head, and the hood fell to her shoulders. "Too much of either one can do it."

"Where did the gold come from?" River asked.

"Oliver was hoarding it. Kept it in long blue coin boxes in that safe he had in his office. He was planning to send it out of the country. She tried to talk him out of it. Pleaded with him," she said. "But when he refused, she took matters into her own hands." Megan smiled. "Got away with it for a long time, too."

"How did she do it?" I asked.

"She got them to let her go shopping alone at night. Then they'd put everything back in the morning, except for the player piano rolls. They let her keep those."

"She loved the piano," I said.

"She loved the gold," Megan said. "She knew the combination to that old safe, so she'd sneak in there, take the gold out of the boxes, and put the piano rolls in. The boxes were the same size. They didn't catch on for a long time. By then she'd put about half of what Oliver was hiding down below and kept a few boxes of gold up here, in the armoire."

"They didn't let her go shopping after she came back with dirt on her shoes, right?" River said. "And her husband figured out that she'd been taking the gold and going outside."

"You've been paying attention to my little stories, River. Yes, that's right."

"He must have been furious," I said. "What did he do?"

Megan smiled. "It was Oliver Wendell's idea to lock

her up. Thought it would make her talk about where she hid the gold," Megan said. "I told her it wasn't worth it, but she was stubborn, Tabitha was. When she decided to keep a secret, wild horses couldn't drag it out of her."

I hesitated for a minute, then blurted out, "Like the secret about Mary Alice?"

Megan looked surprised. She leaned back on Tabitha's pillows and folded her hands. "You figured that out for yourself? I know I never told anyone."

"Mary Alice ran away to West Virginia with her baby's father," I said.

Megan nodded. "That girl was crazy about a boy named Johnny Greene. Deckhand on a coal boat. Her father would have disowned her. She told her mother she was pregnant and what she was going to do. Tabitha gave her a couple of boxes of gold."

"She and Mary Alice exchanged letters," I said.

"You're a smart one," Megan said. "Tabitha had a post office box. She wrote letters all the time. She'd get the nurse drunk, then send her out to post the letters and pick up the mail. Oliver never caught on." She paused and lowered her voice. "Oliver was not the brightest man I ever met."

"Tabitha wrote to the captain of the gunrunning boat, too," I said. "And to his wife. Did she send gold to them, too?"

"Captain Gable," she said. "Yes. She felt bad that her boy had let that man take the blame for everything. Other than paying the nurse and the coins she gave to Mary Alice, that's the only time she dipped into President Roosevelt's money."

"You said Tabitha went 'down below,'" I said. "Did she hide the gold somewhere in the tunnel?"

"Still there," said the witch. "It's in the toy box. Mary Alice has the keys."

"I think the keys may be here in Salem again," I told her. "Mary Alice's grandson and great-granddaughter are here."

The old woman sat up straight and clasped her hands together. "Joseph Greene is here?"

"You know about Joe?" I asked. "You know his name?"

"Of course I do," she said. "I remember when Tabitha got the note saying he'd been born. I remember when his daddy, John Junior, was born, too. Just five months after Mary Alice ran away."

"Did Mr. Trumbull ever know about Mary Alice?" River asked. "That she didn't drown?"

"He never did."

One of the soundmen from the TV station appeared at the door. "'Scuse me, ladies," he said. "We need to run some wires in here." He looked first at Megan, then at River. "The other, uh, people are in the big, empty room."

River stood and helped Megan to her feet. "We'll be out of your way in two seconds," she said. "Let's go, Lee."

"The ballroom, eh?" the old witch said. "It was a grand place for parties, and it'll be a grand place for a magic circle."

River held Megan's arm, and they walked ahead of me into the hall. As I followed them, I wasn't really surprised to see the rocking chair moving back and forth, even though the soundman was nowhere near it.

CHAPTER 30

The sight of all those black-robed witches standing together in the center of the ballroom floor was an eerie one. Megan and River joined them, and there began a low, melodic chanting sound. It seemed as though they were reciting some sort of beautiful poetry, but I couldn't make out the words. I'd never felt more out of place, more the intruder, than I did at that moment. I backed out of there and hurried down a long hall, following the sounds of the voices of the television crew. Mr. Pennington stood in the center of the blue-walled living room, pointing one way, then another with his walking stick, as stagehands moved furniture.

"Ms. Barrett. A delight to see you," he said. "Do you think the Empire sofa should be here by the window? Or next to the Sheraton table?"

"It looks fine right there," I said. "I think I'll go down and see how my class is doing."

"You may tell your students that they'll be seated in the balcony of the ballroom. They'll have a good view of the goings-on from there without being in the way," he said. "And since it appears unlikely that young

Thom will be joining us, I've invited your dear aunt to attend."

"She'll be delighted," I told him and then headed for the stairway leading to the third floor. I rang Pete's number as I walked down to the mezzanine and my classroom.

"You still here?" I asked when he answered. "I've been up in the Trumbull suite. It looks amazing. Wait until you see it."

"I'm in the diner," he said. "Pennington invited me to hang around tonight. He says I'm an invited guest, but I think he's counting on me for extra security. Come have a cup of coffee with me."

"I will," I said. "I'm going to check on my class first—see who's coming tonight and who's not. Wait for me. I have a lot to tell you."

Since the witches had gone up to the ballroom, and the television crew was out of sight, the crowd of curious onlookers had thinned considerably. Therese had done a good job of keeping the class together. She, Primrose, Kelly, and Duke were in their usual seats, and Sammy sat in my chair, under the giant shoe. Seeing them all together that way made me acutely aware of the missing one. I pictured Thom in a jail cell, alone and frightened.

Therese proudly handed me the stack of notebooks she'd collected from the group. "I think we're all pretty good reporters."

I glanced through a few pages of each notebook, determining that everyone had written something. "You've done well on a confusing day," I said. "I'm going to dismiss you early. Get some rest. Kelly, Mr. Pennington has checked with your dad, and he says you may stay with Therese tonight, rather than go home so late. He's had an extra cot moved into her room. Everybody, we'll all be back here by eleven thirty. Got it?"

They all agreed. Duke sounded hesitant but said he'd be there. I grabbed my purse and jacket and went to the diner, where Pete had somehow commandeered a booth for the two of us.

"What a day," I said, sliding in beside him. "I've got so much to tell you, but first, how's Thom?"

"He answered a few questions. Then his dad showed up with a lawyer, so we didn't really get much. Except that he swears he didn't do it."

"And Joe? What's going on there?"

"Joe's not talking, either. Chief told him not to leave town and let him go. Too bad, but we'll probably need Kelly's testimony eventually, and it's unlikely that we'll get it if we arrest her father now. Anyway, moving a body gets lower priority than a murder case."

"I see," I said, hoping Kelly wouldn't ever have to testify against her father *or* her best friend. "I've been up to the top floor, and it looks a lot different than it did when you saw it Christmas night. And I got to talk to Megan today. You're going to enjoy meeting her. She answered all my questions."

"Tell me about it."

"I found out that Tabitha wasn't crazy, and we were right about Mary Alice running away to West Virginia with the baby's father," I said proudly. "And Joe Greene is actually Mary Alice's grandson, and Mary Alice had a couple of boxes of the gold coins. And, Pete, I know where the gold is. It's in a playroom somewhere down in the old tunnel. How's that?"

"Did I ever tell you you'd make a good cop?"

"Several times," I said. "And that's not all. I found out how she was mailing all those letters to the president and to Captain Gable, even though she was locked up."

"Whoa. Wait a minute." He held up his hand. "Who is Captain Gable?"

"Oh, didn't I tell you? He was the captain of the gunrunning boat. When they were trading guns for cocaine."

Pete reached for his notebook and flipped through the pages. "Gable. Here it is. Lee, where is Sammy Trout right now?"

"Sammy? Why? I dismissed the class. Told them all to be back here at eleven thirty."

He tapped the top of the notebook. "Because Sammy's cell mate when he was in prison was one Benny Gable, commercial fisherman."

"Captain Gable is dead, Pete," I said. "Aunt Ibby checked. Do you think Sammy is at the Tabby because of something the captain told him when they were in jail together?"

"It's possible. Either that or it's one huge coincidence."

"You don't believe that," I said.

"I work with facts, Lee. I've seen some awfully strange things happen." He put the notebook in his pocket. "So I'll just say it's possible."

"Megan knows all about Tabitha sending gold to the captain's wife," I said. "Maybe she knows some more about him. Want to go up and meet her?"

"Sure do," he said. "Let's go."

We climbed the three flights of stairs to the Trumbulls' penthouse apartment. I could hardly wait to see Pete's face when he saw the transformation of the place. I wasn't disappointed.

"Wow. It must have looked almost like this when they lived here."

"I know," I said. "It's going to look wonderful on TV

tonight. Come on. I think Megan and the other witches are in the ballroom."

"Isn't that the room with the messed-up piles of furniture?"

"Was," I said. "Not anymore."

I led Pete through the series of revamped rooms to the open double doors of the ballroom. A square table covered with a black velvet cloth had been placed in the center of the room, beneath the glittering chandelier. Men and women stood here and there, their figures reflected in huge gold-framed mirrors. It looked like a normal social gathering, except, of course, for the fact that every person there, other than Pete and I, wore a long hooded black robe.

"Look, there's Megan," I said, pointing. "And River, too."

Megan sat in a throne-like chair, and River, standing by her side, motioned for us to join them. We hurried across the vast polished floor. I knew introductions were in order and desperately wished I'd asked River for the proper form of address for a witch queen or goddess, or whatever Megan's title might be. Thankfully, River bailed me out.

"Lady Megan, goddess of this coven," she said, "may I present my friend Peter Mondello? You already know my friend Lee."

Megan extended her hand. "Welcome, Peter Mondello. We've spoken on the telephone."

"Lady Megan," he said, taking her hand and bowing easily and gracefully, as though he met witch goddesses every day. "My great pleasure."

"You had some questions for me about a map," Megan said, reaching for her lorgnette. "Do you have it with you?"

"I do," Pete said, pulling a rolled paper from his

inside pocket. "You spoke to River about a hidden tunnel you saw when you were a child, somewhere near the waterfront. I hope you can locate it on a map."

He unrolled the paper and held it close to the old woman's face. She peered at it through the handled glasses for a moment. "Yes," she said. "I can point it out if you like, but it's easier to just tell you where it is. I pass by it on my walk every morning."

Pete didn't look surprised very often, but he did then. "You can?" He rolled the paper up and put it back in his pocket. "Where is it?"

"It's in the little hillside behind the house Tabitha gave to Mary Alice. The house Tabitha's grandfather Smith used to own. Of course, I can't see the house anymore. It may have changed over the years, but I know it's still there. There's a trapdoor that goes to the tunnel. It's hidden well, but if you go inside and quite a way to the right, there's a playhouse back in there." She smiled, and for an instant her pale eyes seemed to sparkle. "It had a bright red door. Tabitha had both sets of keys, but she gave one set to Mary Alice."

"Greene's Tavern," I said.

"Both tunnels spread out in all directions. The city engineer says that once there were entrances and exits all over the city." Pete shook his head. "One of them was right under our noses."

River put her hands on the back of Megan's throne. "See?" she said. "I told you she never forgets anything."

"Lady Megan," Pete said, "may I ask one more question?"

"You may, sir."

"We know that Tabitha sent gold coins to the wife of a fisherman named Benny Gable. Do you know about that?"

"Just that the coins were all marked with a tiny letter

T and that she made him promise that neither he nor his wife would ever tell anyone where the coins came from," she said. "By that time it was perfectly legal to have gold coins, you know, so I don't suppose Mrs. Gable had any trouble spending them."

"Maybe the captain told Sammy about the coins," I said. "Maybe that's why he came to the school."

"Could be," Pete said and bowed to the seated witch. "Thank you, Lady Megan. You've been so helpful. Thank you, too, River. We'll be watching you tonight."

"Blessed be, Peter," said the goddess witch. "Blessed be, Maralee."

Pete and I left the ballroom and went back downstairs to the diner.

"Do you want me to try to contact Sammy and ask him to come back?" I asked as we sat at the counter.

"No. Don't want to spook him," Pete said. "Hopefully, he'll show up at eleven thirty with the others, and we'll see if he wants to talk about his old cell mate." He looked at the Coca-Cola clock on the stainless-steel-paneled wall. "That's a few hours away. Do you have to go home and change?"

"I do, and I'd better get going," I said. "Mr. Pennington invited Aunt Ibby to take Thom's spot in the invited guest section, and she'll probably ride back with me."

"I'll just hang out here, then," he said. "See you tonight."

I stopped to check on my classroom and found it empty. Mr. Pennington had ordered the entire building closed to the public at the request of the city fathers. No one wanted to have witch protesters wandering the halls, interfering with the television production. Even the dorm students, except for those who'd made the guest list, had been told to stay in their rooms or to find another venue to watch the show. I headed down to the main floor, wished the guard at the basement entrance a good evening, walked outside, and climbed into my beautiful new car.

When I reached home, my aunt, who had not so long ago pooh-poohed such things as spirits and magic, was as excited as a kid on Halloween at the prospect of the midnight ghost hunt. She and O'Ryan met me in the front hall.

"I can't tell you how pleased I was when Rupert called to invite me to take Thom's place," she said. She paused and put a hand to her mouth. "Not that I'm pleased about that poor boy's trouble—not at all— but I'm excited to witness such a thing. Imagine that. Trying to contact a woman who's been dead these many years."

"Of course there's no guarantee that they'll be successful," I said, "but it'll surely be a fascinating spectacle. Wait until you see what they've done to the old Trumbull penthouse." I told her about the renovated rooms and the newly cleared ballroom. "We'll be sitting in the balcony," I told her, "so we'll have a clear view of everything the witches do, but we'll be out of the way of the television people."

"I can hardly wait," she said. "Rupert said that the witches are already there. That they showed up this afternoon to make their preparations."

"That's right. They've set up some sort of altar, and Megan—she's the goddess—has a throne."

"You've had quite a day," she said. "Thanks for keeping me up to date on all the developments—although I don't quite know how to process them."

"It gets even more interesting," I told her. "I learned today who Ma was. She was M. A. Mary Alice. She kept in touch with her mother all those years. Megan told me everything. You'd better sit down. It's a long story."

I went through everything I'd learned since leaving Greene's Tavern, finally ending with Captain Gable and his cell mate, Sammy Trout.

"Astonishing," she said. "Absolutely astonishing, all of it."

My aunt and I discussed the proper attire for balcony-seated guests at a midnight ghost hunt and decided on comfortable pants, a warm top, and low-heeled shoes. I put on my NASCAR jacket, and Aunt Ibby opted for her favorite long plaid wool cape. "In case those balcony seats are cold," she said. "We don't know how well the heating system works up there after all these years."

At eleven o'clock we piled into the Corvette and headed for the Tabby. I parked in my usual spot, and we stepped out of the car, pausing to gaze up at the upper-floor windows, ablaze with lights.

It was at that moment that I felt warm fur on my ankles and heard a plaintive "mrrow."

CHAPTER 31

We both spoke at once. "O'Ryan!"

"Oh, you naughty boy," my aunt said, bending to scoop up the wayward cat. "I heard the cat door open when you left to get the car, Maralee, but I thought he was just going out to do his business."

I looked at my watch. "We don't have time to take him home and get back. Mr. Pennington's placed the building on lockdown from midnight until the show is over at two. We won't be able to get in if we're even a minute late, and it's too cold to leave him in the car for two hours."

"I'll wrap him up inside my cape, and we'll sneak him in," she said. "I'll hold him on my lap. No one will know the difference."

"I don't like it," I said, "but I don't see what else we can do. Let's go."

I held our "invited guest" passes against the glass door and Aunt Ibby and I, along with our four-footed stowaway, were admitted to the building.

"I'll show you the entrance to the balcony stairway when we get inside the apartment," I said. "Then I'm going to take Therese and Kelly to meet River and

Megan before the program starts. We'll catch up with you—and your furry friend—before midnight."

We took the two elevators up to the Trumbulls' penthouse apartment before I rushed Aunt Ibby through the formal parlor and the long dining room, with a promise to bring her back soon so that she could study the whole place at her leisure. The stairway leading to the balcony was a dainty spiral creation around the corner from the double door of the ballrooms.

"Hold on to the railing," I warned.

I hurried back to the third floor and knocked on Therese's door. "It's Lee Barrett," I called. "Are you girls in there?"

Therese opened the door. "Is it time? Can we see the witches now?"

"If you come with me right away," I said, "I think I can arrange for you to meet a couple of them."

The two tumbled out of the room with much giggling and chatter. I was pleased to hear Kelly's laugh, and Therese's excitement was contagious. I knew they'd enjoy riding in the sumptuous Trumbull family elevator, and I was rewarded with oohs and aahs from both of them as we ascended to the fourth floor and the glittering Trumbull suite.

River and Megan sat together on the Empire sofa in the formal living room. This time I did the introductions.

"Lady Megan, goddess of this coven, and, River North, may I present two of my students, Kelly Greene and Therese Della Monica?"

Kelly said, "How do you do?" but Therese did a curtsy worthy of royalty and knelt in front of Megan with her head bowed. "Lady Megan," she whispered.

Megan reached a gnarled hand in Therese's

direction, touching her blond hair. "Who is this dear little witch?" the old woman said. "Why have I not met her before? Is she new to the coven?"

"Oh, she isn't a witch," I protested. "She's one of my students, but she's very interested in, um, what you do."

"Nonsense, Maralee!" Megan lifted her hand, indicating that Therese should stand. "I know a witch when I meet one. This child is a born witch."

"I am?" Therese's voice wavered.

"Of course you are. Didn't you know it?" Megan reached for Therese's hand. "You'll need some instruction before your initiation into the craft perhaps, but you are aware of your gift, aren't you?"

Therese nodded. "Sometimes I can see . . . things . . . before they happen."

Like the numbers of the keno game!

"There now." Megan turned toward River. "River, see that this child gets some instruction. She is one of us." She faced Therese. "Remember these words. Let it harm none. Do what ye will."

"I always knew you were special, Therese," Kelly whispered. "But I didn't know you were a witch. No wonder you like Salem so much."

The old woman faced Kelly. "You have a sadness about you, Kelly Greene. I know who you are. Believe these words. Perfect love and perfect trust." She nodded in my direction. "Thank you, Maralee, for bringing these children to meet us." She reached for her cane, and River took her arm, helping her to her feet. "We must cast the circle and prepare for the ritual now. Blessed be."

Thus dismissed, I shepherded my two students back toward the ballroom.

"Look, here comes Primrose," Kelly said. "I wonder if the guys are here, too."

"I hope Duke came," Therese said. "He's afraid of ghosts and witches, but I stuck a rose quartz crystal into his hatband this morning, so maybe he'll be brave enough to watch tonight." Her smile was radiant. "I hope he won't be afraid of me, now that I'm a witch."

Primrose joined us at the bottom of the spiral staircase. "I almost didn't come," she said. "I can't stop thinking about what happened to Jonathan . . . Mr. Wilson." The brown eyes were downcast. "And, Kelly, I hope Thom didn't do it. I really do."

"Perfect love and perfect trust," Kelly said. "I trust Thom."

Single file, we climbed the curving staircase. A television screen had been installed over a deep border of crown molding at the front of the balcony, and three rows of folding chairs faced the ballroom. Aunt Ibby sat on the second to the end chair in the back row and had placed her purse on the seat beside her.

"Lee, I saved you a seat," she said. "Good evening, girls." She didn't offer a handshake, and I knew she was holding tight to the wayward cat hidden under her cape.

I recognized the president of the historical society and Bruce Doan, the manager of WICH-TV, who were seated in the front row, along with several more of the special guests Mr. Pennington had invited. My three female students slid into the second row, as did a dour-looking gentleman wearing a clerical collar. Sammy and Duke hadn't arrived yet, but it wasn't quite midnight. I took the end seat next to my aunt.

"How is everything going?" I whispered.

"Everything is relaxed and as quiet as a mouse," she whispered back. "I think everything is sound asleep."

"Let's hope everything stays that way," I said. "Look. Here come the witches."

The ballroom lights dimmed, and a slow procession entered from a side door of the grand room. All wore hoods and a few had heavy veiling covering their faces. One of the mobile TV cameras rolled along beside them, while another followed River as she left the line and moved to the edge of the floor, where Megan sat in her throne-like chair.

"Why the veils?" my aunt asked.

"River told me some of them haven't come out of the broom closet yet. Don't want to be recognized."

As we watched, four of the witches positioned themselves at the corners of the square table. A black iron cauldron was in its center, along with a large gold-colored pentagram. River stood beside Megan, holding a brass pot with smoke rising from it.

"That smells like sage," Aunt Ibby said. "Very pleasant."

A few of the witches, marching in rhythm to a low, humming chant and each carrying a single item, approached Megan and passed the items through the smoke.

Primrose turned in her chair to face me. "What are they doing?"

"It looks like some kind of a cleansing ceremony," I said, watching as the items were then carefully placed in a precise pattern around the cauldron. There were candles, black and white ones, a clear glass chalice, a sharply pointed knife, a chunk of rock, and a wooden wand.

"Do you know what it all means?"

"I don't. Ask Therese later," I said. "Look. Here's Duke."

The big man entered the balcony, removed his hat,

and sat at the other end of the back row. "Hi, every-body," he said. "Sorry I'm late."

I hadn't seen Pete anywhere yet, and Sammy was still among the missing, but it was good to see that Duke had, at least temporarily, overcome his fear of witches and ghosts.

Maybe rose quartz crystals really work.

River's voice sounded over the chanting, and her theme music, *Danse Macabre,* began. "Good evening, friends of the night," she said. "Welcome to this very special edition of *Tarot Time with River North.*" A camera rolled in for a close-up of her face. "This night you will see a coven of witches perform an ancient ritual in an attempt to contact the spirit of Tabitha Trumbull, who once lived in this very building." River lowered her voice, adding a dramatic flair to her words. "As the ritual progresses," she said, "television cameras will roam throughout this apartment, which was Tabitha's home during the final years of her life. Watch for signs of her presence along with us, dear friends, and send good intentions for Tabitha's release from the bonds tying her to this earthly realm."

No one had noticed that Duke had left the door to the balcony ajar. That is, no one except O'Ryan, who took the opportunity to sneak out from under Aunt Ibby's cape and bolt for the spiral staircase.

"O'Ryan! You bad boy!" Of course he ignored me. "Aunt Ibby," I whispered, "if I catch him, I'll just take him back to my classroom and watch the show from there."

She nodded her understanding, and I chased the cat down the curlicue staircase, through the long dining room, into the blue-walled parlor, and out into the fourth-floor foyer. A yellow blur, he tore down the stairs, heading for the third floor, with me thumping along behind him. He sprinted past the dorm rooms, skidded to a stop at the head of the stairs leading down to the second floor, then picked up speed. I huffed and puffed and ran, wishing I hadn't quit going to the gym. I reached the balustrade overlooking the deserted mezzanine and main floor and leaned against the railing, catching my breath.

I spotted Sammy Trout just then, standing directly behind the seated security guard, both men facing a portable television set obviously tuned to *Tarot Time with River North.*

Good old Sammy. Late for the show, but on time to help me catch this crazy cat.

I was about to call down to him when the words caught in my throat. Sammy held a length of rope with the ends coiled tightly around his hands, and those hands were raised above the guard's head. I watched, momentarily frozen with fear and disbelief, as he pulled the rope taut around the man's neck. I backed slowly up the stairs, watching the silent struggle before the guard finally fell to the floor.

Sammy bent, deftly removing a gun from the man's holster. He looked up and locked eyes with me. Shoving the gun under his belt, he lunged toward the main staircase, while I continued backing away. Sammy took the stairs two at a time, rapidly closing the distance between us. I turned, searching for a way out.

The closest door was the one to Mr. Pennington's office. Had the director meant it literally when he said, "My door is never locked"? I had to chance it. My phone was in my purse in the balcony. If I could get into the office and lock the door behind me, I could use the phone there and get help before Sammy could get in. I ran for it.

Mr. Pennington had told the truth. Pushing the

door open, I slammed it shut behind me. Fumbling in the darkness, I twisted the center of the doorknob until it gave a satisfying *click*, then stumbled across the room, bumping into the desk.

I searched my memory. Where did Pennington keep his phone? I remembered an old-fashioned gooseneck lamp with a green shade, and a silver tray with a pen and an inkwell and a letter opener. Desperately, I felt along the broad surface, while Sammy pounded and kicked at the door. I found the lamp and pushed the switch, illuminating the room with a pale greenish glow. The telephone was on the opposite side of the wide desktop. I heard wood splintering behind me as I reached for it and then turned toward the sound. Before long that lock would give way, and he'd have me cornered.

Think fast. There's no time for a phone call now, and there's no one around to hear me scream.

The door began to collapse. I grabbed the letter opener. It wasn't much of a weapon, but it was better than nothing. I ducked behind the safe. I could see Sammy Trout's shadow on the wall.

How can such a small man cast such a huge, wavering shadow?

His voice, that network announcer–quality voice I'd so admired, was harsh and menacing. "Come on out, Lee. I'm going to have to take you with me."

The shadow moved closer, and I could see his legs inches away from where I crouched. I had to take a chance. I plunged the letter opener into his leg.

He groaned and swore, bending to pull it out. "Bitch!" he said. "That's my bad leg. I'll kill you."

I ran for the splintered door and escaped into the hall. He limped close behind, the gun pointed at me. I reached the top of the main stairway, knowing he'd catch up with me in seconds, and barely even thinking about it, I straddled the gleaming wide bannister and slid all the way to the bottom. I ran for the glass doors and freedom.

But the Tabby was in full lockdown mode. I faced three locks, including a dead bolt, and Sammy was gaining on me, blocking my path to the mezzanine and the upper floors. The locks on the doors leading to the diner and to the student theater would be locked just as securely. No time and nowhere to run.

Except to the basement—and the tunnel.

I had to step over the silent form of the guard to open the door with the NO ADMITTANCE sign. No one had locked that one. Why would they, with an armed officer guarding it?

River's voice issued from the television set. "A camera is now entering Tabitha's bedroom. Some of you may remember the player piano, which once entertained Trumbull's shoppers." I glanced at the TV screen as I pulled the door toward me. It was Tabitha's bedroom, all right—and her chair was gently rocking.

I slammed the door shut behind me and ran down the stairs. In the basement, lights blazed and the wall panel was propped open with an ordinary automobile jack. Lifting the panel, I ducked through the opening, kicking the jack aside. The movable panel slid shut just as Sammy appeared at the foot of the stairs. *Now what?* Would the ladder still be in the hole? Would I be able to get to it before Sammy pushed the silver button in the floor?

I stood beneath the stone archway that I'd seen on television, facing toward where I knew the hole leading to the new tunnel was located. But even though small lights glowed in neatly spaced niches, I couldn't see any hole.

Pete told me they'd strung lights down here. I don't see any wires. These look like neat little lamps set into the stone wall.

I heard a small rustling sound nearby.

A small "mrrup" told me that O'Ryan was close by my side. I knelt on the damp floor, hugging the cat. "Good boy," I whispered. "I don't know how you got here, but I'm so glad to see you. Let's get out of here. Come on."

Instead of moving straight ahead to where Bill had fallen into the hole, O'Ryan made an abrupt left turn, then looked back at me. I shaded my eyes and watched as he trotted slowly along what looked like a long brick-lined corridor. I followed, wondering why Pete hadn't told me the digging crew had made so much progress. The brick walls looked clean and new, and I saw the metal tracks imbedded in the hard-packed dirt floor, where bootleggers used to move their cases of illegal whiskey.

Pete had told me that it was like a deep freeze down here, and he was dead right about that. I pulled my jacket close around me and shoved my hands in the pockets. I felt the coin Pete had given me for luck, and fervently hoped it would work. The cat and I walked at a fast clip, moving deeper into the tunnel. Every so often, I paused, listening and looking behind me for any sign or sound of Sammy. Once I thought I heard him calling my name, but the sound was so muffled, it seemed to come from somewhere below the metal tracks.

We'd probably walked about a mile when I saw her.

Tabitha Trumbull, young, smiling, and beautiful in her white wedding dress, stood not ten feet ahead of me at a bend in the tunnel. I stopped and stared, but O'Ryan walked right up to her. She raised a jingling key ring above her head and disappeared around a corner, the cat following behind.

It was exactly the scene I remembered from the vision in the shoe. But the cat wasn't an anonymous tunnel cat. It was O'Ryan, the witch Ariel's cat. The woman wasn't a vague, wispy ghost. She was Tabitha—and following her to wherever she was going seemed like my best option at the moment.

I rounded the corner, almost running, not wanting them to get out of my sight. Then, ahead of me, I saw Sammy. First, I saw his head, then his shoulders, then his trunk and his legs. He seemed to be rising up from the path. He held a very large flashlight in one hand, the gun in the other, and he was closing in on Tabitha and O'Ryan.

The woman and O'Ryan stood against the wall, and Sammy limped right by. Oddly, he didn't seem to notice them. After a moment, Tabitha beckoned me to follow her deeper into the tunnel.

Sammy was not far ahead of us. What if he turned back and saw me, illuminated by the lights in the wall? Would he be able to catch up with me if I reversed direction and ran back to the basement? Didn't matter. He had the gun. If an explosion down there sounded like a door slamming, a gunshot would be like a snap of the fingers.

We walked on. Tabitha stopped and, smiling, pointed over her head. I looked at where she pointed. There was a round shape there in the ceiling, and intermittent flashes of light shone through small opaque windows. I smiled back at Tabitha. It was the sidewalk grating Megan had talked about. We were under Derby Street, and the light came from the cars passing overhead.

That smile faded fast when I heard Sammy call my

name. "Lee, you bitch. There you are!" Somehow, he
was behind me now, with the gun pointed at my
head. I began to run, looking back over my shoulder.
I stopped short, amazed, as Sammy began to disappear
from the bottom up! His legs seemed to melt into the
floor, then his chest and arms and finally his head. Just
as quickly as he'd appeared, he was gone.

I got it.

Impossible as I knew it was, I got it. Tabitha and
O'Ryan and I were in the old tunnel, exactly as it had
been in the 1930s. Sammy was in the new one. Sammy
and I were not just in different tunnels; we were in
different centuries—except for the few places where
the two tunnels merged.

As long as I was with Tabitha in the old tunnel, I was
safe. Sammy couldn't see me, and I couldn't see him.
"The damn thing goes up and down like a roller
coaster," Pete had said. That was why Sammy seemed
to disappear into the floor whenever he entered the
new tunnel. Tabitha knew her way around the old one,
and for some reason, she'd chosen to take me along
with her. I was sure that we were headed for the entrance behind Greene's Tavern, and that both tunnels
ended up there. If we were already underneath Derby
Street, it wouldn't be long before Sammy Trout and I
would be in the same place at the same time—and in
the same century.

CHAPTER 32

I thought about Pete and Aunt Ibby and the witches back there at the Tabby. Was the show over? Had they seen the shattered door to the director's office yet and found that poor man lying in front of the television set? The police would probably search the building first. How long would it take Pete to realize that we were in the tunnel? More importantly, would he figure out where we were going to end up?

I hurried to keep up with the ghost woman and the witch's cat—figuring if I had any chance of getting out of there, it was by sticking with them. I was so close to Tabitha that I could see the details of her dress—the tiny pleats in the sleeves, the satin-covered buttons at the wrists and the collar. Curiously, there wasn't so much as a trace of dust on the gown, even though the train had been dragged across a dirt floor for a couple of miles, while I had splotches of mud on my pants and shoes, and even O'Ryan's yellow coat looked grimy.

I heard the jingle of Tabitha's keys as she rounded another corner. I lost sight of her then and, for a moment, felt a rising sense of panic. A loud meow from

O'Ryan led me to where the two of them waited in front of a bright red door.

The woman bent down and turned one of the keys in a shiny brass keyhole. The door swung open, and I followed her inside. She lit an electric lamp on the wall of the playhouse, then went directly to a red wooden chest. She used the other key and lifted the lid. The chest was filled with long piano-roll boxes, just like the ones I'd seen in the attic room. Soundlessly, she closed the chest and led us back into the tunnel. There she stopped, closed the red door, put a finger to her lips, smiled . . . and began to fade. A pale figure, she moved backward into the tunnel, growing smaller and fainter, until she'd completely disappeared.

As I watched, amazed, the paint on the red door began to fade and peel, and the shiny brass lock became tarnished and rusted. I rubbed my eyes as a brick wall began to appear, hologram-like, between me and the rapidly aging door. I took a step back, and O'Ryan gave a low growl. I caught just a flick of his yellow tail as he darted into a wide crack near the top of the now solid brick wall. I heard a sound behind me, whirled around, and found myself face-to-face with Sammy Trout.

Sammy looked just as surprised as I'm sure I did. "How the hell did you get here ahead of me?" The gun was tucked under his belt, and he put his hand on it. "Never mind. Here. Start digging." He handed me a small trowel and jerked his thumb toward a patch of loose dirt. "And keep quiet, or I'll kill you right here." He shone the flashlight into my eyes, pointing the gun. "You know I can do it."

He's already decided to kill me.

I knelt on the ground. "Where am I supposed to dig?" He pointed. "Right there."

I began to dig. The soil was dark colored, cold, and claylike, but it felt loosely packed, as though it had been disturbed recently.

"I got one of them this morning," Sammy said, his tone surprisingly normal. "There should be at least one more."

"What are we looking for?" I asked, trying hard to sound as though this was an ordinary conversation.

"Shut up and keep digging," he snarled. "Saves me the trouble." He leaned against the brick wall, favoring the injured leg. "As if you don't know what we're looking for."

"The gold, I suppose," I said.

"Gold? What gold? Did you think that dollar sign on the map meant gold? Please. I can turn it into gold, though." He laughed. "At least two kilos. Uncut cocaine. Maybe more."

What does cocaine have to do with anything?

"Y'know," he said, "I don't think Wilson knew what he was looking for, either. By the time I got here, he already had the cover off that bomb shelter thing." He shook his head. "Smart bastard. Had his coat off, his sleeves rolled up, and he was digging away with that little trowel. Hell, he'd already dug up a nice two-pound coffee can full of coke. Looked surprised as hell when he saw what it was." He laughed again. "Not half as surprised as he looked when I shoved his hedge clippers in his throat and took it away from him."

I tried to gauge whether or not I could use the trowel somehow as a weapon and get away. I struggled to keep my voice calm. "Why'd you do that?"

He shrugged. "Had to. He recognized me from the school."

Keep him talking. He's enjoying bragging about what he's done.

"How'd you know about this place, anyway?" I watched his eyes as I dug.

"Keep digging. And keep quiet." His voice was low. "They'll be starting to look around here again in a few hours, when it gets light." He shifted his weight, moving his leg carefully. "It was the map. Guy I met in prison had one just like it. Benny Gable. Kept it under his mattress. The stupid jerk didn't know I looked at it every chance I got." His laugh was harsh.

He went on. "Had that sucker memorized. The guy used to run a boat for Trumbull, trading guns for drugs. He even told me he had a nice clean stash of coke hidden somewhere in Salem. That's how come I picked your school. Salem . . . Trumbull. Funny, but I always thought it was a street map. Then the big, dumb cowboy figured it out. It's a regular maze down here, you know. Blind alleys everywhere. But once I knew what the map was for, it was easy. Now I know where all the exits are." He laughed again. "These stupid bomb shelters are in backyards all over the place. Most people don't even know they're there. But I know!"

I heard a slight clinking sound as the trowel hit something solid. Had Sammy heard it, too? I guessed he hadn't, because he kept talking.

"The hedge clipper thing was kind of messy, but it was all I had to work with." He caressed the gun, and his shrug was casual, indifferent. "I figured I'd better get out of there fast and come back later for the other can. Splashed a lot of blood on my jacket, so I put on Wilson's coat, rolled mine up nice and neat, and stuffed it inside of his. Then I wiped my prints off of everything I'd touched, picked up the coffee can, and strolled on back to school." He smiled. "Just a man in a big fat coat out buying himself some coffee."

"You changed your shirt and came back to class as though nothing had happened."

"Right. Stashed my can of coke and the jackets and went to class like a good boy." His smile was chilling. "I still don't know how Thom got blamed for it, but it works out fine for me!" The trowel clinked again, and this time he heard it.

"What was that? You hit something." He waved the gun. "Get out of my way. Go over there against the wall and don't move."

Sammy propped his flashlight on the floor with a loose brick, aimed the gun at me with his left hand, and snatched the trowel away with his right. "Over there," he said again, motioning toward the wall with the trowel. "Don't move a muscle, or I swear I'll shoot you right here."

He's planning to shoot me, whether here or someplace else.

The tunnel yawned, deep and black, on my left. Gone were the neatly recessed lamps set into the bricks. There was only darkness. Opposite me was another wall, the one with the wide crack at the top. The third wall, I figured, had to be the one with an entrance to the bomb shelter. I peered closely at it, trying not to be too obvious, because Sammy was looking rapidly back and forth between me and the growing hole in the dirt.

At first I couldn't see any opening at all. The wall appeared to be made of bricks, just like the other two. But there was a slight difference in the pattern. There was one section, around five feet high and two feet wide, with bricks stacked one atop the other, instead of in the normal alternating rows. A small black iron ring protruded from the center of the rectangle. It had to be the exit to the bomb shelter.

So near, and yet so far away.

There was a dull *clunk* from the hole in the dirt. I knew Sammy had found something solid. I watched as he pulled a tall coffee can from the hole, laid the trowel aside, and brushed dirt from the bright blue container. He struggled to wrench the top off of it with his free hand, while the gun was still aimed in my direction. The top came free with a jolt, and I heard the *whoosh* of escaping air as he broke the vacuum seal.

He stuck his finger into the can, then put it in his mouth. "Ahhh," he said, licking his lips and replacing the top. "This'll bring me a million bucks on the street."

Leaving the coffee can on the floor, he stood with difficulty, the wounded leg obviously giving him trouble. He backed up against the wall where O'Ryan had ducked out of sight, and leaned heavily against the bricks.

"Pick that up," he said, gesturing at the can with the gun. "You can carry it for me." He bent down, grunting with the effort, and picked up the flashlight. "It's the least you can do after stabbing me, bitch. You'll walk ahead of me."

I picked up the can, and Sammy motioned toward the yawning blackness of the tunnel. "We're not going far. There's another bomb shelter just like this one behind the house across the street. Stupid people don't even know it's there." He laughed that terrible laugh again. "That's where I stashed my other coffee can. There's a big dealer in a boat just offshore, waiting to pick me and my coke up. Your smart-ass cop boyfriend doesn't know that, does he? One wrong move, and I'll shoot you in the back. Don't doubt me."

What difference is it going to make to me if he shoots me here or across the street? Should I make a move now or wait?

O'Ryan decided for me. With a hideous yowl, he leapt from his hiding place, claws extended, onto

Sammy's head. Both the gun and the flashlight thudded to the floor as the man tore in vain at the snarling cat. I snatched the top off the coffee can and, with a warning shout to O'Ryan, threw a handful of uncut cocaine into Sammy Trout's face.

He dug frantically at his eyes, not trying to stop me when I pulled the iron ring. The section of wall gave immediately, and O'Ryan and I were in the Greenes' bomb shelter, where nothing blocked the exit door except a yellow ribbon of police tape. O'Ryan scampered ahead of me, and with a loud sigh of relief, I climbed over the wooden sill and toward the tavern's parking lot, where flashing red, white, and blue lights and the wailing of sirens provided the most welcome sights and sounds I'd ever seen or heard. I shielded my eyes when a spotlight illuminated the hillside where I stood.

"Not so fast, Ms. Barrett." Sammy's voice was in my ear, his gun in the small of my back. "You're my ticket out of here. Slowly now, walk ahead of me."

"Drop the gun, Trout," came the command over a bullhorn. "Don't make the situation any worse than it is." It was Pete's voice, calm and steady.

Sammy held the gun to my head, the coffee can cradled in his other arm. He shouted an answer. "Back off, or I'll kill her. Clear the lot. Leave me a car gassed up, with the engine running."

"Let her go, Sammy," Pete said. "Come on down and we'll talk about it."

"No talking, Pete," Sammy yelled. "If you don't want to see your woman with her pretty head blown off, you'll do what I say. Clear the lot. Give me a car. Now."

"Okay. Okay." Pete still sounded calm. "We're leaving. There'll be a car here with the engine running. Don't hurt Lee."

"No tricks, or she gets it. I'm not kidding," Sammy answered. "And don't try to follow me. Do what I say and I'll let her go later."

The police cars, with lights flashing, pulled away, but the spotlight remained trained on us. A gray Chrysler moved slowly into the center of the lot. Pete climbed out, then raised the bullhorn again.

"Here it is, Sammy. Gassed and ready to go." He turned his back on the whole scene—on me—and walked slowly toward the street.

"Okay," Sammy yelled. "Douse the spotlight. We're coming down."

The light blinked off, and stumbling in the sudden darkness, with the gun prodding my back, I made my way toward the solitary car in the now quiet parking lot. Sammy opened the driver's side door, the gun about two inches from my head.

"Slide across. Don't pull any funny business. You're no good to me dead now. I need a hostage." Again the hoarse laugh. "But trust me, I wouldn't mind shooting your kneecaps out. Hold this." He handed me the can and stood there outside the car, eyes searching the vacant parking lot, with the gun trained on my legs. He activated the door lock from the switch on the driver's side door. "Don't even think about touching that lock," he warned, standing with one foot inside the car, scrutinizing every corner of the silent, darkened lot.

What took place next happened so fast, I'm not sure I can describe it exactly the way it went down. First, there was the unmistakable roar of a sweet V-8 engine, then the glow of high beams. I saw it coming in the rearview mirror, lunging straight at us out of the darkness, tires screeching on damp asphalt. I saw the expression on Sammy's face as it bore down on him, tearing the Chrysler's door clean off and sending him sprawling facedown and unmoving on the pavement.

The pounding rhythm of running feet, the welcome sound of sirens, the comforting flashing of red, white, and blue lights all blurred together. Strong arms pulled me from the ruined car.

"Are you all right?" Pete's voice was ragged with emotion. "Jesus, Lee, don't ever scare me like that again. When I went downstairs to look for you and saw that smashed door and the guard down . . ." His voice broke. He stopped speaking and just held me close for a long moment. I closed my eyes, pressing my face against his shoulder.

I heard another voice nearby. "You have the right to remain silent when questioned. Anything you say or do may be held against you. . . ."

I opened my eyes. "Is . . . is he still alive, Pete?"

"Yeah. The son of a bitch isn't in too good shape, but he's still breathing." Pete's voice was harsh. "He'll be well enough to stand trial. What the hell hit him? Did you see it? Could you tell where it went?"

"No. Too dark," I lied.

I'd seen what hit him. I'd seen it plainly, in clear detail. Sammy Trout had been run down by a bright yellow 1986 Corvette Stingray. I couldn't tell where it went, though. It had faded away into the night sky, growing smaller and fainter, until it disappeared.

CHAPTER 33

"Pete, how did you find me? How did you know where we'd come out of the tunnel?"

"Wilson's map," he said. "It was still in his briefcase. We figured Sammy would come here or to the exit across the street. We had that staked out, too."

"You knew about that exit?" I was surprised.

"Not until we got the map. Then it was easy." He took my hands in his and rubbed them. "You must be freezing. Come on. I'll take you home now. Your aunt is worried sick about you—and O'Ryan."

"O'Ryan! Oh, Pete, he was in there with me. Have you seen him?"

"Sure have." He pointed toward the street. "He's right over there, sound asleep in my car, with the heater and the radio running. Did you know he likes country music?"

An ambulance drove off, taking Sammy to the hospital, in the company of a couple of armed police officers, as Pete and I joined O'Ryan in the Crown Vic. Then Pete drove us home to Winter Street.

"I have to ask you a few questions about tonight, you know." We parked in front of the house and Pete looked over at me, taking in my mud-spattered clothes and bedraggled hair.

"Can the questions wait until I have a nice long hot shower?"

"Absolutely," he said. "And O'Ryan could use a bath, too."

We hurried up the steps and Aunt Ibby met us in the front hall, teary eyed but smiling. "Maralee, oh, my dear child. I've been so worried."

"I'll be fine as soon as I get cleaned up." I handed her the cat. "Do you think O'Ryan will let you give him a bath? He needs one, too."

"I think he will." She stroked O'Ryan's matted coat. "You're sure you'll be okay?"

"I'll be fine," I promised.

"All right then," she said. "Come on, boy."

She carried him toward the kitchen, while Pete ran a hand through my messed-up hair. "You look cute even when you've been through hell."

"Thanks, I guess," I said. "Pete, want to answer a couple of questions for me before I go upstairs?"

"Sure."

"What about the security guard at the Tabby? Is he . . . dead?"

"No. He'll make it. Gonna have a sore throat for a while, but at least we'll get Trout for attempted murder."

"You can get him for Jonathan Wilson's murder, too," I said. "He admitted it to me. Thom didn't do it."

"Thanks, Lee." He wiped a smudge from the tip of my nose. "I'll wait right here and take your statement as soon as you feel up to it."

"You go help with the cat bath, put on a big pot of coffee, and I'll be ready to tell you all about it."

Well, everything except the part about the ghost woman,

my time-travel trip through the old tunnel, and the yellow Corvette.

"Take your time." His kiss was gentle.

The hot shower and the much-needed shampoo felt great. Then, dressed in my good old comfy gray sweats, I went downstairs, restored, and with a few more questions of my own.

Aunt, clean cat, and Pete with his notebook awaited me in the kitchen, the promised coffee percolating. I joined them at the table. O'Ryan, his coat still damp, climbed into my lap.

"Aunt Ibby," I said. "First of all, how did you get home? I know you didn't drive the Corvette."

"I thought about it, but no," she admitted. "Rupert brought me home. And he told me about what happened to that poor guard."

"And, Pete, how did you get the witches and the guests out of the building after the show? The main floor must have been crawling with police."

"Actually, Pennington figured it out," he said. "When the show was over, we stopped all the activity for a while, and he shut off all the lights on the first and second floors. He told everybody there was a problem with the elevator, had them get off at the mezzanine level, and let them out the side door next to your classroom."

Aunt Ibby beamed. "Brilliant. Don't you think so?"

"Brilliant," I agreed. "Okay, Pete. Questions?"

"Quite a few," he said. "This is just informal, you know. You're not under oath or anything. Just remember the best you can. Take me from the time the cat ran away."

I began with how I'd chased O'Ryan down the spiral staircase. I told him about seeing Sammy and almost calling out his name before I saw the rope in his hands.

Aunt Ibby paled and closed her eyes when I described what Sammy had done to the guard.

"Oh, my dear. Oh, good heavens, Maralee."

"Go on," Pete said.

I told them about going into Mr. Pennington's office and stabbing Sammy's leg with the silver letter opener, and about how I'd run to the basement, trying to get away from him.

"Thanks for telling me about the bannister, Aunt Ibby," I said. "I used it, and it sure saved me some needed seconds—and any other time it would have been fun."

"I'm glad if I helped you even a tiny bit, Maralee." She smiled and poured me another cup of coffee. "But how ever did you find your way across town in that tunnel? You'd never been down there before."

Good question.

"I followed the lights along the walls as far as they went," I said. That was true. No need to tell them that the lights I'd followed had probably been lit nearly a century ago and were not the ones the police had strung up last week. "Then, when Sammy caught up with me, he had a flashlight. And a gun." True again. "He knew his way through the tunnel. I just went where he told me to."

Pete nodded and wrote in his notebook. "Tell me exactly what Sammy said about killing Wilson."

"He said that he shoved the hedge clippers into Mr. Wilson's throat," I said, "and that the blood splashed on his jacket."

I heard Aunt Ibby gasp.

Pete continued. "Did he tell you why he did that?"

"Mr. Wilson recognized him. From the class. He knew he wouldn't get away with just grabbing the cocaine and running."

"So Trout was after the cocaine in the coffee can?"

"Yes. That was the second can. He took one out after he killed Mr. Wilson. He said he hid it along with his bloody jacket. Wilson's coat, too."

He nodded. "Yep. We found all that in the shelter across the street from Greene's. Did he tell you how he knew the cocaine was there?"

"He heard about it in jail. From a cell mate. Benny Gable."

Aunt Ibby sat up straight. I knew she'd recognized the captain's name.

"Got it," Pete said. "We know about Gable. How did you get away from Sammy? He had a gun on you."

I told him about O'Ryan jumping on Sammy's head and giving me time to open the door into the bomb shelter. "You know the rest," I said.

He closed the notebook. "That's enough for right now. Chief's going to have questions for you later, though, I'm sure."

"Will you have enough evidence to let Thom go? Sammy said he had nothing to do with any of this."

"It's plain that he didn't kill Wilson," Pete said, "but there's still the matter of moving a dead body. Joe has to answer for that, too, along with that blasting in the tunnel he did. Moving a body without a medical examiner's permission is a felony."

"They've admitted to it?"

"Thom and Joe both swear that they didn't know Bill was dead. Joe was in the tunnel and heard him fall. He says he tried to revive him by pouring some whiskey down his throat, and to warm him up by putting a jacket on him. Joe knew he had no business being down in the tunnel himself, but he couldn't leave Bill there. So he woke Thom up and promised to give him a gold coin worth more than a thousand dollars if he'd help move Bill to the park. And keep quiet about it."

"Thom wanted the money," I said. "So they pretended to be drunk and carried him down the street, right?"

"Singing Christmas carols, in case anyone saw them," Pete said. "But it's still a felony."

"The coin Joe gave him must have been the marked one Friedrich found at the coin show. Did Joe tell you where he got it?"

"He said his grandmother gave him a whole box of them before she died, along with the deed to his house," he said.

"Did he make the nine-one-one call so Bill would be found?"

"That was Thom." Pete stood up. "You get some rest now, Lee. You, too, Miss Russell. I'll call you later."

I went to the door and let him out. Another gentle kiss, and he was gone. I went back to the kitchen. Neither my aunt nor I was ready for bed yet. I poured a fresh cup of coffee and sat down, facing her.

"Now, tell me all about the show. Did Tabitha's ghost ever show up?"

"Yes and no," she said. "The ceremony itself was interesting, and River did kind of a play-by-play of what was going on. We saw the witches cast a magic circle and do some incantations using the things on the altar. One of them drew a huge pentagram in a circle on the floor with blue glitter. That might have been just for effect, but it looked grand on the television."

"But did you ever actually see Tabitha?"

"I think she was there, Maralee. While the witches did their spells and incantations and such, the television cameras moved around, showing the whole apartment, room by room. They played somber music in the background—Toccata in B-flat Minor, I believe. Quite effective." She leaned forward with her elbows on the table, chin in her hands. "Anyway, River talked about orbs and spirit manifestations just about everywhere in the place, but I didn't actually *see* anything until the camera showed Tabitha's room."

"The chair was rocking," I said. "I saw it, too."

"The chair? That was the least of it. Didn't you hear the piano playing 'Sentimental Journey'?" Her eyes widened. "And did you see the picture of President Roosevelt fly off the wall and land upside down on Tabitha's bed?"

"Afraid I missed all that," I said. "Did everybody see the same thing?"

"Uh-huh. They did. Your friend Duke says it was just a TV trick, but Therese thought it was real. Kelly covered her eyes and refused to look, and Primrose didn't say anything. The clergyman started to pray, and the camera cut away from the scene, and they ran a commercial, even though they'd promised there wouldn't be any." She took a deep breath. "What do you think? Was it real?"

"I think it was," I said. "I couldn't tell Pete everything about tonight, so I'm going to tell you now."

I filled her in on all the supernatural details I'd left out earlier.

"That must be why O'Ryan had tiny chips of dried-up old red paint in his fur," she said.

"It must be." I realized I'd been talking for nearly an hour.

Do I dare to tell her about the yellow car? Not yet. Maybe someday.

"So there we were, in the parking lot," I said. "Sammy had pushed me into the car, and he just stood there with his door open, checking the lot to be sure all the police were gone. All of a sudden, another car came whipping across the lot, clipped the door, knocked Sammy onto the ground, and took off."

"That car might have saved your life, Maralee," she said. "Did the police catch whoever it was?"

"Nope. None of them even saw it," I said truthfully. "But one of the officers said he saw tire tracks where the old driveway used to be, on the side street behind the tavern." That was true, too. "Pete thinks it was just a lucky hit-and-run."

"Lucky? I should say so . . . more like a miracle! Tell me, did Pete say anything about the gold?"

"Not much," I said. "He just mentioned that Joe Greene had given Thom a gold coin, and he knew that Mary Alice had given Joe a box of gold. But I suppose Joe must have admitted that he'd been looking around down there for the rest of Mary Alice's gold when he found Bill." I paused and thought about that. "Mary Alice. M. A. It all goes back to her, doesn't it?"

"It really goes back to Tabitha," she said, "and to President Roosevelt's gold."

"Captain Gable never betrayed Tabitha's secret," I told her. "Sammy didn't know about the gold at all, and River thinks I'm supposed to help Tabitha cross over, that she's earthbound because of something that needs to be done—the same way Ariel couldn't leave until her killer was caught. But I don't know for sure what Tabitha wants me to do."

"That's easy," my aunt said. "She wants the president's gold to go back to the United States Treasury."

"Maybe you're right," I said. "The Treasury Department has all those letters from Tabitha stating exactly that. I'll call Pete tomorrow and tell him I'm pretty sure where that gold is hidden."

"You mean you think you can find the playhouse again?"

I thought about where I'd been standing when Tabitha had faded away. We'd been right in front of the red door. One step back, and I'd been facing Sammy. It had to be a spot where the two tunnels met, and it was next to the brick wall with the hole in it where O'Ryan had hidden. The cat had come out of the hole with chips of dried-up red paint on his coat.

"If Pete will take me back into the tunnel, I'm sure I can show them exactly where to take down a wall," I told her. "And I don't have to mention Tabitha's ghost at all."

I did just what I'd told my aunt I'd do. On Saturday afternoon Pete picked me up, and we drove to the Greene's Tavern parking lot.

"You're sure you're ready to go in?" he asked, taking my hand as we approached the bomb shelter. "It's awfully soon after what happened to you there."

"I'm okay," I said. "And Joe will be surprised when he finds out how close he's been to the gold all along."

The bomb shelter doors were open, both front and back. Only two strips of yellow tape separated us from the tunnel entrance. Pete was right about it being awfully soon after the most terrifying moments of my life. I fought back momentary panic, then stepped into the brick-walled area.

"It has to be right behind there," I told Pete, pointing to the wall with the crack in it. "That's where O'Ryan got into the old red paint."

"Megan said the playroom had a red door," he said. "No other reason for red paint to be in the tunnel that I can see. You could be right."

"I'm pretty sure I am," I said, taking one step into the tunnel. I was standing just about here when Tabitha waved good-bye and disappeared, I thought.

I'll never know what prompted me to look down at just that moment. If I hadn't, I would have missed it, and it would have been lost forever in the dirt and clay. It was such a little thing. I bent down and picked up the white satin-covered button and slipped it into my pocket, next to the lucky quarter Pete had given me.

CHAPTER 34

People all over Salem and most of Essex County who'd watched *Tarot Time with River North* that night talked about it for weeks afterward. Some of the big national paranormal programs began calling the school immediately after the show, wanting to arrange for their own crews to visit Tabitha's room. But with the whole apartment so nicely spruced up, Mr. Pennington had begun making plans for accommodating "important personages from the world of music, stars of the stage and screen" in the historic venue, and he wasn't sure a resident ghost would be a welcome amenity.

The director gave me permission to visit Tabitha's room the following Monday morning, before anything had been disturbed. The school's regular cleaning crew had refused to set foot in it, and I'd offered to rehang the picture and straighten out the bedspread, just in case any of those important personages happened by. No one except Therese and Duke had shown up for class, and I invited the two of them to come with me.

"Really? Me?" Therese was thrilled. "I'd love to. I hope Tabitha is still there."

"Don't think I'm afraid to go, because I'm not," Duke said. "But I'd better stay here in case Primrose or Kelly shows up, so I can tell them where you are. Maybe Thom will come back, now that he's out of jail."

Thom was out of jail, but I didn't expect him to join us again yet. According to his lawyer, when he'd run away from New York that night, he had made it all the way to Salem and had hidden far back inside the tunnel, remembering how the doors worked from his Christmas night adventure. But when he'd opened the back door leading into the bomb shelter in the morning, cold and hungry, he'd tripped over Wilson's body. Grabbing the hedge clippers to keep his balance, he'd pulled them loose from the man's throat. Horrified and in understandable shock, Thom had run outside, holding the bloody evidence. Someone had seen him there on the hillside and had called 911.

I told Duke that it would be okay for him to wait for the others if that was what he'd like to do. I already knew that Kelly and Joe were at the police station, pleading Joe's case to Chief Whaley. I knew where Primrose was, too. I'd been right about the secret playhouse. Mr. Pennington's skeleton keys had fit both the door and the toy chest, and the piano-roll boxes full of gold coins had been recovered. Primrose had gone to Boston in an armored car with Mr. Friedrich to deliver them to the Treasury Department.

"Text me if you need me, Duke," I told him. "We won't be gone long."

Therese was close beside me, fairly wriggling with excitement, as we rode the elevator up to the Trumbulls' apartment. We walked through the silent parlor and the dining room and peeked through the open doors of the ballroom, where there were still traces of blue glitter on the floor. Most of the doors in the long hallway leading to Tabitha's room were closed, but hers stood open.

Sunlight streamed through lavender-tinted windows onto the rocking chair, with its new velvet cushion. The recently shampooed Oriental rug's colors seemed to glow, and piano keys gleamed white against polished dark walnut. I picked up the fallen picture frame.

"Lucky the glass didn't break," I said, turning it face up. "The president looks as good as new."

"What's that writing on the back?" Therese asked. "All those numbers?"

I flipped it to the paper-covered back. "They seem to be birth dates. Here's John Junior, 9/4/1951. And Joseph, 11/11/1970," I read. "And look, here's Kelly. 3/9/1993. Tabitha's grandson, great-grandson, and great-great-granddaughter's birthdays."

"How cool is that? But what do these other numbers mean?" Therese pointed to a row of numerals and letters close to the bottom of the frame. She read aloud. "*L* four, *R* six, *L* zero, *R* seven, *L* two."

"It's a combination," I said slowly, "and I'll bet it's the combination to the safe in Mr. Pennington's office. Tabitha must have written it down so she'd remember how to open it."

We rehung the picture and straightened out the bedspread, while I memorized the five-digit safe combination.

"Let's get back downstairs," I said. "I don't want to forget the numbers. Mr. Pennington will be thrilled." I couldn't resist a backward glance toward the silent piano and the motionless rocking chair.

Good-bye, Tabitha.

As I'd expected, Mr. Pennington was delighted when I told him the combination. Therese and I watched as he knelt, almost reverently, in front of the safe, with its round dial and massive handle. He repeated each letter and number aloud as he spun the dial left and right, listening for the sound of falling tumblers. With both hands, he gripped the handle and pulled downward. The door swung open, revealing a single cardboard carton.

"I'm almost afraid to look inside," he said. "Not that it matters a whit what it is. Like with those two old keys, it's been the not knowing that has perturbed me."

He pulled the carton slowly toward him. The top of it was lettered in black marker—PERSONAL PROPERTY OF O. W. TRUMBULL. All three of us held our breath as he peeled back the cover.

I'd never heard Rupert Pennington laugh before, but he had a great laugh—hearty and uproarious. He moved aside so that Therese and I could get a look at Oliver Wendell's personal collection of mint condition *Playboy* magazines—beginning with the very first issue in 1953. He closed the safe, stood up, and patted the top of it. My inner Nancy smiled. With the opening of that safe, the last piece of the puzzle clicked neatly into place.

"There's nothing more to do. The mission was successful." Mr. Pennington paused.

Therese and I waited.

"Hugh Laurie," he said. "*Arthur Christmas*, 2011."

EPILOGUE

Primrose and Duke finished the script, and Kelly and Thom performed as Tabitha and Oliver, as planned. Therese did the voice-over as Tabitha, and Duke surprised everyone by reading Oliver's part in a near-perfect Harvard accent. The documentary was well received both by the local audience and the NEA. In fact, we've received another grant for next year.

Thom and Joe were fined five thousand dollars each and were given a year's probation for moving Bill's body—whether they knew he was dead or not. Joe got an extra six months' probation for obstructing the investigation. The court decided that the gold coins his grandmother had given him as a gift were legally his, so he was able to pay both his and Thom's fines—and for an extremely good lawyer. Thom's picture was in the paper so often during Sammy's trial that a Boston agency picked him up. Even though he can't leave Massachusetts yet, he has plenty of work locally, both in print and television.

Duke and Kelly still work nights at the tavern. Therese is taking special instruction from Lady Megan in the studies of spells, rituals, and meditations, and she's given up wasting her gift on gambling games. Primrose, with a brunette French twist, wire-rimmed glasses, and a wardrobe of business suits and fabulous shoes, accepted an assignment at the John F. Kennedy Presidential Library. Mr. Pennington and Aunt Ibby attended the Woody Allen Film Festival and are still dating. So are Pete and I. We go to Greene's Tavern sometimes. The police never found the hit-and-run car, but one night Pete showed me the tire tracks in the old driveway where he thought it had gone. Could I have imagined the yellow Corvette, because it was what I wanted to see? I still wonder.

The city returned Bill's bag of coins to the Sullivans and sold the *Playboy* collection for enough money to begin building the new sound and light facility in the Tabby's basement—to be named the Jonathan Wilson Studio.

The third floor of the house on Winter Street is almost finished, and Aunt Ibby surprised me with the fact that it's to be my own suite of rooms, with a separate entrance. O'Ryan has already checked it out and seems to approve.

Will having a private space of my own mean that my relationship with Pete might become quite a bit closer?

We'll see.

ACKNOWLEDGMENTS

Special thanks to three strong and beautiful women—fellow authors Liz Drayer, Adele Woodyard, and Laura Kennedy—for their gentle and perceptive critiques throughout the writing . . . and rewriting . . . and rewriting process.

A big thank-you to Chris Dowgin for both inspiration and information from his remarkable book on Salem's secret underground.

Thanks to my editor, Esi Sogah, who unfailingly makes whatever I write a little better, and to the rest of Kensington's extraordinary team of professionals for careful attention to every detail of publication and especially for the gorgeous cover art.

And, of course, eternal gratitude to my parents, Marjorie and Arthur Phelps, for raising me in the magical city of Salem.

Keep reading for
An excerpt from the next book in
The Witch City Mystery series
Available Fall 2015
From
Carol J. Perry
And Kensington Books

"Maralee, come here. You won't believe this!"

I hurried from my sparsely furnished bedroom to the kitchen, where Aunt Ibby sat on an unpainted and slightly wobbly wooden stool. She pointed to the new TV, which was propped against a carton of books on the granite countertop.

"Look," she said. "It's exactly the same, isn't it?"

I pulled up a faded folding beach chair and peered at the screen. "You're right," I said, watching as a tall, gray-haired woman opened and closed the top drawer of an oak bureau. "It looks just like mine. What show is this?"

"*Shopping Salem,*" she said. "It's new. The WICH-TV reporter goes around the city, interviewing shop owners. You should go right over there and buy that bureau before somebody else grabs it." She glanced around the nearly empty kitchen. "Lord knows you need furniture."

I sighed. "I know."

My aunt had recently turned the third floor of our old family home on Salem's historic Winter Street into an apartment for me. I was delighted to have the private space, but selecting furnishings had become an unexpected challenge. Who knew that deciding between red and blue, modern and traditional, oak and walnut could be so bewildering?

So far all I'd bought for my spacious new digs was a king-size bed, the television set, a coffeemaker, and a scratching post for our resident cat, O'Ryan—supplemented with assorted temporary seating brought up from the cellar.

I'm Lee Barrett, née Maralee Kowolski, aged thirty-one, red-haired, Salem born. I was orphaned early, I married once, and I was widowed young. I was raised by my librarian aunt, Isobel Russell, in this house and had returned home, to my roots, nearly a year ago.

"You'd better get going," Aunt Ibby said. "A handsome bureau like that will get snapped up in no time. The shop's Tolliver's Antiques and Uniques, over on Bridge Street. Won't take you but a minute to drive over there." She tossed her paper coffee cup into the recycling bag next to the sink. "And you might pick up some proper coffee cups while you're there."

I had a special reason—besides my obvious dearth of furnishings—to want this particular piece. An identical one had long ago adorned my childhood bedroom and had later been relegated to the attic. Sadly, it had been destroyed by a fire that pretty much ruined the top two floors of our house. The damage to the structure had been nicely repaired, but the contents of the rooms, including my bureau, had proven pretty much irreplaceable.

"Do you suppose hers has little secret compartments, like mine did?" I wondered aloud.

"It does," she said. "The woman on TV said that it

has six and that she'll give whoever buys it directions on how to open them."

"I think I can remember all of them," I said, "but maybe that one is different."

"Only one way to find out," she said, and within minutes I was driving along Bridge Street, convertible top down, enjoying the bright June morning and looking forward to adding one more piece of furniture to my apartment, reclaiming a happy childhood memory at the same time.

Tolliver's Antiques and Uniques wasn't hard to find. The shop's weathered silvery-gray exterior featured a purple door. Bright pink petunias in purple window boxes added more color, and the lavender shield-shaped sign suspended over the doorway spelled out the name of the place in black Old English lettering. I parked on a hot-top driveway next to the building and hurried inside. A bell over the door jingled a welcome, and the gray-haired woman I'd seen on television stepped from behind beaded curtains, right hand extended.

"Hello. I'm Shea Tolliver," she said. "Welcome to my shop." Her handshake was firm, her smile genuine, and the gray hair clearly of the premature variety.

"Hello," I said. "I'm Lee Barrett. I saw you on television this morning. I'm interested in the antique bureau you showed."

"Yes, a lovely piece. It was made by a little-known Salem cabinetmaker back in . . ." She stopped mid-sentence and looked at me intently. "I've seen you on television, too. You were the psychic medium on that *Nightshades* show before it got canceled."

She was right. I'd worked in television, one way or another, ever since I graduated from Emerson College.

I smiled and held up both hands in protest. "That was me," I admitted. "But I promise I'm not a psychic—just played one on TV. These days I'm teaching TV Production 101 at the Tabitha Trumbull Academy of the Arts."

She laughed. "Quite a switch. From soothsayer to schoolmarm."

"You're right," I agreed. "But teachers get the summer off, and I'm planning to spend some of this one furnishing a new apartment."

"Well, you couldn't go wrong with that bureau," she said. "Good-looking, useful, and secret compartments to boot."

"I know. I had one exactly like it when I was a kid. Mine burned up in a fire."

"No kidding. What a shame. The cabinetmaker made just three that we know of. If yours is gone, there may be only two left—mine and one I saw in a New York shop, where the dealer showed me how it worked. I'd never have figured it out by myself." She parted the beaded curtains. "I found this one at an estate sale, and I don't think the owner even knew about the secret spaces. Come on back here and take a look."

I followed her into a back room. What a nostalgia rush! It was as though my own bureau had been magically restored, every curlicue and knob exactly as I remembered. I reached out and stroked the polished top.

"This is it," I said. "How much?"

The price she quoted was steep, but not unreasonable.

"If you'll throw in those white ironstone coffee mugs over there," I said, remembering Aunt Ibby's plea, "you've got a deal. Is a credit card okay?"

"It's a deal, and a credit card is fine."

"Will you hold on to the bureau for a day or so, while I round up a truck and some extra muscle to help me get it home?"

I wasn't sure where the truck was going to come from, but I knew Detective Pete Mondello would be ready and willing to lend the muscle. Pete and I had become kind of a steady item since I'd come home, and I was pretty sure he was looking forward to me having a place of my own as much as I was!

"No worries about that," she said. "My delivery guy is due here any minute. You'll have your bureau by this afternoon. No extra charge. You're sure you remember where all the compartments are?"

"I think so." I touched each spot that I thought might hide a tiny chamber. "That's where mine were. Is it the same?"

"Sure is." She handed me a card. "Just write down your address. And in case you forget, I'll put the directions for opening all of them in the top drawer."

"Perfect," I said.

While I swiped my card she wrapped four mugs in lavender tissue, put them into a purple bag, and handed it to me. "Come back again soon, Lee."

"You can count on it, Shea."

"I will." She smiled. "By the way, there is one thing I guess I should tell you."

"What's that?" I asked.

"The estate your bureau came from . . . A kind of famous murder happened there. That doesn't bother you, does it?"